除了多樣的分類主題，
以及生活化的對話範例，
本書讓你在吸收會話句型與單字之餘，
也能在輕鬆地在笑話和故事中
享受異國文化的洗禮。

本書使用方式

1 高頻口語，靈活表達

取材於日常生活中的慣用英語口語表達，延伸講解了重要詞彙、同義表達、重要片語、片語釋義，迅速增加英語學習者的日常口語語料庫。重點單字配有KK音標，讓讀者迅速掌握單字的正確發音，提高詞彙量。

放鬆心情

Unit 52

Concert
演唱會

歌迷們，與我們的偶像一起互動吧，讓他感受到我們的熱情和對他的喜愛。讓我們與現場的燈光一起，為偶像點亮激情。

精選實用會話例句

1 那場演唱會真令人失望。
The concert was a letdown. Track 972
重要詞彙 letdown [ˋlɛt͵daʊn] n 失望，令人失望的事物

2 我希望將來有一天可以去現場聽戴安娜的演唱會。
I wish I could go to Diana's live concert someday in the future. Track 973
重要詞彙 concert [ˋkɑnsɚt] n 演唱會，音樂會

3 我經常去聽演唱會。I go to a concert frequently. Track 974
同義表達 I often go to a concert.

4 我知道你對音樂有鑒賞力。
I know you have an ear for music. Track 975
重要片語 have an ear for 對……有鑒賞力，對……聽覺靈敏

5 你的偶像對音樂很有天賦。
Your idol has a natural bent for music. Track 976
片語釋義 natural bent 天賦，天生的喜好

6 在音樂方面我是外行。I'm no judge of music. Track 977
重要片語 be no judge of 不能判定

7 我無法忍受搖滾樂。
Rock music is more than I can bear. Track 978
同義表達 I can't stand rock music.

310

2 精彩對話，感知語境

本書摒棄了傳統英語口語學習的弊端，呈現出日常生活中的常用會話，並且增加了加分單字、對話解析和譯文。讓英語學習者在學習日常口語後，感知所使用的語境，把口語的學習放到不同的生活場景中。

① pay a visit to
意為「拜訪，參觀，探望」，後可接人，表示「拜訪某人」，也可接地點，表示「參觀某地」。

② during the day
意為「在這天當中，在白天期間」，特指某一天，而 during a day 則泛指某一天。

③ stress out
意為「承受極大的壓力」，若構成 stress sb out 則指的是「使某人緊張，令某人焦慮不安」。

④ pretend to be
意為「假裝是……」，通常還可構成 pretend to do sth 意為「假裝做某事」，或者 pretend to be doing sth 表示「假裝正在做某事」。

⑤ go back to

看情境學對話 Track 994

	中譯
A: Alan, are you free this Sunday?	A：艾倫，你這週日有空嗎？
B: It seems there is nothing to do that evening, but I need to pay a visit to ① our professor with my classmates during the day ②. What's up?	B：那天晚上貌似沒有事，不過白天我需要跟同學們一起去拜訪教授。怎麼了？
A: Great! I'd like to invite you to a concert.	A：那太棒了。我想邀請你看一場演唱會。
B: What kind of concert is that? And where?	B：那是一場什麼類型的演唱會？在哪裡？
A: It is a rock concert at the sports center near your home.	A：那是一場搖滾音樂演唱會。就在離你家很近的體育中心。

312

3 輕鬆一下，邊「學」邊「玩」

在每個場景下，設置了小笑話、諺語、漫畫等等，讓英語學習者在「玩」中「學」，「學」中「玩」，輕輕鬆鬆學口語。

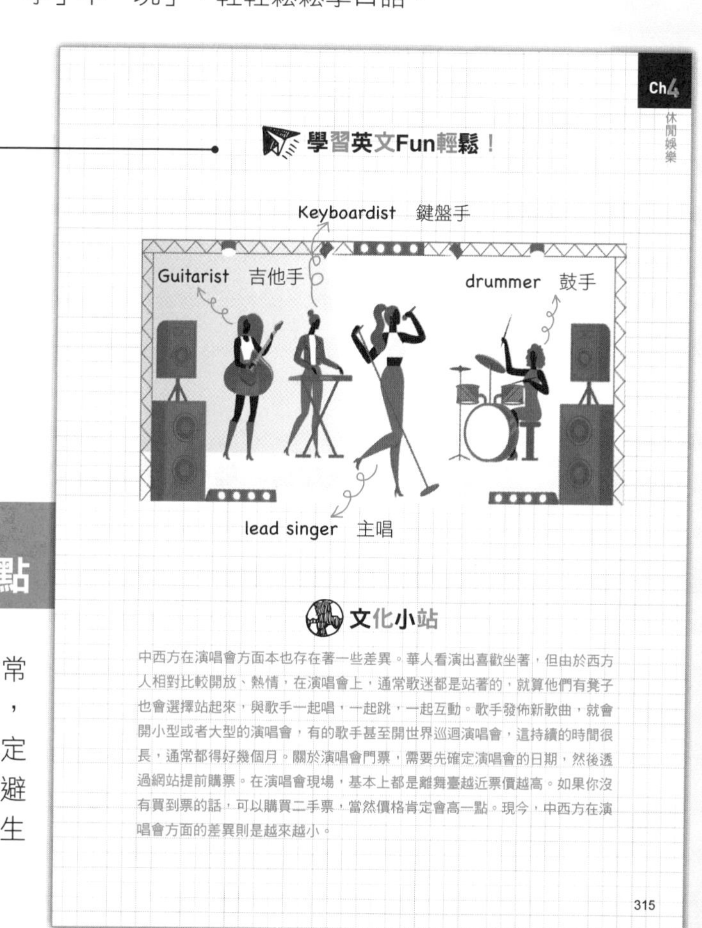

Ch4 休閒娛樂

學習英文Fun輕鬆！

文化小站

中西方在演唱會方面本也存在著一些差異。華人看演出喜歡坐著，但由於西方人相對比較開放、熱情，在演唱會上，通常歌迷都是站著的，就算他們有凳子也會選擇站起來，與歌手一起唱，一起跳，一起互動。歌手發佈新歌曲，就會開小型或者大型的演唱會，有的歌手甚至開世界巡迴演唱會，這持續的時間很長，通常都得好幾個月。關於演唱會門票，需要先確定演唱會的日期，然後透過網站提前購票。在演唱會現場，基本上都是離舞臺越近票價越高。如果你沒有買到票的話，可以購買二手票，當然價格肯定會高一點。現今，中西方在演唱會方面的差異則是越來越小。

315

4 文化小站，介紹文化盲點

讓英語學習者在學習日常口語後，進行文化洗禮，掃清文化盲點，具備一定的英語社會文化底蘊，避免在英語口語交流中產生誤解，鬧出笑話。

“

Preface 前言

英語是當今世界應用最廣泛的語言，也是國際通用的語言之一。無論是在生活還是職場中，能夠用英語流利地同別人交流已經成為現代人必備的技能。越來越多的人亦想借助英語來體驗不一樣的生活，看看是否外國的月亮比較圓。儘管很多人的願望如此，但卻不能達到理想的效果，這是因為一旦碰到外國友人需要交際時，大家都變成了啞巴。講起話來語無倫次，結結巴巴，再加上沒有自信，就會給外國友人留下不怎麼好的第一印象，要知道第一印象對他們來說是很重要的。

那麼到底如何才能學好英語呢？其實，學好英語說到底還就是講好英語，畢竟英語是一門語言，是人與人之間交際的工具。所以要想在口語方面有所突破就需要將口語句子融入到真實的交際情景中，學好理論，然後在實踐中獲得更深層的領悟。

本書就是這樣一本實用的英語口語學習書，全書共有四章，64 個小節。涵蓋了生活中的各個方面，收錄日常生活中所必須的主題和場景。本書不僅羅列了各類實用的主題和場景，還別具匠心地在每個章節內設置了會話例句、情境對話、學習英文Fun輕鬆和文化小站四大模組。除了它們都具有不同的特點外，本書的亮點在於輕學習英文Fun輕鬆和文化小站，前者以漫畫、笑話、諺語或者電影賞析的形式出現，並附帶相關的圖片，為的是給讀者增添學習的趣味性與多樣性；而文化小站則是為了讓讀者在學習口語的同時能瞭解中西方文化的差異，以此豐富讀者的學習內容，避免千篇一律的枯燥。本書力求口語的實用性，幫助讀者積累知識，融會貫通，學以致用。

衷心希望這本書能為廣大讀者在口語交際方面帶來確實幫助。當然，在編寫過程中，難免會有疏漏之處，懇請讀者批評指正！

Contents 目錄

Chapter 1 居家生活

Chapter 2 餐廳用餐

Chapter 3 愛情與婚姻

Chapter 4 休閒娛樂

Chapter 1
居家生活

Part 1 飲食

Part 2 起居

Part 3 外出

Part 4 家庭理財

Part 5 接打電話

飲食
Unit 01

Shopping for Food 買食材

食材是美食的原料，精挑細選才最好。我們挑選的食材要盡量天然健康，這樣做出來的食物才會美味可口，你才有機會抓牢別人的胃哦。

精選實用會話例句

1 這裡的雞肉都很新鮮。
All the chicken is pretty fresh here. Track 001
同義表達 The chicken is very fresh here.

2 蔬果區在哪裡？
Where is the fruit and vegetable section? Track 002
重要詞彙 section [`sɛkʃən] n. 部分，部門

3 我需要買一些食材。
I need to buy some ingredients. Track 003
重要詞彙 ingredient [ɪn`gridɪənt] n. （烹調的）原料

4 你能告訴我肉品櫃檯在哪裡嗎？
Could you tell me where the meat counter is? Track 004
詞組釋義 meat counter 肉品櫃檯

5 你們現在有新鮮的蔬菜出售嗎？
Do you have any fresh vegetables for sale now? Track 005
詞組釋義 for sale 出售，代售

6 我想買一些新鮮的蔬菜。
I'd like to buy some fresh vegetables. Track 006
同義表達 I want to buy some fresh vegetables.

7 你能給我推薦一些做點心用的食材嗎？ **Could you recommend me some ingredients for desserts?** Track 007
重要詞彙 dessert [dɪ`zɝt] n. 甜點

❽ 一共是 20 美元。It's going to be 20 dollars. Track 008

重要片語 be going to 要，會，將要

❾ 你想要點什麼？ What do you want? Track 009

同義表達 What would you like?

❿ 請給我一公斤的牛肉。Please give me a kilo of beef. Track 010

重要詞彙 kilo [ˋkilo] n. 千克，公斤

⓫ 我想知道羊肉是不是新鮮的。
I wonder if the mutton is fresh. Track 011

重要詞彙 wonder [ˋwʌndɚ] v. 想知道

⓬ 一公斤兩美元。They're two dollars per kilo. Track 012

同義表達 Two dollars a kilo.

⓭ 排骨怎麼賣？ How much are the chops? Track 013

重要詞彙 chop [tʃɒp] n. 排骨

⓮ 有點貴了。It's a bit too expensive. Track 014

片語釋義 a bit 稍微，有一點

⓯ 我三美元就可以在我家附近的超市買得到。
I can get it for three dollars at the supermarket near my house. Track 015

重要詞彙 supermarket [ˋsupɚˏmɑrkɪt] n. 超市

⓰ 只要你買得多，就會得到九折的優惠。
Take much and you'll get a 10% discount. Track 016

重要詞彙 discount [ˈdɪskaʊnt] n. 折扣

⓱ 我要買三公斤牛肉。I'll take three kilos of beef. Track 017

同義表達 I'd like to buy three kilos of beef.

⓲ 這兩種排骨有什麼區別？ What's the difference between these two kinds of ribs? Track 018

重要詞彙 difference [ˈdɪfrəns] n. 差別，差異

⓳ 給我一些雞肉。Get me some of this chicken. Track 019

片語釋義 some of 一些

20 我需要付多少錢？**How much do I need to pay?**

Track 020

同義表達 How much shall I pay?

21 我要兩公斤的馬鈴薯和一公斤胡蘿蔔。**I want two kilograms of potatoes and one kilogram of carrots.**

Track 021

重要詞彙 potato [pəˈtetəʊ] **n.** 馬鈴薯

22 這是你的零錢。**Here is your change.**

Track 022

重要詞彙 change [tʃendʒ] **n.** 零錢，變化

23 一公斤的番茄多少錢？
What's the price for a kilo of tomatoes?

Track 023

片語釋義 a kilo of 一公斤

看情境學對話

Track 024

	中譯
A: Can I help you ①, sir?	A：有什麼需要幫您的嗎，先生？
B: I wanna buy some fresh vegetables.	B：我想買一些新鮮的蔬菜。
A: Yeah, all the vegetables on this counter were delivered this morning. I guess they will meet your need ② .	A：這個櫃檯上的蔬菜都是今天早上運過來的。我猜一定符合您的要求。
B: Great.	B：太棒了。
A: What do you need?	A：你想要點什麼？
B: I'd like some carrots and celery. How much are the carrots?	B：我想要點胡蘿蔔和芹菜。胡蘿蔔怎麼賣？
A: Three dollars a kilo.	A：一公斤三美元。
B: It's a little expensive. Why are the vegetables on that counter only one dollar?	B：有點貴啊。為什麼那個櫃檯上的蔬菜只需要一美元？

A: Those are not very fresh. If you want to choose the cheaper one, you can buy some.	A：那些都不大新鮮了。如果你想選擇便宜的，你也可以買一些。
B: Forget it. ③ I will just take fresh vegetables. Two kilograms of carrots and one kilogram of celery.	B：算了。我還是要新鮮的蔬菜吧。給我兩公斤的胡蘿蔔和一公斤的芹菜。
A: OK. Wait a second ④ , please.	A：好的。請稍等。
B: I would also like to know when these leeks were for sale.	B：我還想知道這些韭菜是什麼時候開始賣的。
A: About a day ago. Do you need some?	A：大約一天前。你需要一些嗎？
B: Give me one kilogram. Do you have any cheaper mushrooms?	B：給我來一公斤吧。有沒有便宜一點的蘑菇？
A: Yes. By the way, these mushrooms don't look good, but they have the same nutritional value.	A：有的。順便說一下，雖然這些蘑菇的賣相不好，但營養價值是一樣的。
B: Well. One kilogram, too.	B：好的。也要一公斤。
A: OK, anything else ⑤ ?	A：好的，其他還需要嗎？
B: No, thanks.	B：不用了，謝謝。

【程度提升，加分單字】

★**deliver** [dɪ`lɪvɚ] **v.** 運送，投遞

★**accordance** [ə`kɔrdəns] **n.** 一致，和諧

★**requirement** [rɪ`kwaɪəmənt] **n.** 要求

① **Can I help you?**

在口語中使用頻率很高，用 may 使語氣更加委婉，通常是看見他人需要幫助而詢問對方的用語。需要根據不同的場景來分析其具體的意思，如用在商場中，則可將其譯為「請問買什麼」。

② **meet one's need**

意為「滿足某人的需要」，one's 可用my，his，her 和their等代替。

③ **forget it**

意為「算了吧」，對他人的道歉表示「沒關係」以及表示不想提及某事或者認為某件事無關緊要。有時也有拒絕或否定某事的意思。

④ **wait a second**

意為「稍等一下」，常用在口語中，與 please 連用。其等同於 wait a moment。

⑤ **anything else**

意為「其他東西」，用於口語疑問句，表示「還要別的嗎？」在購物或點餐時經常會聽到。

文化小站

中西方的飲食文化有很大的差異，這也就在某種程度上決定了人們在選購食材時所關注的點不一樣。華人通常習慣於用新鮮的食材做美食，有的人甚至會選擇一天三次去買新鮮的食材，而西方人往往一次性購買一週的食物存放於冰箱中，這些食物基本上都是冷凍食品，而他們食用的罐頭甚至達華人食用的八倍之多。西方人購買的食材通常是穀類、培根、牛奶、麵包、乳酪以及牛排等，最重要的是奶油，還有很多食材通常用來製作冷菜，例如沙拉；而華人購買的食材則大部分都用來製作熱菜。由於西方人追求營養，特別講究食物的營養成分，所以他們購買的蔬菜通常都是能直接食用的，用來製作各類沙拉，所煎的牛排都是半熟的；而華人追求美味，喜歡各類做法的熟食。

飲食

Unit 02

Cooking

烹飪

吃飯十分鐘，做飯兩小時，其瑣碎程度常常讓人望而生畏。但是，烹飪其實充滿了各種樂趣，我們能從中獲得許多成就感。那還等什麼，趕快行動吧！

精選實用會話例句

1. 做麵條是我媽媽的強項。
Making noodles is my mother's long suit. Track 025
同義表達 My mother is good at making noodles.

2. 我受不了油膩食物。 I can't stand greasy food. Track 026
重要詞彙 greasy [ˋgrizɪ] adj. 油膩的，諂媚的

3. 午飯你想吃什麼？
What would you like to eat for lunch? Track 027
同義表達 What do you want to eat for lunch?

4. 能把醋遞給我嗎？
Could you pass me the vinegar? Track 028
重要片語 pass sb sth 給某人遞東西

5. 別忘了鍋裡的魚。Don't forget the fish in the pot. Track 029
同義表達 Remember you are cooking fish in the pot.

6. 先把菜洗了，然後切碎。Wash the vegetables and chop them into little pieces. Track 030
重要詞彙 chop [tʃɒp] v. 切碎，砍

7. 義大利麵是我最喜歡的食物。
Pasta is my favorite food. Track 031
重要詞彙 pasta [ˈpæstə] n. 麵團，義大利麵

8 你能到廚房幫我忙嗎？
Can you help me in the kitchen?
Track 032
同義表達 Could you do me a favor in the kitchen? / Could you lend me a hand in the kitchen?

9 你會做日本料理嗎？
Can you cook Japanese cuisine?
Track 033
同義表達 Do you know how to cook Japanese cuisine?

10 我正忙著做炸雞呢。**I am busy making fried chicken.**
Track 034
重要片語 be busy doing sth 忙於做某事

11 你喜歡什麼口味？ **What flavor do you prefer?**
Track 035
重要詞彙 flavor [`flevɚ] n. 口味

12 你可以在平底鍋裡煎雞蛋。
You can fry the eggs in the pan.
Track 036
重要詞彙 fry [fraɪ] v. 煎，炸 n. 油炸食物

13 現在把番茄切碎。 **Now, cut up the tomatoes.**
Track 037
片語釋義 cut up 切碎，切開

14 你吃很辣的嗎？ **Do you eat a lot of pepper?**
Track 038
重要詞彙 pepper [`pɛpɚ] n. 胡椒

15 你對做飯感興趣嗎？ **Do you like cooking?**
Track 039
同義表達 Are you keen on cooking? / Are you fond of cooking?

16 那對健康不好。**It's not good for your health.**
Track 040
重要片語 be good for 對……好

17 你準備好所有材料了嗎？
Have you got all the ingredients ready?
Track 041
重要詞彙 ingredient [ɪn`gridɪənt] n. 食材

18 我要做牛排給兒子吃。
I'm gonna make a steak for my son.
Track 042
同義表達 I want to make a steak for my son.

19 我需要先把鍋熱一下嗎？
Do I need to heat the wok first?
Track 043
重要詞彙 wok [wɒk] n. 鍋

⑳ 鍋熱了後，放一點油進去。
Put a little oil in the pot once it gets hot. Track 044

同義表達 Put a little oil into the pot as soon as it becomes hot.

㉑ 今天我來給你露一手，你就等著享受美食吧。**I'll give you a show and you just wait for the delicious food.** Track 045

重要片語 give sb a show 給某人露一手

㉒ 你做菜很有天賦。**You have a talent for cooking.** Track 046

重要片語 have a talent for 有……的天賦

看情境學對話

中譯 Track 047

A: John, do you like cooking?	A：約翰，你喜歡做飯嗎？
B: Yes. I love making various meals with different ingredients for my families and friends. It gives me a sense of satisfaction. What about you ①?	B：是的。我喜歡用不同的食材做出豐盛的飯菜，給我的家人朋友們吃，這讓我很有滿足感。你呢？
A: I hate cooking. I think it wastes too much time. Besides, I don't like cleaning up after the meal. It's annoying to do the washing up, drying up and putting away ② the bowls and dishes.	A：我討厭做飯。我認為這太浪費時間了，而且，我不喜歡飯後收拾。洗碗，烘乾，再把碗碟都收起來太煩人了。
B: You will be tired if you do all the washing up yourself. Why not ask others to help? You just have to remind them where everything goes.	B：如果所有的清洗都是你自己做的話就太累了。為什麼不找其他人幫忙呢？你只需要提醒他們所有東西放哪就好。

A: Good idea. ③ So what kind of dishes do you often make?	A：好主意。那麼，你經常做什麼菜呢？
B: I am fond of Italian and Chinese cuisine.	B：我喜歡義大利菜和中式料理。
A: I hear it's hard to get ingredients for Chinese food.	A：我聽說中式料理的食材不好買。
B: Not always. You can buy most of them at supermarket. The way you cook Chinese food is different from that you prepare the western food.	B：也不全是。你可以在超市買到大部分的材料。做中餐和西餐的方式是不同的。
A: Sounds interesting. ④ How long does it take if you cook a meal for four people?	A：聽起來很有趣。你準備四個人的餐點要多久？
B: Well, it depends on ⑤ what I am cooking. Generally speaking, I spend an hour or two.	B：嗯，那要看做什麼飯，一般是一兩個小時。

【程度提升，加分單字】

★**satisfaction** [ˌsætɪsˈfækʃn] n. 滿足，滿意
★**annoying** [əˈnɔɪɪŋ] adj. 討厭的，讓人厭煩的
★**remind** [rɪˈmaɪnd] v. 提醒，使記起

對話解析

① **what about you**

使用頻率很高，表示「你呢？」、「你怎麼想？」、「你怎麼樣？」等，跟前一句緊密相連，問對方的情況或者想法。也可以用 how about you 來替換。

② **put away**

表示「收藏，放好」，後面常跟表示物品的名詞或者名詞片語。

③ **good idea**

表示「好主意，妙計」，是對別人的贊同。一般在對方提出自己的想法、建議後，可以用這句話表示贊許、認可。

④ **sounds interesting**

表示「聽起來不錯」，sound 是感官動詞，後面可以直接跟形容詞。這句話也可以用 sounds great 來代替。

⑤ **depend on**

意思是「依賴，依靠」，其中的介詞 on 也可以用 upon 來代替。 depend on 後面一般要跟名詞、代詞或者名詞片語。

學習英文Fun輕鬆！

1. An apple a day keeps the doctor away.
   每天一個蘋果，疾病遠離我。
2. Diet cures more than doctors.
   自己飲食有節，勝過上門求醫。
3. Leave off with an appetite.
   吃得七分飽，就該離餐桌。
4. Eat at pleasure, drink with measure.
   隨意吃飯，適度飲酒。
5. Some soup before dinner, healthy body forever.
   飯前喝口湯，永遠沒災殃。
6. A close mouth catches no flies.
   病從口入。
7. Wanna be healthy? Do treat yourself a nice breakfast.
   要想身體好，早餐要吃飽。

文化小站

在華人宴席上，人們習慣相互敬酒，相互讓菜、夾菜。而西式飲宴上，食品和酒都是陪襯，宴會的核心在於交際，與鄰座客人互相交談，共結友誼。比如說，中式宴席像是集體舞，而西式宴會就是男女的交誼舞。對於食物的烹飪，中西方的方式也不盡相同。華人喜歡加蔥、薑、蒜、醋、醬油、辣椒，這些佐料可以殺菌、消脂、增進食欲、助消化，而西方人的佐料比較簡單。

飲食

Unit 03 Baking 烘焙

烘焙，火候尤為重要。尤其台灣人非常熱愛甜點。如果你學會了烘焙，你也會獲得很多人的青睞，所以有空就體驗一下烘焙的樂趣吧。

精選實用會話例句

❶ 你如何烤麵包？
How do you bake bread? Track 048
重要詞彙 bread [brɛd] n. 麵包

❷ 你需要一些糖、麵粉和雞蛋，這取決於你想要製作多少。
You need some sugar, flour, and eggs, depending on how much you want to make. Track 049
片語釋義 depend on 取決於，依賴，依靠

❸ 我聽說你是一個專業的烘焙師。
I heard you are a professional baker. Track 050
重要詞彙 professional [prəˈfeʃənl] adj. 專業的，職業的

❹ 對我來說，烘焙是一種令我放鬆的創意形式。**For me, baking is a form of creativity that relaxes me.** Track 051
重要詞彙 creativity [ˌkrieˋtɪvətɪ] n. 創造性，創造力

❺ 就個人而言，我喜歡吃甜食。
Personally, I love desserts. Track 052
同義表達 have a sweet tooth.

❻ 我喜歡甜食，所以做蛋糕對我來說是一種樂趣。**I love sweets, so it ends up being fun making cakes.** Track 053
片語釋義 end up 以……結束，最後成為／變得

7 說到餅乾，我已經好久沒有做了。
Speaking of cookies, I haven't made them for a long time. Track 054
片語釋義 speaking of 談起，提到

8 我不知道你是否知道如何烘焙。
I don't know if you know how to bake. Track 055
重要詞彙 bake [bek] v. 烤，烘焙

9 你有沒有烤過餅乾之類的東西？ Have you ever baked biscuits or anything like that? Track 056
同義表達 Have you ever baked cookies or anything?

10 我確實烤過一個蛋糕。
I did actually bake a cake. Track 057
重要詞彙 actually [ˈæktʃuəlɪ] adv. 實際上，事實上

11 烤幾個大蘋果派正合我意。
Baking some big apple pies is just the thing. Track 058
片語釋義 just the thing 正是想要的

12 你能教我如何烤這個餅乾嗎？
Can you teach me how to bake this cookie? Track 059
重要片語 teach sb sth 教某人某事

13 掌握溫度是至關重要的。
It is vital to master the heat. Track 060
重要片語 it is vital to do sth 做某事至關重要

14 這些餅乾正到火候。The cookies are done to a turn. Track 061
重要片語 done to a turn 烹調得恰到火候

15 我想問你一些關於烘焙的訣竅。
I'd like to ask for some tips about baking. Track 062
重要詞彙 tip [tɪp] n. 訣竅

16 你最好現在就把它放進烤箱裡。
You'd better put it in the oven now. Track 063
重要詞彙 oven [ˈʌvn] n. 烤箱

⑰ 我把這些餅乾放在烤箱裡烤，直到它們變咖啡色。**I put these cookies in the oven until they turn brown.** Track 064

片語釋義 turn broun 變咖啡色

⑱ 我給你解釋一下烘焙過程。

I'll explain the baking process to you. Track 065

同義表達 Let me tell you the baking process.

⑲ 我怎樣操作這個烤箱？

How do I operate the oven? Track 066

重要詞彙 operate [ˈɒpəreɪt] v. 操作，經營，管理

看情境學對話

\中譯/ Track 067

A: You are a baker; can you explain to me ① how to bake bread?	A：你是位烤麵包師，能向我解釋一下如何烤麵包嗎？
B: Of course. First of all, you need some flour, yeast, sugar, cream, salt, and water. The quantities of them depend on how much you want to make.	B：當然可以了。首先你需要準備麵粉、酵母、糖、奶油、鹽和水。他們的量取決於你想製作多少。
A: Okay. And then?	A：好的。然後呢？
B: Then you use the mixer to mix them together. By the way ② , you can't sprinkle salt directly on the yeast because theyeast will lose its effect.	B：然後用機器把它們攪拌在一起。順便說一下，不能直接灑鹽在酵母上，因為酵母會失去功效。
A: OK, I know. And how long do I need to mix?	A：我知道了。需要攪拌多久？

B: About eight minutes until the dough is developed. Then you need to wait for five minutes to let it ferment into the size you want.	B：大約八分鐘直到麵團膨脹起來。然後你需要等待五分鐘讓它發酵成你想要的大小。
A: That sounds interesting. When do I need to put it in the mold?	A：聽起來很有趣。我什麼時候需要把它放進模型裡？
B: After it's fermented, you divide them into ③ what you want and put them in the mold.	B：等它發酵後，你就把它們分成你想要的數量裝進模型裡。
A: Do I need to put them in the oven at this time?	A：這時我就需要把它們放進烤箱裡嗎？
B: Yes.	B：是的。
A: How long do I need to keep it in there?	A：我需要放多長時間？
B: About twenty minutes. Then it's done and you need to take the bread out of ④ the oven.	B：大約二十分鐘。然後你就把麵包從烤箱裡取出來，它就做好了。
A: Okay, I get it. ⑤ How I wish I had a try now.	A：好的，瞭解了。我多麼希望現在就嘗試一下。

【程度提升，加分單字】

★**mixer** [ˋmɪksɚ] **n.** 攪拌器　★**sprinkle** [ˈsprɪŋkl] **v.** 撒，灑

★**ferment** [fɝˋmɛnt] **v.** 使發酵，醞釀　★**mold** [mold] **n.** 模型

對話解析

① **explain to sb sth**

意為「向某人解釋某事」，要牢記 explain後的 to，其等同於 explain sth to sb。若 sth 是代詞 it 的話，要用 explain it to sb。

② **by the way**

意為「順便一提」，通常用在口語中，是為了避免話鋒一轉給人唐突的感覺。

③ **divide sth into...**

意為「將某物分成……」，指的是把整體分成若干個相對應的部分，也可以直接用作 divide into 意為「分成，分為」。

④ **take sth out of sth**

意為「把某物從……中取出來」，of 後面跟的是從什麼裡面拿出， take 後跟的是要拿出的東西。

⑤ **get it**

意為「瞭解，懂得」，通常用在口語中 I get it，意為「我明白了」，在美語中既可以用現在時的 I get it，也可以用過去時的 I got it 。

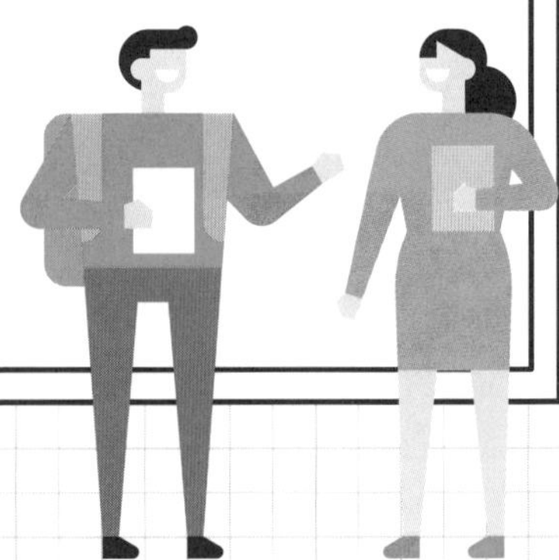

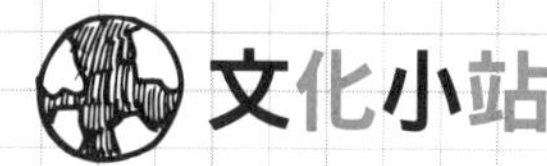

文化小站

烘焙，作為蛋糕、麵包之類的製作流程之一，在西方國家佔據著十分重要的位置。烘焙食品除了營養高之外，還富含氨基酸和蛋白質，易於吸收，因此烘焙食品幾乎成了西方國家飲食的代名詞。眾所周知，烘焙食品是西方人生活的必需品，麵包和餅乾等在西方家庭的飲食中佔據著主要地位。在西方，烘焙行業的市場規模很大，幾乎趨於穩定。當你漫步於街道上時，你會發現自產自銷的糕點房比比皆是。烘焙食品在西方三餐中都扮演著重要的角色，由此可看出其重要性，值得一提的是，在西方國家裡，幾乎每一個家庭主婦都會製作點心。當她們與親朋好友在家聚餐時就會呈上自製的各類點心，尤其是蛋糕和蘋果派，以表達出她們的誠意。在西方人的觀念中，在美景的襯托下享用點心和各類飲料，會具有浪漫和溫馨的情調，是一種極致的享受。由此我們可看出，烘焙食品已然成了一種西方文化的象徵。

飲食
Unit 04

Dining
用餐

俗話說，民以食為天。這足以證明吃飯在日常生活中起著重要的作用。一日三餐很重要，即使你屬於愛賴床的懶鬼行列也要按時吃飯哦，健康才是你應當考慮的重點。

精選實用會話例句

1. 我們什麼時候吃飯？ **When shall we eat?** Track 068
   重要詞彙 shall [ʃəl] v. 應該，將要

2. 請把辣椒遞給我。**Pass me the hot pepper, please.** Track 069
   重要片語 pass sb sth 把某物遞給某人

3. 約翰，幫我擺一下餐具。
   Help me set the table, John. Track 070
   片語釋義 set the table 擺桌子，擺餐具

4. 如果你在上面撒一些胡椒粉就會更好吃了。**It would be more delicious if you sprinkle some pepper on it.** Track 071
   重要詞彙 delicious [dɪˈlɪʃəs] adj. 美味的，可口的

5. 炒飯是我喜歡吃的料理。**Fried rice is my cup of tea.** Track 072
   片語釋義 cup of tea 喜愛的人或事物

6. 你想再來點薯條嗎？
   Would you like some more fries? Track 073
   重要詞彙 fries [fraɪz] n. 炸薯條

7. 我早飯想吃漢堡。
   I feel like a hamburger for breakfast. Track 074
   片語釋義 feel like 想要

❽ 該吃飯了。It's time to eat.

同義表達 Time for dinner.

Track 075

❾ 吃光你盤子裡的東西。Clean up your plate.

片語釋義 clean up 清空，大撈一筆

Track 076

❿ 你應該把盤子裡的食物吃光。

You should eat up all the food on your plate.

片語釋義 eat up 吃光，耗盡

Track 077

⓫ 你洗手了嗎？ Did you wash your hands?

重要片語 wash one's hands 洗手

Track 078

⓬ 別用手拿，用你的勺子吃飯。Don't pick the food with your fingers, just use your spoon.

重要詞彙 spoon [spun] n. 匙

Track 079

⓭ 請自便。Help youeself.

同義表達 Make yourself at home.

Track 080

⓮ 不要這麼狼吞虎嚥的。

Don't pig out.

片語釋義 pig out 狼吞虎嚥，大吃特吃

Track 081

⓯ 你做的飯真好吃！

What delectable food you cook!

重要詞彙 cook [kʊk] v. 烹調 n. 廚師

Track 082

⓰ 我覺得你最好強迫自己吃掉。

I think you'd better force yourself to eat them.

重要片語 force oneself to do sth 強迫自己做某事

Track 083

⓱ 你想再來一碗飯嗎？

Would you like another bowl of rice?

重要詞彙 bowl [boʊl] n. 碗

Track 084

⓲ 我真希望能再吃點，但是我吃不下了。

I wish I could eat more, but I am full.

重要詞彙 wish [wɪʃ] v. 希望，想要

Track 085

⑲ **我很高興你喜歡吃。**

I'm glad you enjoy it. Track 086

重要詞彙 glad [glæd] **adj.** 令人高興的

⑳ **你能邀請我真是太好了。**

It's very nice of you to invite me. Track 087

重要片語 it's very nice of sb to do sth 某人能做某事真的很好

㉑ **開飯了。Dinner is served.** Track 088

同義表達 Dinner is ready.

看情境學對話

\中譯/ Track 089

A: We haven't seen each other in ages. How have you been recently? Please take a seat ①.	A：我們好多年沒見了，你最近過得怎麼樣？請坐。
B: Very well, thank you. Daniel, I'm glad you could invite me to dinner ②.	B：我很好，謝謝。丹尼爾，很高興你能邀請我來吃飯。
A: I heard you have been working abroad for years, so I guess you'd like to eat at home. Then I had Amy make her special dishes. I don't know if it's your cup of tea.	A：我聽說你近幾年一直在外工作，所以我猜你一定想在家裡吃飯。然後我就讓艾米做了自己最拿手的菜。我不知道這是否符合你的胃口。
B: Wow. It's delicious. I love it.	B：哇，太美味了。我很喜歡。
A: I'm glad you like it. Would you like some whiskey first?	A：很高興你能喜歡。你想先要一點威士忌嗎？

B: No, thank you. I've quit drinking. But would you give me a glass of drink?	B：不了，謝謝。我已經戒酒了。不過給我一杯飲料好嗎？
A: Here you go ③ . Anything else?	A：給你。還要其他的嗎？
B: No, thank you. To be honest, what makes me most happy is that there is salad, which I like best. French fries and chicken are what I often eat. I also have a sweet tooth.	B：不了，謝謝。老實說，令我最高興的是這裡有我最喜歡吃的沙拉。炸薯條和雞肉也是我經常吃的。我還很喜歡吃甜點。
A: Great. Please make yourself at home ④. Would you like some more rice?	A：請別客氣，請自便。你想再要一碗飯嗎？
B: No, thank you. I wish I could eat more, but I am quite full.	B：不用了，謝謝。我還想再吃，但是我實在太飽了。
A: Here is to our friendship. Cheers.	A：這一杯敬我們的友誼。乾杯。
B: Cheers. Thank you again. I had a nice dinner.	B：乾杯。再次感謝。我吃了一頓很美味的晚餐。
A: Please feel free ⑤ to call me if you want to come over again.	A：如果你想再來我這裡的話，請隨時打給我。
B: Okay, thank you.	B：好的，謝謝你。

【程度提升，加分單字】

★**abroad** [əˋbrɔd] **adv.** 在國外
★**special** [ˋspɛʃəl] **adj.** 特殊的，專門的
★**thirsty** [ˋθɝstɪ] **adj.** 口渴的，缺水的

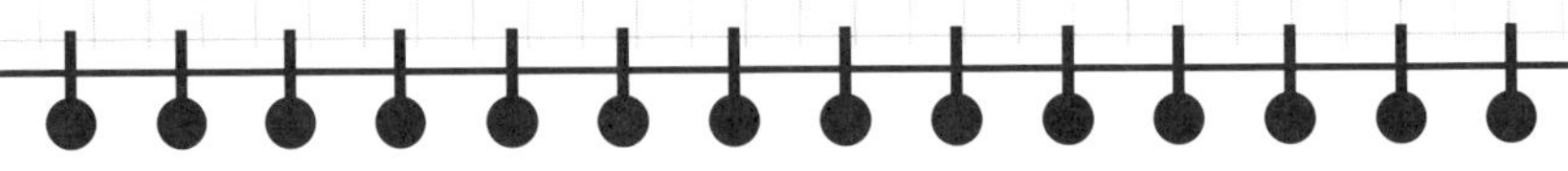

對話解析

① **take a seat**

意為「請坐」，通常是家裡來客人時一種比較客氣的說法，與其相區別的 have a seat 指的是一種狀態。

② **invite sb to sth**

意為「邀請某人做某事，參加某活動」，我們經常見到的關於 invite 的用法是 invite sb to do sth 意為「邀請某人做某事」。

③ **here you go**

意為「給你」，在口語中很常見，等同於 here you are，例如在速食店裡店員給你東西的時候就可以使用，其還有「做得好，就是這樣」的意思。

④ **make yourself at home**

意為「就當自己家一樣，請不要客氣」，通常是主人為了客人能在家裡感到自在而說的客氣話，常與 please 搭配使用。

⑤ **feel free**

意為「請便，隨自己之意」，其後通常接 to do sth。

文化小站

中西方文化的差異也體現在餐桌上，這也就是所謂的餐桌禮儀。就餐時餐具的差異是中西方餐桌文化的基本差異。眾所周知，西方人用刀叉，東方人用筷子。通常，人們認為使用刀叉就意味著分吃，這也就體現了西方人的分食制，以此衍生出他們講究獨立的文化。而筷子在東方則象徵了團結與合作。有一點相似的是，不管是筷子還是刀叉，人們吃飯時都不能用其比手畫腳，而應將其放在合適的位置，尤其是在發言時。另外，華人在餐桌吃飯時講究座次，也就是說，華人在吃飯時依據尊重長者，長幼有序的標準來安排座位，常選擇圓桌來體現團圓。西方人就餐時通常選擇長桌，主人喜歡坐於長桌兩端，然後遵循「女士優先」、「右為上」的習慣，首先讓女主賓坐在自己的右手邊。東西方餐桌文化還有一點不同的是「鬧」與「靜」的差異。在西方的餐桌上每個人都有一份自己的食物，不用干擾鄰座用餐的人，只有調料是公用的，所以他們是「靜」，而東方人在餐桌上吃飯時體現出的是一種熱情與和睦，氣氛很熱烈，所以是「熱鬧」。

飲食

Unit 05 Cleaning 收拾碗筷

飯後收拾碗筷，做個勤勞的主人。要養成飯後收拾碗筷的習慣，或許你能體會到家務帶來的喜悅心情。

精選實用會話例句

1 請幫我清理一下桌子。
Please help me clean the table. Track 090
片語釋義 clear the table 清理餐桌，收拾桌子

2 輪到誰來收拾碗筷了？
Whose turn is it to clean the dishes? Track 091
重要片語 it is one's turn to do sth 輪到誰做某事

3 你能幫我洗盤子嗎？
Can you help me to do the dishes? Track 092
同義表達 Can you wash the dishes for me?

4 輪到你來洗餐具了。**It's your turn to do the dishes.** Track 093
片語釋義 do the dishes 洗餐具（飯後）

5 吃完飯你會洗餐具嗎？
Will you wash the dishes after the meal? Track 094
重要詞彙 meal [mil] n. 餐，飯

6 晚飯後我不想洗餐具。
I don't feel like doing the dishes after dinner. Track 095
片語釋義 after dinner 晚餐後

7 把餐具放進水槽裡。**Put the dishes in the sink.** Track 096
重要詞彙 sink [sɪŋk] n. 洗滌槽

❽ 你把它們放入洗碟機。
You load the dishwasher. Track 097
重要詞彙 dishwasher [ˋdɪʃˏwɑʃɚ] n. 洗碗機

❾ 把每樣物品都放好。
Put everything away. Track 098
片語釋義 put away 收起來，放好

❿ 你能告訴我為什麼這些汙漬洗不掉嗎？**Can you tell me why these stains can't be removed?** Track 099
同義表達 Can you tell me why these stains won't come out?

⓫ 在我看來，收拾餐具使我放鬆。
The way I see it, tidying up makes me relax. Track 100
片語釋義 the way I see it 在我看來

⓬ 收拾餐具時要小心些。
Be careful when you clean up the dishes. Track 101
重要片語 be careful 注意，當心，小心

⓭ 當你洗盤子時用一點洗滌劑。**Use a little detergent when you wash the dishes.** Track 102
重要詞彙 detergent [dɪˋtɝdʒənt] n. 洗滌劑，去垢劑

⓮ 把這些盤子放回原位。
Put these dishes back. Track 103
片語釋義 put back 放回原處

⓯ 為什麼你不幫你媽媽收拾碗筷？
Why don't you help your mom with the dishes? Track 104
重要詞彙 dish [dɪʃ] n. 盤，餐具

⓰ 我在等著你把盤子放進櫥櫃裡。**I'm waiting for you to put the dishes in the cupboard.** Track 105
重要詞彙 cupboard [ˋkʌbəd] n. 櫥櫃

⓱ 如果我幫你洗碗，你能給我一點零用錢嗎？
Could you give me some pocket money if I help you wash the dishes? Track 106
片語釋義 pocket money 零用錢

⑱ 記得把盤子放在一起。

Remember to get the dishes all together. Track 107

片語釋義 all together 一起

⑲ 我不喜歡洗碗盤。

I don't like washing the dishes. Track 108

重要片語 don't like doing sth 已成習慣不喜歡做某事

看情境學對話

\中譯/ Track 109

A: Have you finished eating?	A：你吃完了嗎？
B: Not yet. What's up? ①	B：還沒有。怎麼了？
A: Is it your turn to wash the dishes today?	A：今天輪到你洗盤子了嗎？
B: No, it's Jenny.	B：不是，是珍妮。
A: But Jenny is not at home today. Can you help me clean up the dishes?	A：但是珍妮今天不在家，你能幫我收拾碗筷嗎？
B: No way. I can help you wash the vegetables, but I don't like washing the dishes. You know, I hate washing dishes.	B：不可能。我能幫你洗菜，但是我不願意洗盤子。你知道的，我討厭洗盤子。
A: I know. If you had to wash the dishes or cook, which would you choose?	A：我知道。假如你必須洗盤子和做飯，你會選擇哪樣？
B: I'd rather cook than ② wash the dishes.	B：我寧願做飯也不想洗盤子。

A: All right. Let's make a deal. ③ If you wash the dishes today, I'll give you an extra five dollars for your pocket money, is it OK?	A：這樣吧，我們來做個交易。如果你今天洗盤子的話，我會給你額外五美元的零用錢，怎麼樣？
B: No, at least ten dollars.	B：不行，最少 10 美元。
A: Done. By the way, if I find a stain on the plate, I'll take away your pocket money.	A：成交。順便說一下，如果我發現盤子上有汙漬的話就會沒收你的零用錢。
B: OK, but as I see it, you will find a way to take my ten dollars.	B：可以。不過在我看來，你一定會想辦法拿走我的十美元。
A: No, I'm a person of my word. ④ And your father can testify it. What's more, remember to put clean dishes in the cupboard.	A：不會的。我是一個說話算數的人，你爸爸可以作證。另外，記得把乾淨的盤子放進櫥櫃裡。
B: Fair enough. ⑤ By the way, where's our new detergent?	B：好的。對了，我們的新清洗劑在哪裡？
A: It's on the right side of the cabinet.	A：就在櫥櫃的右側。

【程度提升，加分單字】

★**pocket** [ˋpɒkɪt] **n.** 口袋
★**stain** [steɪn] **n.** 汙點，瑕疵
★**testify** [ˋtestɪfaɪ] **v.** 作證
★**cabinet** [ˋkæbɪnət] **n.** 櫥櫃

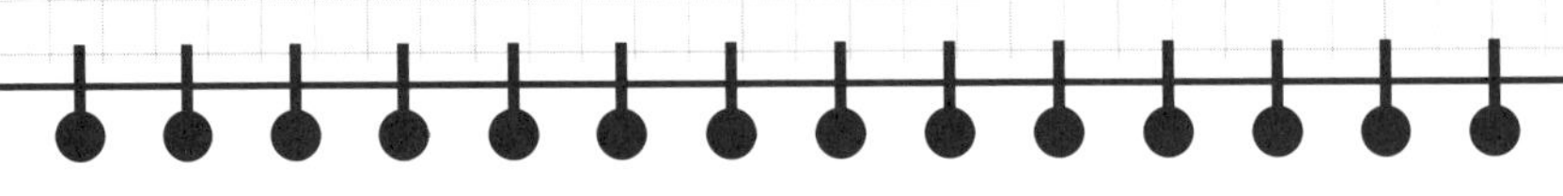

對話解析

① **What's up?**

意為「怎麼了？近來如何？」是美國人常用的寒暄語，是一種打招呼的方式。若當「近來如何」使用時，回答「沒什麼事」就用 not much 或者 nothing來表示。等同於 How's it going?/ How are you doing?

② **would rather do A than do B**

意為「寧願做 A 而不願做 B」，其等同於 would do A rather than do B。

③ **make a deal**

意為「成交，達成交易」，常出現在口語中，表示與某人做交易。但若是碰見 make a big deal 則要意為「小題大做，大驚小怪」，注意其翻譯。

④ **I'm a person of my word.**

意為「我是一個說話算話的人，我是一個講信用的人」，這裡的 I 可以替換成 He 和 She，my 也可以替換成 his 和 her 等。

⑤ **fair enough**

意為「好吧，說的對，有道理，可以」，是很流行的口語用語，用於同意對方的話或要求等。

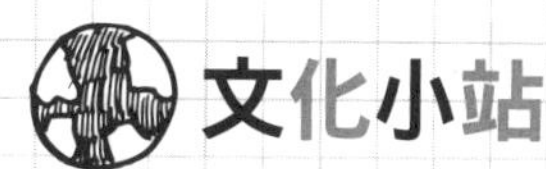

文化小站

飯後我們都有收拾餐具的習慣。不僅是為了乾淨衛生，也是為了給人留下好印象。在西方，人們用餐結束後會將刀叉平行並排放於餐盤中央，垂直於自己，這表示自己用餐結束了。而他們的家用洗碗機就如同冰箱和洗衣機一樣常見。他們認為用洗碗機可以節省下時間來做其他的事情。無論是中還是西，客人一般都會主動提出收拾餐具、清洗餐具的提議，以表達自己的感激之情和心意。

飲食
Unit 06

Eating Habits 飲食習慣

飲食習慣很重要，為了健康要謹慎。在生活中我們要養成良好的飲食習慣。

精選實用會話例句

❶ 通常你都吃什麼早餐？
What do you usually have for breakfast? Track 110
重要詞彙 breakfast [ˋbrɛkfəst] n. 早餐

❷ 你最好遵循一種你能堅持的健康飲食習慣。**You'd better follow a healthy diet that you can stick to.** Track 111
片語釋義 stick to 遵循，忠於

❸ 醫生建議我保持健康的飲食習慣。
The doctor advised me to keep a healthy diet. Track 112
片語釋義 keep a healthy diet 保持健康的飲食

❹ 我建議你改變自己的飲食習慣。
I suggest you change your eating habits. Track 113
片語釋義 eating habits 飲食習慣

❺ 你應該停止你那不好的飲食習慣。**You are supposed to stop your bad eating habits.** Track 114
同義表達 You'd better stop your bad eating habits now.

❻ 我猜沒人會有這樣的飲食習慣。
I guess no one goes on that kind of diet. Track 115
重要詞彙 diet [ˈdaɪət] n. 飲食

❼ 你過重就應該節食。
You are so heavy that you should go on a diet. Track 116
片語釋義 go on a diet 節食，減肥

❽ 我通常會在早飯前喝一杯咖啡。
I usually have a cup of coffee before breakfast. Track 117
片語釋義 have coffee 喝咖啡

❾ 我早餐只吃吐司麵包和雞蛋。
I only have toast and eggs for breakfast. Track 118
重要詞彙 toast [tost] n. 烤麵包，乾杯 v. 烤，為……祝酒，為……乾杯

❿ 通常情況下，我在 12 點出去吃午餐。
Normally, I go out for lunch at 12:00. Track 119
片語釋義 go out for lunch 出去吃午飯

⓫ 所以你是說你吃辣椒？So you say you eat chili? Track 120
片語釋義 So you say 所以你說，是你這麼說的嘛

⓬ 這種飲食習慣適合你的生活方式。
This kind of diet fits into your lifestyle. Track 121
片語釋義 fit into 適合，與……融為一體

⓭ 這個飲食方式會讓你的身體不健康。
This diet will make you unhealthy. Track 122
重要詞彙 unhealthy [ʌnˈhɛlθɪ] adj. 不健康的，對健康有害的

⓮ 你通常下午會喝一杯紅茶嗎？Do you usually have a cup of black tea in the afternoon? Track 123
片語釋義 black tea 紅茶

⓯ 我有一個方便的辦法來創造健康的飲食方式。I have a convenient way to make a healthy diet. Track 124
重要詞彙 convenient [kənˋvinjənt] adj. 方便的

⓰ 這不符合我的飲食習慣。It doesn't fit my eating habits. Track 125
重要詞彙 fit [fɪt] v. 適合

⓱ 我已經逐漸戒掉了肉食習慣。
I have gradually given up eating meat. Track 126
同義表達 I have moved away from a daily meat-based diet.

⓲ 你可以飯前喝一杯溫水。You can have a glass of warm water before dinner. Track 127
片語釋義 warm water 溫水

⑲ 我不吃肉的話就總覺得很餓。
I'll always feel hungry if I don't eat meat. Track 128
重要詞彙 meat [mit] **n.** 肉

⑳ 我試著保持這一種飲食。**I manage to keep this diet.** Track 129
重要片語 manage to do 設法做成某事

㉑ 我每天晚上都會吃一個漢堡。
I eat a hamburger every night. Track 130
片語釋義 every night 每夜

看情境學對話

Track 131

	中譯
A: Alan, do you know that good eating habits will make you stay productive at work?	A：艾倫，你知道好的飲食習慣能讓你在工作時保持高效嗎？
B: I have no idea. Can you explain to me what eating habits can make me effective at work? Thank you in advance.	B：我不太懂。你能解釋一下什麼樣的飲食習慣能讓我在工作上有效率嗎？先感謝你。
A: My pleasure. ① First of all, don't eat junk food because it can make you less alert at work, and make you feel sluggish and lethargic, that is to say ②, you may want to sleep during working hours.	A：我的榮幸。首先你不要吃垃圾食品。因為它會讓你在工作中失去警覺性，而且會讓你感到懶散乏力、昏昏欲睡，也就是說你可能會在上班時間想睡覺。
B: Oh. And then? ③	B：哦。然後呢？
A: Be careful with caffeine. If you drink too much coffee, it will affect your productivity. So I suggest you consume small amounts of caffeine.	A：小心咖啡因。如果你喝了過量的咖啡，它也會影響你的工作效率，所以我建議你每天攝入少量的咖啡因。

B: Actually, I don't like coffee very much. I prefer tea.	B：其實，我不太喜歡喝咖啡，我更喜歡喝茶。
A: Good habit. What's more, you should develop the habit of ④ eating breakfast every day so that you can get to work as soon as possible. Even if you drink a glass of orange juice or eat a bit of bread, it will be good for your efficiency.	A：好習慣。另外，你要養成每天吃早餐的習慣，這樣你能儘快進入工作狀態。即使你只是喝一杯柳橙汁或者吃了一點麵包也會對你的效率有幫助。
B: You are right. I feel the same way, so I eat breakfast almost every day now. What about fruit?	B：你說的對。我也有這樣的感受，所以我現在基本上每天都會吃早餐。那關於水果呢？
A: Fruit can be good for ⑤ you. If you don't have something to eat, you can use it instead of other dairy products. It's not only easy to digest, but also keeps you productive all day long.	A：水果對你很有益，如果你沒有東西可吃時就可以用水果來代替其他的乳製品，它不僅易於消化，還能讓你整天持久高效。
B: Sounds interesting.	B：聽起來很有意思。
A: Yes, I learned it from a lot of books, so you should remember these good eating habits.	A：我也是讀了很多書才瞭解到的，所以你應該記住這些好的飲食習慣。
B: OKAY.	B：好的。

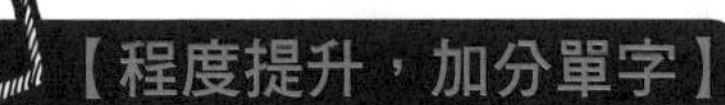

【程度提升，加分單字】

★**productive** [prəˋdʌktɪv] **adj.** 富有成效的，多產的
★**sluggish** [ˋslʌgɪʃ] **adj.** 懶散的
★**lethargic** [lɪˋθɑrdʒɪk] **adj.** 昏睡的，無精打采的
★**caffeine** [ˋkæfiɪn] **n.** 咖啡因
★**dairy** [ˋdɛrɪ] **adj.** 牛奶的，奶製的

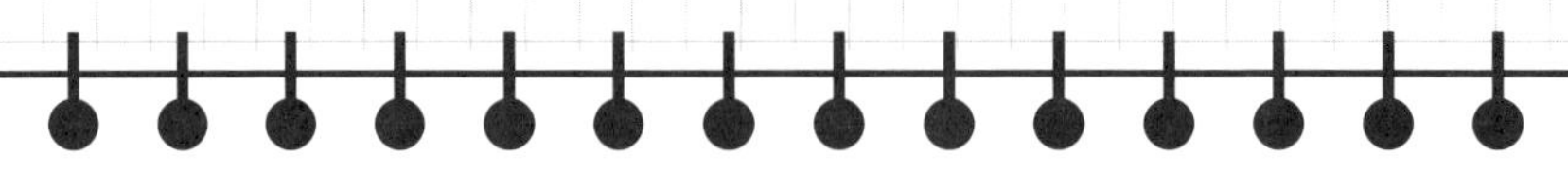

對話解析

① **my pleasure**

意為「我的榮幸，好的」，其是 it's my pleasure 的簡寫，通常是別人感謝你的幫忙時你說的話，而與其相似的 with pleasure 則指別人請你幫忙時你很樂意的態度。

② **that is to say**

意為「換句話說，即，就是」，可作插入語使用，其後接的內容通常是對上一句話的解釋。

③ **And then?**

意為「然後呢？」在口語中出現的頻率很高，表示對某事好奇。

④ **develop the habit of...**

意為「養成……習慣」，of 後接動詞的話是動名詞形式，有時 develop 也可以替換為 form。

⑤ **be good for**

意為「對……有好處，對……有益」，有時會構成 be good for sb to do sth，意為「對某人來說做某事是有好處的」。

文化小站

中西方在飲食習慣上存在著很明顯的差異。由於飲食習慣的不同，華人通常會圍繞著一個桌子吃飯，採取「共用」的方式，而西方人則每人有自己的一份食物。在西方宴席上，主人通常只會替客人夾一次菜，之後都是客人選擇菜品食用，若客人不要，主人也不會勉強，但在華人的思想中，勸酒和夾菜是一種熱情好客，由此來顯示自己的待客之道。

起居

Unit 07

Sleeping

睡覺

夜已深，你在做什麼呢？是否還在抱著手機呢？又或者你在因為工作而熬夜加班？熬夜傷身，睡眠對我們何其重要，快快放下手機或工作，來和周公約會吧。祝你好夢！

精選實用會話例句

1 該睡覺了。**It's time to go to bed.** Track 132

同義表達 It's time for bed.

2 我睡覺前會洗個熱水澡。

I always take a hot bath before I go to bed. Track 133

片語釋義 take a bath 洗澡

3 我閉上眼睛就睡著了。

As soon as I close my eyes, I fall asleep. Track 134

片語釋義 as soon as 一……就

4 睡覺前檢查一下瓦斯。

Check the gas before you go to bed. Track 135

重要詞彙 gas [gæs] n. 瓦斯

5 你應該在睡覺前關窗戶。**You should close the window before you go to bed.** Track 136

同義表達 Remember to close the window before you go to bed.

6 我昨晚直到半夜才睡著。

I didn't fall asleep until midnight last night. Track 137

重要片語 not until 直到……才

7 我睡覺的時候常常打呼。**I often snore when I sleep.** Track 138
重要詞彙 snore [snor] v. 打呼，打鼾

8 我昨晚因為你失眠了。
I lost sleep last night because of you. Track 139
片語釋義 lose sleep 失眠

9 請小聲一點，他在睡覺。**Be quiet; he's sleeping.** Track 140
同義表達 Keep your voice down. He's sleeping.

10 昨晚的吵鬧聲吵得我睡不著。
I was kept awake by the noise last night. Track 141
同義表達 The noise kept me up last night.

11 我睡得很香，什麼也沒有聽到。
I had a sound sleep and didn't hear anything. Track 142
重要詞彙 sound [saʊnd] adj. 完好的 n. 聲音

12 我睡覺的時候會翻來覆去。
I flip around when I sleep. Track 143
片語釋義 flip around 翻轉

13 我習慣在 11 點之前睡覺。
I'm used to going to bed before 11:00. Track 144
片語釋義 be used to 習慣於

14 你打算熬夜嗎？**Are you going to stay up late?** Track 145
片語釋義 stay up late 熬夜

15 你看起來沒睡好。
You don't seem to have a good sleep. Track 146
同義表達 You don't seem to sleep well.

16 我睡得晚是因為我要哄孩子。**I stayed up late because I had to put my baby to bed.** Track 147
片語釋義 stay up 熬夜

17 我痛得整夜睡不著覺。
I had a pain that kept me awake all night. Track 148
同義表達 The pain stopped me from sleeping all night.

⑱ 我很少在午夜前睡覺。

I seldom go to bed before midnight. Track 149

同義表達 I don't often go to bed before midnight.

⑲ 我現在一點也不睏。**I'm not sleepy at all.** Track 150

同義表達 I don't want to sleep.

⑳ 我睡覺的時候做了噩夢。

I had nightmares while I was sleeping. Track 151

重要詞彙 nightmare [ˋnaɪt͵mɛr] **n.** 噩夢

㉑ 我睡覺前忘記關燈了。**I forgot to turn off the light before I went to sleep.** Track 152

片語釋義 turn off 關掉

㉒ 早點睡，否則你明天會很睏。

Go to bed early, or you'll be sleepy tomorrow. Track 153

同義表達 If you don't sleep early, you will be sleepy tomorrow.

㉓ 現在馬上躺下睡覺。**Now lie down and sleep.** Track 154

片語釋義 lie down 躺下

看情境學對話

Track 155

	\中譯/
A: Jack, you don't look refreshed. Didn't you sleep well last night?	A：傑克，你看起來沒有精神，昨晚沒睡好嗎？
B: You are right. I stayed up late last night because I was writing a report.	B：你說對了，我昨晚熬夜，因為我要寫一份報告。
A: No wonder ①. But staying up late is bad for your health. Why don't you ② write the report the next day?	A：難怪，但是熬夜對健康不好，為什麼不隔天再寫呢？

B: Because I had to give it to the manager when I got to work today. There's not much time.	B：因為今天上班的時候就要把報告交給經理了，時間很緊迫。
A: I got it. ③ You must be sleepy right now.	A：明白了，你現在肯定很睏吧？
B: I'm used to staying up. What about you? Did you sleep well?	B：我已經習慣晚睡了。你呢？你睡得好嗎？
A: Yeah. I seldom go to bed after 12:00, so I have plenty of ④ sleep every day. And staying up is bad for my skin, which I care a lot about.	A：是的，我很少在 12 點之後睡覺，所以我每天都有充足的睡眠。而且晚睡對皮膚不好，我很在意這點。
B: It's true that women always care about it.	B：的確，女性總是很在意這件事。
A: Why don't you go to bed earlier? Not only is it good for your health, it also makes you more efficient at work. ⑤	A：你為什麼不早點睡覺呢？不僅對健康有益，還能讓你工作更有效率。
B: I have tried, but I couldn't fall asleep.	B：我嘗試過，但我總是睡不著。

★**refresh** [rɪˋfrɛʃ] v. 使精神，使振作
★**report** [rɪˋport] n. 報告
★**skin** [skɪn] n. 皮膚

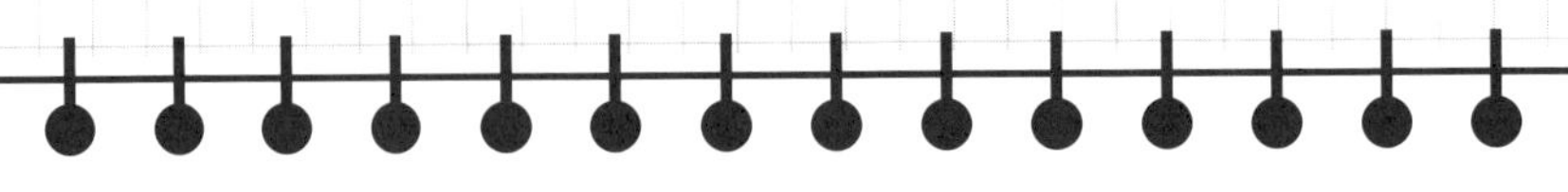

對話解析

① **no wonder**

在口語中可單獨使用，意為「難怪，怪不得」，可後接 that 引導的子句，一般情況下 that 被省略。

② **why don't you**

是一個提出建議的句型，相當於 why not，兩個句型後都接動詞原形。

③ **I got it**

是 I've got it 的簡寫，在口語中常用作 I got it 這種形式，意為「我知道了，我明白了」。另一種表達方式 you got it 則表示「照你說的辦」。

④ **plenty of**

表示「充足的，大量的」，相當於 a lot of，其後可接可數和不可數名詞。

⑤ **not only ... but also**

用在句首句子要用部分倒裝，即把 not only 句子的動詞提至主詞之前， but also 後的句子不需要倒裝。

學習英文Fun輕鬆！

1. Early to bed and early to rise makes a man healthy.
   早睡早起身體好。
2. Sleep is the tonic of life.
   睡眠是生命的滋補品。
3. It's better to sleep than to eat.
   食補不如覺補。
4. Sleep can strengthen one's health.
   睡眠能強身健體。
5. Good sleep will benefit the brain.
   良好的睡眠有益於大腦。

文化小站

睡覺是人類的一種不可缺少的生理現象。在美國，由於上班的時間比較短，所以他們基本上不會午睡，一般都是吃了飯後繼續工作，不過他們也會選擇在累了或者瞌睡的時候「take a nap」，也就是「小睡一下」。關於睡覺，還有一點值得提及，儘管睡眠並沒有固定的時間，但是現代人普遍睡眠都較少，有一部分人每天只睡四五個小時，而醫生們則認為「六到八小時的睡眠時間」是最為健康的養生之道。

Getting Up 起床

一天之計在於晨，早起的鳥兒有蟲吃。各位起床困難的人們，趕緊為了自己的夢想和生活起床吧。

精選實用會話例句

❶ 鬧鐘響了，該起床了。
The alarm goes off, and it's time to get up. Track 156
片語釋義 go off 作響

❷ 你現在得起床了。**You have to get up now.** Track 157
同義表達 You must get up now.

❸ 我們要在太陽出來之前起床。
We have to get up before the sun comes out. Track 158
片語釋義 come out 出來

❹ 我通常在七點半起床。
I usually get up at half past seven. Track 159
同義表達 I always get up at 7:30.

❺ 媽媽總是在七點叫我起床。
Mom always wakes me up at seven. Track 160
片語釋義 wake up 叫醒

❻ 我起晚了以至於上班遲到了。
I got up late and was late for work as a result. Track 161
片語釋義 as a result 結果

❼ 你今天幾點起床了？
What time did you get up today? Track 162
同義表達 What time did you wake up today?

❽ 我起床就把睡衣脫了。
I got up and took my pajamas off. Track 163
重要詞彙 pajama [pəˋdʒæməs] n. 睡衣

❾ 早起是我的習慣。It's my habit to get up early. Track 164
重要詞彙 habit [ˋhæbɪt] n. 習慣

❿ 我不願意早起。I am not willing to get up early. Track 165
重要片語 be willing to 願意

⓫ 鬧鐘壞了，所以我沒有按時起床。The alarm clock was broken, so I didn't get up on time. Track 166
重要詞彙 alarm [əˋlɑrm] n. 鬧鐘，警報

⓬ 我非常討厭在冬天早起。
I hate getting up early in winter. Track 167
同義表達 I am sick of getting up early in winter.

⓭ 我今天起床很早。I showed a leg early today. Track 168
重要片語 show a leg = get up起床

⓮ 我一起床就刷牙了。
I brushed my teeth as soon as I got up. Track 169
重要詞彙 brush [brʌʃ] v. 刷 n. 刷子

⓯ 天剛亮我們就起床了。We just got up before dawn. Track 170
重要詞彙 dawn [dɔn] n. 黎明

⓰ 你起床後會疊被子嗎？
Do you fold the comtorter after you get up? Track 171
重要詞彙 comtorter [ˋkʌmfɚtɚ] n. 被子

⓱ 媽媽總是比爸爸起得早。
Mom always gets up earlier than Dad. Track 172
同義表達 Mom always gets up before Dad.

⓲ 我每天叫妹妹起床。I wake my sister up every day. Track 173
同義表達 I woke up my sister every single day.

⑲ 我起晚了，錯過了第一班公車。

I got up late and missed the first bus. Track 174

同義表達 I got up late and didn't catch the first bus.

⑳ 我一大早就起床了。**I rose with the lark.** Track 175

重要片語 rise with the lark 早起

看情境學對話

Track 176

	中譯
A: Hurry up! ① It's seven o'clock now. We'll be late.	A：快點！現在已經 7 點了，我們要遲到了。
B: Don't worry. We have an appointment at nine. We still have plenty of time.	B：別著急，我們的約定是在 9 點，還有足夠的時間。
A: If you don't get up, we will certainly be late.	A：如果你不起床，我們一定會遲到。
B: I stayed up last night. I'm so tired. Let me sleep another half an hour. Please. ②	B：我昨晚睡晚了，我還很累呢。讓我再睡半個小時吧，求你了。
A: No way. ③ You should get up and have breakfast.	A：想得美，你應該起床吃早飯了。
B: I'm not going to have breakfast. I'm going to sleep. You can prepare for ④ the picnic first and wake me up in half an hour.	B：我不吃早飯了，我要睡覺。你可以先為野餐做準備，半個小時後叫我。

A: I'll drive later and you can sleep in the car. We have to set out ⑤ early.	A：待會兒我開車，你可以在車裡睡覺。我們得早點出發。
B: There may be a traffic jam downtown today.	B：今天市中心可能會塞車。
A: Well, I'm getting up now. Pass me my sportswear.	A：好吧，我現在就起床。把我的運動服遞給我。
B: The temperature is a little low outside today. You'd better wear more.	B：今天外面的溫度有點低，你最好穿多一點。
A: Okay, I'll wear a coat.	A：好吧，我穿一件外套。
B: OKAY.	B：好的。

★**appointment** [əˈpɔɪntmənt] **n.** 約定，約會
★**certainly** [ˋsɝtənlɪ] **adv.** 當然，肯定

① **hurry up**

是表示催促別人的用語，意為「趕快」，常常單獨使用，hurry 作動詞是「催促」的意思，只能用在句子中。

② **please**

在口語中單獨使用時，可表示「求你了，拜託」，常用來表示懇求別人。

③ **no way**

在口語中單獨使用，表示堅決的否定語氣，意為「絕不」，多用來拒絕別人的請求。

④ **prepare for**

是常用片語，意為「為……做準備」，其後常接名詞或動名詞。

⑤ **set out**

是一個多義詞組，有「出發，陳述，陳列」的意思。作「出發」解時，和 set off「出發」的用法相似。

學習英文Fun輕鬆！

1. Dawn is the starter for a day.
   一天之計在於晨。
2. Get up early and stay away from depression.
   早早起床，遠離抑鬱。
3. If you don't rise early, you never do a good day's work.
   早起三光，晚起三慌。
4. Sleepy head, get out of bed.
   小懶蟲，起床了。
5. Rise and hear the crow of the rooster.
   聞雞起舞。
6. Get up when a chicken crows.
   雞啼時就起床。
7. Let your dreams wake you up.
   讓夢想叫醒你。

起居

Unit 09

Housework

家事家務

媽媽每天做家務辛苦了，我們應該主動為媽媽分擔一點，讓媽媽放鬆一下。你都會做什麼家務呢？我們來比一比吧。

精選實用會話例句

1. 該你打掃房間了。**It's your turn to clean the room.** Track 177
   同義表達 It's time you cleaned the room.

2. 你能幫我倒垃圾嗎？
   Can you help me with the garbage? Track 178
   重要詞彙 garbage [ˋgɑrbɪdʒ] n. 垃圾

3. 我現在沒時間洗衣服。
   I don't have time for laundry right now. Track 179
   重要詞彙 laundry [ˋlɔndrɪ] n. 洗衣店，洗衣服

4. 我們輪流做家事。
   Let's take turns doing housework. Track 180
   片語釋義 take turns 輪流

5. 趕快把你的房間收拾乾淨。
   Hurry up and tidy up your room. Track 181
   片語釋義 tidy up 收拾，整理

6. 我太忙了，不能幫你。**I'm too busy to help you.** Track 182
   同義表達 I'm occupied and I can't help you.

7. 夫妻共同分擔做家事。**Husband and wife share housework in my family.** Track 183
   同義表達 Husband and wife do all the housework in my family.

❽ 我決定雇人來做家事。
I decide to hire someone to do the housework. Track 184
重要詞彙 housework [ˋhaʊsˏwɝk] n. 家務

❾ 我會儘快打掃客廳的。
I'll clean the living room as soon as possible. Track 185
重要片語 as soon as possible 儘快

❿ 一會兒我就幫你拖地。
I'll help you mop the floor in a minute. Track 186
重要詞彙 mop [mɒp] v. 拖地

⓫ 你能幫我分擔家事嗎？
Can you share the housework with me? Track 187
同義表達 Can you help me with the housework?

⓬ 我有一堆衣服要洗。
I have a pile of clothes to wash. Track 188
片語釋義 a pile of 一堆

⓭ 你把家事都留給我了嗎？
Did you leave all the housework to me? Track 189
同義表達 Do you want me to do all the housework?

⓮ 我們來洗碗吧。**Let's wash the dishes.** Track 190
同義表達 Shall we do the dishes?

⓯ 我不知道怎麼清理冰箱。
I don't know how to clean the fridge. Track 191
重要詞彙 fridge [frɪdʒ] n. 冰箱

⓰ 我馬上就把衣服洗完了。
I'll finish the laundry at once. Track 192
片語釋義 at once 馬上

⓱ 我厭倦拖地板了。**I'm tired of mopping the floor.** Track 193
重要片語 be tired of 厭倦

⑱ 我要把臥室裡的灰塵清一下。**I'll dust the bedroom.** Track 194

同義表達 I'll wipe out the dust in the bedroom.

⑲ 請先把我的襯衫熨一下。
Please iron my shirt in advance. Track 195

片語釋義 in advance 提前

⑳ 洗衣精用完了。**The detergent has run out.** Track 196

片語釋義 run out 用完，耗盡

㉑ 我打算把牆壁重新粉刷一遍。
I'm going to repaint the wall. Track 197

重要詞彙 repaint [ri`pent] **v.** 重新粉刷

㉒ 水龍頭一直在滴水。**The faucet has been dripping.** Track 198

重要詞彙 faucet [`fɔsɪt] **n.** 水龍頭

㉓ 你每天要把陽臺的花澆一遍。**You have to water the flowers on the balcony once a day.** Track 199

重要詞彙 balcony [ˈbælkənɪ] **n.** 陽臺

㉔ 你的髒衣服都成堆了。
Your dirty clothes have piled up. Track 200

片語釋義 pile up 堆積，堆放

㉕ 你為何不去幫媽媽掃地？
Why don't you sweep the floor for Mom? Track 201

同義表達 Why not sweep the floor for Mom?

看情境學對話

Track 202

	中譯
A: Jenny, what are you doing? Let's go shopping. ①	A：珍妮，你在做什麼？我們去逛街吧。
B: I really want to, but I've got a lot of housework to do today. I have to do the laundry and clean the house.	B：我真的很想去，但是我今天有很多家事要做。我要洗衣服，打掃房子。

A: Isn't your husband home? You should share the housework with him fifty-fifty. ②	A：你丈夫不在家嗎？你應該和他平分家事。
B: I know, but my husband never does housework. My daughter sometimes helps me with cooking.	B：我知道，但是我丈夫從不做家事，我女兒有時幫我做飯。
A: You should change your mind. Equality lies between men and women, and men should also do housework. In my opinion ③ , housework is not just woman's business.	A：你應該改變想法了，男女平等，男人也應該做家事。在我看來，家事不只是女人的事情。
B: You're right. But I'm going to finish the housework today because there's a visitor coming in the afternoon.	B：你說的對，但是我今天要把家事做完，因為下午有人會來拜訪。
A: Who is it?	A：誰呀？
B: He is one of my husband's friends. We haven't seen each other for many years, and he's going to come back from abroad today.	B：我丈夫的一位朋友，我們已經很多年沒見過面了，他今天回國。
A: In that case④ , you do what you have to do. We'll make another appointment next week.	A：既然這樣，你就忙吧，我們下週再約。
B: That's settled ⑤ . I just want to to buy some clothes.	B：一言為定，我正想買幾件衣服呢。

【程度提升，加分單字】

★**equality** [iˈkwɒlətɪ] **n.** 平等
★**business** [ˈbɪznəs] **n.** 事務，生意

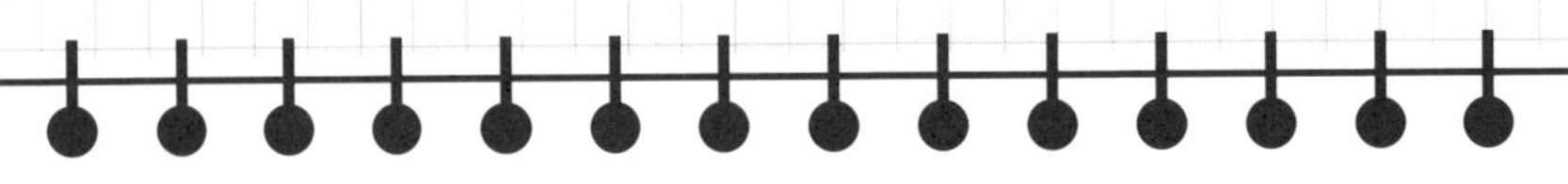

對話解析

① **Let's go Ving.**

是提出建議的句型，在口語中非常常見，通常的回覆有 Sure.、Good idea.、Sounds nice. 等。

② **fifty-fifty**

相當於副詞，意為「平分」，常用於平分錢或工作。

③ **in my opinion**

是固定用法，意為「在我看來」，常用來表示自己的觀點，相當於 in my view 和 from my perspective。

④ **in that case**

和 in this case 在句中多用逗號與後面的內容隔開，表示「既然這樣，這樣的話」。

⑤ **That's settled.**

意為「一言為定」。多用在表示贊成並決定支持的場景中。

學習英文Fun輕鬆！

1. Housework is never done.
家事是永遠做不完的。
2. As long as you practice, you can do housework well.
只要練習，就會做好家事。
3. Labor is the most glorious.
勞動最光榮。
4. Do housework often and exercise practical ability.
勤做家事，鍛煉實作能力。
5. Do housework and take on your own family responsibilities.
做家事，承擔自己的家庭責任。
6. Housework is the basis for enriching knowledge of life.
家事是豐富生活知識的基礎。

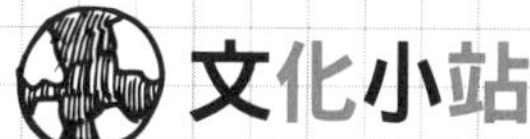

文化小站

做家事，在一般人看來，是女人做的事情。女人在家裡辛苦帶孩子，買菜做飯，飯後要打掃衛生，洗碗刷盤，這在很多男人看來是理所當然的事，因為他們認為自己在外上班很辛苦，女人就應該操持家裡的一切。然而，在當今社會，大部分的女性也是要外出上班的。美國俄亥俄州立大學的一項研究表示，女性下班回家後有 30% 的時間用在了做家務上，只有 10.6% 的時間用在娛樂上，由此可知女性在做家務上的「地位」，他們還稱長期下來會對女性的健康產生影響，因為她們一直挑著家裡的重擔。不過，幸運的是，隨著人們意識的改變，男人也逐漸開始分擔家事，體會她們的辛苦，體驗做家務的快樂。這在中西方都有很明顯的變化。

Before Going Out

外出前

大家都需要外出。外出前我們要做什麼呢？準備行李、檢查車子、接受來自不同親人的叮囑等等。不過，最重要的是，我們要記得回家的路。

精選實用會話例句

1. 我要外出一段時間。**I'm going out for a while.** Track 203
   同義表達 I'm going out for a period of time.

2. 我幫你準備了幾件衣服。
   I have packed some clothes for you. Track 204
   同義表達 I have prepared some clothes for you.

3. 外出前把房子檢查一遍。
   Check the house before you go out. Track 205
   重要詞彙 check [tʃɛk] v. 檢查，核實

4. 你打算怎麼去外地？
   How are you going to get out of town? Track 206
   同義表達 How do you intend to get out of town?

5. 我的重要文件都裝在行李箱裡了。**My important papers have been placed in the suitcase.** Track 207
   重要片語 place in 把……放進

6. 你先檢查一下車子是否有油。
   You should check if the gas tank is full. Track 208
   重要片語 gas tank 油箱

7. 你確定你鎖門了嗎？
   Are you sure you locked the door? Track 209
   同義表達 Can you make sure you have locked the door?

❽ 你能開車把我送到機場嗎？
Can you drive me to the airport? Track 210
重要詞彙 airport [ˋɛrˏport] n. 機場

❾ 我好像把鑰匙落在家裡了。
I seem to have left the keys at home. Track 211
同義表達 It looks I have left the keys at home.

❿ 記得把你的錢包看好。Remember to watch your wallet. Track 212
重要詞彙 wallet [ˈwɒlɪt] n. 錢包

⓫ 到了那裡後一定要打電話給我。
Be sure to give me a call when you get there. Track 213
重要片語 be sure to 一定要

⓬ 我已經在網路上訂好票了。I've booked tickets online. Track 214
同義表達 I've bought tickets through the Internet.

⓭ 到那裡的時候你能告訴我一下嗎？
Can you let me know when you get there? Track 215
同義表達 Could you please tell me when you get there?

⓮ 我已經把你的行李箱放在後車箱裡了。
I've put your suitcase in the trunk. Track 216
重要詞彙 trunk [trʌŋk] n. 後車箱

⓯ 要下雨了，你最好帶一把傘。It's going to rain.
You'd better bring an umbrella. Track 217
重要片語 had better 最好

⓰ 我有件事要處理，要出去一趟。I've got something
to deal with and I need to go out. Track 218
片語釋義 deal with 處理

⓱ 何不等天放晴了再出去？
Why don't you go out when it clears up? Track 219
片語釋義 clear up 放晴

⓲ 我不建議你此時外出。
It's not a good idea to go out at this time. Track 220
同義表達 You'd better not go out at this time.

⑲ 天晴了，我們去郊外野餐吧。**The sky's clear. Let's go for a picnic in the suburb.** Track 221

重要詞彙 suburb [ˋsʌbɝb] **n.** 郊區

⑳ 看來你只能坐計程車去車站了。**Looks like you'll have to take a taxi to the station.** Track 222

片語釋義 take a taxi 坐計程車

㉑ 你介意等我半個小時嗎？**Would you mind waiting for me for half an hour?** Track 223

重要詞彙 mind [maɪnd] **v.** 介意 **n.** 心智

㉒ 快點，我們來不及了。**Come on; we're gonna be late.** Track 224

同義表達 Hurry up; it's late.

㉓ 不要忘記帶你的重要文件。**Don't forget to bring your important papers with you.** Track 225

同義表達 Remember to bring your important papers with you.

㉔ 禁止你晚上十點之後在外面。**You are not allowed to stay outside after ten in the evening.** Track 226

重要詞彙 allow [əˋlaʊ] **v.** 允許

看情境學對話

Track 227

	中譯
A: Honey, I'm going out for a few days.	A：親愛的，我要外出幾天。
B: Oh, my God. It's really not good news. We've already booked a ticket to Denmark for holiday.	B：噢，天哪。這可真不是一個好消息，我們已經訂了去丹麥度假的機票了。
A: I'm so sorry. But there's something wrong with the project I'm in charge of ①, and my boss asked me to go on a business trip tomorrow.	A：我很抱歉，但是我負責的一個專案出了點問題，老闆讓我明天出差去解決這件事。

B: All right, your job matters most. How many days are you going to be away for?	B：好吧，你的工作最重要。你要去幾天？
A: A week at most ② . I'll take the trip with you after I get back.	A：最多一個星期。等我回來，我一定陪你去旅行。
B: Well, plans always fall behind changes ③ . I'll help you with the luggage.	B：唉，計畫趕不上變化。我來幫你準備行李。
A: By the way ④ , it's winter in the city I'm going to. Please prepare some heavy clothes for me.	A：對了，我要去的城市現在是冬季，請幫我準備幾件厚衣服。
B: I see. Who are you going with?	B：知道了。你和誰一起去呢？
A: This time I will go alone, because my secretary has taken the marriage leave ⑤.	A：這次只有我自己去，因為我的秘書請了婚假。
B: You must take good care of yourself and drink more water. I've put some cold medicine in the suitcase for you.	B：你一定要照顧好自己，多喝水。我在行李箱裡為你放了一些感冒藥。
A: It's very considerate of you ⑥ . Thank you, my dear.	A：你真是考慮得太周到了。謝謝你，親愛的。
B: Remember to buy a present for me when you come back.	B：回來的時候記得給我買禮物。

【程度提升，加分單字】

★**project** [ˋprɑdʒɛkt] **n.** 專案，計畫　★**secretary** [ˋsɛkrəˏtɛrɪ] **n.** 秘書
★**considerate** [kənˋsɪdərət] **adj.** 考慮周到的，體貼的

對話解析

① **be in charge of**

是一個常用片語，意為「負責，掌管」，相當於 be responsible for。

② **at most**

意為「最多」，其反義詞組是 at least，意為「至少」。

③ **plans always fall behind changes**

意為「計畫趕不上變化」，也可以用 plans can't always catch up with changes 來表示。

④ **by the way**

意為「對了，順便說一下」，表示說話者轉移話題或者插入一個新話題，多是用來補充一些重要的事情。

⑤ **take leave**

是「請假」的意思，相當於 ask for leave， leave 在此處作名詞。

⑥ **it's + 形容詞 + of sb...**

是一個常用口語句型，意為「某人真是太……了」，一般根據某人所說的話或做的事而評價某人。

文化小站

眾所周知，西方人在出門前會選擇洗澡，而東方人較沒有早上洗澡的習慣。西方男性也較注重自己的形象，因此他們會在出門前整理好自己的儀容，一般情況下，需要靠儀容為自己加分的大多數人會選擇注重外表形象，如商務人士，業務，講師等，他們通常在出門前會花很大一部分時間在儀容上。就習慣而言，許多英國人都淋雨不撐傘的。在西方，人們出門前會喝一杯咖啡或者柳橙汁，而東方人則習慣喝熱的茶水等。

外出

Unit 11

After Getting Home

回家後

在外面奔波了一天，是否很累了？回到家中，你最想做的事情是什麼？洗個熱水澡，打開電視，聽聽音樂，放鬆全身，這真是再美好不過的事情了。

精選實用會話例句

1 我知道你快累死了。I know you're exhausted. Track 228

重要詞彙 exhausted [ɪg`zɔstɪd] adj. 筋疲力盡的

2 糟糕，我把鑰匙落在辦公室了。
Oh, no. I left my keys in the office. Track 229

同義表達 Oops. I left my keys in the office.

3 我要洗個熱水澡。I need a hot bath. Track 230

同義表達 I'll take a hot bath.

4 他們在家裡熱情地迎接我。
They met me warmly at home. Track 231

重要詞彙 warmly [`wɔrmlɪ] adv. 熱情地，溫暖地

5 讓我訝異的是，家裡什麼人都沒有。
To my surprise, there's no one at home. Track 232

重要片語 to one's surprise 讓某人驚訝的是

6 我回到家裡什麼也不想做。I don't want to do anything when I go back home. Track 233

同義表達 I want to do nothing after I go back home.

7 我回到家的時候已經半夜了。
It was midnight when I got home. Track 234

同義表達 I didn't get home until midnight.

8 我剛回到家，還沒來得及做飯。
I just got home before I could cook. Track 235
同義表達 I just got home and I didn't cook.

9 我回到家發現一片狼藉。**I found the house was in a mess when I got back home.** Track 236
片語釋義 in a mess 一片混亂

10 我在客廳裡等你一起聊工作。**I'm waiting for you to talk about work in the living room.** Track 237
片語釋義 talk about 談論

11 你回家後會去健身嗎？
Will you work out after you get home? Track 238
片語釋義 work out 解決，運動健身

12 爸爸一到家就開始看新聞。**Dad started watching the news as soon as he got home.** Track 239
同義表達 No sooner had Dad got home than he started watching the news.

13 你能幫我打開熱水器的開關嗎？
Can you turn on the water heater for me? Track 240
重要詞彙 heater [ˋhitɚ] n. 熱水器

14 我找不到電視遙控器。**I can't find the TV remote.** Track 241
重要詞彙 remote [rɪˋmot] n. 遙控器 adj. 偏遠的

15 把電視的聲音關小一點。**Turn down the TV.** Track 242
片語釋義 turn down 關小，拒絕

16 現在你不適合喝冰的飲料。
An iced drink is not good for you right now. Track 243
同義表達 You should not have an iced drink right now.

17 我不想驚動家人。
I don't want to make my family worried. Track 244
重要詞彙 worry [ˋwɝɪ] v. 使擔心

⑱ 我回到家才聽說你病了。
When I got home, I heard you were sick. Track 245

同義表達 I heard you were sick as I got home.

⑲ 我被淋濕了，我需要換衣服。**I got wet. I need to change.** Track 246

重要詞彙 wet [wɛt] adj. 濕的

⑳ 我回來後就一直待在房間裡。
I stay indoors after I came back. Track 247

片語釋義 keep indoors 待在家裡

㉑ 不要躺在沙發上睡覺。**Don't sleep on the couch.** Track 248

重要詞彙 couch [kaʊtʃ] n. 沙發

㉒ 我要把濕衣服晾在陽臺上。**I'm going to hang my wet clothes on the balcony.** Track 249

重要詞彙 hang [hæŋ] v. 懸掛，晾

㉓ 我在行李箱裡放了一件易碎品。
I put a fragile item in the suitcase. Track 250

重要詞彙 fragile [ˈfrædʒaɪl] adj. 易碎的

㉔ 晚飯後我們去散步吧。**Let's go for a walk after dinner.** Track 251

同義表達 Let's take a walk after dinner.

㉕ 我把禮物放在了你的梳妝檯上。
I put the gift on your dresser. Track 252

重要詞彙 dresser [ˋdrɛsɚ] n. 梳妝檯

看情境學對話

Track 253

	中譯
A: David, I just got home, and I found the house a mess. What's going on?①	A：大衛，我剛回到家，我發現家裡一片狼藉。這是怎麼回事？
B: It's out of the question. ② I just cleaned the house yesterday.	B：不可能，我昨天剛剛打掃了房子。

A: Did someone break in? Should I call the police?	A：難道有人闖入來家裡行竊了？我要不要報警？
B: Jenny, look if our valuables are in the safe. There should be some cash in the drawer in the bedroom, and you should check it out.	B：珍妮，你先看看我們的貴重物品在不在保險櫃裡，還有臥室的抽屜裡應該有一些現金，你看看在不在。
A: Okay. No, David, all the things were stolen. The cash is gone, but there's no sign of ③ the safe being damaged.	A：好的，大衛。糟糕，所有東西都遭竊了。現金不見了，但是保險櫃沒有被損害的痕跡。
B: This is a blessing in misfortune. ④ Don't worry. I'll ask for a leave right now to get home.	B：這是不幸中的萬幸了。你別著急，我現在馬上請假趕回家。
A: What should I do? Shall I clean the house?	A：我應該做什麼？我要把房子打掃一遍嗎？
B: No, we have to call the police, so we need to keep the scene.	B：不需要，我們要報警，所以要保留現場原樣。
A: Okay, I take your point. ⑤ How long will it take you to get home?	A：好的，我聽你的。你大概多久能到家？
B: Half an hour is OK if there is no traffic jam.	B：如果不塞車的話大約要半個小時。

【程度提升，加分單字】

★**valuables** [ˋvæljuəblz] **n.** 貴重物品

★**drawer** [ˋdrɔɚ] **n.** 抽屜

★**scene** [sin] **n.** 場景，風景

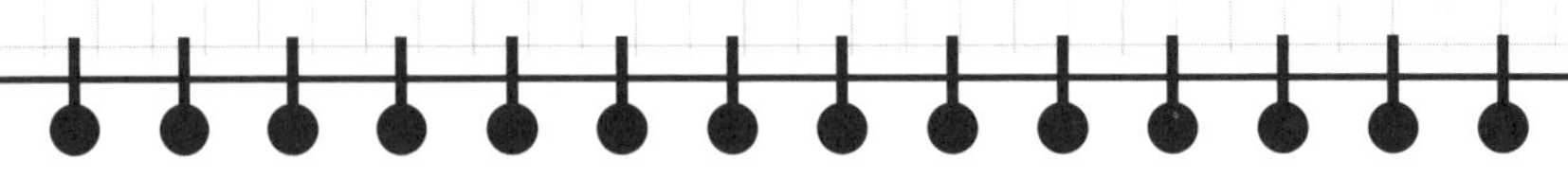

對話解析

① **What's going on?**

意為「怎麼回事？發生什麼事了？」多用來對現場發生的一些不好的事進行詢問。

② **It's out of the question.**

是一個常用的口語句子，意為「這是不可能的。」相當於 No way. 表示對某種情況的堅決否認。

③ **there's no sign of**

意為「沒有……的跡象」，there's no way of 意為「沒有辦法……」，兩個句型後都是接名詞或動名詞。

④ **This is a blessing in misfortune.**

是一句俗語，意為「不幸中的萬幸」。也可以用 Lucky in unlucky. 來表示。

⑤ **I take your point.**

相當於 I listen to you. 意為「我聽你的」。也可以用 I follow your words. 來表示，表示願意按照對方的話來行事。

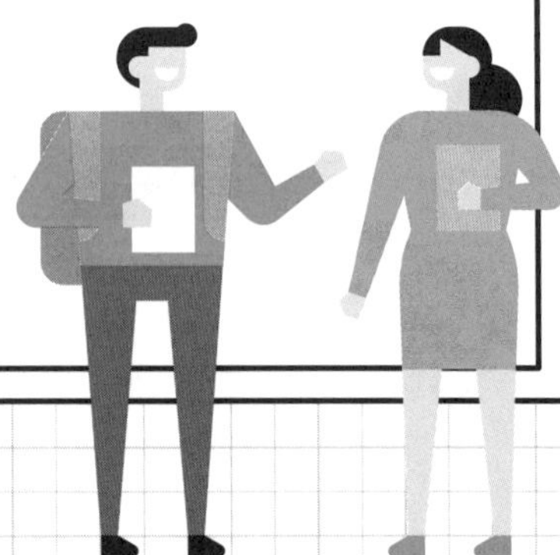

學習英文Fun輕鬆！

Husband: Dear, what are we going to eat today?

Wife: What do you want to eat today?

Husband: What dishes are you going to cook?

Wife: Fried eggs with tomatoes.

Husband: Anything else?

Wife: None.

Husband: Then what should I choose?

Wife: To eat or not.

丈夫：親愛的，我們今天吃什麼？

妻子：今天你想要吃什麼？

丈夫：你要做什麼菜呢？

妻子：番茄炒蛋。

丈夫：別的呢？

妻子：沒了。

丈夫：那我要選什麼啊？

妻子：吃或者不吃。

家庭理財

Unit 12

Investment

投資

與其把多餘的金錢放在銀行獲取微薄的利息，不如選擇合適的投資專案來錢生錢。早日投資，你也就離成為富翁不遠啦。

精選實用會話例句

1 我不建議你投資股票。
I don't suggest you invest in stocks. Track 254
重要詞彙 invest [ɪn`vɛst] v. 投資

2 你認為買黃金作為投資怎麼樣？What do you think of buying gold for investment? Track 255
同義表達 What's your opinion about purchasing gold as an investment?

3 因為錯誤投資，我們的公司可能會破產。With wrong investment, our company might go bankrupt. Track 256
片語釋義 go bankrupt 破產

4 我當然要投資一個利潤大的項目。
I'll certainly invest in a profitable project. Track 257
重要詞彙 profitable [`prɑfɪtəbəl] adj. 有利的，賺錢的

5 比起股票我更願意投資藝術品。
I prefer to invest in art than in stocks. Track 258
片語釋義 prefer to 偏好

6 我沒有多餘的錢來做投資。
I don't have extra money to invest. Track 259
同義表達 I have no spare money to invest.

⑦ 投資股票的風險比房地產大。Investing in stocks is more risky than investing in real estate. Track 260

重要詞彙 estate [ɪs`tet] n. 房地產，不動產

⑧ 我不相信這支股票有巨額回報。
I don't believe this stock has a huge return. Track 261

同義表達 I don't think this stock has a huge return.

⑨ 沒有人會支持你投資新餐廳。No one will support your investment in a new restaurant. Track 262

重要詞彙 support [sə`port] v. 支持

⑩ 你能幫我草擬一份投資合約嗎？Can you draw up an investment contract for me? Track 263

重要片語 draw up 草擬

⑪ 股票被認為是最常見的投資項目。Stock is regarded as the most common investment. Track 264

片語釋義 regard as 認為，當作

⑫ 你投資不當就會損失一大筆錢。If you don't invest properly, you'll lose a lot of money. Track 265

重要詞彙 properly [`prɑpəlɪ] adv. 恰當地，正確地

⑬ 不要慫恿他買股票。
Don't entice him to buy stocks. Track 266

重要詞彙 entice [ɪn`taɪs] v. 慫恿，誘惑

⑭ 我覺得投資股票不明智。
I don't think it is wise to invest in stocks. Track 267

同義表達 I don't think investing in stocks is wise.

⑮ 我們打算在古董上投資十萬美元。We're going to invest in antiques about 100,000 dollars. Track 268

重要詞彙 antique [æn`tik] adj. 古老的 n. 古董

⑯ 我們傾向於投資零風險的專案。
We tend to invest in zero-risk projects. Track 269

片語釋義 tend to 傾向於

⑰ 你的這項投資不可靠。

Your investment is not reliable. Track 270

重要詞彙 reliable [rɪˋlaɪəbəl] adj. 可靠的，可信任的

⑱ 我們不敢貿然投資股票。

We dare not venture into stocks. Track 271

重要詞彙 venture [ˋvɛntʃɚ] v. 冒險

⑲ 我們決定投資一家旅館。

We decide to invest in a hotel. Track 272

同義表達 We make up our minds to invest in a hotel.

⑳ 對於投資，再小心也不為過。

You can't be too careful about investing. Track 273

同義表達 You have to be careful to invest.

看情境學對話

\中譯/ Track 274

A: Steve, I heard you made a lot of money by investing in the Internet. Is that true?	A：史蒂夫，我聽說你投資網路大賺了一筆，是真的嗎？
B: It's an exaggeration, but I did benefit a lot. Are you interested in investing?	B：太誇張了，但是的確獲益了不少。你有沒有興趣投資啊？
A: Actually, I know nothing about ① investing. My wife and I put our money in the bank because we think it is the safest.	A：老實說，我對投資一竅不通，我和妻子的錢都存到了銀行裡，因為我們覺得那樣最安全。
B: Come on ② , bank interest rates are getting lower and lower, and most people tend to make other investments.	B：得了吧，銀行的利息越來越低，大多數人都傾向於做其他投資。

A: Do you have any suggestions? Many investments are risky now.	A：你有什麼建議嗎？現在很多投資專案都有風險。
B: Indeed. But the higher the risk is, the more returns you get. ③	B：的確是這樣。但是風險越高，回報就越多。
A: I don't dare to take risks. ④ I just want to invest in low-risk projects. Do you have any good ideas?	A：我可不敢冒險，我只想投資風險低的專案。你有什麼好的想法嗎？
B: You can buy bonds, mutual funds or foreign curency. These targets are with particularly lower risks, but with longer return cycle.	B：你可以購買債券、共同基金或者外幣。這些項目的風險特別低，但是回報的週期特別長。
A: Which one is best for us?	A：哪一個最適合我們呢？
B: The wisest option is to put the eggs in different baskets. If you invest in each one, it is the safest.	B：最明智的選擇是把雞蛋放在不同的籃子裡。若你想要每一個都投資一點，這樣最保險。
A: It makes sense. ⑤ I'll go back and discuss it with my wife.	A：有道理。我要回去和妻子商量一下。
B: Well, call me if you have any other questions	B：嗯，如果你還有什麼疑問，可以打電話問我。

【程度提升，加分單字】

★**exaggeration** [ɪg͵zædʒə`reʃən] **n.** 誇大，誇張
★**return** [rɪ`tɝn] **n.** 回報，報酬
★**option** [`ɑpʃən] **n.** 選項，選擇

① **know nothing about**

是一個固定片語，意為「對 …… 一無所知、一竅不通」know nothing about。

② **come on**

在英語口語中非常實用。come on 是多義詞組，有「拜託，快點」的意思，在該對話中意為「得了吧」，表示對別人說的話或做的事不贊同。

③ **the more... the more**

是比較級的特殊用法，the more 後面加形容詞或副詞的比較級形式，也可以加名詞。

④ **dare to**

表示「敢於做……」。dare 也常用作情態動詞，後面原形動詞。

⑤ **make sense**

意為「有道理」。it doesn't make any sense 意為「沒有道理」，該句型後可接 that 子句。

學習英文Fun輕鬆！

1. The stock market has only the present and the future.
   股市只有現在和將來。
2. There are risks in the stock market, and investment should be cautious.
   市有風險，投資需謹慎。
3. Never miss a good chance.
   切勿坐失良機。
4. A wise investor must learn to wait.
   明智的投資者必須學會等待。
5. Don't be optimistic about stocks.
   不要對股票持有樂觀態度。
6. The game is lost by a single mistake.
   一著不慎，滿盤皆輸。
7. Only the greedy don't make money.
   只有貪婪者賺不到錢。

文化小站

美國人的投資選擇包括股票、房產、政府企業債券、保險和金融衍生品等，選擇廣泛，投資管道多樣化。很多美國人會拿出 10% 的工資用於退休計畫，這些錢可以用來買賣股票和債券，也可以交由商業機構代為理財，以達到增值保值的目的。西方人投資房產和東方人投資房產的概念不同，西方人通常選擇商業房產，而東方人則選擇住宅房產。此外，東方人的投資傾向於個人控制，而西方人則比較喜歡選擇專業的投資管理機構。

家庭理財

Unit 13

Expenditure

開銷

我們的衣食住行都離不開金錢，我們每日都要花錢，但是我們的錢花到哪裡了呢？你知道你的錢去哪裡了嗎？趕快算一算吧。

精選實用會話例句

1 這個月的開銷太大了。

We have spent a lot this month. Track 275

同義表達 We have a big expense this month.

2 我們得縮減我們的開銷了。

We need to cut back on our expenses. Track 276

片語釋義 cut back on 縮減

3 房租占了我薪水的三分之一。

The rent accounts for one third of my salary. Track 277

片語釋義 account for 占，導致，說明

4 我們的支出遠遠超過了收入。

Our expenditure far exceeds our income. Track 278

重要詞彙 exceed [ɪk`sid] v. 超過，勝過

5 你的開銷與預算不符。

Your expenses are not in line with the budget. Track 279

重要片語 be in line with 和……相符

6 下個月我們得存點錢了。

We need to save some money next month. Track 280

同義表達 We need to draw in our expenditure next month.

7 不要亂花錢。**Don't dip into your purse.** Track 281

片語釋義 dip into 動用，浸入

❽ 我每個月幾乎存不了錢。
I can hardly save money every month. Track 282
同義表達 I spend almost all my money every month.

❾ 你要學會控制自己的消費。You have to learn to control your own consumption. Track 283
重要詞彙 consumption [kənˈsʌmpʃn] n. 消費，消耗

❿ 控制你的開銷吧，否則你會入不敷出。
Keep your expenses under control, or you will not make ends meet. Track 284
重要片語 make ends meet 收支平衡

⓫ 我們來算一下這個月的開銷。
Let's review the expenses of this month. Track 285
片語釋義 review 檢視

⓬ 這些開銷花了我半個月的工資。
These expenses cost me half a month's salary. Track 286
重要詞彙 salary [ˈsælərɪ] n. 薪水

⓭ 為了省錢，我打算坐公車上班。
To save money, I'm going to go to work by bus. Track 287
同義表達 I'll go to work by bus in order to save money.

⓮ 為了控制開銷，我們總是購買打折商品。In order to control our expenses, we always buy discounted goods. Track 288
片語釋義 in order to 為了

⓯ 你上個月揮霍了不少錢。
You squandered a lot of money last month. Track 289
重要詞彙 squander [ˋskwandə] v. 浪費，揮霍

⓰ 低收入限制了我們的支出。
Low income limits our spending. Track 290
同義表達 Our spending is limited by low income.

⓱ 為了還清債務，我們縮減了一切不必要的開支。In order to pay off our debts, we cut all unnecessary expenses. Track 291
片語釋義 pay off 還清

18 你總是花錢買奢侈品。**You always spend money on luxury goods.** Track 292

同義表達 You spend too much on luxury goods.

19 關於那筆開支我們有了爭論。**We had an argument about the expense.** Track 293

重要詞彙 argument [ˋargjəmənt] n. 爭論，辯論

20 為了買房子我們花光了所有的積蓄。**We spent all our savings on the house.** Track 294

同義表達 We spent all our money on the house.

21 我們在車子上的開支很大。**We spent a lot on the car.** Track 295

同義表達 The car costs us a lot.

22 與收入相比，我們的開銷太大了。**Our spending is too big compared to our income.** Track 296

重要片語 compared to 與……相比

看情境學對話

\中譯/ Track 297

A: I ran out of ① money again, but it is still a week before I get paid.	A：我的錢又花完了，但是離拿薪水還有一個星期。
B: Don't worry; I'll lend you some money. But I think you should balance your expenses and income.	B：別擔心，我借給你一些。但是我覺得你應該平衡一下你的花費和收入了。
A: Yes, but I can't always make ends meet.	A：是的，但我總是入不敷出。
B: I think you have a lot of unnecessary expenses, and if you cut them down ② , you won't be living beyond your means ③ .	B：我覺得你有很多不必要的開支，如果你把那些開銷縮減掉，你就不會入不敷出了。

A: What expenses are unnecessary?	A：哪些支出是不必要的呢？
B: For example, you always take a taxi to work, which is a big expense. Why don't you take the bus?	B：舉例來說，你總是乘坐計程車去上班，這就是一筆大的開支了。你何不乘坐公車呢？
A: Well, that's a good suggestion. Any thing else?	A：好吧，這是一個好的建議。還有嗎？
B: Of course ④ . You always eat out. That's your biggest expense. I suggest you cook by yourself, which is both healthy and economical.	B：當然了。你總是在外面用飯，這就是你最大的開支了。我建議你自己做飯，既健康又省錢。
A: I'm not good at cooking.	A：我不擅長做飯。
B: Cooking is actually very easy, and I can give you some simple recipes. I spend no more than ⑤ 300 dollars a month on meals.	B：做飯其實很簡單的，我可以教你一些簡單的做法。我每個月在吃飯上花費的錢不超過 300 美元。
A: It's too small. I spend at least 500 dollars on eating a month.	A：這也太少了，我每個月至少花費 500 美元吃飯。
B: See, that's why your money is never enough.	B：看吧，這就是你的錢總是不夠花的原因。

【程度提升，加分單字】

★**balance** [ˈbæləns] **v.** & **n.** 平衡
★**economical** [ˌikəˋnɑmɪkəl] **adj.** 節約的，經濟的
★**actually** [ˈæktʃuəlɪ] **adv.** 實際上

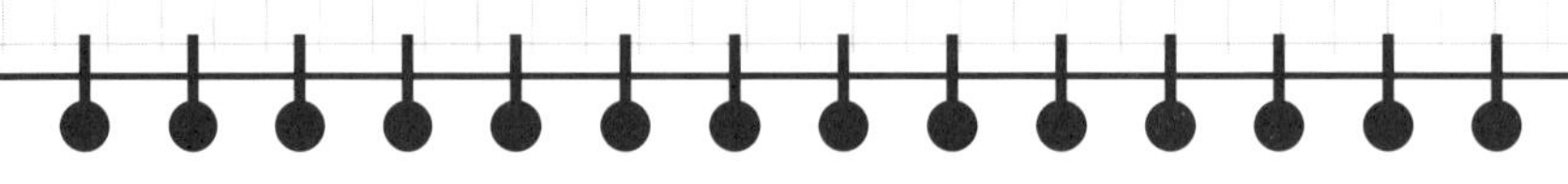

對話解析

① run out of

意為「用完」，其主詞要是人而非物。而 run out 也意為「用完」，主詞為物，表示被動含義。例如：The juice had already run out yesterday. 果汁昨天就沒了。

② cut down

意為「砍倒，削減」，如果其受詞是代名詞，需置於兩者之間。

③ live beyond one's means

意為「入不敷出」，相當於 not make ends meet。

④ of course

是常用的口語句，意為「當然」，在對話中通常用來回答別人的話，有時與not 連用構成 of course not 表示「當然不」。

⑤ no more than

意為「不超過，不多於」，not more than 意為「最多」。no less than 意為「不少於」，not less than 意為「至少」。

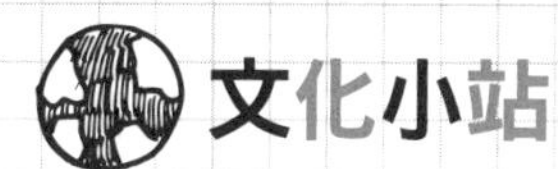

文化小站

西方人的開銷普遍都很大，這不僅在於他們花錢的方式很多，還在於他們很願意將錢花在休閒娛樂上，很注重享受。相對的，東方人願意節省存錢，而不會將大部分的錢花在休閒娛樂上，基本上不會把每月的薪水花完，要留一部分錢用於其他的計畫中。東方人比較顧及將來，包括後代的未來，而西方人則普遍享受當下。除此之外，西方人開銷大還因為成年人大都不依靠父母，自己買房、租房等，自己獨立生活。

家庭理財

Unit 14

Savings 儲蓄

儲蓄理財很安全，只是利息有點低。儲蓄也作為理財的一種方式，有著風險小，收益低，靈活方便的特點。如果你還沒有考慮好如何將自己的錢合理投資，就不妨先儲存起來。

精選實用會話例句

1 你想存多少？How much do you want to deposit? Track 298

重要詞彙 deposit [dɪˈpɒzɪt] v. 儲蓄

2 你能告訴我一些有關儲蓄的事情嗎？Could you tell me something about the deposit? Track 299

同義表達 Would you mind telling me something about deposit?

3 活期存款的利率是多少？What's the interest rate for current deposit? Track 300

片語釋義 current deposit 活期存款

4 我想存些錢。I wanna deposit some money. Track 301

重要詞彙 wanna [ˈwɒnə] v. 想要 = want to

5 你想存多長時間？How long do you want to deposit your money in the bank? Track 302

重要片語 deposit...in 在……儲存

6 我建議你開一個定期存款帳戶。I suggest you have a time deposit account. Track 303

片語釋義 time deposit 定期存款

7 請填寫一個存款單。Please fill in a deposit slip. Track 304

重要詞彙 deposit slip 存款單

❽ 定期存款的利率肯定要比活期存款的高一些。
The interest rate of the time deposit must be higher than the current deposit. Track 305
重要詞彙 current [ˈkʌrənt] **adj.** 最近的，現在的

❾ 你可以先開一個帳戶。
You can open an account first. Track 306
片語釋義 open an account 開戶

❿ 如果我存款五年的話我能得到多少利息？
How much interest would I get if I saved my money for five years? Track 307
重要詞彙 interest [ˈɪntrəst] **n.** 利息，興趣

⓫ 凱莉說服我把錢存在銀行裡。Kelly talked me into keeping my money in the bank. Track 308
重要片語 talk sb into doing sth 說服某人做某事

⓬ 我覺得把錢存在銀行裡是一種浪費。I think it's a waste to have money in the bank. Track 309
同義表達 I think keeping money in the bank is a waste.

⓭ 這種儲蓄存款的利率高嗎？Does this kind of saving deposit have high interest rate? Track 310
片語釋義 savings deposit 儲蓄存款

⓮ 請把存單收好。
Please keep the deposit receipt carefully. Track 311
片語釋義 deposit receipt 存款收據，存單

⓯ 它已經存入您的帳戶了。
It has been paid into your account. Track 312
重要片語 pay sth into an account 存入帳戶

⓰ 我覺得活期存款更適合您。I think the demand deposit is more suitable for you. Track 313
片語釋義 demand deposit 活期存款

⓱ 你們這裡辦理什麼類型的存款？
What type of deposit do you have here? Track 314
重要詞彙 type [taɪp] **n.** 類型

⑱ **我能辦理存款嗎？Can I make a deposit here?** Track 315

片語釋義 make a deposit 存款

⑲ **我聽說最近央行的利率上升了。I heard that bank rate has risen recently.** Track 316

片語釋義 bank rate 央行利率

看情境學對話

Track 317

	中譯
A: Good morning. Can I help you?	A：早安。您想辦理什麼業務？
B: Good morning. I want to make a deposit ①.	B：早安。我想存錢。
A: Would you like to choose time or current deposit?	A：您想存定期的還是活期的？
B: I don't know much about current and time deposits. Can you tell me something about ② them?	B：我對活期存款和定期存款不是很瞭解，你能告訴我一些關於它們的資訊嗎？
A: OK. First, time deposit means you can't withdraw money at any time unless the deposit is mature. And current deposit refers to ③ you can withdraw money at any time. In general, the longer you keep your savings, the higher your return will be ④.	A：好啊。首先，定期存款指的是除非存款到期，否則您不能隨時領錢。活期存款指的是你可以隨時提領。一般來說，您存款的時間越長，得到的回報就越高。
B: What about the interest rate?	B：那利率呢？
A: The interest rate of the time deposit is much higher than the current deposit.	A：定期存款的利率高於活期存款的利率。

B: Well, if I choose time deposit, will the interest rate be the same?	B：哦，那如果我選擇定期存款的話，利率都是一樣的嗎？
A: No, it depends on how long you keep the certificate. This is the specific information about the deposit.	A：不是的。這取決於您存多長時間。這是有關存款的具體資訊。
B: OK. But I only have 3,000 dollars. Which do you think suits me better?	B：好的。不過我只有三千美元，你認為哪種更適合我？
A: Do you have any plans in recent years?	A：您近幾年內有什麼打算嗎？
B: No.	B：暫時沒有。
A: Then I suggest you select time deposit. Besides, if you don't have any plans in recent years, you can save your money for five years, and then you will get a good return.	A：那我建議您選擇定期存款。此外，如果您近幾年都沒有什麼計畫的話，可以將您的錢存上五年，您會得到一個很好的報酬。
B: Okay. I choose this.	B：好的。那我就選這個吧。
A: All right. Please fill in ⑤ the deposit slip first.	A：好的。請先填一下存款單。

【程度提升，加分單字】

★**withdraw** [wɪð`drɔ] v. 拿走，（從銀行）取（錢）
★**return** [rɪ`tɝn] n. 回報
★**certificate** [sɚ`tɪfəkɪt] n. 單據

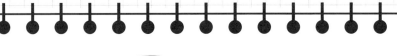

① **make a deposit**

意為「存款」， deposit 在這裡作名詞，還可以作動詞用 deposit money，表示「存款」。

② **Can you tell me something about...?**

意為「你能告訴我一些……嗎？」about 後跟的是名詞。

③ **refer to**

意為「指的是，參考，涉及」，作「指的是」解時，等同於 mean。

④ **the longer...the higher...**

意為「……越長……越高」，構成「the + 比較級，the + 比較級」形式。

⑤ **fill in**

意為「填寫（表格）」，強調的是把表格中必要的資訊填寫清楚，而與其都有「填寫」意思的 fill out 則強調完整填寫。

接打電話

Unit 15 Calling

通話

電話已經成為人們聯繫的重要工具，接打電話也成為日常生活中必不可少的行為。掌握禮貌的電話技巧非常重要，就讓我們來學習吧！

精選實用會話例句

1 我是南西。**Nancy speaking.** Track 318

同義表達 This is Nancy.

2 我老師正想給他打電話呢。

My teacher is just about to phone him. Track 319

片語釋義 be about to 剛要，正打算

3 請問你是哪位？**May I have your hame, please?** Track 320

同義表達 Who is calling?

4 你能讓蒂娜接電話嗎？

Could you let Tina answer the phone? Track 321

片語釋義 answer the phone 接電話

5 請稍等。**Hold on, please.** Track 322

重要詞彙 hold [hold] v. 保留，拿住，握住

6 真抱歉這麼晚打電話過來。

I'm so sorry to phone you so late. Track 323

同義表達 I'm sorry that I make such a late phone call. / I'm sorry to call so late.

7 有你的電話。**Here is a call for you.** Track 324

同義表達 You've got a call.

8 你想和誰說話？**Who do you want to speak to?** Track 325

同義表達 Whom are you calling?

9 對不起，你所撥打的電話已關機。
Sorry, the number you dialed is turned off. Track 326
片語釋義 turn off 關機

10 請叫你的老闆回電話給我。
Please ask your manager to call me back. Track 327
重要片語 call sb back 給某人回電話

11 傑克要求轉接跟艾咪通話。
Jack has asked to be put through to Amy. Track 328
片語釋義 put through 轉接

12 那個打電話的人已經等通話三分鐘了。
The caller has been on hold for three minutes. Track 329
片語釋義 on hold 等著通電話

13 秘書試著給他回電，但是他正在通話中。**The secretary tried to call him back, but he was engaged.** Track 330
重要詞彙 secretary [ˋsɛkrəˏtɛrɪ] **n.** 秘書

14 你兒子知道你的電話號碼嗎？
Does your son know your phone number? Track 331
片語釋義 phone number 電話號碼

15 你的電話號碼是多少？
May I have your number, please? Track 332
同義表達 Could you tell me your number, please?

16 我妻子上週查看了我的通話記錄。
My wife checked my call records last week. Track 333
重要詞彙 record [ˋrɛkɚd] **n.** 記錄，記載

17 自從上次通話之後傑森就一直在想這個問題嗎？
Has Jason been thinking about the matter since his last call? Track 334
片語釋義 think about 考慮

⑱ **沒有什麼要緊的，我爸爸等等會再打過來的。**
It is not urgent; my father will call back later. Track 335
重要詞彙 urgent [`ɝdʒənt] **adj.** 緊急的，急迫的

⑲ **信號問題導致了視頻通話的中斷。**
The signal problem caused the interruption of the video call. Track 336
重要詞彙 interruption [ˌɪntə`rʌpʃən] **n.** 中斷，打斷

⑳ **昨天晚上那個時候，我妹妹沒有和任何人通話。**
My sister didn't talk to anyone at that time yesterday evening. Track 337
片語釋義 at that time yesterday evening 昨天晚上那個時候

看情境學對話

Track 338

	中譯
A: Hello. This is Steven. May I speak to Robert?	A：你好。我是史蒂芬。我能和羅伯特說話嗎？
B: Robert speaking.	B：我就是羅伯特。
A: Why didn't you answer your phone one hour ago? I've been trying to phone ① you dozens of times.	A：你為什麼一個小時以前不接電話？我打了很多次電話給你。
B: I am so sorry. I was having an important meeting at that time ② . What's up? ③	B：很抱歉，那個時候我正在開一個很重要的會議。有什麼事嗎？
A: Your company purchased our machines three years ago. I am following up to confirm if they are still in good condition.	A：貴公司在三年前買下了我們的機器。我打電話是想確認它們是否狀況良好。

B: Let me check. Yes. They are still in good condition.	B：讓我看看，是的。它們狀況很不錯。
A: That is wonderful. They are in first-rate quality and performance. In addition, they are also made with advanced technology.	A：那太棒了。它們的品質和性能都是一流的。此外，它們還採用了先進的技術製造。
B: Have you developed any new products?	B：你們開發更新的產品了嗎？
A: Of course. By the way, there will be ④ a trade fair of our new products in the International Exhibition Center next week. Would you like to come?	A：當然。順便說一下，我們的新產品下週將在國際展覽中心展出。你要來參加嗎？
B: My pleasure.	B：我很樂意。
A: I'll prepare the tickets for you. See you then. ⑤	A：我會提前替你準備好票。下週見。

★**purchase** [ˋpɝtʃəs] **v.** 購買，採購
★**performance** [pɚˋfɔrməns] **n.** 表演，表現
★**technology** [tɛkˋnɑlədʒɪ] **n.** 科技

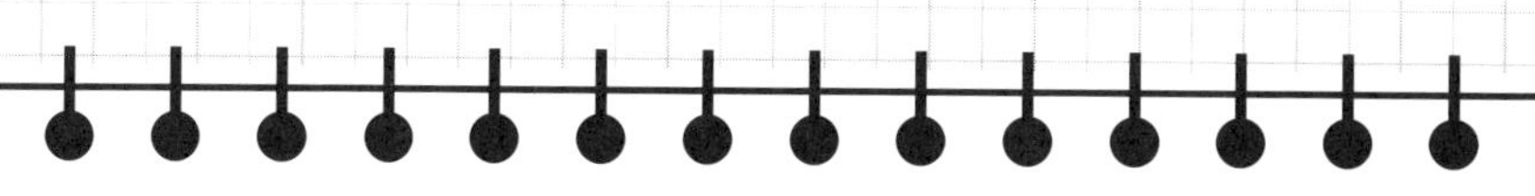

對話解析

① try to do sth

try to do sth 表示「努力做某事」，強調付出努力但不一定成功；表示「嘗試做某事」，強調試試看。

② at that time

表示「在那個時候」，相當於 at that moment。但是前者強調時間段，後者強調時間點。

③ What's up?

是一句很常用的口語，表示「怎麼了？最近怎麼樣？」如果沒什麼事就回答「Not much. / Nothing.」

④ there will be...

是 there be 句型的將來時，也可以是 there is going to be...。

⑤ see you then

表示「到時候見」，類似的還有：see you later 待會見；see you next time 下次見。

接打電話

Unit 16

Leaving Messages

留言

當你打電話時無人接聽或你要找的人不在，你會怎麼處理呢？留言也許是個不錯的選擇，透過紙條或者錄音的方式，把事情傳達給對方。讓我們看看怎麼留言吧！

精選實用會話例句

1. 有一條給你媽媽的留言。
   There is a message for your mother. Track 339
   重要詞彙 message [ˋmɛsɪdʒ] **n.** 資訊，消息

2. 你晚點再打電話給他，還是留言？
   Could you call him later or leave a message? Track 340
   片語釋義 leave a message 留言

3. 你可以留言給她秘書。
   You can leave a message for her secretary. Track 341
   重要片語 leave sth for sb 給某人留某物

4. 學校裡沒有給你的留言。
   There were no messages for you at school. Track 342
   片語釋義 at school 在學校

5. 我們會轉達他的口信。
   We will relay his oral message. Track 343
   重要詞彙 relay [rɪˋle] **v.** 轉播，傳達

6. 你可以幫我留個言嗎？
   Could you take a message for me, please? Track 344
   同義表達 Would you like to leave a message, please?

⑦ 起初沒有人能弄懂這個神秘留言。At first, nobody could figure out the secret message. Track 345

片語釋義 figure out 弄懂，想出

⑧ 你收到我想跟你聯繫的留言了嗎？Did you get an message that I was trying to reach you? Track 346

重要片語 try to do sth 努力做某事

⑨ 你那時候把手機關掉了嗎？
Did you turn off the phone at that time? Track 347

片語釋義 turn off 關掉

⑩ 他寫信是想確認一下你是否聽到我的語音留言。
He is writing to confirm whether you have heard my voice messages. Track 348

重要詞彙 confirm [kən`fɝm] **v.** 確認，批准

⑪ 提姆告訴我可以在這個答錄機上留言。Tim told me that I can leave a message on this answering machine. Track 349

片語釋義 answering machine 答錄機

⑫ 你有什麼需要我幫你傳達給你父母的嗎？
Is there anything you would like me to tell your parents? Track 350

同義表達 Do you have anything to tell your parents? / Is there anything that you want to tell your parents?

⑬ 在留言板上留言請點擊這裡。Please click here to leave a message on the message board. Track 351

同義表達 Have your say on our message board by clicking here.

⑭ 琳達留言給你說她人已經到達了。Linda messaged you saying she had already arrived. Track 352

重要詞彙 together [tə`gɛðɚ] **adv.** 在一起

⑮ 這個女孩已在留言板上發布了一個問題。The girl has posted a question on the message board. Track 353

片語釋義 message board 留言板

⑯ 傑森得回放，把留言又聽了一遍。Jason has to rewind and listen to the message again. Track 354

重要詞彙 rewind [ri`waɪnd] v. 倒帶

⑰ 你哥哥買了一台留言的電話答錄機。Your brother has bought an answering machine for. Track 355

重要詞彙 machine [mə`ʃin] n. 機器

⑱ 如果有人打電話，你能不能立刻記下留言？If someone calls, could you write down the message at once? Track 356

片語釋義 write down 寫下，記下

⑲ 電話響了好幾次，艾咪才聽到留言。The telephone rang many times before Amy heard the recorded voice. Track 357

重要詞彙 voice [vɔɪs] n. 嗓音，聲音

⑳ 你爸爸一回來就請他打電話給我。Ask your father to give me a call as soon as he returns, please. Track 358

片語釋義 as soon as 一……就

看情境學對話

Track 359

	中譯
A: Hello. May I speak to Mr. Smith?	A：你好！我想找史密斯先生？
B: May I have your name?	B：你叫什麼名字？
A: This is Rachel Johnson.	A：我是瑞秋・強森。
B: Hold on, please. I am sorry that he is out of the office right now ①. Could you call back later or leave a message?	B：請稍等。很抱歉他現在不在辦公室。你晚點再打來還是留言？

A: Okay. Let me leave a message for him. But it is just a little complicated. I am Mr. Smith's friend. I was supposed to meet ② him for dinner at 7:30 at the Hilton with a friend of us, Miss Green.	A：好吧，讓我給他留言吧，但是有些複雜。我本來要在 7:30 和我們的一個朋友格林小姐在希爾頓酒店和史密斯先生共進晚餐。
B: Miss Green...at 7:30 at the Hilton...OK.	B：格林小姐……在 7:30 希爾頓酒店。好的。
A: But Miss Green's flight was delayed, so I need to pick her up at the airport ③ now. Please tell him that the dinner time is put off to 8:00.	A：但是格林小姐的飛機誤點了。所以我現在需要去機場接她。請告訴他晚餐時間延後到八點了。
B: Okay. May I have your telephone number?	B：好的。你能告訴我你的電話嗎？
A: 547-556-379.	A：547-556-379。
B: Is there anything else you would like me to tell Mr. Smith?	B：你還想讓我告訴史密斯先生什麼嗎？
A: Please tell him not to take reservations for dinner; I have already done it.	A：請告訴他不要為晚餐訂位，我已經訂過了。
B: Got it.	B：知道了。
A: That's all. ④ Thank you. Good bye.	A：就這些。謝謝你，再見。
B: Bye-bye.	B：再見。

【程度提升，加分單字】

★**complicatd** [ˋkɑmplə͵ket] **v.** 使複雜化 **adj.** 複雜的

★**suppose** [səˋpoz] **v.** 假定，猜想　★**airport** [ˋɛr͵port] **n.** 機場

① **right now**

表示「現在，此時此刻，目前」。類似的表達還有：at present，at the moment。

② **be supposed to do sth**

表示「應該要做某事」。

③ **at the airport**

表示「在機場」，at 後面常常加小地點，比如：at school（在學校），at home（在家）。in 後面常常加大地點，比如：in New York（紐約）。

④ **that's all**

表示「就這些，就這樣」，常常出現在句子結尾。

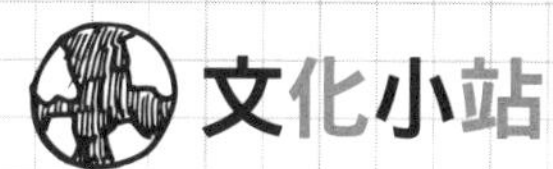

文化小站

隨著手機的普及，電話留言也越來越受人們的歡迎。當不能及時找到對方的時候，如果有事情要通知對方，人們一般會選擇留言的方式告知對方。在西方國家，電話留言是一個非常重要的商業交流工具。人們喜歡用電話留言功能，這種場景我們也經常在美劇中看到。西方人喜歡把生活和工作鮮明地分開，自己生活的時候一般不喜歡接聽工作的電話，所以他們只好選擇留言了。

接打電話

Unit 17

Wrong Number

打錯電話

你有過打錯電話嗎？打錯電話是一件很尷尬的事情。那麼怎樣禮貌地告知對方打錯電話了呢？我們一起來學習吧！

精選實用會話例句

1 你的電話號碼是錯誤的嗎？
Did you get the wrong number? Track 360
重要詞彙 wrong [rɔŋ] adj. 錯誤的，不正確的

2 提姆被告知要打的就是那個號碼。
That is the number Tim was asked to ring. Track 361
重要片語 ask sb to do sth 要求某人做某事

3 對不起，我打錯電話了。
I'm sorry. I have the wrong number. Track 362
片語釋義 have the wrong number 打錯電話

4 艾利克斯一定撥錯了區號。
Alex must have dialed the wrong area code. Track 363
片語釋義 area code 區號

5 你一定把這個電話號碼和蘇珊的弄混了。
You must confuse the number with Susan's. Track 364
重要詞彙 confuse [kən`fjuz] v. 使困惑

6 你能核對一下電話號碼嗎？
Could you check the telephone number? Track 365
同義表達 Could you tell me whether the telephone number is correct?

❼ 我們公司沒有叫琳達的。There isn't any Linda working here in our company. Track 366

同義表達 There is no Linda in our company.

❽ 湯姆撥的電話號碼是多少？
What number is Tom trying to reach? Track 367

同義表達 What number is Tom calling?

❾ 那個女士建議我查一下電話簿。
The lady suggested me look in the phone book. Track 368

片語釋義 phone book 電話簿

❿ 你應該向查詢台詢問一下。You are supposed to check with directory assistance. Track 369

片語釋義 check with sb 與某人核對

⓫ 辦公室裡沒有您說的這個人。
There is no one in the office by that name. Track 370

同義表達 There's nobody of that name in the office.

⓬ 很遺憾電話號碼不同了。I am sorry that the telephone number was different. Track 371

重要詞彙 change [tʃendʒ] v. 改變，變更

⓭ 很抱歉，您打錯電話了。
I am sorry this isn't the number you want. Track 372

同義表達 Sorry, you've got the wrong number.

⓮ 很遺憾，他們的分機號碼沒撥對。
I'm sorry they have the wrong extension. Track 373

重要詞彙 extension [ɪk`stɛnʃən] n. 電話分機，伸展，擴大

⓯ 那個人要的電話號碼是什麼？
What number is the man trying to dial? Track 374

重要詞彙 dial [ˋdaɪəl] v. 撥打

⓰ 你確定你撥的號碼是對的嗎？
Are you sure you're calling the right number? Track 375

同義表達 Are you sure you are dialing the right number?

⑰ 當我丈夫接電話時，他發現電話打錯了。
When my husband answered the call, he found that was a wrong number. Track 376
片語釋義 answer the call 接電話

⑱ 傑瑞會在他的電話本裡查詢正確的電話號碼。
Jerry will look up the correct number in his telephone directory. Track 377
片語釋義 look up 查找

⑲ 溫蒂會再次檢查電話號碼。
Wendy will check the telephone number again. Track 378
重要詞彙 check [tʃɛk] v. 檢查，核對

⑳ 抱歉打擾到你了。**Sorry to have bothered you.** Track 379
重要片語 sorry to do sth 抱歉做某事

看情境學對話

Track 380

	中譯
A: Hello. May I speak to Lisa?	A：你好！我要找麗莎。
B: There is no Lisa in our company ①. I am afraid that you have dialed the wrong number.	B：我們公司沒有叫麗莎的。恐怕你打錯電話了。
A: That's not true. I called last week and she was there and answered the phone. Are you sure? ②	A：這不可能。我上個禮拜打過來，她還在這裡接電話了。你確定嗎？
B: Yes. I feel quite sure that you have the wrong number. Our company has been using this telephone number for more than ③ ten years.	B：是。我相當肯定你打錯電話了。因為我們公司使用這個電話已經十多年了。
A: That's impossible. This phone number must be correct.	A：那不可能。這個電話號碼一定是正確的。

B: What number are you trying to reach?	B：你所撥打的電話號碼是多少？
A: 488-566-997.	A：488-566-997。
B: Sorry. Our telephone number is 488-566-977. It seems that ④ you have dialed the wrong number.	B：抱歉。我們的電話號碼是 488-566-977。看來是你撥錯號了。
A: Oh, my goodness. Sorry to have bothered you.	A：噢，我的天啊。抱歉打擾到你了。
B: It doesn't matter. This kind of thing happens to ⑤ everyone.	B：沒關係。這種事情常遇到。
A: I am really sorry.	A：真的很抱歉。
B: It's all right.	B：這沒什麼。

★**quite** [kwaɪt] **adv.** 相當，很，非常
★**correct** [kə`rɛkt] **adj.** 正確的，合適的
★**reach** [ritʃ] **v.** 到達，走到

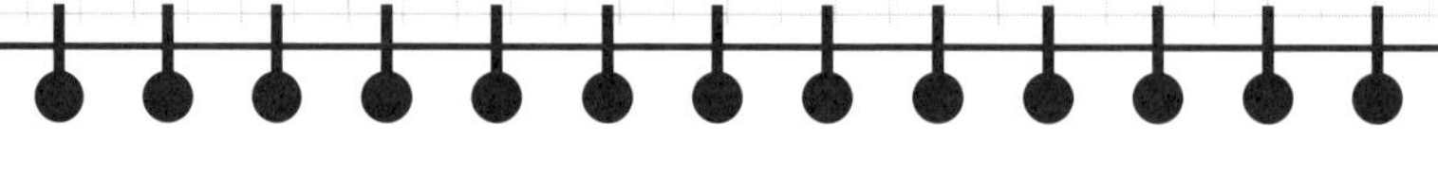

① There is no...

後面加單數名詞，表示「沒有……」，如果後面是複數名詞，要使用There are no...

② are you sure

表示「你確定嗎」，一般使用在口語或非正式的語言環境中。

③ more than

表示「超過，不僅僅」，後面可以接名詞、數詞。 more than 也可用在一些習慣用語中，如：more often than not （經常）。

④ It seems that...

表示「似乎……，看來……」。

⑤ happen to sb

表示「某事發生在某人身上」。這裡發生的「某事」通常指「不好的事情」，對話中的意思則是這種事會發生在所有人身上，也就是大家難免都會遇到的意思。

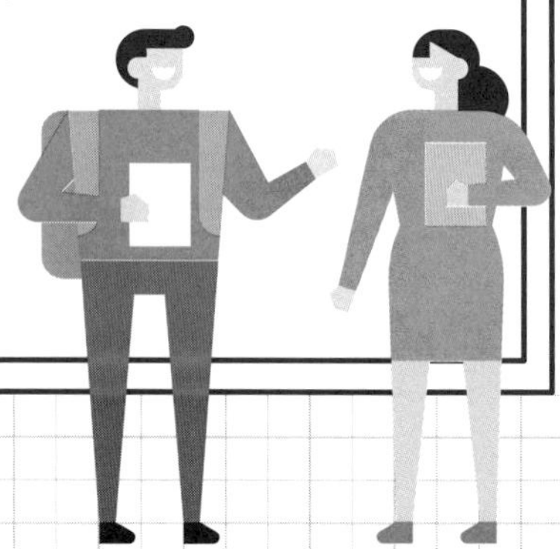

接打電話 Unit 18

Finishing A Call
掛斷電話

當你遇到緊急的事情，不得不掛斷電話的時候，你能否禮貌地掛斷電話呢？如何禮貌地掛斷電話？讓我們一起學習吧！

精選實用會話例句

1 你現在得掛電話了。**You have to hang up now.** Track 381
片語釋義 hang up 掛斷

2 我能晚些給你打電話嗎？**Can I call you later?** Track 382
同義表達 Can I talk to you later? / Can I get back to you later?

3 我現在得掛斷電話了。**I must ring off now.** Track 383
片語釋義 ring off 掛斷

4 我應該讓你去忙了，晚些時候再打給你。
I had better let you go. I'll call you later. Track 384
重要片語 let sb go 讓某人離開

5 抱歉，我得掛電話了。**I am sorry that I'd better go.** Track 385
同義表達 Sorry, I have to end the conversation.

6 你可不可以今天晚上再打來？
Could you call again this evening? Track 386
重要詞彙 evening [`ivnɪŋ] n. 傍晚，晚上

7 我不耽誤他的時間了。**I won't keep him any longer.** Track 387
同義表達 I won't take any more of his time.

8 我馬上要上班了。
I'm sorry that I have to go to work right now. Track 388
片語釋義 go to work 去上班

9 你有另一通電話打進來了嗎？
Do you have another call coming in? Track 389
片語釋義 come in 進來，到達

10 我想知道能不能晚點再打給你。
I wonder whether I could call you back later. Track 390
重要詞彙 whether [ˋwɛðɚ] **conj.** 哪一個，是否

11 恐怕我打擾您太久了。
I'm afraid I've taken up a lot of your time. Track 391
片語釋義 take up 接受，佔用，開始從事

12 我們可不可以晚一點再談？
Could we talk a little later? Track 392
片語釋義 a little later 晚一點

13 抱歉，我得掛斷了，我朋友正在等我。**Sorry, I have to ring off; my friend is waiting for me.** Track 393
重要片語 wait for sb 等某人

14 我們何不明天再談會議呢？
Why don't we talk about the meeting tomorrow? Track 394
重要詞彙 tomorrow [təˋmɔro] **adv.** 明天

15 抱歉，我一分鐘之後要參加一個活動。**Sorry, I have exactly one minute before I'm due at an activity.** Track 395
重要詞彙 exactly [ɪgˋzæktlɪ] **adv.** 精確地，確切地

16 我得掛了，到那裡了我再打電話給你。
I have to go; I will call you when I get there. Track 396
片語釋義 I have to go. 我得掛電話了

17 我得掛斷電話，因為我現在有個客戶要見。**I've got to hang up as I have a client to meet right now.** Track 397
片語釋義 hang up 掛電話

18 湯姆必須掛斷電話了，因為他得趕火車。
Tom has to ring off; he has to catch the train. Track 398
片語釋義 catch the train 趕火車

⑲ 這位女士說她已經把該說的說完了。**The lady said that she had finished what she had to say.** Track 399

重要片語 say that... 某人説……

⑳ 請別掛斷電話，我去看看經理在不在。**Please hold the line while I see if the manager is here.** Track 400

片語釋義 hold the line 不掛斷電話

看情境學對話

Track 401

	中譯
A: Hello, Modern Line. How may I help you?.	A：你好！Modern Line公司，有何為您服務的嗎？
B: Hi, I would like to speak ① to Mr. Green, please.	B：你好！我想找格林先生。
A: May I have your name, please? All of the callers should check in first ② .	A：請問你是哪一位？所有的來訪者都需要先登記一下。
B: Okay. My name is Jack Smith from WTK Company.	B：好的。我是WTK公司的傑克．史密斯。
A: Thank you. Mr. Smith. Please wait just a few seconds. Sorry to have kept you waiting. Mr. Green is just coming ③ .	A：謝謝你。史密斯先生。請稍等。抱歉讓你久等了，格林先生馬上就來。
C: Hi, Mr. Smith. This is Green. How can I help you? ④	C：你好，史密斯先生。我是格林。請問你找我有什麼事情嗎？
B: I want to talk about some new products. I don't know whether you are interested or not ⑤ ?	B：我想跟你談談開發新產品的事宜。我不知道你是否感興趣。

C: I see, Mr. Smith. Our company is considering developing our own new product. Sorry, I have exactly one minute before I'm due at a meeting. Let's make an appointment to meet and talk about it in detail.	C：我明白了，史密斯先生。我們公司也正在考慮開發新產品。很抱歉我一分鐘之後要參加一個會議。讓我們約個時間見面詳細談一談吧。
B: No problem. How about next Monday?	B：沒問題。下週一怎麼樣？
C: OK.	C：好的。
B: I will be in your company on time.	B：我會準時到你們公司的。

★**product** [`prɑdəkt] **n.** 產品
★**appointment** [ə`pɔɪntmənt] **n.** 約會，任命
★**detail** [`ditel] **n.** 詳細，詳述

① **would like to do sth**

表示「希望做某事」，相當於 want to do sth。would like doing sth 表示「樂意做某事」。

② **check in**

表示「登記，簽到」，可以表示辦理入住手續，是指填寫入住表格，也可以表示辦理登機手續，指托運行李，預訂座位，列印登機牌等。

③ **just coming**

該句是現在進行時表示將來，常常表示「意圖，安排，打算」等。現在進行時表示將來，所使用的動詞多是 go 或 come。

④ **How may I help you?**

此句使用率非常頻繁，常見於電話或是服務業中，有時也可以省略開頭的 How，意思是一樣的。

⑤ **whether...or not**

表示「不管，是否，無論如何」， or not 放在句末，通常與 whether 連用。

接打電話

Unit 19

Network Issues

線路故障

出現線路故障，你會怎麼辦呢？是自己動手解決，還是打電話叫維修工呢？讓我們一起來學習遇到線路故障應該怎麼處理。

精選實用會話例句

1. 蒂娜無法聯絡上你。**Tina can't get through to you.** Track 402
   重要片語 get through to sb 通過電話與某人取得聯繫

2. 很抱歉線路出現問題了。
   I'm sorry the line is out of order. Track 403
   片語釋義 out of order 故障

3. 或許線路串聯了。**Perhaps we have a crossed line.** Track 404
   同義表達 The lines seem to be crossed.

4. 對不起，你所撥打的這個號碼占線。
   I'm sorry the number you dialed is engaged. Track 405
   重要詞彙 engage [ɪn`gedʒ] v. 從事，銜接

5. 似乎我們之間電話連接不好。**There seems to be a bad connection between us.** Track 406
   重要詞彙 connection [kə`nɛkʃən] n. 連接，聯繫

6. 或許是聽筒沒放好。
   Perhaps the receiver is off the hook. Track 407
   重要詞彙 receiver [rɪ`sivɚ] n. 話筒

7. 電話線路出現嚴重干擾。
   There is a terrible interference on the line. Track 408
   片語釋義 terrible interference 嚴重干擾

❽ 我的線路出了故障。There is a fault on my line. Track 409

同義表達 My line is broken.

❾ 你們已經檢查線路了嗎？
Have you checked the line? Track 410

重要詞彙 check [tʃɛk] v. 檢查，核對

❿ 我們也許能掛斷電話再試一次。
Maybe we should hang up and try again. Track 411

重要片語 Maybe we should 也許應該

⓫ 我爸爸的電話被打斷了。
My father has been disconnected from a call. Track 412

重要詞彙 disconnect [ˌdɪskə`nɛktɪd] v. 切斷，斷開

⓬ 現在還沒有回音。There's no answer right now. Track 413

片語釋義 right now 立即，此刻，目前

⓭ 電話裡有一種有趣的噪音。
There is a funny noise on the phone. Track 414

同義表達 There is an interesting noise on the phone.

⓮ 線路一定超負荷了。The lines must be overloaded. Track 415

重要詞彙 overload [ˌovɚ`lod] v. 使超載

⓯ 這線路不能運作。 The network isn't working. Track 416

重要詞彙 work [wɝk] v. 運作；運行

⓰ 電話打不通。 I couldn't get through. Track 417

片語釋義 get thorugh 接通

⓱ 你能告訴我是不是他的電話機出了問題。
Can you tell me if there's something wrong with his cellphone? Track 418

重要片語 tell sb sth 告訴某人某事

⓲ 我幾乎聽不到你在說什麼。I can hardly hear what you are saying. Track 419

重要詞彙 hardly [`hɑrdlɪ] adv. 幾乎不

⑲ 你能掛斷電話再打過來嗎？

Can you hang up and call back? Track 420

片語釋義 call back 回電話

⑳ 你能聽到持續的嗡嗡聲嗎？

Can you hear the continuous beeping sound? Track 421

重要詞彙 continuous [kən`tɪnjʊəs] **adj.** 連續的

㉑ 我想知道你的電話是否出現了故障。

I want to know whether there is anything wrong with your telephone. Track 422

重要詞彙 telephone [`tɛlə͵fon] **n.** 電話

㉒ 昨天湯尼的電話有什麼故障？**What troubles did Tony's cellphone have yesterday?** Track 423

同義表達 What was the failure of Tony's cellphone yesterday?

看情境學對話

Track 424

	中譯
A: You are late.	A：你來晚了。
B: I know. I tried to call you back, but I couldn't get through ① to you. No one seems to hear ② the cellphone ring.	B：我知道。但是我聯繫不到你，似乎沒有人聽到手機鈴聲。
A: Really? I have no idea. I didn't hear the ringing of my cellphone. Let me check my cellphone. Yes, it's dead.	A：真的嗎？我一點都不知道。我沒有聽到我的手機鈴聲。讓我檢查一下我的手機。是的，它沒電了。
B: I knew I would be late because the car wouldn't start. It was too cold and I had to warm it up in the garage with a heater. That's why I'm late.	B：我知道我會遲到，因為我的車沒法發動，天氣實在太冷了，我必須在車庫用暖爐熱車，這就是為何我會遲到。

A: This is terrible. I'm waiting for an important call. But my cellphone is out of batteries.	A：這下慘了，我正在等一個重要的電話。但是我的手機沒電。
B: About what?	B：關於什麼的電話？
A: IBM will call me and discuss the plan about developing new software. If I don't have my cellphone, what should I do? ③	A：IBM 公司會打電話給我，討論開發新軟體的計畫。如果我沒有電話，該怎麼辦？
B: You can find a socket and charge it quickly.	B：你可以找個插座快快充電。
A: But I don't have a phone charge.	A：但是我沒有充電線。
B: You can borrow it from ④ the hotel front desk.	B：你可以借用旅館櫃臺的線。
A: That's a good idea. Thank you.	A：真是一個好主意。謝謝。
B: You're welcome.	B：不客氣。

【程度提升，加分單字】

★**garage** [gəˋrɑʒ] **n.** 車庫
★**heater** [ˋhitɚ] **n.** 加熱器
★**software** [ˋsɔftˏwɛr] **n.** 軟體

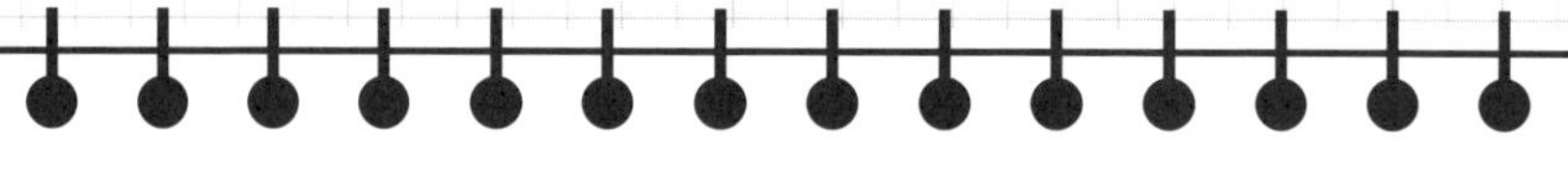

對話解析

① get through to sb

表示「與某人取得聯繫」，get through with sb 表示「與某人做了結」，get through (with) sth 表示「戰勝（困難），結束（某事）」。

② seem to do sth

表示「看起來做某事」，是對事物的主觀判斷。 seem doing sth表示「看起來像做某事」。

③ What should I do?

表示「我該怎麼辦？」是一個獨立的特殊疑問句，用於詢問對方該怎麼辦。

④ borrow sth from...

表示「向……借……」，是一個很常見的結構。

Chapter 2

餐廳用餐

流程

Unit 20

Reservation

預訂

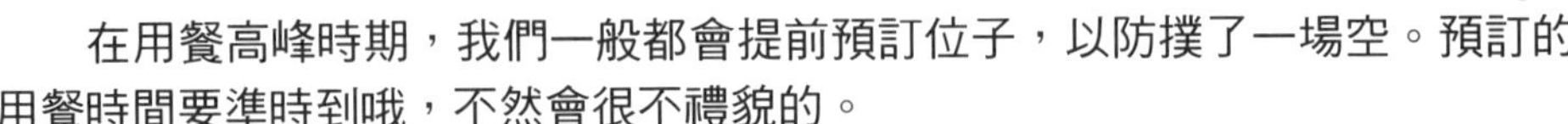

在用餐高峰時期，我們一般都會提前預訂位子，以防撲了一場空。預訂的用餐時間要準時到哦，不然會很不禮貌的。

精選實用會話例句

❶ 需要預約嗎？**Do you need a reservation?** Track 425

重要詞彙 reservation [ˌrɛzɚ`veʃən] n. 預訂，預約

❷ 您要預訂幾個位子？

How many tables would you like to reserve? Track 426

重要片語 would like to do sth 想要做某事

❸ 我想預訂今晚八點三個人的位子。**I want to make a reservation for three at eight tonight.** Track 427

同義表達 I'd like to reserve a table for three at eight tonight.

❹ 昨天晚上這家餐廳的客人相當多。**The restaurant had so many guests yesterday evening.** Track 428

片語釋義 yesterday evening 昨天晚上

❺ 你什麼時候能到餐廳？

When will you arrive at the restaurant? Track 429

同義表達 When can you get to the restaurant?

❻ 請告訴我你的姓名和電話號碼。**Give me your name and telephone number, please.** Track 430

片語釋義 telephone number 電話號碼

❼ 有幾位呢？**How many people are coming?** Track 431

同義表達 How many people are in your party?

❽ 有能容納十人的桌子嗎？Do you have a table that will accommodate ten? Track 432

重要詞彙 accommodate [əˋkɑmə͵det] v. 容納，使適應

❾ 他們下午 7 點之前會到。
They will be here just before 7 p.m. Track 433

同義表達 They will arrive before 7 p.m.

❿ 我的客戶想坐在靠窗的位置。
My clients want to sit by a window. Track 434

重要詞彙 client [ˋklaɪənt] n. 客戶，顧客

⓫ 請為我們準備餐桌好嗎？
Would you please have our table ready for us? Track 435

同義表達 Can you set a table for us?

⓬ 我想預訂一個遠離吸煙區的位子。I want to book a table far away from the smoking section. Track 436

片語釋義 far away from 遠離

⓭ 我想訂包廂。I would like a table in a private room. Track 437

同義表達 I want to set up a room.

⓮ 秘書會預訂晚餐。
The secretary will make a dinner reservation. Track 438

重要詞彙 secretary [ˋsɛkrə͵tɛrɪ] n. 秘書

⓯ 請問你叫什麼名字？May I have your name, please? Track 439

同義表達 Can I get your name?

⓰ 我期待您這個週五的光臨。
I look forward to seeing you this Friday. Track 440

重要片語 look forward to doing sth 期盼做某事

⓱ 首先，你應該預訂一個位子。
First of all, you should book a table. Track 441

片語釋義 first of all 首先

⓲ 餐廳在什麼位置？Where is the restaurant? Track 442

同義表達 What's the location of the restaurant?

⑲ **我想在這附近訂一家便宜的餐廳。I want to book an inexpensive restaurant near here.** Track 443

重要詞彙 inexpensive [ˌɪnɪkˋspɛnsɪv] adj. 不貴的，便宜的

⑳ **這附近是否有中餐廳？**
Is there a Chinese restaurant around here? Track 444

片語釋義 Chinese restaurant 中餐廳

㉑ **你們有在角落的桌子嗎？**
Do you have a table in the corner? Track 445

片語釋義 in the corner 在角落

㉒ **你能安排一張靠窗的桌子嗎？**
Can you arrange a table near the window? Track 446

重要詞彙 arrange [əˋrendʒ] v. 安排，整理

看情境學對話

Track 447

	中譯
A: This is Conrad Hotel. Can I help you ①?	A：這是康拉德飯店。請問有什麼需要嗎？
B: I want to make a reservation for a dinner this Friday.	B：我想預訂這個星期五的晚餐。
A: How many ② people are in your party?	A：有多少人？
B: About ten people. And do you have a table that will accommodate ten?	B：大概十個人。有能容納十人的桌子嗎？
A: Of course ③ we have. When will you arrive on Friday?	A：當然有。你們星期五什麼時候到？
B: We will be here just before 7 p.m.	B：我們下午 7 點之前能到。
A: We will have your table ready for you in advance. May I have your name and phone number?	A：我們會預先為您準備好桌子。能告訴我您的姓名和電話號碼嗎？

B: My name is John Smith and the telephone number is 9-8-4-3-2-7-3.	B：我叫約翰・史密斯，電話號碼是 9-8-4-3-2-7-3。
A: OK, John Smith, a table for ten at about seven this Friday. Is there anything else?	A：好的，約翰・史密斯，這個星期五 7 點左右預訂一張 10 個人的位子。還有別的事嗎？
B: Can you arrange a table near the window so that we can enjoy the evening view?	B：你能安排一張靠窗的桌子讓我們欣賞晚上的景色嗎？
A: No problem. I will arrange it for you.	A：沒問題。我會給您安排的。
B: By the way ④, it is really best to manage a table far away from the smoking section.	B：順便說一句，最好是離吸煙區很遠的位子。
A: Don't worry. I will do it. I look forward to ⑤ seeing you this Friday.	A：別擔心。我會安排的。期待這個星期五見到你。
B: Thank you very much.	B：非常感謝。

★**view** [vju] n. 風景，看法

★**manage** [`mænɪdʒ] v. 辦理，應付，解決

★**section** [`sɛkʃən] n. 部分，部門

① **Can I help you?**

在英語口語中使用頻率很高，表示「需要我幫忙嗎？」常常用於向對方提供幫助。類似的表達還有：May I help you? What can I do for you?

② **how many**

常常用於詢問「多少」，後面通常跟可數名詞的複數。how much 也可用於詢問「多少」，但是後面通常跟不可數名詞。

③ **of course**

在英語中是一個使用頻率高的片語，表示「當然」，相當於 sure。

④ **by the way**

表示「順便問一下，順便說一下」，常常用逗號與句子的其他成分隔開。

⑤ **look forward to**

表示「期待，盼望」，後面一般跟名詞或者是動名詞。

學習英文Fun輕鬆！

1.Success is in favor of the person who is prepared.
成功是留給有準備的人的。

2.The early bird catches the worm.
早起的鳥兒有蟲吃。

3.A good beginning is half done.
良好的開始是成功的一半。

4.No preparation is preparing to fail.
沒有準備的人，就是在準備失敗。

5.The best preparation for tomorrow is doing your best today.
對明天最好的準備就是今天做到最好。

6.The future belongs to people who start preparing now.
未來屬於現在就開始準備的人。

文化小站

中西方餐桌禮儀存在很大的差異，並且各有特色。在東方餐桌傳統文化中體現了「群體意識」，比如圓形餐桌很受歡迎，因為圓桌可以讓大家面對而坐。而在西方餐桌文化中體現了「個體意識」，長形餐桌可以很清楚地通過座位辨認地位，同時每個人有自己的一份食物，各吃各的。在座次安排中，中西方餐桌禮儀也不盡相同。在東方餐桌上都是客人入座上席，客人需要有主人的邀請才可入座，入座要從椅子的左邊進入，入座之後切記不可先動筷子，更不可以隨便走動。主人要注意不要讓客人坐在上菜的位置。在西方餐桌禮儀中，女主人宣佈晚宴開始，男主人引領客人入座。有時餐桌上會有名卡，讓客人很清楚地知道自己的位置。在預訂餐廳中，守時也是非常重要的，因為在星級餐廳中位置是很搶手的，用餐時間也是有限制的。如果預訂之後遲到或者不去，這是很不禮貌的。另外沒有按時到達餐廳，餐廳就會視你主動放棄用餐。

流程

Unit 21

Placing an Order

點菜

你會點菜嗎？點菜看似是一件很平常的事情，裡面也有很深的學問。點菜時，不僅要有葷有素，冷熱搭配，而且也要注意有些特殊人群對飲食的禁忌。

精選實用會話例句

1 你需要看菜單嗎？
Would you like to look at the menu? Track 448
重要詞彙 menu [`mɛnju] n. 菜單

2 你現在要點餐嗎？**Are you ready to order now?** Track 449
同義表達 Would you like to order now?

3 我要三份牛排和一份沙拉。
I'll have a beef steak and a salad. Track 450
同義表達 I'd like to order three beef steaks and a salad.

4 我們點餐之前要來點開胃酒。
We need an aperitif before we order. Track 451
重要詞彙 aperitif [ɑperi`tif] n. 開胃酒，餐前酒

5 你能讓我看看中文的菜單嗎？
Do you have menu Chinese? Track 452
重要片語 show sb sth 把某物展示給某人

6 我不喜歡太油膩的菜。**I don't like greasy food.** Track 453
重要詞彙 greasy [`grizɪ] adj. 油膩的

7 您有什麼特殊飲食需求嗎？
Are you on a special diet? Track 454
片語釋義 special diet 特殊飲食

❽ 你想嚐嚐本地菜嗎？
Would you like to try some local food? Track 455
片語釋義 local food 當地菜品，本地菜

❾ 您今天可以免費品嚐我們店的特色菜。**You can have a taste of our specialty for free today.** Track 456
同義表達 You can try our specialty for free today.

❿ 您最喜歡吃什麼食物？
What kind of food do you like best? Track 457
同義表達 What sort of food do you like best?

⓫ 你的牛排要幾成熟？**How do you like your steak?** Track 458
重要詞彙 steak [stek] **n.** 牛排

⓬ 您最喜歡哪種沙拉？
What kind of salad do you like better? Track 459
同義表達 Which kind of salad do you prefer?

⓭ 他們正在等一個朋友。**They are waiting for a friend.** Track 460
重要片語 wait for sb 等待某人

⓮ 餐廳是否供應素食餐點？
Do you have vegetarian dishes? Track 461
片語釋義 vegetarian dishes 素菜

⓯ 我推薦一些主菜給你們。
I will recommend you some main courses. Track 462
片語釋義 main course 主菜

⓰ 他還沒想好要點什麼。
He hasn't decided what to order. Track 463
重要詞彙 decide [dɪˈsaɪd] **v.** 決定，決心

⓱ 先生，你還要點別的嗎？
What else would you like to order, sir? Track 464
重要詞彙 order [ˋɔrdɚ] **v.** 下訂單，訂購

⓲ 這位女士想來點清淡些的。
The lady prefers something lite. Track 465

重要詞彙 prefer [prɪˋfɝ] v. 更喜歡，寧願

⓳ 我想吃點海鮮。**I'd like to have some seafood.** Track 466

片語釋義 sea food 海產食品，海鮮

⓴ 今天的特色菜是什麼？
What is the specialty of the day? Track 467

片語釋義 special cuisine 特色菜

看情境學對話

Track 468

	中譯
A: Excuse me ①, could I see the menu, please?	A：打擾一下，我能看看菜單嗎？
B: OK, here you are ②.	B：當然，給您。
A: What would you recommend? Can you recommend us some main courses?	A：你有什麼要推薦的？能給我們推薦一些主菜嗎？
B: I would suggest the sirloin steak, which is the specialty of our restaurant. It tastes delicious and is very popular among our customers.	B：我建議您嚐嚐沙朗牛排，這是餐廳的特色菜。它的味道很好，而且在顧客中很受歡迎。
A: It sounds great. We will try it.	A：聽起來不錯。我們會試試的。
B: How would you like your steak? Medium rare, medium, or well-done?	B：牛排要三分熟、五分熟還是全熟？
A: Medium, please. Please don't make the steak too greasy ③.	A：五分熟，請不要做得太油膩了。

B: OK. What else would you like? Would you need an aperitif?	B：好的，還想點些什麼？需要開胃酒嗎？
A: Not today, thanks. Do you have vegetarian dishes?	A：今天不要了，謝謝。你們有素菜嗎？
B: Of course. You can see this menu. What would you like to order?	B：當然有。您可以看看這個功能表。想點些什麼？
A: We'll have a mixed green salad.	A：我們要一份綜合蔬菜沙拉。
B: Would you like anything to drink?	B：想喝什麼飲料？
A: A cup of coffee and two bottles of sparkling water. ④	A：一杯咖啡和兩瓶氣泡水。
B: Is that all? ⑤	B：就這些嗎？
A: Yes. Thank you.	A：是的。謝謝。
B: Are you on a special diet?	B：有什麼忌口的嗎？
A: No. Thank you very much.	A：沒有。非常感謝。

★**recommend** [ˌrɛkəˋmɛnd] **v.** 推薦，勸告
★**specialty** [ˋspɛʃəltɪ] **n.** 專長，特點 **adj.** 特色的，專門的
★**delicious** [dɪˋlɪʃəs] **adj.** 美味的，可口的
★**aperitif** [ɑperiˋtif] **n.** 開胃酒

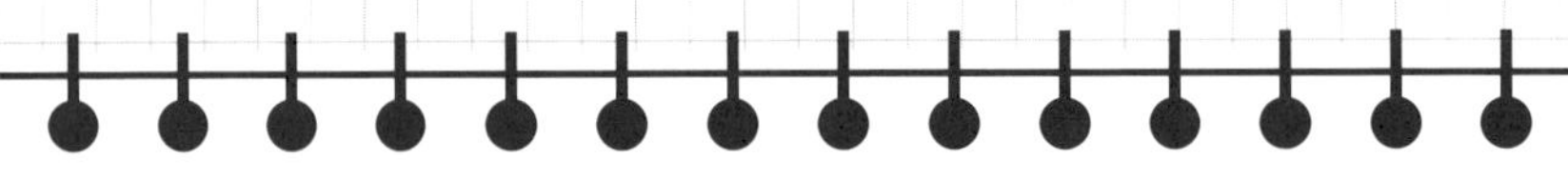

對話解析

① **excuse me**

表示「請問，對不起，打擾一下」，使用的場合有多種：可以用於問路，客氣地打斷別人說話，中途退席，對自己的不禮貌行為道歉等。

② **here you are**

是一個倒裝結構，表示「給你」。類似的表達還有：here it is, here they are。

③ **too greasy**

表示「太油膩」，too 表示一種不認同的語氣，也含有否定的意思。

④ **a cup of coffee**

表示「一杯咖啡」， two bottles of sparkling water 表示「兩氣泡水」， coffee 和 sparkling water 都是不可數名詞，在表示數量時要借助量詞 cup 和 bottle。

⑤ **Is that all?**

表示「就這些嗎？」常常用於說話者詢問資訊是否已經完整。

流程 Unit 22

Waiting for the Meal 等待上菜

等待上菜對於一個饑腸轆轆的人來說，無疑是一件煎熬的事情。但是若一味地催促做菜速度，難免菜品質量會無法保障。為了享受一頓美食，有時候等待也是值得的。

精選實用會話例句

1 我們趕時間，你們能馬上上菜嗎？We are in a hurry. Can you bring our order at once? Track 469

片語釋義 in a hurry 立刻，急切

2 請快點上菜。Please rush our orders. Track 470

重要詞彙 rush [rʌʃ] V. 催促，急速進行

3 你能和主廚核對我點的菜嗎？Can you check my order with the chef? Track 471

片語釋義 check with 核對

4 他們對這家餐廳的上菜慢很生氣。They are angry about the slow service of this restaurant. Track 472

重要片語 be angry about... 對……生氣

5 請享用您的晚餐。Please enjoy the dinner. Track 473

重要詞彙 enjoy [ɪn'dʒɔɪ] V. 享受

6 為什麼這些菜要花這麼長時間？Why are the dishes taking so long? Track 474

重要詞彙 take [tek] V. 拿，採取，接受，花費

7 這是您的沙朗牛排。Here is your sirloin steak. Track 475

片語釋義 sirloin steak 沙朗牛排

❽ 這位女士半小時前點的餐。
The lady ordered her meal half an hour ago. Track 476
片語釋義 half an hour ago 半小時以前

❾ 我們的餐點還沒有來。**Our meal still hasn't come.** Track 477
同義表達 Our meal has not come yet.

❿ 湯姆已經等了三十分鐘。
Tom has been waiting for thirty minutes. Track 478
片語釋義 wait for 等待

⓫ 能不能快點啊？**Can you hurry up?** Track 479
重要詞彙 hurry [ˈhʌrɪ] v. 倉促，催促

⓬ 很抱歉，你點的牛排需要花費更長的時間。**I'm sorry, the steak you ordered will take a longer time.** Track 480
片語釋義 take a longer time 花費更長的時間

⓭ 這不是我們點的菜。**It is not the dish we ordered.** Track 481
同義表達 This is not our order.

⓮ 恐怕主廚弄錯了。
I am afraid that the chef has made a mistake. Track 482
片語釋義 make a mistake 犯錯

⓯ 孩子們都餓壞了，上菜吧。
The kids are starving! Serve it up! Track 483
片語釋義 serve up 上菜

⓰ 服務生上最後一道菜了。
The waiter is serving the last dish. Track 484
重要詞彙 serve [sɝv] v. 服務，招待，端上

⓱ 經理會催一下廚師的。
The manager will ask the cooks to hurry. Track 485
重要片語 ask sb to do sth 要求某人做某事

⓲ 我們的主廚擅長做海鮮。
Our chef is good at cooking seafood. Track 486
重要片語 be good at... 擅長做……

⑲ **這道魚以味道鮮美而聞名。**
The fish is famous for being fresh and tasty. Track 487
重要詞彙 tasty [ˋtestɪ] adj. 美味的，可口的

⑳ **這道蔬菜湯用了八種原料。**
The vegetable soup is made with 8 ingredients. Track 488
重要詞彙 ingredient [ɪnˋgridɪənt] n. 原料，因素

㉑ **你能告訴我怎麼吃嗎？Can you tell me how to eat it?** Track 489
同義表達 Could you please tell me how to eat it?

㉒ **你能把這些空盤子撤走嗎？**
Can you take the empty dishes away? Track 490
片語釋義 take away 拿開，撤走

㉓ **他說你的菜很快就好了。**
He said your order would be ready soon. Track 491
重要詞彙 ready [ˋrɛdɪ] adj. 準備好的，現成的，即將的

看情境學對話

Track 492

	中譯
A: Excuse me. We have been waiting for half an hour. Could you please tell the cooks to hurry up?	A：我們已經等半個小時了。你能催一下廚師嗎？
B: We are so sorry to keep you waiting ① . Your order will be ready soon. The fish you ordered will take more time because the chef makes it with fresh fish.	B：很抱歉讓您久等了。您的菜馬上就好了。您點的魚要花更多的時間，因為廚師用鮮魚做的。
A: That's fine. ② Could you bring us some aperitif ?	A：好吧。能給我們來點開胃酒嗎？
B: Certainly. Here you are. Here is your steak, vegetable salad and red wine. Please enjoy your dinner.	B：當然可以。給您。這是您的牛排、蔬菜沙拉和紅酒。請慢慢享用您的晚餐。

A: Thank you. By the way, can you take the plates away? ③	A：謝謝。順便問一下，你能把盤子拿走嗎？
B: Of course.	B：當然。
A: That tastes delicious ④ . What's that?	A：嚐起來很好吃。那是什麼？
B: The fish is boneless, nutritious and transparent. Please try the white shrimp. It is the instant-boiled white shrimp.	B：這種魚沒有骨頭，營養豐富，透明。請嚐嚐白蝦。這是用快火煮的白蝦。
A: Yes, the shrimp tastes very tender, but it is a bit too small.	A：是的，這蝦味道很嫩，但它有點小。
B: The shrimp can't grow very big and the size is good to eat. Here is your vegetable soup.	B：這種蝦是不能長太大的。這樣大小的白蝦正是味道最好的。這是您的蔬菜湯。
A: It is not the dish we ordered ⑤ . Perhaps you are mistaken.	A：這不是我們點的菜。也許你弄錯了。
B: I am sorry. I will take it away. This is the complete course and the fruit combination will be served later.	B：很抱歉。我會把它拿走。菜已經上齊了，水果拼盤將在稍後提供。

★**chef** [ʃɛf] **n.** 廚師，主廚

★**nutritious** [nju`trɪʃəs] **adj.** 有營養的

★**shrimp** [ʃrɪmp] **n.** 蝦，小蝦

★**complete** [kəm`plit] **adj.** 完全的，完整的

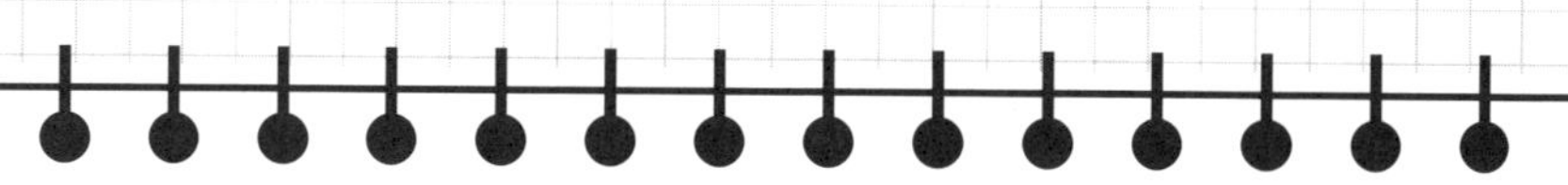

① **keep sb doing sth**

表示「讓某人持續做某事」，要與 keep sb from doing sth（阻止某人做某事）區別開來。

② **that's fine**

表示「不錯，好吧，可以」，可以用於回答「How about...?」、「Is that OK?」之類的問題。

③ **take away**

表示「拿走，拿開，帶走」，這裡的受詞可以是物也可以是人，如果是代名詞必須放在 take 和 away 的中間。

④ **taste delicious**

表示「嚐起來很美味」，此處的 taste 是一個感官動詞，後面可以直接跟形容詞。

⑤ **It is not the dish we ordered.**

該句是一個強調句，其結構是：It is + 被強調部分 + that + 其他 . 該句中省略了that，而且是一個否定句。

流程

Unit 23

Bottoms Up

勸酒夾菜

宴請中的「勸酒」和「夾菜」你會嗎？光喝酒不吃菜不行，光吃菜不喝酒也不行，如何做到「勸酒」和「夾菜」呢？讓我們一起去看看吧！

精選實用會話例句

1 請隨便吃。**Please help yourselves.** Track 493

重要片語 help oneself 請自便

2 你想再來一杯酒嗎？

Would you like another cup of wine? Track 494

重要詞彙 another [əˋnʌðɚ] adj. 另一個，再一個

3 別不好意思。**Don't be shy.** Track 495

同義表達 Don't be embarrassed.

4 我們一直在夾菜呢。

We have already been helping ourselves. Track 496

重要詞彙 already [ɔlˋrɛdɪ] adv. 已經，先前

5 你想嚐嚐菜嗎？**Would you like to try that dish?** Track 497

同義表達 Do you want to try that dish?

6 讓我們為升職喝一杯。**Let's drink to the promotion.** Track 498

重要詞彙 promotion [prəˋmoʃən] n. 升職

7 這道菜有點辣，但是很美味。

The dish is a little hot, but very delicious. Track 499

重要詞彙 hot [hɑt] adj. 熱的，辣的，激動的

8 如果她堅持的話，麥克斯就會再來一杯。

Max will have another cup if she insists. Track 500

片語釋義 have another cup 再來一杯

❾ 我爸爸不喜歡一個人喝酒。
My father doesn't like to drink alone. Track 501
重要詞彙 alone [ə`lon] adj. 單獨的，孤獨的 adv. 單獨地

❿ 讓我們為這頓大餐乾杯。Let's toast to the big meal. Track 502
片語釋義 toast to 祝酒，乾杯

⓫ 讓他為你丈夫倒啤酒吧。
Let him pour the beer for your husband. Track 503
重要詞彙 pour [por] v. 湧出，傾，倒

⓬ 據說這裡的牛排很出名。
It is said that the steak here is very famous. Track 504
重要片語 It is said that... 據説……

⓭ 過分勸酒你會變得不禮貌。
It's impolite to urge people to drink. Track 505
重要片語 be impolite to do... 做……不禮貌

⓮ 為她的成功乾一杯。Here's to her success. Track 506
重要詞彙 success [sək`sɛs] n. 成功，成就

⓯ 謝謝你的熱情款待。Thank you for your hospitality. Track 507
重要詞彙 hospitality [ˌhɑspɪ`tælətɪ] n. 熱情好客，招待，款待

⓰ 我希望我早知道那家餐廳。
I hope I had known the restaurant earlier. Track 508
同義表達 I wish I had known the restaurant before.

⓱ 你兒子想來點冰淇淋嗎？
Would your son like some of the ice cream? Track 509
同義表達 Does your son want some of the ice cream?

⓲ 我們對飯菜很滿意。
We are satisfied with the dishes. Track 510
重要片語 be satisfied with... 對……滿意

⓳ 老闆特別喜歡這條魚。
The boss especially likes the fish. Track 511
重要詞彙 especially [ə`spɛʃəlɪ] adv. 尤其地，主要地

20 **這家餐廳果然名不虛傳。**

The restaurant deserves its reputation. Track 512

重要詞彙 deserve [dɪ`zɝv] v. 應受，應得，值得

21 **你想嚐嚐那瓶啤酒嗎？**

Would you like to try that beer? Track 513

同義表達 Could you please try that beer?

看情境學對話

Track 514

	中譯
A: Please help yourself ① to the dishes. If you have some problems, please ask me.	A：請自便。如果你有什麼問題，儘管問我。
B: Thank you. We have already been helping ourselves. These dishes taste very delicious.	B：謝謝。我們一直在吃呢。這些菜的味道都很好。
A: Look at this fish. It is the special cuisine ② of this restaurant. It is made with the fresh fish and 8 ingredients. The soup is very tasty and nutritious.	A：看看這道魚。這是這家餐廳的特色菜。它是用新鮮的魚和 8 種原料製成的。這湯也很美味，很有營養。
B: That sounds great. My mouth is watering.	B：聽起來很不錯。我都流口水了。
A: This dish is terrific. Would you like some of this? It tastes a bit hot, but very nice. I like hot dishes; my hometown is in Sichuan. Most people like spicy food.	A：這道菜太好吃了。你想來點嗎？它嚐起來有點辣，但味道很好。我喜歡辣的，我的家鄉是四川的。大多數人喜歡辛辣的食物。

B: Would you like to try another cup ③ of red wine?	B：你想再來一杯紅酒嗎？
A: I will have another cup if you insist. But I don't want the red wine. I want a cup of beer.	A：如果你堅持的話，我再來一杯。但我不想要紅酒。我想喝杯啤酒。
B: Today is a special day. Tony has become the manager of our department. Let's toast to his promotion. ④	B：今天是個特別的日子。托尼已經成為我們部門的經理。讓我們為他的晉升乾杯。
A: Cheers. This is a wonderful restaurant. I wish I had known it before.	A：乾杯。這是一家很棒的餐廳。我真希望我以前就知道了。
B: Thanks a lot to bring me here.	B：謝謝你帶我來這裡。
A: You're welcome. ⑤ Try this.	A：你太客氣了。嚐嚐這個。
B: I am full. Thank you for your hospitality.	B：我已經飽了。謝謝你的熱情款待。

★**cuisine** [kwɪ`zin] **n.** 烹飪，菜餚
★**terrific** [tə`rɪfɪk] **adj.** 極好的，了不起的
★**spicy** [`spaɪsɪ] **adj.** 辛辣的

對話解析

① **help yourself**

表示「請自便」，yourself 是一個反身代詞，表示「你自己」。 help yourself 相當於 enjoy yourself。

② **special cuisine**

表示「特色菜」， special 是一個形容詞，在此處修飾 cuisine。 specialty 也可以表示「特色菜」。

③ **another cup**

表示「再來一杯」，此處的 another 表示「另一個，再一個」，特指三者或以上的數目。

④ **let sb do sth**

表示「讓某人做某事」，該句是一個由 let 引導的祈使句。let 之後出現的動詞要使用原形。

⑤ **You're welcome.**

表示「不客氣」。用於回答別人的感謝。相當於 It's my pleasure. 或者 My pleasure.

文化小站

酒在華人的歷史源遠流長，逐漸形成了「酒文化」。在華人傳統酒席宴上，酒是必不可少的存在。俗話說的好：酒品看人品。宴席之間的勸酒也就成為了一道獨特的風景線。華人對於酒有自己的一套相應的規則：敬酒，倒酒，祝酒，飲酒。其中敬酒是最為重要的一個環節。宴席上人們地位、職務、親疏、年齡的不同，在碰杯時酒杯的位置需要有所體現。華人習慣在酒桌上頻繁敬酒，以體現自己的熱情與尊重。於是「勸酒」就成了酒席宴上很重要的一個環節。在中國餐桌上還有「夾菜」一說。主人或者長輩會夾菜給客人或晚輩，以表達自己的關懷之意。這在華人的餐桌上是很常見的。

流程

Unit 24

Wrap Up
打包外帶

你經常會打包剩餘的食物嗎？有句話說的好：「誰知盤中餐，粒粒皆辛苦。」這告誡我們要節約糧食。節約從自己做起，讓我們一起行動吧！

精選實用會話例句

1. 請給我們一個打包盒。**Please give us a to-go-box.** Track 515
   同義表達 Please give a to-go-box to us.

2. 你想要一個打包袋嗎？**Do you want a doggy bag?** Track 516
   片語釋義 doggy bag 打包袋

3. 你點的太多了。**You have ordered too much.** Track 517
   重要詞彙 order [ˋɔrdɚ] v. 命令，訂購，下訂單

4. 吉米不想浪費食物。**Jimmy doesn't want to waste the food.** Track 518
   片語釋義 waste the food 浪費食物

5. 你能把剩下的食物打包讓我們帶走嗎？**Would you mind packing the rest of the food for us to go?** Track 519
   重要片語 pack sth for sb 為某人打包某物

6. 昨天他們吃飯剩下了好多菜，就全都打包回家了。**They left so much food yesterday that they took it home.** Track 520
   重要詞彙 yesterday [ˋjɛstɚde] n. 昨天

7. 我需要一個打包袋。**I need a doggy bag.** Track 521
   同義表達 I need a packing bag.

❽ 這位女士想把食物從餐廳裡打包帶走。The lady wants to take food out of the restaurant. Track 522

重要片語 take sth out of... 把某物從……帶走

❾ 你能請那個年輕人把剩下的食物打包嗎？Could you ask the young man to pack the rest of the food? Track 523

重要片語 ask sb to do sth 請求某人做某事

❿ 你應該要拿一個打包袋。
You should have asked for a doggy bag. Track 524

重要片語 should have done sth 應該做某事

⓫ 這家餐廳的食物可以外帶嗎？
Can we order food to go in the restaurant? Track 525

重要詞彙 food [fud] n. 食物，食品

⓬ 傑瑞想點一些食物外帶。
Jerry wants to order some food to go. Track 526

重要片語 want to do sth 想要做某事

⓭ 不要浪費食物，把它們帶回家。
Don't waste the food. Take it home. Track 527

重要詞彙 waste [west] v. 浪費，損耗

⓮ 把剩下的食物用打包袋裝起來。
Pack the rest of the food with the doggy bag. Track 528

片語釋義 the rest of 剩下的

⓯ 打包之後帶回你家。
Wrap it up and take it to your home. Track 529

片語釋義 wrap up 包裹

⓰ 有些人在飯店用餐完畢後，經常打包走一些食物。
Some people often leave a restaurant with the rest of the food to take away. Track 530

重要詞彙 leave [liv] v. 離開，出發

⓱ 這位女士拒絕吃打包的食物。
The lady refused to eat the packed food. Track 531

重要片語 refuse to do sth 拒絕做某事

⑱ 在某些餐廳你不能打包食物帶走。**You can't take the rest of the food to go in some restaurants.** Track 532

同義表達 You can't pack food to take away in some restaurants.

⑲ 今天唯一可以外帶的食物只有漢堡。
The only take-out food for today is hamburger. Track 533

重要詞彙 hamburger [`hæmbɝgɚ] n. 漢堡

⑳ 他們需要買外帶食物嗎？
Do they need to buy take-out? Track 534

重要片語 need to do sth 需要做某事

看情境學對話

Track 535

	中譯
A: Do you often take the leftover food home from a restaurant?	A：你經常從餐廳打包食物回家嗎？
B: Not very often ①. The doggie bags are quite uncommon in most cities.	B：不常。打包袋在大多數城市都是很少見的。
A: What happens to the rest of the food?	A：那剩飯剩菜怎麼處理呢？
B: It usually goes to the dump.	B：通常就會直接倒掉。
A: What an awful waste! People should have ordered fewer dishes so that ② they can reduce the waste of the food at the end of ③ the meal.	A：真是太浪費了！人們應該少點菜，這樣他們就可以減少飯後食物的浪費。
B: Why don't people order fewer dishes?	B：為什麼人們不能少點些菜呢？
A: It is a tradition to order a lot of food in a restaurant.	A：在餐廳裡點很多食物是一種傳統。

B: Then it is better to take the leftovers home.	B：那最好還是打包剩下的飯菜。
A: However, many people are unwilling to do it ④ . But if you want, you can take the leftovers home.	A：然而，很多人不願意這樣做。但如果你願意，你可以把剩菜帶回家。
B: Yes, maybe it is the best way to reduce the waste.	B：是的，也許這是減少浪費的最好方法。
A: If you want to pack the rest of the food, the waiter will provide you with a doggie bag. ⑤	A：如果你需要打包剩餘的食物，服務生會提供給你打包袋。
B: I know. The service in a restaurant is excellent.	B：我知道。餐廳的服務一般都很好。
A: But my wife refuses to eat the packed food. That makes me very confused.	A：但我的妻子不喜歡打包的食物。這讓我很困惑。
B: That's OK. So does my wife.	B：還好吧。我妻子也是這樣的。

【程度提升，加分單字】

★**leftover** [ˋleftˏovɚ] **adj.** 剩餘的 **n.** 剩餘物
★**uncommon** [ʌnˋkɑmən] **adj.** 不尋常的，罕見的
★**tradition** [trəˋdɪʃn] **n.** 傳統，慣例

① **not very often**

在口語中，使用頻率很高，表示「不經常」。

② **so that**

表示「以便，為了」，在句中引導的是一個表示目的的狀語子句。 so...that... 表示「如此……以致於……」。

③ **at the end of**

表示「在……的末端，在……的盡頭」， at the end of 後面可以加名詞短語，也可以加時間名詞。

④ **be unwilling to do sth**

表示「不願意做某事」，其反義的結構是：be willing to do sth 表示「願意做某事」。

⑤ **If you want to...**

該句是一個主從複合句，if 引導的是條件子句，主句是 the waiter will provide you with a doggie bag，使用了未來式。

文化小站

隨著社會經濟的高速發展，人們的生活水準越來越高。在中國，餐桌浪費由來已久。據報導，每年餐桌浪費就有 2000 多億元。這相當於 2 億多人一年的口糧。人們為什麼沒有把剩餘的食物打包帶回家？人們為什麼不能少點些菜呢？這都受「面子文化」的影響。中國人講究面子、排場，這就導致了奢華浪費的吃飯方式。這一現象，在西方也很常見。西方人生活很揮霍，食品浪費很嚴重。在西方，聚會之後剩餘的食物很少有人打包，因為剩飯剩菜沒有人吃，最後就只能倒進垃圾桶。在法國，很少有人會打包剩餘食物。法國人從小就形成了不打包食物回家的觀念，因此食物浪費的情形很嚴重。有些人想打包，也只能偷偷摸摸進行。法國人覺得，打包剩菜很不衛生，而且顯得小氣、不禮貌。很多法國人承認，打包是很環保的。但是在實踐中卻很少有人主動去做。食品浪費已成為全球問題，打包也許不是解決這個問題的唯一方法，但也是很有必要去做的。

流程

Unit 25

Check, please.

結帳

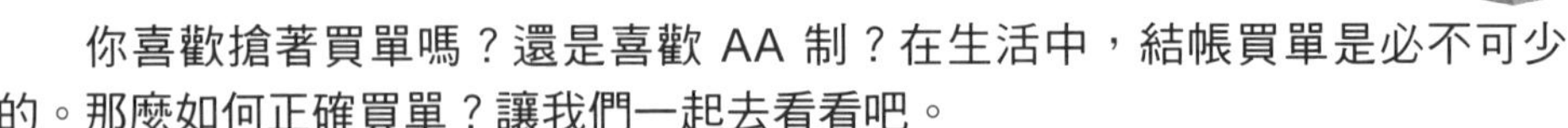

你喜歡搶著買單嗎？還是喜歡 AA 制？在生活中，結帳買單是必不可少的。那麼如何正確買單？讓我們一起去看看吧。

精選實用會話例句

❶ **最好先結帳。I had better check out first.** Track 536

片語釋義 check out 結帳離開

❷ **我想刷卡結帳。I want to pay with a credit card.** Track 537

片語釋義 credit card 信用卡

❸ **您能幫我們開個發票嗎？**
Could you give us a receipt, please? Track 538

重要詞彙 receipt [rɪ`sit] **n.** 收據，發票

❹ **這是找給你的零錢。Here's your change.** Track 539

重要詞彙 change [tʃendʒ] **n.** 變化，零錢 **v.** 改變，變換

❺ **我能看看帳單嗎？May I see the bill, please?** Track 540

同義表達 Can I have the check, please? / Please give me the bill.

❻ **很抱歉你得付現金。**
I am sorry you have to pay in cash. Track 541

片語釋義 pay in cash 付現金，現金支付

❼ **誰會去買單？Who will pay for the bill?** Track 542

同義表達 Who is going to pay the money?

❽ **這個年輕人身上沒有帶現金。The young man doesn't have any cash on him.** Track 543

同義表達 The young man has no cash with him.

❾ 他的帳單一共是 215 美元。
His bill comes to 215 dollars. Track 544
片語釋義 come to 到達，共計

❿ 今天邁克請客，請把帳單給他。
This is Mike's treat; please give him the bill. Track 545
重要詞彙 treat [trit] n. 款待，招待

⓫ 您是要一起結帳還是分開結帳呢？**Would you like one single bill or separate bill?** Track 546
同義表達 Do you want one single bill or separate bill?

⓬ 先生，請問在哪裡結帳？**Where is the cashier, sir?** Track 547
重要詞彙 cashier [kæ`ʃɪr] n. 收銀員

⓭ 新來的服務生把帳單算錯了。
A mistake is made on the bill by a new waiter. Track 548
同義表達 The bill is added up wrong by a new waiter.

⓮ 不用找零了。**Just keep the change.** Track 549
同義表達 You can keep the change. / No need to give me the change.

⓯ 艾米想要怎麼樣付款？
How would Amy like to settle the bill? Track 550
同義表達 How is Amy going to pay?

⓰ 這是你的帳單，一共是 135 美元。
Here is your bill and 135 dollars in all. Track 551
片語釋義 in all 合計

⓱ 你可以到收銀台付帳。
You can come to the cashier counter. Track 552
同義表達 You can pay at the cashier counter.

⓲ 總共多少錢？**How much is it altogether?** Track 553
重要詞彙 altogether [͵ɔltə`gɛðɚ] adv. 全部地

⑲ 這家餐廳收信用卡和現金。The restaurant accepts credit cards and cash. Track 554

重要詞彙 accept [ək`sɛpt] v. 承認，接受

⑳ 婷娜信用卡的信用額度不足。There is no sufficient credit limit in Tina's credit card. Track 555

重要片語 There is no... 沒有……

㉑ 我們各付各的。Let's go Dutch. Track 556

片語釋義 go Dutch 各付各的賬

㉒ 麗娜向服務生招手，想要買單。Lena waved at the waiter to try to get the check. Track 557

重要片語 try to do sth 試圖幹某事

㉓ 這包括紅酒的費用了嗎？Does the bill include the charge for the red wine? Track 558

重要詞彙 include [ɪn`klud] v. 包括，包含

看情境學對話

Track 559

	中譯
A: Have you finished your offee?	A：你咖啡喝完了嗎？
B: Not yet. ① The food in this restaurant is excellent. I'm still enjoying it.	B：還沒有。這個餐廳的食物真的很好吃。我還在享受呢。
A: Take your time. ② We have enough time to go to the movie theater. Would you like some desserts?	A：慢慢來。我們有足夠的時間去電影院。你要來點甜點了嗎？
B: No, thank you. I have had enough. Let me pay for ③ the bill today.	B：不，謝謝了。我已經吃飽了。今天讓我買單吧。

A: No, this is my treat; please give me the bill.	A：不，今天我請客。請把帳單給我吧。
B: It's unfair. What about going Dutch?	B：那就不公平了。要不我們各付各的吧。
A: Please let me pay the bill. You paid last time because I didn't have any cash on me. Remember?	A：讓我買單吧。因為我身上沒有帶現金，上次是你買單。還記得嗎？
B: Oh, come on ④ . I almost forgot.	B：噢，算了吧。我已經忘記了。
A: Could I have the bill, please?	A：能把帳單給我嗎？
C: Here is your bill. Would you like to pay in cash or with a credit card?	C：這是您的帳單。您用現金付帳還是用信用卡？
A: I'd like to pay in cash. Does the bill include the charge for drinks?	A：我想付現。這包括酒水的費用了嗎？
C: Yes. The total amount is 187 dollars.	C：是的。總數是 187 美元。
A: Here is 200 dollars. You don't need to give me the change. Thank you.	A：這是 200 美元。你不需要給我零錢。謝謝。
C: My pleasure ⑤.	C：不用謝。

★**excellent** [`ɛksələnt] adj. 傑出的，卓越的

★**movie theater** [`muvɪ `θɪətɚ] n. 電影院

★**amount** [ə`maʊnt] n. 數量，量

① not yet

表示「尚未，還沒有」。yet 常常出現在否定句和疑問句中。

② take your time

表示「別著急慢慢來」， 常常用於讓人做事放鬆，不用很趕時間。類似的還有 take it easy 表示「別緊張，放鬆」。

③ pay for

表示「付錢」，pay for sb 表示「為某人付款」。

④ come on

其表達的意思也有多種，如：表示鼓勵「加油」，表示催促別人「快點」，表示責備「得了，算了吧」。

⑤ My pleasure.

表示「我很樂意。」用作對謝意的客氣回答，完整的表達是 It's my pleasure.

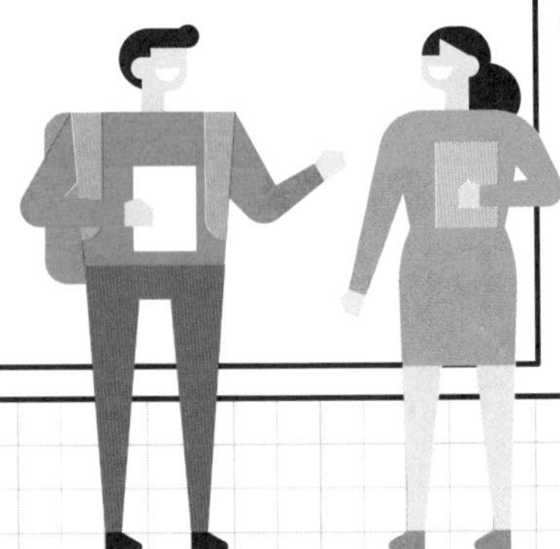

學習英文Fun輕鬆！

1.Gold will not buy anything.
黃金不能買盡一切。

2.Time is money.
時間就是金錢。

3.Let's go Dutch.
分開付帳。

4.Money is the root of evil.
金錢是罪惡的根源。

5.All things are obedient to money.
一切事物都服從於金錢。

6.Money is the key that opens all doors.
金錢是打開一切門戶的鑰匙。

文化小站

在東方，宴席之後，大部分人會搶著買單，這對於西方人而言是匪夷所思的。那麼為什麼中西方會存在如此的差異呢？主要取決於三個方面的不同：文化，用餐方式，用餐目的。在東方傳統文化中，很看重人與人之間的關係。人們為了表達深厚的感情，又或者體現自己的社交氣度，通常情況下都會搶著買單。各付各的在東方人看來，是很小氣的表現。同時搶著買單也可以體現出和諧的人際關係。這對西方人來說是很困惑的一件事情。西方人提倡個人主義，更側重於獨立自主。在西方某些地區，夫妻之間都會算的很清楚，但這並不代表西方人與人之間的感情不深厚。對西方人而言，就算人與人之間的感情很深，也不會主動請客吃飯。

流程

Unit 26

Tips

小費

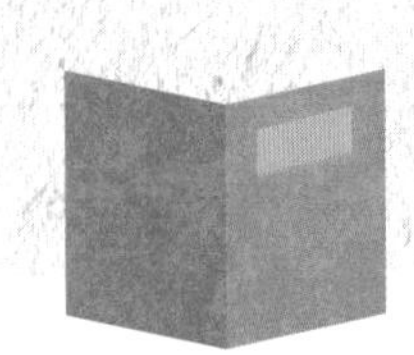

成大事者，不惜小費。在美國服務行業中有給小費的規定。你有給小費的習慣嗎？讓我們學習怎麼給小費吧！

精選實用會話例句

1. 這位女士給你留了多少作為小費啊？
How much tip did the lady leave you? Track 425
重要詞彙 tip [tɪp] **n.** 小費

2. 謝謝你周到的服務，不用找了。**Thank you for your kind service and keep the change.** Track 426
片語釋義 keep the change 不用找零錢了

3. 這是您的小費。**Here is your tip, please.** Track 427
同義表達 Your tip, please.

4. 我該付多少錢？**How much do I owe you?** Track 428
重要詞彙 owe [o] **v.** 欠債，感激

5. 你可以把多出來的錢留作你的小費。
You can keep the extra money as your tip. Track 429
重要片語 keep sth as... 把……當作……

6. 這家餐廳是不收小費的。
They don't accept tips in this restaurant. Track 430
同義表達 This restaurant doesn't accept tips.

7. 帳單的 5% 作為小費在這個國家太低了。
5% of the bill as a tip is too low in this country. Track 431
重要詞彙 country [ˈkʌntrɪ] **n.** 國家

❽ 這個年輕人除了工資外，還能得到很多小費。
The young man can get a lot of tips in addition to his wage. Track 432

片語釋義 in addition to 除……之外

❾ 給服務生、導遊和司機小費是很常見的。
It is common to tip waiters, guides and drivers. Track 433

重要詞彙 guide [gaɪd] v. 指路 n. 導遊

❿ 這個機構加了 5% 的服務費以代替小費。**This agency added 5% service charge in lieu of tipping.** Track 434

片語釋義 in lieu of 代替

⓫ 今天早上經理扣留了所有人的小費。
The manager kept all the tips this morning. Track 435

片語釋義 this morning 今天早上

⓬ 很多外國人給小費很大方。
Many foreigners are usually big tippers. Track 436

重要詞彙 foreigner [ˋfɔrɪnɚ] n. 外國人

⓭ 我可以給服務生小費嗎？
May I offer gratuities to the server? Track 437

同義表達 May I tip the waiter?

⓮ 老太太忘了給小費。
The old lady forgot to give a tip to the server. Track 438

重要片語 forget to do sth 忘記做某事

⓯ 你們國家允許給理髮師小費嗎？**Is one allowed to tip hairdressers in your country?** Track 439

重要片語 allow sb to do sth 允許某人做某事

⓰ 他因給小費出手慷慨很受服務生的歡迎。
He is popular among the servers for being a big tipper. Track 440

片語釋義 be popular among... 受……歡迎

⑰ 你給服務生小費了嗎？

Have you given a tip to the waiter? Track 441

同義表達 Did you tip the waiter?

⑱ 傑森忘了把小費也算進去了。

Jason forgot to add in the tip. Track 442

片語釋義 add in 加進去，包括

⑲ 我們拒絕給服務生小費，因為他真的很不友善。

We refused to tip the waiter because he was really unfriendly. Track 443

重要詞彙 unfriendly [ʌnˈfrendlɪ] **adj.** 不友好的，不友善的

⑳ 少於五十美元就足夠給服務生小費了。

Less than fifty dollars should be more enough to tip the waiter. Track 444

片語釋義 less than 小於，不足

Track 445

	中譯
A: It is reported that ① a church congregation ordered one $6 pizza and tipped their Dominos delivery man $1,000.	A：據報導，一家教會點了一份六美元的披薩，然後給了達美樂披薩店的送餐員1000美元的小費。
B: It's absolutely amazing. I can't believe it. Why did the church congregation do like that?	B：這簡直太棒了！我真不敢相信。為什麼這家教會會這麼做呢？
A: They are trying to spread a message about generosity. But they complained about ② the onions in the pizza when the delivery man left.	A：他們傳達的是關於慷慨的訊息。但是在送餐員走之後，他們抱怨披薩添加了洋蔥。

B: This is the first time I heard someone tipped so much money. But the church will use the money to do good deeds in the world.	B：這是我第一次聽到有人給了這麼多小費。但是教會會用這筆錢在世界上做好事。
A: There's no doubt ③ that tipping can get complicated. That's why more and more people want to get rid of the tippping system.	A：給小費毫無疑問是個挺複雜的事。這就是為什麼越來越多的人想要去掉小費制度。
B: But the income of servers will decrease if there are no tips.	B：但是如果沒有小費，服務生的薪水就會減少。
A: And instead, the restaurant can give the servers a decent wage by raising the price of ④ his food.	A：作為替代，餐廳可以藉由食物漲價，給服務生漲工資。
B: Maybe some of the customers don't want to have to pay higher prices.	B：也許有些顧客不想支付更高的價格。
A: Most people hate tipping ⑤ .	A：大部分人是討厭付小費的。
B: I couldn't agree with you more.	B：我非常同意。

【程度提升，加分單字】

★**absolutely** [ˋæbsə͵lutlɪ] **adv.** 絕對地
★**generosity** [͵dʒɛnəˋrɑsətɪ] **n.** 慷慨
★**complicate** [ˋkɑmplə͵ket] **adj.** 複雜的
★**salary** [ˈsælərɪ] **n.** 薪水

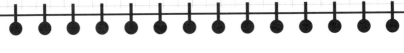

① **it is reported that**

表示「據報導」，that 引導子句。

② **complain about**

表示「抱怨，對……不滿」，後面可以直接跟名詞或動名詞。complain of 可以表示「抱怨」，也可以表示「抗議，訴說病痛」。

③ **There's no doubt...**

表示「……毫無疑問」，後面可以直接跟 that 子句。類似的表達還有：It is no doubt...

④ **the price of**

表示「……的價格」，後面一般跟名詞。at the price of 表示「以……的代價」。

⑤ **hate doing sth**

表示「討厭某種行為」，是一個習慣性的動作；hate to do sth表示「討厭做某事」，是一個偶然性的動作。

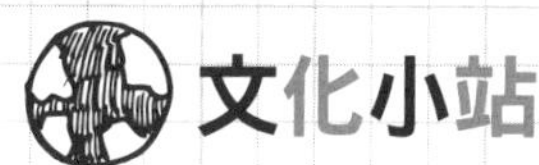

文化小站

在服務行業中，小費就是客人為優質服務支付的報酬。在西方國家，小費尤其盛行，支付小費給服務生的現像是很常見的。不管是去餐廳、酒店、理髮店還是旅遊、搬家都是需要支付小費的。因此，小費所涉及的行業很廣泛，比如：餐飲業，旅遊業，家庭教育，酒店行業。據報導，西方國家服務人員70%的工資是由小費組成的，小費的多少一般是由服務品質與行業決定的。在西方國家，付小費是一種自願行為，沒有強制性的制度。

其他場合就餐

Unit 27

Buffet

自助餐

說到自助餐，扶著牆進，扶著牆出，可算是吃貨的最高境界。愛吃自助餐的朋友們是不是控制不住了？讓我們一起去吃自助餐吧！

精選實用會話例句

❶ 你能告訴我附近最近的自助餐廳在哪裡嗎？**Can you tell me where the nearest buffet restaurant is around here?** Track 425

重要詞彙 cafeteria [ˌkæfəˈtɪərɪə] n. 自助餐廳

❷ 你去過自助餐廳嗎？**Have you ever been to the buffet restaurant?** Track 426

重要片語 have been to... 去過某地

❸ 我們想找一個價格適中的自助餐廳。**We want to find a buffet restaurant with moderate prices.** Track 427

片語釋義 moderate prices 價格適中

❹ 自助餐每個人的收費是多少？**How much does the buffet charge for each person?** Track 428

同義表達 What is the charge of buffet for one person?

❺ 因為隊伍很長，他們不得不等候。
They have to wait because of the long line. Track 429

片語釋義 wait in line 排隊等候

❻ 自助餐廳確實有點人手不足。**The buffet restaurant actually a bit short-handed.** Track 430

重要詞彙 actually [ˈæktʃuəlɪ] adv. 實際上，事實上

⑦ 我們在自助餐廳吃點東西吧。
Let's have something to eat in the cafeteria. Track 431
片語釋義 in the cafeteria 在自助餐廳裡

⑧ 在自助餐廳中，你可以一邊走一邊選擇食物。**You can select your food as you go along the plates.** Track 432
片語釋義 walk through 步行穿過

⑨ 你可以在自助餐廳中隨意夾取食物。**You can help yourself to the food in the buffet restaurant.** Track 433
同義表達 You can pick up food at random in the cafeteria.

⑩ 在自助餐廳，你可以以大眾化的價格得到高品質的享受。**You can get a high quality enjoyment at a popular price in the buffet restaurant.** Track 434
片語釋義 popular price 大眾化的價格

⑪ 你可以選甜點了。**You can choose a dessert.** Track 435
重要詞彙 dessert [dɪ`zɝt] n. 餐後甜食，甜點

⑫ 吃自助餐時浪費食物是不禮貌的。
It is impolite to waste food in the buffet. Track 436
重要詞彙 buffet [bu`fe] n. 自助餐廳

⑬ 吉米發現附近有自助餐廳。
Jimmy found a buffet restaurant around here. Track 437
同義表達 Jimmy noticed there is a cafeteria nearby.

⑭ 在那家自助餐廳中有很多種可供選擇的食物。**There are many kinds of food to choose in that buffet.** Track 438
片語釋義 at choice 可供選擇

⑮ 自助餐廳的收費取決於時間。
The charge of buffet depends on the time. Track 439
片語釋義 depend on 取決於，依靠，依賴

⑯ 你喜歡吃什麼就吃什麼。
You can eat whatever you like. Track 440
同義表達 You can choose whichever you want.

⑰ 人們經常在自助餐廳吃得太多。

People often overeat in the buffet. Track 441

同義表達 People often eat too much in a buffet.

⑱ 大多數人喜歡吃自助餐。

Most people like to eat in a buffet. Track 442

重要片語 like to do sth 喜歡做某事

⑲ 你們要在飯店吃自助餐嗎？

Will you have the buffet at the hotel? Track 443

片語釋義 at the hotel 在酒店

⑳ 海鮮是進口的，你驚訝嗎？

Are you surprised that the seafood is imported? Track 444

重要詞彙 surprised [sə'praɪzd] **adj.** 驚奇的

看情境學對話

Track 445

	中譯
A: Let's have something to eat ① in the buffet restaurant. Do you like it?	A：我們在自助餐廳吃點東西吧。你喜歡吃自助餐嗎？
B: I often eat buffet with my family, because we can have ditterent styles of food at the same time ②.	B：我經常和家人一起吃自助餐，因為我可以同時吃很多食物。
A: I found a buffet restaurant around here. There are many kinds of foods. ③	A：我在這附近發現了一個自助餐廳。在那裡有很多種可供選擇的食物。
B: Let's go there. How much does the buffet charge for each person?	B：我們去那裡吧。自助餐每人多少錢？

A: It depends on ④ lunch, afternoon tea, or dinner. On average, it is about 46 dollars for one person.	A：這取決於是午餐、下午茶，或是晚餐。一般來說，一個人大約是 46 美元。
B: Wow, there are so many people! We have to wait in line at the moment. The food smells delicious. That makes my mouth water.	B：哇！餐廳裡有這麼多人。我們現在只好排隊等候。食物聞起來真香。我都流口水了。
A: There are varieties of fruits, meat, and ice cream, so I can't wait to ⑤ dig in!	A：這裡有各種各樣的水果、肉類和冰淇淋，所以我迫不及待想吃了！
B: Every time people eat buffet, they will eat as much as possible. Because they want to let the food deserve the money they pay.	B：每當人們吃自助餐時，都會盡可能多地吃。因為他們想讓食物值他們所付的錢。
A: But overeating may hurt one's stomach. I think the money I pay is to enjoy the food instead of hurting my stomach.	A：但吃得過多可能會使胃受到傷害。我想我所付的錢是為了享受食物而不是傷害我的胃。
B: You are right. That's the problem about buffet.	B：你是對的。這就是自助餐廳的問題。

【程度提升，加分單字】

★**family** [ˈfæməlɪ] **n.** 家庭
★**charge** [tʃɑrdʒ] **v.** 要價
★**deserve** [dɪˋzɝv] **v.** 值得

對話解析

① **have something to eat**

表示「吃點東西」， have something to 後面直接加動詞原形。have something to do with 表示「與……有關」。

② **at the same time**

表示「同時，一起，與此同時」，作時間狀語，在句中的位置，句首、句中、句末都可以。

③ **There are many kinds of foods.**

該句是 there be 句型，表示某處存在某人或者某物。其結構是 there + be 動詞 + 名詞。

④ **depend on**

表示「依靠，取決於」，後面可以跟名詞或代詞。類似的表達還有： rely on。

⑤ **can't wait to do sth**

表示「迫不及待做某事」。

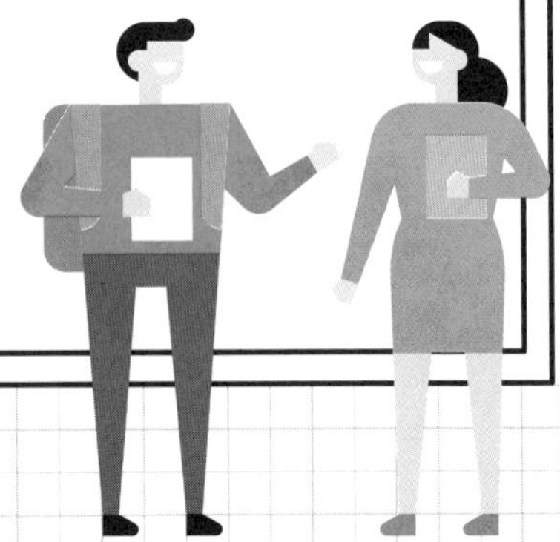

文化小站

自助餐因為形式多樣化，菜式豐富，營養全面，價格低廉深受消費者的喜愛。自助餐常常不提供正餐，就餐者在用餐時自行選擇食物、飲料，可以與他人坐在一起或是獨自一人用餐。之所以叫自助餐，是因為餐廳不提供菜單，自享菜餚。中式自助餐常常以中式的涼菜、熱炒、湯、點心和主食為主。而西式自助餐通常以沙拉、涼菜、烤肉、披薩、甜點和水果為主。也有中西式自助餐，包含中式菜餚和西式菜餚的混合形式。自助餐發展迅速，目前已有海鮮、烤肉、日料、火鍋等餐飲主題。在享用自助餐時，注意不要暴飲暴食。

其他場合就餐

Unit 28 Cafe 咖啡館

午後，一杯咖啡，一本書，兩三首音樂，品味人生。這樣的生活你喜歡嗎？

精選實用會話例句

1 你想來杯咖啡嗎？**Would you like a cup of coffee?** Track 446

片語釋義 a cup of coffee 一杯咖啡

2 請給她來杯咖啡。
Bring her a cup of coffee, please. Track 447

重要詞彙 coffee [`kɔfɪ] n. 咖啡

3 您想喝點什麼？**What would you like for a drink?** Track 448

重要詞彙 drink [drɪŋk] v. 喝 n. 飲料

4 我妻子想要一杯白咖啡加兩塊糖。**My wife would like a white coffee with two sugars, please.** Track 449

片語釋義 white coffee 白咖啡

5 請給我們來一杯摩卡和兩杯拿鐵。
A cup of mocha and two cups of latte, please. Track 450

重要詞彙 mocha [`mokə] n. 摩卡咖啡

6 你喜歡濃的還是淡的？
Do you prefer the coffee strong or weak? Track 451

重要詞彙 prefer [prɪ`fɝ] v. 偏好

7 蒂娜想要一杯牛奶咖啡，謝謝。
Tina would like a cup of milk coffee, thanks. Track 452

片語釋義 milk coffee 牛奶咖啡

❽ 我想要一杯拿鐵瑪奇朵咖啡。
I'll have a cup of Latte macchiato. Track 453
重要詞彙 Latte [ˈlateɪ] n. 拿鐵咖啡

❾ 你想要白咖啡還是黑咖啡？
Would you like white coffee or jnst black? Track 454
同義表達 Which one do you want to choose, white coffee or black coffee?

❿ 您想再來一杯咖啡嗎？**Would you like to have another cup of coffee?** Track 455
同義表達 Do you want to have another cup of coffee?

⓫ 可以請你再喝杯咖啡嗎？
Shall we have another cup of coffee, please? Track 456
重要詞彙 shall [ʃəl] v. 應該

⓬ 您的咖啡需要加糖嗎？
Do you want sugar in your coffee? Track 457
同義表達 Would you like some sugar in your coffee?

⓭ 請在咖啡裡面放少糖。
Less sugar in the coffee, please. Track 458
同義表達 Easy on the sugar in the coffee, please. / Low on sugar in the coffee please.

⓮ 這間咖啡館是我最喜歡的，它整個都被裝飾成了義大利風格。**This is my favorite café; it is decoratedin Italian style.** Track 459
重要詞彙 decorate [ˋdɛkəˏret] v. 裝飾；佈置

⓯ 請給我來一個芝士漢堡和一杯冰咖啡好嗎？
May I have a cheese burger and a cup of iced coffee, please? Track 460
片語釋義 cheese burger 芝士漢堡

⓰ 你想要點甜點嗎？
Would you like something for dessert? Track 461
同義表達 Do you want to eat dessert?

⑰ **請給他來一杯拿鐵咖啡好嗎？**
Could you make a cup of latte for him, please? Track 462
重要片語 make sth for sb 給某人做某物

⑱ **給我來一杯咖啡，少放糖和牛奶。Please give me a cup of coffee and easy on the sugar and milk.** Track 463
重要詞彙 sugar [`ʃʊgɚ] **n.** 糖

⑲ **湯姆昨天晚上在咖啡館巧遇到他的高中同學。Tom met his high school classmates by accident in the cafe last evening.** Track 464
片語釋義 by accident 偶然地，不經意地，意外地

⑳ **您可以在咖啡廳享受安靜舒適的環境。You can enjoy a quiet and comfortable environment at the café.** Track 465
重要詞彙 environment [ɪnˋvaɪrənmənt] **n.** 環境

看情境學對話

Track 466

A: Hi, Jessica. Long time no see. How have you been?	A：嗨，潔西卡。好久不見。一切都還好嗎？
B: Not bad. I am busy with ① decorating the coffee shop. I'm exhausted, but it is nearly finished.	B：還不錯。我正忙著裝修咖啡店。真是快累死了，還好就快完成了。
A: Congratulations. I heard the coffee shop is near the park. It is a great convenience for ② most people.	A：恭喜你。我聽說咖啡店在公園附近。這對於大多數人來說，是一種極大的方便。
B: Do you like drinking coffee?	B：你喜歡喝咖啡嗎？
A: Of course. Coffee is a good thing that can make my brain work.	A：當然了。咖啡是個好東西，能讓我的大腦保持清醒。

B: Yes. What kind of ③ coffee do you prefer, the white one or the black one?	B：是啊。你喜歡哪種咖啡，白咖啡還是黑咖啡？
A: Black coffee. But my wife likes it with milk and two sugars. What it kind of coffee have you got?	A：黑咖啡。但是我妻子更喜歡加奶和兩塊糖。你們的咖啡廳都有什麼咖啡啊？
B: We have espresso, cappuccino, latte, soy latte, and Americano.	B：我們有意式濃縮咖啡、卡布奇諾、拿鐵咖啡、豆漿拿鐵咖啡，還有美式咖啡。
A: You have so many choices! But the environment is essential to ④ a coffee shop.	A：這麼多種啊。但是環境對於咖啡店來説是很重要的。
B: You are right. A good café can give people a comfortable environment.	B：對啊。一家好的咖啡館能給人一個舒適的環境。
A: Hum, may be. It is reported that drinking coffee is good for health.	A：嗯，或許吧。根據報導顯示，喝咖啡對健康是有益的。
B: Coffee is not harmful, and in some cases ⑤ , it may have health benefits.	B：咖啡不僅無害，而且在某些情況下還有益處。

★**decorate** [ˋdɛkəˏret] **v.** 裝飾，佈置
★**congratulation** [kənˏgrætʃuˈleʃn] **n.** 祝賀，恭賀
★**harmful** [ˋharmfəl] **adj.** 有害的

① **be busy with sth**

表示「忙於某事」，be busy doing sth 表示「忙於做某事」。

② **be a convenience for sb**

表示「對某人來說……很方便」；另外 be convenient for sb to do sth 表示「對某人來說做某事很方便」。

③ **what kind of**

表示「哪一種，哪一樣」，後面常常跟可數名詞單數或者不可數名詞。 what kinds of 後面只跟可數名詞複數。

④ **be essential to**

表示「對……重要的，對……必不可少」，其後如果跟動詞要跟動詞原形。

⑤ **in some cases**

表示「在某些情況下，有時候」，類似的表達還有 in certain conditions。

文化小站

咖啡，是世界三大飲品之一，清晨來一杯咖啡已經成為很多國家的日常飲食習慣。由於地域不同，每個國家的咖啡文化也是不一樣的。對於西歐和北歐的人來說，人們喜歡清淡口味的咖啡，咖啡豆也只是烘焙成褐色而不是黑色。而在南歐的某些地區，人們習慣早晚各飲一杯咖啡，並且鍾愛義大利式咖啡，咖啡豆通常是深度烘焙的，沖出來的咖啡也是帶著焦味的。對於法國人來說，喝咖啡是一種休閒方式，牛奶咖啡在他們的早餐中是不可或缺的飲品。在日本，人們對冰咖啡格外情有獨鍾。冰咖啡主要有：添加牛奶為主的冰咖啡牛奶系列，加巧克力醬為主的冰摩卡咖啡，以霜淇淋為基礎的聖代咖啡，還有充滿成年人風味的雞尾酒冰咖啡系列。有如此多的冰咖啡系列，由此可見日本人對冰咖啡的狂熱。

其他場合就餐

Unit 29

Bakery

麵包店

你喜歡吃麵包嗎？會烘焙麵包嗎？想成為一名麵包師嗎？那還等什麼，趕快行動吧！

精選實用會話例句

❶ 你想買切片麵包嗎？**Would you like to buy sliced bread?** Track 467

片語釋義 slice 切片

❷ 你能幫我買一條酸麵包嗎？**Could you help me to buy a loaf of sourdough bread?** Track 468

重要詞彙 sourdough [ˋsaʊrˏdo] **n.** 酵母，發酵的麵團

❸ 傑森想買一打可頌麵包。**Jason wants to buy a dozen croissants.** Track 469

重要詞彙 croissant [krwɑˋsɑn] **n.** 可頌麵包

❹ 歡迎選購。**Welcome to our store.** Track 470

同義表達 Welcome to the bakery.

❺ 我侄子想吃全麥麵包。**My nephew wants to eat the whole wheat bread.** Track 471

片語釋義 whole wheat bread 全麥麵包

❻ 麵包店裡有各種各樣的生日蛋糕。**There are various birthday cakes at the baker's shop.** Track 472

片語釋義 birthday cake 生日蛋糕

❼ 麗娜要去麵包店嗎？**Is Lena going to the baker's?** Track 473

重要詞彙 baker [ˋbekɚ] **n.** 麵包師

8 我的小兒子走到麵包店去買蛋糕。
My little son walks to the bakery to buy cakes. Track 474
重要詞彙 bakery [`bekərɪ] n. 麵包房，麵包店

9 你還記得麵包店裡的那個女孩嗎？
Do you remember the girl in the bakery? Track 475
片語釋義 in the bakery 在麵包店

10 你可以在那家麵包店買法式麵包。
You can buy French bread in that bakery. Track 476
片語釋義 French bread 法式麵包

11 這家麵包店的生意出奇地好。The business in this bakery is surprisingly good. Track 477
重要詞彙 surprisingly [sə`praɪzɪŋlɪ] adv. 驚人地

12 我妹妹去年在麵包店做過兼職。My sister did a part-time job in the bakery last year. Track 478
片語釋義 part-time job 兼職

13 這間麵包店要倒閉了。
The bakery is going to close down. Track 479
片語釋義 close down 倒閉，停業

14 這家麵包店在這個城市已經存在了十年。The bakery has existed for ten years in the city. Track 480
同義表達 This bakery has been in the city for ten years.

15 吉姆中午在麵包店買了一條麵包當午飯。Jim bought a loaf of bread at the bakery for lunch at noon. Track 481
片語釋義 a loaf of bread 一條麵包

16 這個年輕人想有一天成為一個麵包師。The young man wants to be a baker some day. Track 482
重要片語 want to do sth 想做某事

17 麵包師正在烤你的生日蛋糕。
The baker is baking your birthday cake. Track 483
重要詞彙 bake [bek] v. 烤，烘焙

⓲ 這位女士把麵包放在櫃檯上，離開了麵包店。
The lady put the bread on the counter and left the bakery. Track 484

片語釋義 on the counter 在櫃檯上

⓳ 生日蛋糕的包裝很精美。**The package of the birthday cake is wrapped well.** Track 485

重要詞彙 package [ˈpækɪdʒ] n. 包裝，包裝袋 v. 包裝

⓴ 五年前這條街上有三家麵包店。**There were three bakeries along the street five years ago.** Track 486

片語釋義 along the street 沿街

看情境學對話

Track 487

	中譯
A: Welcome to ① our bakery. What can I do for you?	A：歡迎來到我們的麵包店。我能為你做些什麼？
B: I want to make a birthday cake for my son. Do you customize cakes?	B：我想給我兒子做一個生日蛋糕。你們這裡有客製蛋糕嗎？
A: Sure. I am a baker. I can teach you. Are you ready to ② choose the desrgn?	A：當然。我就是麵包師。你準備選擇設計樣式了嗎？
B: Almost. Being a baker is pretty cool. You can make different varieties of bread and cakes.	B：差不多了。成為一名麵包師是很酷的。可以做不同種類的麵包。
A: Yeah, but my specialty is making bread, donuts, and cake.	A：是啊，但是我的強項是做麵包、甜甜圈、蛋糕。

B: That sounds great. What is the routine of ③ a baker? Do you have to get up early?	B：聽起來很棒。那麵包師的作息是怎樣的？你們是不是需要早起？
A: I often come in and open up the shop at 4 am. Then I fire up the ovens and start mixing the bread dough. The customers can get fresh baked bread at eight in the morning and desserts.	A：我經常在早上四點來開門，然後打開烤箱，開始攪拌麵包麵團。顧客早上八點可以買到新鮮的烤麵包。
B: It is hard work ④. But you can enjoy that part of baking, making those kinds of products.	B：真辛苦啊。但是你可以享受這種烘焙各種麵包的過程。
A: Yes, I do ⑤ enjoy it. I like the smell of fresh bread.	A：我確實很享受。我喜歡新鮮麵包的味道。
B: Let's get started.	B：讓我們開始做蛋糕吧。
A: Okay. The first thing we are going to do is to prepare the ingredients. Please have apron on.	A：好的。我們要做的第一件事就是烤蛋糕。請穿上圍裙。
B: Got it.	B：知道了。

【程度提升，加分單字】

★**donut** [ˋdo͵nʌt] **n.** 甜甜圈
★**oven** [ˋʌvn] **n.** 烤箱
★**dough** [do] **n.** 生麵團
★**apron** [ˋeprən] **n.** 圍裙

① **welcome to**

表示「歡迎……」，後面可以加地點名詞。但是如果後面跟 here，there，home 地點副詞時，要省略 to。

② **be ready...**

表示「做好……的準備了」，可以用成 be ready to (for)，也可以用 get

③ **the routine of**

此為常用片語，後面多接一個事件，用來表示該事件的流程。

④ **It is hard work.**

在英語中的使用頻率很高，表示某件事情需要耗費很多心力，或者用來回覆對方所描述的事情表達認可。

⑤ **do**

加上助動詞 do/ does 為強調用法，表示「確實」、「的確」之意。

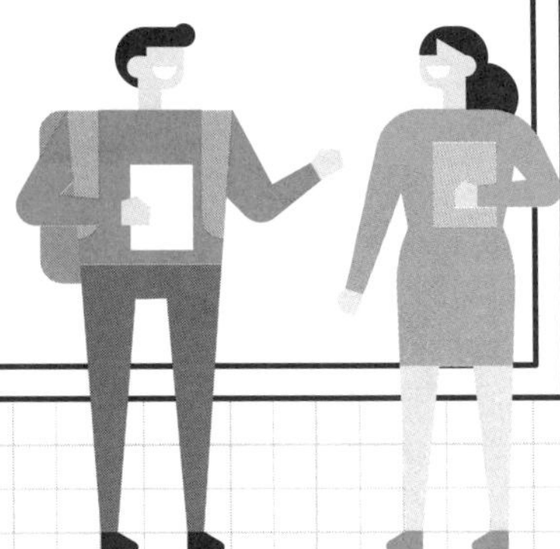

學習英文Fun輕鬆！

1.Dogs wag their tails not so much in love to you as your bread.

狗搖尾巴，愛的是麵包。

2.Do not argue with your bread and butter.

不要自找麻煩。

3.Bread is the staff of life.

民以食為天。

4.The knife cuts bread and fingers.

水能載舟，亦能覆舟。

5.Each day brings its own bread.

天無絕人之路。

文化小站

麵包，是經過發酵的烘焙食品。麵包起源於西方國家，是用小麥粉、酵母、水、糖、油脂、乳品等做成的。同樣以小麥為原料做成的食品，在東方叫作饅頭、麵餅等。麵包的種類也有很多，如：吐司類、甜麵包類、丹麥類、起酥類等。在西方國家，麵包歷史悠久，普及迅速。在東方，如今麵包店也已經遍及中國各地，成為了人們生活中普通的一部分。但是人們也只是將麵包作為點心，而非主食。近些年來，隨著人們健康意識的提高，全麥麵包、硬歐等比較健康的麵包，很受消費者的青睞。在西方國家，麵包、牛奶是早餐的一個不錯的選擇。在東方，雖然麵包早餐有了一席之地，但並不是主要的選擇，很受歡迎的早餐還是油條、包子、燒餅、蛋餅等。除此之外，西方人在食物的溫度喜好方面和東方人也存在著差異，他們鍾愛生食、冷食。而在東方，卻是截然相反的，人們喜歡吃熱的，所以總喜歡說「趁熱吃！」西方人吃麵包是從來不考慮溫度的，而東方人不喜歡吃冷了的包子或饅頭。

其他場合就餐

Unit 30

Western Restaurant 西餐廳

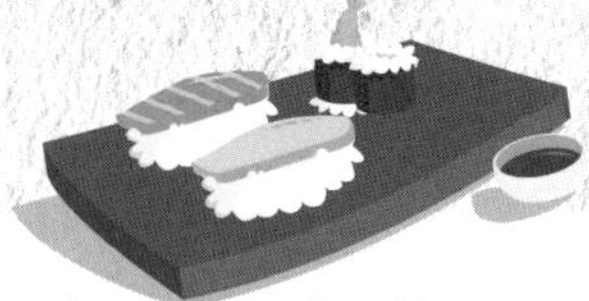

生活要有儀式感，去西餐廳就餐也許是一個不錯的選擇。舒適的環境，美味的大餐，會不會讓你心動呢？

精選實用會話例句

1. 到西餐廳你最好先熟悉一下菜單。**You had better check the menu first in a western restaurant.** Track 488
   片語釋義 western restaurant 西餐廳

2. 你要點西餐嗎？
   Would you like to order western food? Track 489
   同義表達 Do you want to order western food?

3. 主廚特餐很受歡迎。
   The chef's special is very popular. Track 490
   片語釋義 chef's special 主廚特餐

4. 你能告訴我怎麼去最近的西餐廳嗎？**Can you tell me how to get to the nearest western restaurant?** Track 491
   同義表達 Can you tell me where the nearest western restaurant is?

5. 你媽媽想吃點什麼，中餐還是西餐？
   What does your mother want to eat, Chinese food or Western food? Track 492
   片語釋義 Chinese food 中餐

6. 湯姆覺得吃西餐怎麼樣？
   What does Tom think of having western food? Track 493
   同義表達 How does Tom feel about western food?

❼ 你開胃菜想吃什麼？
What do you want for appetizers? Track 494
重要詞彙 appetizer [`æpə͵taɪzɚ] n. 開胃菜

❽ 你們最棒的主菜是什麼？What's your best entrées? Track 495
重要詞彙 entrées [`ɑntre] n. 主菜

❾ 我希望我的牛排可以附上蔬菜，且我不想要其他配菜。
I'd like to have my steak served with vegetables, and I don't want other side dishes. Track 496
片語釋義 side dishes 配菜

❿ 飯店的二樓供應西餐。The second floor of the hotel offers western food. Track 497
重要詞彙 second [`sekənd] adj. 第二的，次要的

⓫ 這種調料主要用於西餐。This kind of seasoning is mainly used for western food. Track 498
重要片語 be used for... 用來做……

⓬ 我們可以在飛機上吃到西餐。
We can have western food on the plane. Track 499
重要詞彙 plane [plen] n. 飛機

⓭ 有些航班提供免費的西餐。
Some flights offer free western-style meals. Track 500
重要詞彙 free [fri] adj. 自由的，免費的

⓮ 我能預訂下週一晚上 6 點在那間新西餐廳的位子嗎？
Can I book a table at that new western restaurant at 6 p.m. next Monday? Track 501
片語釋義 next Monday 下週一

⓯ 這條街上有一家不錯的西餐廳。There is a nice western restaurant on this street. Track 502
片語釋義 on this street 在這條街上

⑯ 我們昨天晚上七點正在西餐廳吃晚飯。**We were having our dinner at seven yesterday evening in the western restaurant.** Track 503

重要詞彙 yesterday [`jɛstɚde] **n.** 昨天

⑰ 這家西餐廳位於郊區。**This western restaurant is located in the suburbs.** Track 504

重要片語 be located in... 位於……

⑱ 他們打算在我們學校開西餐廳。**They are going to open a western restaurant in our college.** Track 505

重要片語 be going to do sth 打算做某事

⑲ 傑森看不懂西餐廳的菜單。**Jason can't read the menu of the western restaurant.** Track 506

片語釋義 the menu of... ……的菜單

⑳ 一家大飯店裡至少有兩家西餐廳。**There are at least two western restaurants in a big hotel.** Track 507

片語釋義 at least 至少

看情境學對話

Track 508

	中譯
A: I don't know how to use the forkand knife. Can you teach me?	A：我不知道如何使用叉子，你能教我嗎？
B: Just remember this. You can use your left hand for the fork and right hand for the knife.	B：記住這一點。用你的左手拿叉子，右手拿刀。
A: I got it ① . It is real trouble to have western food. I've been practicing for many times but still can't really get it.	A：我知道了。吃西餐可真麻煩啊。我已經學習很多次了，但還是沒學會。

B: But you should learn more about ② western culture.	B：但是你應該瞭解更多的西方文化。
A: You are right. Which restaurant shall ③ we go to tonight?	A：對啊。我們今天晚上去哪家餐廳呢？
B: I have reserved a table for us at the city centre. The environment there is really pleasant.	B：我在市中心的一家餐廳預訂了位子。那家餐廳的環境真的很不錯。
A: Great. I believe in ④ your taste. I had better iron your black suit first.	A：不錯。我相信你的品位。我最好先燙一下你的黑色西服。
B: I will go to the bank to withdraw some money.	B：那我去銀行領點錢吧。
A: There is no need to do that ⑤ . We can use the credit card.	A：沒必要那麼做。我們可以使用信用卡。
B: That sounds great. I'll take care of the order.	B：好主意。那我負責點餐吧。
A: Don't forget about the dessert.	A：不要忘記點甜點。
B: Do not worry, I will not.	B：知道了，我不會忘記的。

★**fork** [fɔrk] **n.** 叉子
★**culture** [`kʌltʃɚ] **n.** 文化
★**tonight** [tə`naɪt] **adv.** 今晚
★**believe** [bɪ`liv] **v.** 相信，認為

① **got it**

是英語中高頻出現的口語，表示「明白了，知道了」，比較口語化。相當於：I see，I know。

② **learn about**

表示「學習，瞭解，知道」，learn more about 表達了在程度上更進一步，其含義是「學習或者瞭解更多的」。

③ **shall**

作為助動詞，一般只用於第一人稱 I 和 we。如果表示將來的動作，構成未來式，shall 之後要接動詞原形。

④ **believe in**

表示「信仰，信賴」， believe in 也可用於 believe in doing sth 表示「相信做某事」。

⑤ **there is no need**

表示「沒必要」，後面可以跟介詞短語，也可以跟不定式。

學習英文Fun輕鬆！

He's a Western Restaurant Member

While dining in the western restaurant in the city centre, my wife and I lost our appetites when a rat scurried past up. "Waiter!" I said, pointing to the rodent. "What are you going to do about that? " "It's all right, sir, " he said unfazed. "I've already confirmed he's a western restaurant member."

他是西餐廳的會員

我和太太在市中心的一個西餐廳裡吃飯，看到一隻老鼠從身邊竄過，頓時沒了胃口。我指著老鼠問侍者：「你準備怎麼處置？」他毫不在意地說：「先生，這沒什麼。我已經確認過他是我們西餐廳的會員。」

文化小站

因受地理、歷史、民族等多種因素的影響，中餐和西餐存在很大的差異。首先使用的餐具是不一樣的。中餐使用的是碗筷，而西餐常常使用刀和叉。中餐一般使用炒的烹調方法，西餐的烹調方法主要是煎、烤、燜、燴等。西方人用餐側重個人點菜，個人品嚐，份量適中，重視自我喜好。中餐是一桌菜大家共同享用，菜品種豐富，更多地重視整體，點菜也要儘量滿足不同人的口味。西方人用餐結束時需要把所有的菜吃完，如果點了太多而浪費，這是很不禮貌的。在吃西餐時，要考慮是否要預先留點肚子空間以便最後吃一些甜品。吃西餐時，可以選擇一些如雞尾酒、葡萄酒或天然礦泉水等，作為就餐搭配。去西餐廳就餐，要提前預約，說明人數和時間，除此之外，守時也很重要。另外，去高檔的西餐廳，著裝也是需要注意的。一般而言，男士需要穿正式的服裝，女士要穿套裝和高跟鞋。進入餐廳時，男士需要先開門，請女士進入。

其他場合就餐

Unit 31

Fast Food Restaurant

速食店

提到速食，就會想到全家桶、炸雞腿、漢堡包、薯條等速食食物。是不是都要流口水啦？那我們就一起去吃速食吧！

精選實用會話例句

1 你喜歡速食嗎？Do you like fast food? Track 509

片語釋義 fast food 速食

2 我們有足夠的時間吃速食。

We have enough time for a hasty snack. Track 510

同義表達 We have enough time to eat fast food.

3 火車站附近哪裡有速食店？Where is the fast food restaurant near the railway station? Track 511

片語釋義 railway station 火車站

4 我叔叔午飯時通常只吃一份點心。

My uncle usually has a snack at lunch time. Track 512

片語釋義 lunch time 午飯時間

5 客人又要了一份速食餐點。

The guest ordered another fast food meal. Track 513

重要詞彙 guest [gɛst] n. 客人

6 我們在談論我們最喜歡的速食。We are talking about our favorite kinds of fast food. Track 514

重要片語 talk about sth 談論某事

7 你想吃什麼，速食還是正餐？What would you like to eat, a small snack or a main meal? Track 515

片語釋義 main meal 正餐

❽ 我姐姐認為速食是一種垃圾食品。My sister thought the fast food is a kind of junk food. Track 516

片語釋義 junk food 垃圾食品

❾ 肥胖的主要原因是速食的歡迎程度越來越高。
The main reason for obesity is the increasing popularity of fast food. Track 517

重要詞彙 reliance [rɪˈlaɪəns] n. 依靠，依賴

❿ 我女兒在速食店點了薯條和漢堡包。My daughter ordered both french fries and a hamburger in the fast-food restaurant. Track 518

重要詞彙 sandwich [ˈsænwɪtʃ] n. 三明治

⓫ 琳達喜歡魚堡勝過蔬菜堡。
Linda prefers fish burgers to veggie burgers. Track 519

片語釋義 fish burger 魚堡

⓬ 這個區域沒有速食店。
There is no fast food restaurant in this area. Track 520

重要詞彙 area [ˋɛrɪə] n. 地區，區域

⓭ 我的堂兄在一家速食店工作。
My cousin works at a fast food restaurant. Track 521

重要詞彙 cousin [ˈkʌzn] n. 堂（表）兄弟姐妹

⓮ 越來越多的孩子喜歡吃速食。
More and more children like to eat fast food. Track 522

片語釋義 more and more 越來越多

⓯ 我們怎麼去附近的速食店？How can we get to the hot dog restaurant around here? Track 523

重要詞彙 restaurant [ˋrɛstərənt] n. 餐廳

⓰ 你需要一份薯餅嗎？Do you need hash browns and orange Juice for breaktast? Track 524

重要片語 hash browns 薯餅

⑰ **這家速食店供應漢堡、披薩、冰淇淋和三明治。**
The fast food restaurant serves burger, pizza, ice cream and sandwich. Track 525

重要詞彙 pizza [ˋpitsə] n. 披薩

⑱ **這家速食店有鎮上最棒的炸雞。This fast food restaurant serves the best fried chicken in town.** Track 526

重要詞彙 serve [sɝv] v. 提供

⑲ **您要升級薯條和可樂到最大份嗎？Would you like to supersize your coke and fries?** Track 527

重要詞彙 supersize [ˋsupɚsaɪz] v. 升級

⑳ **這家速食店的營業時間是什麼時候？What are the opening hours of the fast food restaurant?** Track 528

片語釋義 opening hours 營業時間

看情境學對話

＼中譯／ Track 529

A: Could you introduce some popular fast food restaurants in your city?	A：你能介紹我一些你們城市裡受歡迎的的速食店嗎？
B: There are McDonald's, Burger King, and KFC. Do you like to eat fast food?	B：有麥當勞、漢堡王和肯德基。你喜歡吃速食嗎？
A: Yes. I often have a snack at lunch time ①. I can save a lot of time to rest.	A：喜歡啊。我經常在午飯時間吃速食。我可以省很多時間來休息。
B: But eating fast food is bad for ② our health. Fast food is a really good way to save time, but it is not the proper way for nutrition.	B：但是吃速食對我們的健康有害。速食確實是節省時間的好方法，但是卻沒有充分的營養。

A: Why?	A：為什麼這麼說？
B: Because compared with ③ home-made food, the nutrition provided by fast food is far less. Some most common diseases and other side effects are caused by fast food, like obesity and heart disease.	B：因為與家庭製作的食物相比，速食提供的營養要少得多。一些最常見的疾病和其他的副作用由速食引起，比如肥胖和心臟病。
A: I never expected these bad effects. Maybe I should change my eating habits.	A：我從沒想過會有這樣的壞影響。也許我該改變飲食習慣。
B: Fast food is convenient sometimes ④ in our lives, but we can't eat it very often.	B：速食有時在我們的生活中是必要的，但我們不能經常吃。
A: In my opinion ⑤ , fast food restaurants should develop and provide more and more fresh and healthy food.	A：在我看來，速食店應該研發和提供越來越多的營養食品。
B: And the government should strengthen the supervision of food making.	B：政府應加強對食品生產的監督。
A: Thank you for telling me about these.	A：謝謝你告訴我這些。
B: My pleasure.	B：客氣了。

★**provide** [prə`vaɪd] **v.** 提供，供應
★**obesity** [o`bisətɪ] **n.** 肥胖，肥胖症
★**strengthen** [`strɛŋθən] **v.** 加強，鞏固

對話解析

① at lunch time

表示「在午飯時間」，at 之後可以加時間，也可以加地點，但是地點必須是小地點如機場車站。

② be bad for...

表示「對……不好」，類似的表達還有 be harmful for，反義的表達是 be good for。

③ compared with

表示「與……相比」，在句中作狀語，相當於一個時間或者條件狀語子句。 compare A with B 表示「把 A 和 B 相比較」。

④ sometimes

表示「有時」，是一個頻率副詞。常見的頻率副詞還有：always（總是），usually（通常），often（經常）等。

⑤ in my opinion

表示「在我看來」，類似的表達還有：in my view，as far as I am concerned。

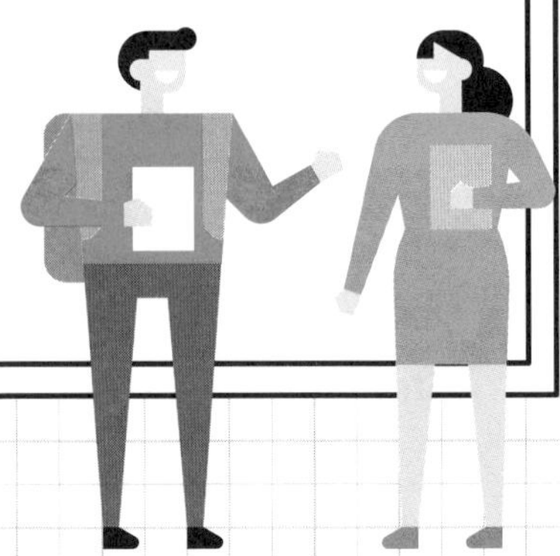

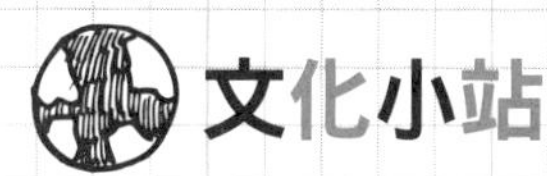

文化小站

由於餐飲文化的差異，中西方速食業不盡相同。西式速食主要以漢堡、薯條、炸雞，還有一些西式飲料等為主。西式速食通常是標準化生產，發展已經步入了成熟的階段。

其他場合就餐

Unit 32

Japanese Restaurant

日式料理

去一家日本餐廳，享受一頓日式料理，是一次不錯的生活體驗。壽司、生魚片、日式火鍋等，讓我們一起品嚐吧！

精選實用會話例句

❶ 我妻子喜歡吃日式料理。
My wife likes to eat Japanese cuisine. Track 530
片語釋義 Japanese cuisine 日式料理

❷ 日式烹飪的主要特點是低脂肪。**The main feature of Japanese cuisine is low in fat.** Track 531
同義表達 The cuisine of Japan is low in fat.

❸ 這家餐廳以生魚片出名。
The restaurant is famous for its sashimi. Track 532
重要詞彙 sashimi [sɑ`ʃimɪ] n. 生魚片

❹ 壽司吧料理，作為主要的消費場所，深受消費者的歡迎。
Sushi Bar, as a main consuming place, is popular among the guests. Track 533
片語釋義 consuming place 消費場所

❺ 你想吃壽司還是拉麵？
Would you like to eat sushi or Ramen? Track 534
重要詞彙 Ramen n. 拉麵

❻ 你點日式雞排飯了嗎？**Have you ordered Japanese Style Chicken fillet Rice?** Track 535
片語釋義 Japanese Style Chicken fillet Rice 日式雞排飯

❼ 這家餐廳提供日式服務標準。**The restaurant provides Japanese standard service.** Track 536

重要詞彙 standard [ˋstændɚd] n. 標準，規格

❽ 你聽說過日本紙火鍋嗎？
Have you heard of Japanese paper hot pot? Track 537

同義表達 Do you know Japanese paper hot pot?

❾ 這家餐廳的裝修風格是以日式為主的。**The decoration of this restaurant is mainly Japanese style.** Track 538

重要詞彙 decoration [͵dɛkəˋreʃən] n. 裝修，裝飾

❿ 你想和我們一起去日本餐廳嗎？**Would you like to go to a Japanese restaurant with us?** Track 539

片語釋義 Japanese restaurant 日本餐廳

⓫ 這家酒店有一間大餐廳供應日式料理。**There is a large dining room serving Japanese cuisine in this hotel.** Track 540

片語釋義 dining room 餐廳

⓬ 這家餐廳以美味的日式料理而聞名。**The restaurant is noted for its excellent Japanese cooking.** Track 541

重要片語 be noted for... 因……而聞名

⓭ 這家餐廳的海鮮新鮮又好吃。**The seafood in this restaurant is fresh and tasty.** Track 542

同義表達 It takes more time to set up a Japanese restaurant

⓮ 有些人很愛芥茉。
Some people like wasabi very much. Track 543

重要詞彙 wasabi n. 芥茉

⓯ 這道日式料理做得絕對出色。
This Japanese cuisine is absolutely excellent. Track 544

重要詞彙 absolutely [ˋæbsə͵lutlɪ] adv. 絕對地

⓰ 紫菜是日本料理的必需品。
Seaweed is a necessity for Japanese cuisine. Track 545

同義表達 Seaweed is essential for Japanese cuisine.

17 在日本，我一定要品嚐不同的丼飯和拉麵。**In Japan, I must try different kinds of don and Ramen.** Track 546

重要詞彙 Japanese [͵dʒæpəˋniz] **n.** 日本人 **adj.** 日本的

18 我們可以在這家餐廳品嚐各式各樣的日本酒類。
We can enjoy a variety of popular Japanese wine and beer in this restaurant. Track 547

同義表達 We can taste all kinds of Japanese food in this restaurant.

19 烤鰻魚是日本料理中比較貴的一道菜。**Grilled eel is a relatively expensive dish in Japanese cuisine.** Track 548

重要詞彙 expensive [ɪkˋspɛnsɪv] **adj.** 昂貴的

20 你能教我如何做炸天婦羅和炸雞嗎？**Could you teach me how to make fried tempura and chicken?** Track 549

重要片語 teach sb sth 教某人某事

看情境學對話

Track 550

中譯

A: I heard you have learned how to make Japanese food. Could you tell me something about the Japanese cuisine?	A：我聽說你學習了如何做日本料理。你能告訴我一些關於日本料理的事情嗎？
B: Certainly. Japanese cuisine is famous for its centuries-old cooking techniques and seasonal ingredients.	B：當然。日本料理因其歷史悠久的烹飪技術和季節性食材而聞名。
A: Sounds exciting! I'm about to take a trip ① to Japan. Could you introduce some Japanese cuisine to me?	A：聽起來很不錯。我正在考慮去日本旅行。你能給我介紹一些日本料理嗎？
B: Japan has long been famed for ② its sushi. In addition ③ , Ramen and Tempura are also popular.	B：日本長期以來因壽司聞名。拉麵和天婦羅也很受歡迎。

A: Do you know any food in Japan that is great but not as well-known to foreigners?	A：你還知道什麼外國人不熟悉但很好吃的日本美食？
B: Sure, I'm going to show you some desserts ④ .	B：當然，我給你介紹一些甜點。
A: That sounds terrific. I love desserts very much.	A：那太棒了。我非常喜歡吃甜點。
B: The Japanese fruit parfait is famous for being really cute, unique and delicious. Besides, you must check out Japanese crepe.	B：日本的水果冷甜品，又可愛又特別還非常好吃，很有名。還有你一定要嚐嚐日本的可麗餅。
A: My mouth is watering. Have you heard of ⑤ Japanese hot pot?	A：我都要流口水了。你聽說過日式火鍋嗎？
B: This is my favorite one. Make sure to try that in Japan. When are you going to Japan?	B：這是我最喜歡的。去日本一定要嚐嚐。你打算什麼時候去日本？
A: In the summer.	A：這個夏天。
B: Hope you have a good trip.	B：祝你旅途愉快。

★**technique** [tɛk`nik] **n.** 技巧，技能
★**parfait** [pɑr`fe] **n.** 凍糕
★**summer** [`sʌmɚ] **n.** 夏天

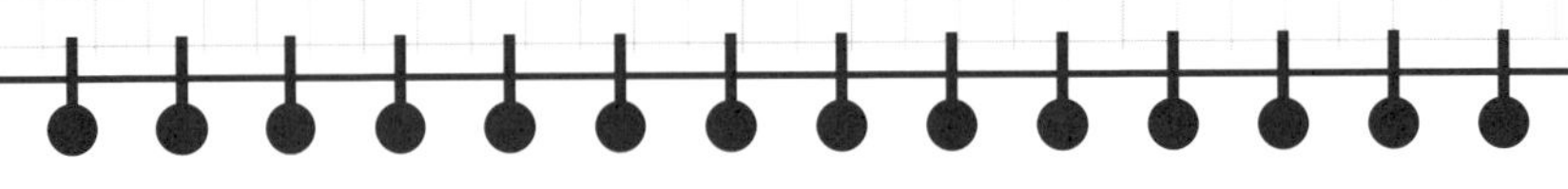

對話解析

① **be about doing sth**

表示「準備做某事」，等同於 be about to do sth

② **be famed for...**

表示「以……而出名」，類似的表達還有：be famous for...

③ **in addition**

表示「另外，除此之外」，常常出現在句首，後面接完整的句子。in addition to 表示「除……之外」，後面要接受詞。

④ **show sb sth**

表示「給某人展示某物」，show 後面接雙受詞，show sb sth 等於 show sth to sb。

⑤ **hear of**

表示「聽說過，聽到」，類似的表達還有：hear about。兩者的區別是，hear of 表示對聽說的事非常瞭解，後者表示只是聽到知道而已。

文化小站

日本是一個海島型國家，人們相當偏愛海產品。日本料理也逐漸發展成為獨具日本特色的菜餚。日本料理主要是指日本和食和日本洋食。說到日本料理，人們便會聯想到壽司和生魚片。這是日本自己發明的食物就稱為和食。從外國引進的，經過日本人改造之後的料理就是洋食。同樣，日本也改造了一些中式餐點，比如：日式拉麵、日式煎餃等。日本的主食與中國相似，也是以米飯和麵條為主。日本料理在製作上，講究選材新鮮，注重「色、香、味、器」，很重視視覺享受。日本料理主要包含三類：本膳料理、懷石料理和會席料理。日本料理由切、煮、烤、蒸、炸五種基本的調理法做成。日本料理通常講究飲食的精緻和健康。日本料理的主要精神是自然原味，烹調方式也是細膩精緻。在日本餐廳吃飯，吃是一方面，氛圍、情調和環境也是很重要的。

Chapter 3

愛情與婚姻

愛情

Unit 33

Falling in Love

墜入愛河

在很多年輕人的心裡，他們把愛情放在第一位。當兩個人墜入愛河的時候，就會不顧一切。那麼，就讓我們來感受一下他們的愛情吧！

精選實用會話例句

1 因為她的溫柔漂亮，我愛上了她。**I fell in love with her for her tenderness and beauty.** Track 551

同義表達 I was in love with her because of her tenderness and beauty.

2 莉莉單戀他很多年了。**Lily has carried a torch for him for many years.** Track 552

重要片語 carry a torch for sb 單戀某人

3 凱特是一個沉溺於愛情中的傻瓜。**Kate is a fool addicted to love.** Track 553

重要詞彙 addict [ə'dɪkt] v. 沉溺於

4 她不知道我已經暗戀她五年了。**She doesn't know that I have had a crush on her for five years.** Track 554

重要片語 have a crush on sb 暗戀某人

5 愛情的力量是相當偉大的。**The power of love is quite great.** Track 555

重要詞彙 power [`paʊɚ] n. 力量，權力

6 傑克給的驚喜讓她很開心。**The surprise that Jack gave really delighted her.** Track 556

同義表達 She was so delighted because Jack gave her a surprise.

⑦ 我想像不到他是這麼一個浪漫的人。I can't imagine him being such a romantic person.

Track 557

重要詞彙 romantic [rə`mæntɪk] adj. 浪漫的，浪漫主義的

⑧ 我們對彼此的情感很強烈。

We have strong affections toward each other.

Track 558

重要詞彙 affection [ə`fɛkʃən] n. 情感

⑨ 你知道約翰在追你嗎？Do you know that John tries to win your affections?

Track 559

重要片語 try to win one's affections 追求某人

⑩ 他對艾米有好感。He has been coming on to Amy.

Track 560

重要片語 come on to 對……有好感

⑪ 這場暗戀使他很痛苦。

This unrequited love made him suffer.

Track 561

片語釋義 unrequited love 單相思，暗戀

⑫ 我最好的朋友暗戀著克麗絲。

My best friend is a secret admirer of Chris.

Track 562

片語釋義 secret admirer 愛慕者，暗戀者

⑬ 羅賓暗戀過她。Robbin bore a secret love for her.

Track 563

同義表達 Robbin fell in love with her secretly.

⑭ 艾拉把對他的感情埋藏於心裡。Ella keeps her love for him corked up inside her.

Track 564

片語釋義 cork up 封鎖，埋藏

⑮ 我不會放棄對他的愛戀。

I won't give up my love for him.

Track 565

片語釋義 give up 放棄

⑯ 喬治到底為什麼喜歡她？

Why on earth does George like her?

Track 566

片語釋義 on earth 究竟，到底

⑰ **他最終贏得了這個女孩的愛慕。**
He finally won the girl's admiration. Track 567
重要片語 win one's admiration 贏得某人的愛慕

⑱ **他們已經相愛五年了，但是還沒有結婚。**
They've been in love for five years, but they're not married yet. Track 568
重要詞彙 marry [ˈmærɪ] v. 結婚

⑲ **我想追求奧利維亞，但是我沒有勇氣。**
I want to court Olivia, but I have no courage. Track 569
重要片語 court sb 追求某人

⑳ **他下定決心去追求愛麗絲。**
He made up his mind to pursue Alice. Track 570
重要片語 make up one's mind to do sth 下定決心做某事

㉑ **在我看來，愛情使她變得比以前更加幸福。In my opinion, love makes her happier than ever.** Track 571
重要片語 in one's opinion 在某人看來

看情境學對話

Track 572

	中譯
A: Hello, Stephen. Did you go to Emily's birthday party yesterday?	A：嗨，史蒂芬。你昨天去參加艾米麗的生日派對了嗎？
B: Yes, I was late for ① her party. You had gone home already.	B：是的。我去的比較晚。你都已經回家了。
A: So do you know the girl who had been standing by Emily?	A：那你知道一直站在艾米麗身邊的那個女孩嗎？

B: Yes, she is Emily's cousin. What's the matter? ② Could it be said that you like her?	B：是的，她是艾米麗的表妹。怎麼了？難道你喜歡上她了？
A: I fell in love with her at first sight ③ , so I decide to show her my love. Do you know the girl's phone number?	A：我對她一見鍾情，所以我想向她表白。你知道這個女孩的電話號碼嗎？
B: I don't know. But I heard that she just got married last week.	B：我不知道。但是我聽說她上週剛剛結婚。
A: That's a pity! ④ If only I had known her earlier!	A：那真是太遺憾了！要是我早點認識她該多好啊！
B: I have a beautiful sister. I can introduce her to you if you like.	B：我有個姐姐也很漂亮。如果你願意，我可以把她介紹給你。
A: Forget it, but thank you. I'm not in the mood ⑤ right now.	A：算了吧，但還是謝謝你。因為我現在沒心情。
B: It's okay.	B：沒關係。

【程度提升，加分單字】

★**cousin** [ˋkʌzn] **n.** 堂（表）兄弟姐妹
★**pity** [ˋpɪtɪ] **n.** 遺憾的事，同情
★**introduce** [ˏɪntrəˋdjus] **v.** 介紹
★**mood** [mud] **n.** 心情

對話解析

① **be late for**

表示「遲到，來晚」，for 後面一般跟名詞或者動名詞。late 還有一種用法為 too late to do sth，表示「做某事太晚了」。

② **what's the matter**

詢問對方「你怎麼了」。它相當於what's wrong 和what's up。

③ **fall in love with sb at first sight**

表示「對某人一見鍾情」，比較口語化的表達為 love sb at the first sight。

④ **That's a pity!**

表達的是一種遺憾的感情，它的同義句為 What a pity! 或者 What a shame!

⑤ **be not in the mood**

表示「沒有心情」，相當於 be in a bad mood。be in the mood 和 be in a good mood 表示「心情好」。

學習英文Fun輕鬆！

1.Love lives in cottage as well as in courts.
愛情不分貧賤與高貴。

2.Love me, love my dog.
愛屋及烏。

3.Beauty lies in the eyes of the beholder.
情人眼裡出西施。

4.Unlucky in love, lucky at play.
情場失意，賭場得意。

5.Love makes the world go around.
愛讓世界轉動。

6.Where there is great love, there are great miracles.
哪裡有愛，哪裡就有奇跡。

7.Love is hard to get into, but harder to get out of.
愛很難投入，但一旦投入，便更難走出。

愛情

Unit 34 Confessions 深情表白

當對對方產生了一定的愛意時，需要鼓足勇氣去深情地表白。只有表白後，兩人才能開始感受甜蜜的愛情。女生們都喜歡那些浪漫的表白，那麼我們就來學習一下男生們是如何表白的吧。

精選實用會話例句

1. 我不敢向溫蒂表白。
I dare not confess my love for Wendy. Track 573
同義表達 I dare not tell Wendy I love her.

2. 我已經喜歡你七年了。**It has been seven years since I fell in love with you.** Track 574
同義表達 I have loved you for seven years.

3. 你向簡表白了嗎？
Have you spoken out your love for Jane? Track 575
同義表達 Have you confessed your love for Jane?

4. 他鍾情於蘇珊。**He is deeply in love with Susan.** Track 576
重要片語 be deeply in love with sb 鍾情於某人

5. 我沒有信心去表白。**I have no confidence to confess.** Track 577
重要詞彙 confidence [ˋkɑnfədəns] n. 信心，信任

6. 讓我告訴你，你是這個世界上獨一無二的人。**Let me tell you that you are the only one in the world.** Track 578
重要詞彙 only [ˋonlɪ] adj. 僅有的，唯一的

7. 你是如此獨特，以至於我被你吸引了。
You're so unique that I'm attracted to you. Track 579
重要片語 be attracted to sb 被某人吸引

❽ 大衛沒有莉莉就無法活下去。
David can't live without Lily. Track 580
重要詞彙 without [wɪˈðaʊt] **prep.** 缺乏，沒有

❾ 你是我見過最優雅的女人。
You're the most elegant woman I've ever seen. Track 581
重要詞彙 elegant [ˋɛləgənt] **adj.** 優雅的，優美的

❿ 愛麗絲讓我神魂顛倒。I'm infatuated with Alice. Track 582
重要片語 be infatuated with sb 迷戀某人

⓫ 我日日夜夜都在思念你。I miss you day and night. Track 583
片語釋義 day and night 日日夜夜

⓬ 我說的都是真心話。What I'm saying is true. Track 584
同義表達 What I say is true.

⓭ 我無法停止對你的愛。I can't stop loving you. Track 585
重要片語 stop doing sth 停止做某事

⓮ 答應我不要拋棄我，我不能離開你。Promise me not to abandon me. I can't leave you. Track 586
重要片語 promise sb to do sth 答應某人做某事

⓯ 他可以不惜一切代價為我做任何事。
He can do anything for me at all costs. Track 587
片語釋義 at all costs 不惜一切代價

⓰ 請允許我無論到哪裡都牽著你的手。Please allow me to hold your hand everywhere you go. Track 588
重要片語 hold one's hand 牽某人的手

⓱ 我發自內心的愛著那個可愛的女生。I love the lovely girl from the bottom of my heart. Track 589
重要片語 from the bottom of one's heart 發自某人的內心

⓲ 我確定她就是我喜歡的類型。
I'm sure that she's my type. Track 590
重要詞彙 type [taɪp] **n.** 類型

⑲ 他沒有去表白，因為他害怕被拒絕。**He didn't confess his love for fear of being rejected.** Track 591

同義表達 He didn't confess his love because he was afraid to get rejected.

⑳ 難道你不認為這是在表白嗎？

Don't you think this is a confession? Track 592

重要詞彙 confession [kən`fɛʃən] **n.** 表白，承認

㉑ 我不相信她接受了湯姆的愛。

I can't believe she accepted Tom's love. Track 593

重要詞彙 accept [ək`sɛpt] **v.** 接受，同意，承認

㉒ 如果上帝能再給我一次機會，我一定會向她表白。

If God could give me another chance, I would tell her I love her. Track 594

重要詞彙 chance [tʃæns] **n.** 機會，機遇

看情境學對話

Track 595

	\中譯/
A: Jessica, I need to talk to you.	A：潔西卡，我有話想和你説。
B: What do you want to say?	B：你想説什麼？
A: Are you dating anyone ① at present ② ?	A：你現在有男朋友嗎？
B: Not yet. What's wrong?	B：還沒有。怎麼了？
A: What kind of person do you think I am?	A：在你看來，我是一個什麼樣的人？
B: I think you're kind, and what's more ③ , you are so masculine. But what do you mean ④ by asking me these questions?	B：我認為你很善良，而且很有男子氣概。但是你問我這些問題是什麼意思？

A: Because you're the most kind of girl that I've ever seen, and I have carried a torch for you for a long time.	A：因為你是我見過的最善良的女孩，我已經喜歡你很久了。
B: Really?	B：真的嗎？
A: Of course. I've never loved someone so much.	A：當然了。我從來沒有如此深愛著一個人。
B: Well, we can try to hang out for a while.	B：我們可以試著相處一段時間。
A: Are you telling the truth? I can't believe it. That's very kind of you.	A：你說的是真的嗎？我簡直不敢相信。你真是太好啦。
B: You are welcome ⑤ .	B：不用客氣。

★**date** [det] v. & n. 約會
★**present** [ˋprɛznt] n. 現在，禮物
★**masculine** [ˋmæskjəlɪn] adj. 男子氣概的，像男人一樣的
★**while** [hwaɪl] n. 一段時間
★**truth** [truθ] n. 事實，真相，真理

① **Are you dating anyone?**

表示詢問對方是否有男朋友，相當於 Do you have a boyfriend?

② **at present**

表示「目前，現在」，它可以和 now 相互替換。

③ **what's more**

表示「而且」，而 what's worse 表示「更為糟糕的是」。

④ **What do you mean?**

表示「你是什麼意思？」相當於 What are you talking about? 或者是 What's your point?

⑤ **You are welcome.**

是別人感謝的回覆語，類似的回答還有 It's my pleasure. / That's all right.

學習英文Fun輕鬆！

Thirsting for Love

Thurston was in the habit of visiting his girlfriend's apartment from time to time, but always managed to get home at a decent hour with a plausible excuse. But this time, both he and his girlfriend had fallen asleep, and it was 2:00 am when Thurston woke up. Thinking fast, he immediately called home, and when his wife answered, panted, "Don't pay the ransom! I've escaped!"

渴望愛情

瑟斯頓經常去他女友的公寓，但他總是設法找個理由以免太晚回家。但這一次，他和女朋友都睡著了，當他醒來時都已經凌晨兩點了，瑟斯頓腦筋一轉，立刻打電話回家，當他太太接電話時，他故意喘著氣說：「千萬不要付贖金！我已經安全逃出來了！」

愛情

Unit 35 Dating 交往約會

約會在時間、地點、方式等的選擇上也是有講究啊。讓我們來策劃一場完美的約會吧。

精選實用會話例句

❶ 我們在哪裡見面，瑞秋？
Where shall we meet, Rachel? Track 596
重要詞彙 meet [mit] V. 相遇，相識，滿足

❷ 你真的要和麥克斯約會嗎？
Are you really having a date with Max? Track 597
重要片語 have a date with sb 和某人約會

❸ 我能和你約會嗎？**May I ask you out?** Track 598
同義表達 Would you go on a date with me?

❹ 我能開車去接你嗎？**May I go to pick you up?** Track 599
片語釋義 pick up 撿起，接載，學會，逮捕

❺ 你是想和我約會嗎？
You want to have a date with me? Track 600
同義表達 Are you asking me out on a date?

❻ 今晚瑪麗要和傑森約會嗎？
Does Mary want to go out with Jason tonight? Track 601
重要片語 go out with sb 和某人約會

❼ 這是我第一次和女孩約會。
This is the first time that I date with a girl. Track 602
同義表達 This is my first date with a girl.

❽ 我明天晚上和琳達有個約會。
I've got a date with Linda tomorrow evening. Track 603
重要詞彙 date [det] n. 日期，日子，約會

❾ 這個男孩在中學的時候不常約會。**The boy did not date very much in high school.** Track 604
同義表達 The boy seldom dated in high school.

❿ 湯姆告訴我他有一個重要的約會。**Tom told me that he had an important appointment.** Track 605
重要詞彙 appointment [əˈpɔɪntmənt] n. 約會，任命，職位

⓫ 我哥哥上大學的時候才真正開始和女孩子約會。
My brother only really started having a date with girls at college. Track 606
片語釋義 at college 在大學

⓬ 他生病了，不得不取消和那個女孩的約會。
He had to cancel the date with the girl because of illness. Track 607
重要詞彙 illness [ˋɪlnɪs] n. 疾病

⓭ 傑克和蘿絲已經約會半年了。
Jack and Rose have been dating for half a year. Track 608
片語釋義 half a year 半年

⓮ 你願意和傑瑞一起去看電影嗎？
Would you like to go to the cinema with Jerry? Track 609
片語釋義 go to the cinema 去看電影

⓯ 他們的約會進行得怎麼樣？**How did their date go?** Track 610
同義表達 How was their date?

⓰ 今晚是我第一次約會，你能給我一些建議應該穿什麼衣服嗎？**Could you give me some suggestions about what to wear for my first date tonight?** Track 611
重要詞彙 suggestion [səˋdʒɛstʃən] n. 意見，建議

⑰ 妮娜想知道之後經理要去哪裡約會。
Nina wondered where the manager was going for the rendezvous afterwards. Track 612

重要詞彙 rendezvous [`randə͵vu] v. 約會

⑱ 我昨晚的約會很棒。
I had a wonderful date night yesterday. Track 613

片語釋義 date night 約會之夜

⑲ 尼克和艾米交往有三年了。**Nick and Amy have been knocking around together for three years.** Track 614

同義表達 Nick and Amy have been dating for three years.

⑳ 你們決定正式交往了嗎？**Have you decided to put your relationship on a formal footing?** Track 615

重要詞彙 relationship [rɪ`leʃən`ʃɪp] n. 關係，聯繫

看情境學對話

Track 616

	中譯
A: What do you think an ideal date should be like?	A：你認為理想的約會應該是什麼樣的？
B: My ideal date? First of all ①, I think the guy should make a plan for everything. He should not rely on me to make the suggestions because it's very attractive when a guy makes the plans.	B：我理想的約會？首先，我認為男生應該安排計畫。他不應該依賴我提出建議，因為男生安排計劃是非常有吸引力的。
A: That sounds like a good first step.	A：聽起來是個不錯的第一步。

B: Secondly, I would probably want him to pick me up ② to the places, or could go on public transportation together, as long as ③ he has a plan.	B：第二，我可能想他開車帶著我去約會，或是我們也可以一起坐公共交通工具，只要他有計劃就行。
A: Okay. Do you have the third step?	A：好。你還有第三步驟嗎？
B: The last one, I think the guy should pay for the date.	B：最後一條，我認為他應該支付約會費用。
A: Pay for the date?	A：支付約會的費用？
B: Yeah. It is his responsibility because it is his pleasure to take a girl out. And the date should also be fun and not be boring, and it should end with ④ giving presents to each other if it goes well. If it doesn't, we should also say goodbye politely.	B：是的。這是他的責任，因為帶一個女孩出去是他的榮幸。約會應該很有趣，不應該無聊。如果約會順利的話，結束的時候會互送禮物。如果進展不順利的話，我們也應該禮貌的告別。
A: But a guy like that is hard to find ⑤, and it's actually unfair and unrealistic. Good luck finding your ideal partner.	A：但是那樣的男生很難找，而且這其實不太公平也不實際。祝你找到你理想中的對象。
B: Thank you.	B：謝謝你。

【程度提升，加分單字】

★**ideal** [aɪˋdiəl] **adj.** 理想的，完美的
★**arrangement** [əˋrendʒmənt] **n.** 安排，約定
★**responsibility** [rɪˌspɒnsəˋbɪlətɪ] **n.** 職責，責任

① **first of all**

表示「首先」，強調次序。類似的表達還有：in the first place，above all，firstly。

② **pick up**

表示「撿起，接載，學會」，是一個動詞短語。代詞要放在 pick up 的中間，如：pick me up。

③ **as long as**

在該句中表示「只要」之意，類似的表達還有：only if。但是 only if 要as long as 的語氣強。

④ **end with**

表示「以……結束」，類似的表達還有：end in。前者強調以某件事的發生而告終，後者強調以什麼樣的結果而告終。

⑤ **be hard to do sth**

表示「做某事很困難」，相反的表達是：be easy to do sth 表示「做某事很簡單」。

愛情

Unit 36

Sweetness of Love

甜情蜜意

陪伴是最長情的告白，相守是最溫暖的承諾。愛情是需要保鮮的，如何才能做到甜情蜜意呢？讓我們一起看看吧！

精選實用會話例句

1 傑克告訴蘿絲他會永遠愛她。
Jack tells Rose that he will love her forever. Track 617
重要詞彙 forever [fɚˋɛvɚ] adv. 永遠地

2 這個男人深愛自己的妻子。
The man loved his wife deeply. Track 618
重要詞彙 deeply [ˋdiplɪ] adv. 深深地

3 那個年輕人深情地望著他的妻子。**The young man gazes with deep feeling at his wife's face.** Track 619
片語釋義 gaze with 注視，凝視

4 我很感動我丈夫沒有忘記我們的紀念日。
I was touched that my husband didn't forget our anniversary. Track 620
重要詞彙 touch [tʌtʃ] v. 接觸，觸動，感動

5 我們應該心甘情願地愛著彼此。
We should love each other out of our own will. Track 621
重要片語 out of our own will 願意做某事

6 情人節給我們提供了一個表達感情的機會。
Valentine's Day provides us with a chance to express our feelings. Track 622
片語釋義 Valentine's Day 情人節

❼ 我們可以看出提姆深愛他的妻子。
We could see Tim's deep love towards his wife. Track 623
同義表達 We can see that Tim loves his wife so much.

❽ 托尼把對她的感情深藏於心。Tony keeps his love for her corked up inside him. Track 624
片語釋義 cork up 抑制，封鎖

❾ 這個女孩總是帶著十分甜美的微笑。
The girl always has a smile of great sweetness. Track 625
重要詞彙 sweetness [`switnɪs] n. 甜蜜，美妙

❿ 這位老太太仍然深情懷念著她死去的丈夫。The old woman still deeply missed her dead husband. Track 626
重要詞彙 dead [dɛd] adj. 死去的

⓫ 毫無疑問，我對你有深厚的感情。
It is no doubt that I hold deep feelings for you. Track 627
片語釋義 hold deep feelings for 對……有深厚的感情

⓬ 她已經感覺到自己甜蜜的淚水湧了出來。She has felt the sweet release of her own tears. Track 628
重要詞彙 release [rɪ`lis] v. 釋放，放開，發佈，發行

⓭ 這個男人享受著甜蜜愛情。
The man enjoys the happy love. Track 629
片語釋義 happy love 甜蜜愛情

⓮ 這位男士告訴我愛情混雜著甜蜜和苦澀。
The man tells me that love is a mixture of honey and bitterness. Track 630
重要詞彙 bitterness [`bɪtɚnɪs] n. 苦味，痛苦

⓯ 這本相冊記錄了我們的甜蜜愛情。This photo album has recorded the sweet love of us. Track 631
片語釋義 photo album 相簿

⓰ 任何時候鮮花都代表了我們的甜蜜愛情。
Flowers represent our sweet love at any time. Track 632
片語釋義 at any time 任何時候

⑰ **傑森對露西感到一種深情。**
Jason feels a great tenderness for Lucy. Track 633
重要詞彙 tenderness [ˋtɛndɚnɪs] n. 柔軟，溫和，親切

⑱ **我們進行了持續到深夜的深情交談。We had an emotional conversation that lasted long into the night.** Track 634
片語釋義 emotional conversation 深情交談

⑲ **老太太深情地撫摸著她丈夫的臉頰。The old lady caresses her husband's cheek affectionately.** Track 635
重要詞彙 caress [kəˋrɛs] v. 撫摸

⑳ **他們祝願我們擁有甜蜜的愛情和成功的事業。**
They wish that we will have happy love and a successful career. Track 636
片語釋義 successful career 成功的事業

看情境學對話

Track 637

	\中譯/
A: What do you think of long distance relationships?	A：你怎麼看待異地戀？
B: A long distance relationship is a trial of patience for two people in love. I had a long distance relationship three years ago. That made me very upset.	B：異地戀對於相愛的兩個人來說是一種考驗。三年前，我有過一段異地戀。那真的讓我非常苦惱。
A: I think you're kind of ① like me. I have to ② see the person often.	A：我想你和我是一樣的。我必須能常常見到那個人。
B: That is correct. So our relationship came to an end ③ soon. How do you feel about the never-ending love?	B：沒錯。因此我們的戀愛關係很快就結束了。你對永恆的愛怎麼看？

A: That sounds very sweet. It is also a romantic idea.	A：聽起來很甜蜜。也是一個浪漫的想法。
B: I believe that I can find someone to live with forever.	B：我相信我可以找到那個共度一生的人。
A: What a romantic thing it is! ④	A：多麼浪漫的一件事啊！
B: How is the relationship between you and your wife?	B：你和妻子之間的關係怎麼樣？
A: At the beginning, both of us felt very happy and sweet. But there were still some problems between us. Fortunately, we solved the problems. We are willing to love each other.	A：剛開始的時候，我們都感覺幸福甜蜜。但是我們之間仍然存在一些問題。幸運的是，我們解決了這些問題。我們心甘情願的愛著彼此。
B: I am jealous of ⑤ you.	B：我真羨慕你。
A: I'd like to invite you to my house next Sunday.	A：我想下週日邀請你來我們家做客。
B: Thank you.	B：謝謝你。

★**distance** [ˋdɪstəns] **n.** 距離，路程
★**relationship** [rɪˋleʃənˋʃɪp] **n.** 關係，聯繫
★**romantic** [rəˋmæntɪk] **adj.** 浪漫的

對話解析

① **kind of**

表示「稍微，有一點」，後接形容詞或者副詞。要與 kinds of 區分開， kinds of 表示「各種各樣的」。

② **have to**

表示「必須，不得不」，強調客觀上需要做某事，後面要接動詞原形。 have to 有人稱、數和時態的變化。

③ **come to an end**

是一個固定搭配用法，表示「結束，終止，完事」，往往強調事物自然地發展到了盡頭，結束了。

④ **What a romantic thing it is!**

表示「多麼浪漫啊！」是 what 引導的感歎句。相當於 How romantic it is!

⑤ **be jealous of**

表示「妒嫉」，在該句中翻譯成了「羨慕」，相當於 envy。後面可以接名詞或者動名詞。

文化小站

人都會快樂、生氣、寂寞、悲傷，也會去愛去恨。由於文化背景等的不同，中西方人表達感情的方式也就天差地遠。西方國家的大部分人都心直口快，富於表現。說話時並不喜歡拐彎抹角，總是直截了當地來一句「yes」或者「no」。而東方人講究含蓄美，常常善於隱藏自己的感情，不喜歡直接表達出來，有時會讓人摸不著頭緒。西方人從不吝嗇對別人表達自己的讚美，「You are pretty」、「You are wonderful」是他們掛在嘴邊的話語，被讚美的人也會大方地說一句「Thank you」，而東方人是比較謙虛謹慎的，被誇獎時總會客套地回覆「過獎了」、「我還不夠好」或者「哪裡哪裡」。

愛情
Unit 37

Argument
爭吵矛盾

有句話：「打是情罵是愛，不打不罵是禍害」。爭吵是日常生活中不可避免的，如何正確解決生活中的矛盾呢？讓我們一起去學習吧！

精選實用會話例句

1 真是讓人討厭！What a nuisance!
重要詞彙 nuisance [`njusns] n. 討厭的東西
Track 638

2 提姆氣死我了。Tim pisses me off.
片語釋義 piss off 使……討厭
Track 639

3 我再也忍不下去了。This is the last straw.
同義表達 I can bear it no longer.
Track 640

4 不要找任何藉口。No more excuses.
重要詞彙 excuse [ɪk`skjuz] n. 藉口，道歉 v. 原諒
Track 641

5 請從我的面前消失。Please get out of my face.
同義表達 I never want to see you again.
Track 642

6 你要報復他嗎？Do you want to get even with him?
片語釋義 get even with 報復
Track 643

7 你讓我在公共場所感到很丟人。
You made me embarrassed in public.
重要詞彙 embarrass [ɪmˈbærəs] v. 使局促不安，使窘迫
Track 644

8 琳達不想再聽見你說的任何話。
Linda doesn't want any more words out of you.
同義表達 Linda doesn't want to hear anything you say.
Track 645

⑨ 不要和你爸爸頂嘴。
Don't answer back to your father. Track 646
片語釋義 answer back to 頂嘴，回覆，應答

⑩ 少管閒事。**It's none of your business.** Track 647
同義表達 It doesn't concern you. / I don't need your two cents.

⑪ 我丈夫快要氣炸了。
My husband is about to explode. Track 648
重要詞彙 explode [ɪk`splod] v. 使爆炸，推翻，爆發

⑫ 不要試圖把你的妻子當成傻瓜。
Don't try to make your wife look foolish! Track 649
同義表達 Don't treat your wife as a fool.

⑬ 傑森怎麼敢那樣對南西說話！
How dare Jason speak to Nancy like that! Track 650
重要片語 dare do sth 敢於做某事

⑭ 我永遠不會饒恕他。**Never shall I forgive him.** Track 651
同義表達 I'll never forgive him.

⑮ 我再也沒有耐心了。
My patience has completely run out. Track 652
同義表達 I've run out of patience.

⑯ 這位女士對她的丈夫極為生氣。
The lady is so infuriated at her husband. Track 653
片語釋義 be infuriated at 對……極為憤怒

⑰ 你做得太過分了！**You've gone too far.** Track 654
同義表達 That's too much.

⑱ 看看他都做了些什麼？
What on earth has he done? Track 655
同義表達 Just look at what he has done!

⑲ 別告訴我該做什麼！**Don't be a back seat driver.** Track 656
同義表達 Don't tell me what I should do.

⑳ 妮娜不想再聽他說的謊話。
Nina doesn't want to hear any more of his lies. Track 657
重要詞彙 lie [laɪ] v. 説謊，躺 n. 謊言

㉑ 你在玩弄他吧！**You're making fun of him!** Track 658
同義表達 Are you trying to make a fool out of him?

㉒ 讓我靜一靜。**Leave me alone.** Track 659
重要詞彙 alone [ə`lon] adj. 單獨的 adv. 單獨地

看情境學對話

Track 660

	中譯
A: You look very unhappy. What's the matter with you? ①	A：你看起來很不開心。怎麼了？
B: I can't stand living with you anymore. I'm sick of ② your drinking and indolence. Let's get divorced.	B：我再也受不了和你生活在一起了，我討厭你的酗酒和懶惰。我們離婚吧！
A: Please just give me another chance. I swear I'll never drink again.	A：請再給我一次機會吧。我發誓再也不會喝酒了。
B: I have given you a lot of chances. For so many years, there has been nothing changed. I have given up on you ③ .	B：我已經給你很多機會了。這麼多年了，沒有任何的變化。我已經放棄你了。
A: You know I'm trying hard to stop drinking. I don't know how to live without you; I won't let you go.	A：你知道的，我很努力在戒酒。沒有你我不知道該怎麼生活，我是不會讓你走的。

B: Don't you understand? It's not just for your drinking, but you are lacking of sense of responsibility.	B：難道你不懂嗎？不僅是因為你酗酒，還有你缺乏責任感。
A: I have to make money to support our family, so I don't have enough time to stay with you.	A：我得賺錢養家啊，所以我沒有足夠的時間和你待在一起。
B: Even if ④ I really need you, you don't have time to be with me.	B：即使我真的很需要你，你也沒有時間陪我。
A: It happened to be a very important meeting, or I'd be there for you.	A：那次是正好有很重要的會要開，否則我一定會陪你的。
B: I can't trust you any more.	B：我再也不能相信你了。
A: I understand. I'm gonna ⑤ change. Please think it over.	A：我明白了。我一定會改的。請再考慮考慮。

★**indolence** [ˋɪndələns] n. 懶惰
★**understand** [ˏʌndəˋstænd] v. 理解
★**support** [səˋport] v. 支持，支撐，維持

① **What's the matter with sb?**

常常用於詢問對方怎麼了，類似的表達還有：What's wrong with sb?

② **be sick of...**

表示「對……厭倦」，後面可以接名詞或動名詞。類似的表達還有：be tired of。

③ **give up on sb / sth**

表示「對……絕望，對……不抱希望」，give up 是一個固定搭配，表示「放棄」。

④ **even if**

表示「雖然，即使」，用來引導把握不大的事情；even though 也可以表示「即使」，但引出的是事實。

⑤ **gonna**

常常出現在口語之中，gonna（going to）一般是日常生活中朋友之間使用的，類似的還有 wanna（want to）。

愛情

Unit 38 Making Up 和好如初

中國成語「破鏡重圓」常常用來比喻夫妻出現矛盾後重新講和。那麼怎樣才能和好如初？讓我們一起來學習吧！

精選實用會話例句

1 他幫助我平息了爭執，我們又和好如初了。
He helped me to patch up our tiff again. Track 661
片語釋義 patch up 解決，修補

2 讓我們忘掉過去的爭吵。
Let's forget the quarrels of the past. Track 662
重要詞彙 quarrel [`kwɔrəl] n. 爭吵

3 我們和好吧！**Let's make up!** Track 663
片語釋義 make up 組成，補足，化妝

4 托尼的婚姻破裂，已無法和好如初。**The breakdown of Tony's marriage has been irretrievable.** Track 664
重要詞彙 irretrievable [͵ɪrɪ`trivəbəl] adj. 不能挽回的，不能復原的

5 傑克和蘿絲已經設法彌合了他們的分歧。**Jack and Rose tried to patch up the differences.** Track 665
重要詞彙 difference [`dɪfərəns] n. 差別，分歧

6 現在要和好如初是不可能的。
It is impossible to make peace now. Track 666
重要片語 be impossible to do sth 不可能做某事

7 他的妻子回來了，他們可以和好如初。
His wife has come back and they can make up. Track 667
片語釋義 come back 回來

❽ 我和我丈夫吵架了，但現在我們已和好如初。
I quarrelled with my husband, but now we are completely reconciled. Track 668
片語釋義 quarrel with 和……爭吵

❾ 湯姆的父母和好如初了。**Tom's parents are on just as good terms as ever.** Track 669
片語釋義 as...as 和……一樣

❿ 他們昨天和好了嗎？
Did they manage to patch it up yesterday? Track 670
重要詞彙 manage [ˈmænɪdʒ] v. 使用，經營，辦理

⓫ 這位女士已經表現出與丈夫和好的願望。
The lady has already evinced a desire to be reconciled with her husband. Track 671
重要詞彙 desire [dɪˋzaɪr] n. 願望，希望

⓬ 麗娜似乎想要和好，結束他們之間的爭吵。
Lena seems to want to make peace and patch up their quarrel. Track 672
片語釋義 make peace 講和，言和

⓭ 傑瑞和南西兩人已暫時和好。**The relations between Jerry and Nancy have been patched up.** Track 673
同義表達 Jerry and Nancy have made up for a while.

⓮ 傑森和他的妻子和好了嗎？
Did Jason make peace with his wife? Track 674
重要片語 make peace with sb 和某人講和

⓯ 麥克斯是真心願意與妻子言歸於好嗎？**Was Max sincere about reconciling with his wife?** Track 675
重要詞彙 sincere [sɪnˋsɪr] adj. 真誠的，真心的

⓰ 只要父母不干涉，這對夫婦會和好如初的。
The couple will come to terms, if their parents keep their nose out. Track 676
片語釋義 come to terms 妥協，讓步

⑰ **在多年分離之後，這對夫婦終於言歸於好了。**
The couple came together after years of separation in the end. Track 677

重要詞彙 separation [ˌsɛpəˋreʃən] **n.** 分開，分離

⑱ **為什麼他們不能解決矛盾言歸於好呢？**
Why can't they solve the conflict and make up? Track 678

重要詞彙 conflict [ˋkɒnflɪkt] **n.** 衝突，矛盾

⑲ **羅伯特和露西已經和好了嗎？Have Robert and Lucy reconciled with each other yet?** Track 679

同義表達 Have Robert and Lucy made up yet?

⑳ **那個男人放棄了他妻子提供和解的機會。The man has thrown away the chance that his wife offered for the reconciliation.** Track 680

片語釋義 throw away 扔掉，浪費，錯過

看情境學對話

Track 681

	中譯
A: You look so upset. What's wrong with you?	A：你看起來很沮喪。怎麼了？
B: I quarrelled with my wife yesterday. So she has run away from home ① for about ten hours. I immediately regretted. I really want to make peace and patch up our quarrel. I didn't figure out ② how to do it.	B：昨天我和我妻子吵架了。所以她已經離家出走大約十個小時了。我立刻就後悔了。我真的想言歸於好，結束我們之間的爭吵。我不知道該怎麼辦。
A: Listen to me ③ . First of all, you should keep looking for her until you find her.	A：聽我說。你應該一直找，直到你找到她。

B: But I don't know where she is. I didn't find her in our house and her mother's.	B：我不知道她在哪裡。我在家裡和她媽媽家裡都沒有找到她。
A: There is an off chance of finding her at your house. You might go to her friend's house.	A：很少有希望在家裡找到她。你可以去她朋友家裡找找。
B: I will give a try ④ .	B：我會試一試。
A: Secondly, you should think carefully about what is the key point of contention. And whose fault is it?	A：其次，你還需要考慮清楚你們爭論的焦點是什麼。到底是誰的錯？
B: I understand. I don't know if she can give me another chance.	B：我明白了。我不知道她是否還能再給我一次機會。
A: Don't think about it too much ⑤ . The most important thing for you is to find her first. I will help you.	A：別想太多。對你來説最重要的還是先找到她。我會幫你的。
B: Thank you very much.	B：非常感謝。

【程度提升，加分單字】

★**regret** [rɪ`grɛt] **n.** & **v.** 遺憾，後悔
★**contention** [kən`tɛnʃən] **n.** 爭論
★**fault** [fɔlt] **n.** 錯誤，缺點

對話解析

① **run away from home**

表示「離家出走」，run 的過去式是 ran，過去分詞是 run。其中 run away 是一個片語，表示「逃跑，走掉」。

② **figure out**

表示「計算出，解決，想出，弄明白」，外國人在表達「想通一個問題或者是解決一個問題」時，很喜歡用 figure out。

③ **listen to me**

表示「聽我說」，listen to sb 是一個固定的用法，表示「聽某人說」，強調聽的動作。

④ **give a try**

表示「嘗試做某事」， 想要表達不能預測成功與否也要試一試，就可以give it a try。此時 try 表示「嘗試」，也可以用 shot 來取代。

⑤ **too much**

表示「太多的事情」，too much 表示「過多」，後面可以接不可數名詞，也可以單獨使用做主語或者受詞。

學習英文Fun輕鬆！

1.A broken mirror joined together.
破鏡重圓。

2.Endurance can make a true man, flexible, gentleman.
能忍能讓真君子，能屈能伸大丈夫。

3.Forgive many things in others, nothing in yourself.
寬恕他人之種種，你罪無存。

4.A person who is not tolerant does not deserve other people's tolerance.
不會寬容人的人，是不配得到別人的寬容的。

5.Generous spirit is the greatest of all things.
寬宏精神是一切事物中最偉大的。

婚姻

Unit 39

Proposal 求婚

每個女孩都渴望一次浪漫的求婚。如何策劃一場求婚呢？在著裝、地點選擇和求婚用詞方面都是有講究的。

精選實用會話例句

1 你想成為我的妻子嗎？
Would you want to be my wife? Track 682
同義表達 Will you be my wife?

2 你願意嫁給我嗎？**Will you marry me?** Track 683
重要詞彙 marry [ˈmærɪ] v. 結婚，娶，嫁

3 傑克向琳達求婚了嗎？
Did Jack propose to Linda? Track 684
重要詞彙 marriage [ˈmærɪdʒ] n. 結婚，婚姻

4 有人向海倫求婚了。
Helen has had an offer of marriage. Track 685
片語釋義 offer of marriage 求婚

5 邁克跪著向瑞秋求婚。
Mike proposed to Rachel on bended knee. Track 686
片語釋義 on bent knees 屈膝跪著

6 你願意與我共度餘生嗎？**Would you like to share the rest of your life with me?** Track 687
同義表達 Do you want to grow old with me together?

7 羅伯特五週之後向瑪麗求婚了。
Robert proposed to Mary five weeks later. Track 688
重要片語 propose to sb 向某人求婚

❽ 那個年輕人隨即向我們老師求婚。The young man thereupon asked our teacher to marry him. Track 689

重要詞彙 thereupon [ˏðɛrəˋpɑn] **adv.** 於是，隨即

❾ 莉莉拒絕了好幾次求婚。
Lily has repulsed several offers of marriage. Track 690

重要詞彙 repulse [rɪˈpʌls] **v.** 拒絕

❿ 我姐姐拒絕了他的求婚。
My sister repulsed his offer of marriage. Track 691

同義表達 My sister refused his proposal of marriage.

⓫ 哈威準備向艾米求婚時非常緊張。
Harvey was very tense when he planned to ask for Amy's hand in marriage. Track 692

重要詞彙 tense [tɛns] **adj.** 緊張的 **n.** 時態

⓬ 兩天以來，麗娜一直在認真考慮傑森的求婚。
Lena has pondered Jason's marriage proposal for two days. Track 693

重要詞彙 ponder [ˋpɑndɚ] **v.** 思索，考慮

⓭ 這位女士勉強答應了這樁婚姻。
The lady reluctantly agrees to the marriage. Track 694

片語釋義 agree to 同意

⓮ 我哥哥上週向菲奧娜求婚，她同意了。
My brother proposed marriage last week and Fiona accepted him. Track 695

重要詞彙 propose [prəˋpoz] **v.** 求婚，打算，建議

⓯ 湯姆說服妮娜接受了他的求婚。Tom persuaded Nina to accept his marriage proposal. Track 696

重要片語 persuade sb to do sth 勸某人做某事

⓰ 戀愛沒多久，那人向她求婚了。The man asked her to marry him after a short courtship. Track 697

重要詞彙 courtship [ˋkortʃɪp] **n.** 追求期，戀愛期

⑰ 經過六天的掙扎，我決定嫁給他。
I have made a decision to marry him after struggling with myself for six days. Track 698
片語釋義 make a decision 做決定

⑱ 要是他向我求婚了怎麼辦？
What if he has proposed to me? Track 699
重要片語 What if...? 要是……怎麼辦？

⑲ 幾個月以來，麥克斯一直努力想鼓起勇氣求婚。
Max has been struggling for months to pluck up the courage to pop the question. Track 700
片語釋義 pluck up the courage 鼓起勇氣

⑳ 這位女士總是想像她的男朋友向她求婚。
The lady is always imagining her boyfriend proposing marriage to her. Track 701
重要片語 be always doing sth 總是做某事

看情境學對話

Track 702

	\中譯/
A: You know how I feel about you. I have fallen in love with you ① . I want to share the rest of my life with you ② . So I want to ask you a very important question.	A：你知道我對你的感覺。我已經深深地愛上了你。我想和你共度餘生。因此我想問你一個很重要的問題。
B: Okay. But why are you getting down on one knee?	B：好吧。但是你為什麼要單膝下跪呢？
A: Will you marry me?	A：你願意嫁給我嗎？
B: Is this an offer of marriage?	B：你這是在求婚嗎？

A: Yes. I'm serious. I want you to know that I've made this decision after a lot of thought. I'm convinced that we're made for each other ③ .	A：是的。我是認真的。我想讓你知道，我慎重考慮過了。我們兩人是天生的一對。
B: I know. But I'm not ready for ④	B：我知道，可我還沒有準備好……
A: We can have a lavish wedding, if you accept my proposal. I really love you and want you to be my wife ⑤ .	A：如果你答應我的求婚，我們可以舉行盛大的婚禮。我真的很愛你，想讓你成為我的妻子。
B: You are really nice. You really touched my heart.	B：你人真的很好。你真的很讓我感動。
A: So, will you marry me?	A：那麼，你願意嫁給我嗎？
B: It's not a proper time for marriage. We have only been on three dates!	B：現在還不是結婚的時候。我們只約會了三次！
A: If you don't mind, I want you to think about it for more time.	A：如果可以的話，我希望你再多考慮考慮。
B: I will.	B：我會的。

【程度提升，加分單字】

★**important** [ɪm`pɔrtnt] **adj.** 重要的
★**convince** [kən`vɪns] **v.** 使相信，說服
★**touch** [tʌtʃ] **v.** & **n.** 觸摸，觸碰

對話解析

① **fall in love with sb**

表示「愛上某人」，強調一個人單方面的愛戀。表示「相愛」的是：fall in love with each other。

② **share sth with sb**

表示「和某人分享某物」， with sb 在整個句子中作受詞補語。

③ **each other**

表示「互相」，通常出現在動詞或者介系詞的後面，用作動詞或者介系詞的受詞。

④ **be ready for...**

表示「為……做好準備」，後面常加名詞，強調狀態。get ready 也有「準備」之意，但強調的是動作。

⑤ **want sb to do sth**

表示「想要某人做某事」，強調這件事還沒有完成。

學習英文Fun輕鬆！

1.Marriage is a lottery.
婚姻之事難預測。

2.One man's meat is another man's poison.
甲之蜜糖，乙之砒霜。

3.Every couple is not a pair.
成對未必成雙。

4.Marry too soon, and you'll repent too late.
結婚過急，悔之晚矣。

5.First thrive and then wive.
先立業，後成家。

6.Beauty lies in the eyes of the beholder.
情人眼裡出西施。

婚姻

Unit 40

Wedding

婚禮

每個女孩都渴望一次浪漫的求婚。如何策劃一場求婚呢？在著裝、地點選擇和求婚用詞方面都是有講究的。

精選實用會話例句

❶ 樂隊開始演奏婚禮進行曲。
The band began to play the wedding march. Track 703
重要片語 begin to do sth 開始做某事

❷ 他們的婚禮籌備得怎麼樣了？
How is their wedding plan going? Track 704
同義表達 How are they getting on with their wedding preparation?

❸ 麗娜彷彿聽到了她婚禮的鐘聲。
Lena could hear her wedding bells. Track 705
片語釋義 wedding bells 婚禮鐘聲

❹ 在這個教堂裡將會有一場很棒的婚禮。
There will be a terrific wedding in this church. Track 706
重要詞彙 church [tʃɝtʃ] n. 教堂

❺ 草坪留給瑪麗舉行婚禮用。**The lawn was consigned to them for Mary's wedding.** Track 707
重要詞彙 consign [kənˈsaɪn] v. 委託，用作

❻ 為了籌備婚禮大家都忙得團團轉。
Everyone was busy with the wedding. Track 708
重要片語 be busy with sth 忙於做某事

❼ 那將是一場神聖的婚禮。**It will be a holy wedding.** Track 709
重要詞彙 holy [ˋholɪ] adj. 神聖的，聖潔的

❽ 那對夫婦決定低調舉行他們的婚禮。The couple decided that their wedding should be a very low-key affair. Track 710

重要詞彙 affair [ə`fɛr] n. 事情，事件

❾ 你什麼時候開始籌備婚禮的？
When did you start planning this wedding? Track 711

重要片語 start doing sth 開始做某事

❿ 我的朋友邀請我在她的婚禮上當伴娘。My friend asked me to be the bridesmaid at her wedding. Track 712

重要詞彙 bridesmaid [`braɪdz͵med] n. 伴娘

⓫ 婚禮前夕，瑞秋心情十分緊張。Rachel was very flustered on the eve of her wedding. Track 713

片語釋義 on the eve of 在……的前夕

⓬ 內特將出席他最好朋友的婚禮並當伴郎。
Nate will attend the wedding of his best friend and serve as the best man. Track 714

片語釋義 serve as 擔當，擔任

⓭ 婚禮只是新生活的開始。
A wedding is only the beginning of a new life. Track 715

重要詞彙 wedding [`wɛdɪŋ] n. 婚禮，婚宴

⓮ 史密斯先生將給他心愛的女兒舉辦一場完美的婚禮。
Mr. Smith will hold a perfect wedding for his beloved daughter. Track 716

片語釋義 hold a wedding 舉行婚禮

⓯ 琳達確實希望你能來參加婚禮。
Linda hopes you can come to the wedding. Track 717

同義表達 Linda wishes you'll be able to come to the wedding.

⓰ 這對夫婦一門心思籌備自己的婚禮。The couple has been immersed in planning their nuptials. Track 718

重要詞彙 nuptial [`nʌpʃəl] n. 婚禮 adj. 婚姻的，婚禮的

⓱ 傑森將會錯過這場盛大的婚禮。Jason will miss out on the theatricality of a wedding. Track 719

片語釋義 miss out 遺忘，錯過機會

⑱ 婚禮的準備工作是秘密進行的。Preparations for the wedding were carried out under a cloak of secrecy. Track 720

片語釋義 carry out 執行，進行

⑲ 南西還沒通知我們她的喜宴日期。Nancy hasn't informed us of the date of her wedding banquet. Track 721

重要片語 inform sb of sth 告知某人某事

⑳ 在結婚典禮上，新娘的父親把女兒交給新郎。
The father of the bride gives his daughter to the groom at the wedding ceremony. Track 722

重要詞彙 groom [grum] n. 新郎

㉑ 婚禮是一生中最重要的時刻。A wedding is the most important moment of life. Track 723

重要詞彙 moment [`momənt] n. 瞬間，片刻

看情境學對話

Track 724

	中譯
A: I heard that you are getting married ① . When is the wedding date?	A：我聽說你就要結婚了。婚禮日期是什麼時候？
B: On July the ninth ② . I will invite you to the wedding in due course.	B：在 7 月 9 日。到時候我會邀請你參加。
A: That's wonderful. How is your wedding plan going?	A：那太好了。你們的婚禮籌備得怎麼樣了？
B: I didn't have enough time to prepare for ③ my wedding. So I found a wedding planning company. You know what? They asked me how much ④ money I was going to spend on my wedding.	B：我沒有足夠的時間籌備婚禮，所以找到了一家婚慶公司。你知道嗎？他們首先詢問我打算花多少錢辦婚禮。

A: That is a really embarrassing question. Which wedding do you prefer, the church wedding or the lawn wedding?	A：那真是一個令人尷尬的問題。你更喜歡哪種婚禮，教堂婚禮還是草坪婚禮？
B: The church wedding. The wedding company will bring their own priests, but they're not real priests.	B：教堂婚禮。婚慶公司會帶他們自己的牧師，但他們並不是真正的牧師。
A: It will be a holy wedding. Would you wear some special clothes?	A：那將是一場神聖的婚禮。你會穿特別的衣服嗎？
B: Like a morning suit, you know like in England we have a grey morning suit, top and tails, but mine is black.	B：我穿的是日間禮服，你知道在英國我們一般穿灰色的日間禮服，包括禮帽和燕尾服，可我的禮服是黑色的。
A: That sounds cool. That must be a memorable moment.	A：聽起來很酷。那一定會是值得紀念的時刻。
B: I hope so. ⑤	B：但願是吧。

★**date** [det] **n.** 日期，日子
★**prepare** [prɪˋpɛr] **v.** 準備，預備
★**memorable** [ˋmɛmərəbl] **adj.** 值得紀念的

對話解析

① **get married**

表示「結婚」，強調動作是短暫性的，不能與一段時間連用。be married 表示延續性的動作，可以與一段時間連用。

② **July the ninth**

表示「7 月 9 日」，表示「幾月幾日」通常用月份 + 序數詞。幾月幾日的前面要用介系詞 on。

③ **prepare for...**

表示「為……做準備」，prepare 在此處是一個不及物動詞。

④ **ask**

也可以作及物動詞，後面直接加人或者事物。

⑤ **how much**

在該句中表示「多少」， how much 也可以引導疑問句，後面接不可數名詞。

⑥ **I hope so**

表示「希望如此」，表達一種肯定的希望，其中 so 代表上文所提到的事情。其反義的表達是：I hope not.

學習英文Fun輕鬆！

Wedding

At a wedding, a little boy asked his mother, "Mommy, why does the girl wear white?" She answered, "The bride wears white because this is the happiest day of her life." The boy thought about this and said: "Why is the groom wearing black?"

婚禮

在一場婚禮上，一個小男孩問他的母親：「媽媽，為什麼那女孩穿白衣服？」她回答：「新娘穿白衣服，是因為今天是她一生中最快樂的一天。」這個男孩想了想然後說：「那為什麼新郎穿黑衣服？」

文化小站

由於中西方文化的不同，婚禮在形式、服飾等方面也是不盡相同的。中式婚禮服飾，通常會選擇紅色的服裝，因為紅色在中國象徵喜慶、幸福、吉祥如意。在傳統的中式婚禮上新娘都需要穿紅色的禮服，而且龍鳳圖案的服飾也是必不可少的。西方服飾強調浪漫和純潔，白色在西方象徵著吉利、平安、善意、富貴和童貞。新娘都會選擇白色的婚紗，代表對新郎的忠貞。新郎則會選擇西裝。由於受中西方文化融合的影響，中式婚禮越來越受西方人的歡迎。在中國，婚禮當天新娘很多時候也會穿白色的婚紗。

婚姻

Unit 41

Marriage

婚姻生活

有人說，婚姻是愛情的墳墓。是嗎？當然不對。婚姻是另一種生活的開始，彼此認真經營，婚後也是一種幸福的生活。

精選實用會話例句

1. 他們的婚姻生活怎麼樣？How's their married life? Track 725
   片語釋義 married life 婚姻生活

2. 蒂娜剛剛結婚。Tina is a newlywed. Track 726
   同義表達 Tina just got married.

3. 婚姻是終身大事。
   Marriage is the big event of a lifetime. Track 727
   片語釋義 the big event of a lifetime 終身大事

4. 我們夫妻倆性格相似。
   We two are of a kind. Track 728
   同義表達 Like husband, like wife.

5. 這個女士想要建立家庭。
   The lady wants to start a family. Track 729
   片語釋義 start a family 建立家庭

6. 這對夫婦很般配。The couple is well-matched. Track 730
   重要詞彙 well-matched [`wɛl`mætʃt] adj. 匹配的，和諧的

7. 這個年輕人不懂婚姻生活。
   The young man doesn't know what married life is. Track 731
   同義表達 The young man doesn't understand marriage.

❽ 大衛是個顧家的男人。
Dave is a family-centered man. Track 732
同義表達 David is a family man.

❾ 他們共度了有喜有憂的時光。**They got through the good and bad times together.** Track 733
片語釋義 get through 穿過，共度

❿ 婚姻幸福的條件是信任和尊重。**The conditions of a happy marriage are trust and respect.** Track 734
重要詞彙 condition [kən`dɪʃən] n. 條件，環境，狀況

⓫ 他們過著幸福的生活。
They are leading a happy life. Track 735
片語釋義 a happy life 幸福的生活

⓬ 你如何看待婚姻生活？
How do you like married life? Track 736
同義表達 What do you think of married life?

⓭ 在整個婚姻生活中沒有任何改變。
Nothing has changed in the whole married life. Track 737
重要詞彙 whole [hol] adj. 全部的，所有的

⓮ 結婚以後卡倫成為了家庭主婦。**Karen became a housewife after she got married.** Track 738
重要詞彙 housewife [ˋhaʊswaɪf] n. 家庭主婦

⓯ 瑪麗在婚姻生活中努力做一個完美的妻子。
Mary tried to be a perfect wife in the marriage. Track 739
重要片語 try to do sth 努力做某事

⓰ 我姐姐總是渴望未來的婚姻生活。**My sister is always eager for her married life in future.** Track 740
重要詞彙 future [`fjutʃɚ] n. 未來

⓱ 婚姻並不總是稱心如意的。
Marriage is not always a bed of roses. Track 741
片語釋義 a bed of roses 稱心如意的境遇

⑱ **我爸爸說婚姻是需要經營的。My father says that marriage needs patience and good care.** Track 742

重要詞彙 patience [`peʃəns] **n.** 耐心，耐性

⑲ **麥克斯和瑪麗對他們的婚姻生活很滿意。**
Max and Mary are happy with their marriage. Track 743

重要片語 be happy with sth 對……滿意

⑳ **幸福的婚姻需要我們共同努力。**
Happy marriage life needs the joint efforts. Track 744

片語釋義 joint efforts 共同努力

㉑ **婚姻生活並沒有減少傑克和蘿絲之間的感情。**
Marriage has not dimmed the passion between Jack and Rose. Track 745

重要詞彙 passion [`pæʃən] **n.** 熱情，感情

看情境學對話

Track 746

	\中譯/
A: You mentioned that your wife is Chinese.	A：你說你的妻子是華人。
B: That is correct.	B：沒錯。
A: How long ① have you been married?	A：你們結婚多長時間了？
B: We got married in October of 2000, but it took us three years to get to that stage.	B：我們是在 2000 年 10 月結婚的，不過我們結婚前談了三年的戀愛。
A: Okay, what's it like being in an ② international marriage?	A：跨國婚姻的感覺怎麼樣？

B: I really enjoy it. There are many different challenges because we have different cultures, different backgrounds, and different languages. But that makes it fun.	B：我非常享受。這種婚姻有多種挑戰。我們有不同的文化、不同的背景和不同的語言，但是這讓婚姻更有樂趣。
A: You said that your wife speaks to you in Chinese ③ and you speak to her ④ in English?	A：你說過你妻子和你說中文，而你和她說英語？
B: It's fifty-fifty really.	B：實際上是一半一半。
A: So how did you know each other?	A：那你們是怎麼認識的？
B: Through my friend in China. It's been a long time.	B：透過我在中國的朋友。很長時間了。
A: Is there any difficulty in your marriage?	A：你們的婚姻有沒有什麼困難的事情？
B: I think the hardest ⑤ thing is that one of us is always away from the family.	B：我覺得最困難的事情就是其中一個人會一直遠離家人。
A: That's really tough.	A：那確實很難。
B: And this problem seems very permanent to me.	B：而對我來說這是一個永遠存在的問題。

★**stage** [stedʒ] **n.** 階段，舞臺
★**challenge** [`tʃælɪndʒ] **n.** 挑戰
★**background** [ˈbækgraʊnd] **n.** 背景

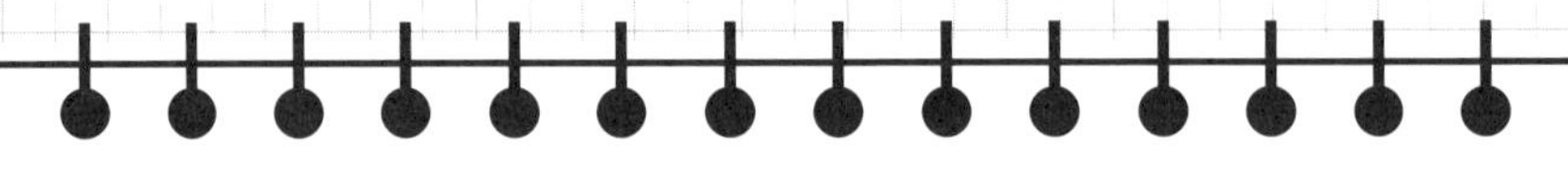

對話解析

① **how long**

可以表示「多長時間」，主要用於對一段時間的提問。how long 還可以用於提問某東西有多長。

② **an**

是一個不定冠詞，表示泛指，常常用於首字母發音是母音的單字前面；a 也是一個不定冠詞，用於首字母發音是子音的單字前面。

③ **in Chinese**

表示「用中文」，in 是一個介系詞，用法有多種，in + 語言表示「用某種語言」，如：in English（用英語）。

④ **speak to sb**

表示「同某人講話」，強調說話。talk to sb 表示「找某人談話」，強調交談。

⑤ **hardest**

是形容詞 hard 的最高級，最高級的前面一定要加 the。

學習英文Fun輕鬆！

1. Marriage is the tomb of love.
   婚姻是愛情的墳墓。
2. Marriage is a lottery.
   婚姻是一樁難於預測的事。
3. Love is an ideal thing, marriage a real thing.
   愛情是理想的事情，婚姻是現實的事情。
4. To marry is to halve your rights and double your duties.
   結婚是權利減半，責任加倍。
5. Marriage is not a ritual or an end.
   婚姻並不是一項儀式，也不是結束。
6. Marriage comes by destiny.
   姻緣命中定。
7. Life is a flower of which love is the honey.
   生活是花，愛情如蜜。

婚姻

Unit 42

Anniversary

結婚紀念

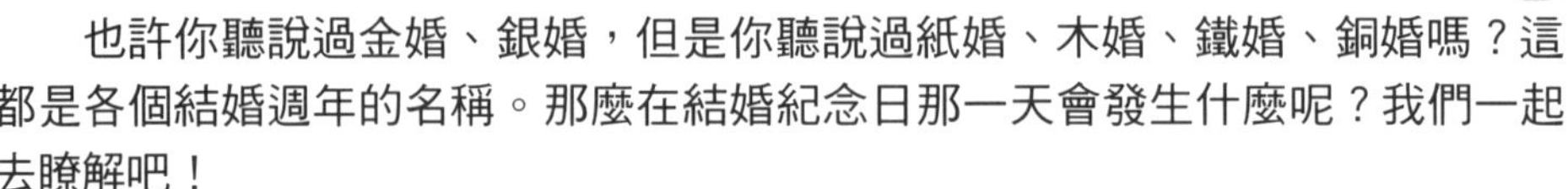

也許你聽說過金婚、銀婚，但是你聽說過紙婚、木婚、鐵婚、銅婚嗎？這都是各個結婚週年的名稱。那麼在結婚紀念日那一天會發生什麼呢？我們一起去瞭解吧！

精選實用會話例句

1 你們的結婚紀念日是什麼時候？
When is your wedding anniversary? Track 747
片語釋義 wedding anniversary 結婚紀念日

2 他們將在七月慶祝他們的金婚。**They will celebrate their golden wedding in July.** Track 748

3 下個月是他們結婚五週年紀念。
Next month is their fifth wedding anniversary. Track 749
片語釋義 in July 在七月

4 我們即將慶祝我們結婚10週年。
We are celebrating our 10 years of marriage. Track 750
同義表達 We are about to celebrate the tenth anniversary of our marriage.

5 我們剛剛慶祝了結婚十週年紀念日。**We have just celebrated the tenth wedding anniversary.** Track 751
重要詞彙 anniversary [ˌænə`vɝsərɪ] **n.** 週年紀念日

6 很榮幸邀請你來參加我們的結婚紀念。**It's my great honor to invite you to our wedding anniversary.** Track 752
重要詞彙 honor [`ɑnɚ] **n.** 尊敬，榮幸

7 下個月是他們結婚五週年紀念。
Next month is their fifth wedding anniversary. Track 753
片語釋義 fifth wedding anniversary 五週年紀念

❽ 你想透過旅遊來慶祝我們的結婚紀念日嗎？Would you like to celebrate our wedding anniversary by travelling? Track 754

重要片語 would like to do sth 想做某事

❾ 我能帶個朋友來參加你父母的結婚紀念日嗎？Could I bring a friend to your parents' wedding anniversary? Track 755

同義表達 Can I take a friend to your parents' wedding anniversary?

❿ 所有人都站起來，一起為他們的金婚紀念日喝彩。
All people rose to their feet, applauding for their golden wedding anniversary. Track 756

重要片語 rise to one's feet 站起來

⓫ 這對夫妻每年都到馬爾代夫旅行以慶祝他們的結婚週年紀念日。The couple travel to Maldives annually for their wedding anniversary. Track 757

片語釋義 travel to 去旅行

⓬ 你可以來參加他們的結婚週年慶典嗎？Would you do him the favor of attending their wedding anniversary? Track 758

重要詞彙 attend [əˋtɛnd] v. 出席，參加

⓭ 我丈夫在我們結婚十週年紀念日那天給我買了一輛車。
My husband bought me a car on our tenth wedding anniversary. Track 759

重要片語 buy sb sth 給某人買某物

⓮ 結婚週年紀念日是個慶祝愛和信任的時候。The wedding anniversary is a time to celebrate love and trust. Track 760

重要詞彙 celebrate [ˋsɛlə͵bret] v. 慶祝

⓯ 由於工作壓力，她完全忘了結婚紀念日的事了。
Due to the pressure from work, their wedding anniversary completely slipped her mind. Track 761

重要片語 slip one's mind 忘記，忽略，忘掉

⓰ 全家必須團聚，以慶祝父母的20週年結婚紀念日。
The family must come together for the parents' 20-year wedding anniversary. Track 762

片語釋義 come together 聚在一起

⑰ 尼克在結婚20週年紀念日那天給他的妻子買了一枚鑽戒。
Nick bought his wife a diamond ring on the twentieth wedding anniversary. Track 763

重要詞彙 diamond [ˋdaɪəmənd] **n.** 鑽石 **adj.** 鑽石的

⑱ 你願意來參加我父母的金婚紀念嗎？**Would you like to attend my parents' golden wedding anniversary?** Track 764

片語釋義 golden wedding anniversary 金婚紀念

⑲ 馬克送給安娜一枚鑽石胸針，來慶祝他們的金婚紀念日。
Mark sent Anna a diamond brooch to celebrate their golden wedding anniversary. Track 765

重要詞彙 brooch [brotʃ] **n.** 胸針

⑳ 金婚紀念總能勾起人們的懷舊和回憶。
Golden wedding anniversary is always an occasion for nostalgia and reminiscing. Track 766

重要詞彙 nostalgia [nɑsˋtældʒɪə] **n.** 懷舊，對往事的懷戀，鄉愁

㉑ 銀婚紀念總能勾起人們的懷舊和回憶。
The silvery wedding anniversaries are always occasions for nostalgia and reminiscing. Track 767

片語釋義 silvery wedding anniversary 銀婚紀念

看情境學對話

Track 768

	中譯
A: Why did you prepare a candlelight dinner? Is there anything special to celebrate?	A：你為什麼準備了燭光晚餐？有什麼特別的事情要慶祝嗎？
B: You won't forget what day it is, will you? ①	B：你不會忘記今天是什麼日子了吧？
A: Of course I remember. It was on this very day last year that we tied the knot ②.	A：我當然記得。就在去年的今天我們結為夫婦。

B: To tell you the truth ③, I'm very impressed that you remember. I thought for sure you would forget.	B：說實話，你還記得，我很感動。我還以為你肯定忘了呢。
A: How could I forget such an important day ④ ? This is our wedding anniversary. Look at that case over there.	A：我怎麼會忘記這麼重要的一天呢？這是我們的結婚紀念日。看看那邊的那個盒子。
B: What's in it?	B：裡面是什麼？
A: Please open it.	A：打開看看。
B: Oh, my god. A diamond ring. It looks very beautiful. You're so nice to me. I really like it very much. But it must be ⑤ expensive.	B：噢，天啊。是鑽戒。看起來真的很漂亮。你對我真是太好了。我真的非常喜歡它。但是這一定很貴吧。
A: Don't worry about the price. I just want you to be happy. You are more beautiful than this diamond ring.	A：不要擔心價格。我只想讓你開心。你比這個鑽戒更好看。
B: I don't know what's going on, but I love you more now than the day we got married. Thank you very much.	B：我不知道怎麼回事，但是我比結婚那個時候更愛你了。謝謝你。
A: Happy anniversary! I love you.	A：結婚紀念日快樂！我愛你。
B: Happy anniversary!	B：結婚紀念日快樂！

【程度提升，加分單字】

★**candlelight** [ˋkændllaɪt] **n.** 燭光

★**impress** [ɪmˋprɛs] **v.** 給……深刻印象

★**expensive** [ɪkˋspɛnsɪv] **adj.** 昂貴的

① **will you?**

該句是一個反義疑問句，表示懷疑對方忘記了什麼事而詢問對方。反義疑問句是由兩部分構成，前部分是陳述句，後部分是疑問句。

② **tie the knot**

字面意思是「打結」，引申為「永結同心」，在該句中表示「結婚」之意，是一個既通俗又地道的表達。

③ **to tell you the truth**

是一個固定搭配，表示「說實話」，類似的表達還有：to be honest，actually。

④ **such**

表示「如此的」，其用法是：such + a / an + 形容詞 + 可數名詞，such + 形容詞 + 不可數名詞。

⑤ **must be**

在此處是一個肯定的推測，表示「一定……」，表示否定的推測時，要用： can't be。

學習英文Fun輕鬆！

Wedding Anniversary

A couple went out to dinner to celebrate their 50th wedding anniversary. On her way home, she noticed the tears in his eyes and asked him if he was wistful about the good time they had celebrated together. "No," he replied. "I was thinking about the time before we got married. Your father threatened me with a gun and said that if I didn't marry you, he would send me to prison for fifty years."

結婚週年

一對夫婦出去吃飯慶祝他們的五十週年結婚紀念日。在回家的路上，她注意到他的眼裡含著淚水，於是問他是否在感傷他們慶祝五十年在一起的美好時光。他回答說：「不，我在想我們結婚前的時光。你的爸爸用槍威脅我，說如果我不娶你，他會把我送進監獄蹲五十年。」

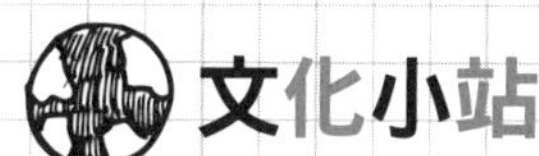

文化小站

所謂結婚紀念日，就是婚後紀念結婚的日子。在華人文化，人們普遍重視金婚和銀婚。所謂金婚就是結婚50週年，所謂銀婚就是結婚25週年。金婚銀婚都會很隆重地慶祝，一般會邀請親朋好友參加宴會。現在，一些年輕人也比較喜歡過結婚週年。西方一些國家，比如美國，很重視結婚紀念日。每到結婚紀念日，都會舉行結婚週年會。50年——金婚；60年——鑽石婚；70年——白金婚；75年——金剛石婚，不同的物品命名的結婚紀念日代表了不同的婚齡，也代表了不同的可貴性。

婚姻

Unit 43

Education
教育孩子

望子成龍，望女成鳳。這是每個家長的心願。孩子是國家的花朵，也是每個家庭的希望。但是教育孩子卻非一件簡單事。

精選實用會話例句

1 必須教育孩子們遵守法律。
Children must be educated in obeying the law. Track 769
重要詞彙 obey [ə`be] v. 服從，遵守

2 父母應該教育孩子不要和陌生人說話。**Parents should teach their children not to talk to strangers.** Track 770
重要片語 teach sb not to do sth 教某人不要做某事

3 孩子們應該尊敬自己的父母。**Children should show respect towards their parents.** Track 771
片語釋義 show respect toward 對……表示尊重

4 我們的首要任務是教育孩子。
Our primary aim is to educate our children. Track 772
片語釋義 primary aim 首要任務

5 傑森一直在自己教育孩子。
Jason has been schooling his kids himself. Track 773
同義表達 Jason has been teaching his children by himself.

6 教育孩子要尊敬父母和老師。**Children must be educated to respect their parents and teachers.** Track 774
重要詞彙 respect [rɪ`spɛkt] v. & n. 尊敬，尊重

7 孩子應該遵守學校的紀律。**Children should comply with school disciplines at school.** Track 775
片語釋義 comply with 服從，遵守

❽ 我們應該教育孩子要當心車輛。**We should teach our children to be careful of traffic.** Track 776

片語釋義 be careful 注意，小心

❾ 我們應該教育孩子不要玩火。**We should teach our children not to play with the fire.** Track 777

片語釋義 play with the fire 玩火

❿ 教育孩子對我國的未來至關重要。**Educating children is essential to the future of our country.** Track 778

同義表達 Educating children is important for the future of our country.

⓫ 這對夫婦教育他們的孩子長大以後為國家服務。**The couple teach their children to serve their country when they grow up.** Track 779

片語釋義 grow up 長大

⓬ 教育孩子注意個人衛生。**Children must be educated to pay attention to their personal hygiene.** Track 780

重要詞彙 hygiene [`haɪdʒin] n. 衛生

⓭ 教育孩子要尊敬長者。**Children are taught to show honor to the elders.** Track 781

重要片語 show honor to sb 對某人表示尊敬

⓮ 父母應確保子女接受良好的教育。**Parents should ensure that their children have a good schooling.** Track 782

重要詞彙 schooling [`skulɪŋ] n. 學校教育

⓯ 這個男孩被教育不要在人前說髒話。**The boy is educated not to swear in front of people.** Track 783

片語釋義 in front of 在……前面

⓰ 父母應教育孩子舉止得體。**Parents should teach children to behave acceptably.** Track 784

重要詞彙 behave [bɪ`hev] v. 表現，舉止

⓱ 父母在教育孩子方面有著重要的作用。**Parents play an important role in educating their children.** Track 785

重要片語 play an important role in... 在……中起重要作用

⑱ 你最好為教育孩子做好準備。**You had better make good preparation for children's education.** Track 786

重要詞彙 preparation [ˌprepəˈreɪʃn] **n.** 準備

⑲ 父母會認真教育孩子。**Parents are conscientious about rearing their children.** Track 787

同義表達 Parents will seriously educate their children

⑳ 我不知道怎麼在教育我兒子的同時又能保持他的天真。
I don't know how to teach my son while letting him be a kid. Track 788

同義表達 I don't know how to educate my son while preserving his nature.

看情境學對話

Track 789

	中譯
A: I can't control my temper when my kids don't behave very well. Could you share some tips with me ① about educating kids?	A：孩子們表現不好的時候，我無法控制自己的脾氣。你能和我分享一些關於教育孩子的方法嗎？
B: Children education is a tough work. You need more patience and understanding.	B：教育孩子可是一件苦差事。你需要更多的耐心和理解。
A: You know, sometimes when we eat, if it is something my son doesn't like, he would spit it out and throw it into other dishes. I can't help spanking ② him sometimes.	A：你知道，有時候我們吃飯，如果是我兒子不喜歡吃的，他就會吐出來，扔到其他菜裡。有時候我忍不住打他的屁股。

B: But you can't change a child's behavior by using force. You have to be patient with ③ him and teach him.	B：但是武力不能改變一個小孩的行為。你得耐心教他。
A: I know, but it's hard. Our public schools here are not very good and private schools are too expensive ④ .	A：我知道，但是很難。我們這裡的公立學校不是很好，私立學校又很貴。
B: I have been reading up on home schooling and it has a lot of ⑤ advantages.	B：我讀了有關家庭教育的書，發現有很多的好處。
A: Like what?	A：比如什麼？
B: We can home school our children. We can teach them everything they learn in school in a more relaxed and fun way. I think that having a one-on-one class is much better since we can focus more on our kids' strengths or weaknesses.	B：我們可以在家教育孩子。能夠用一種更加輕鬆和好玩的方式教他們在學校裡學到的一切。我覺得一對一的教學方式可以有針對性地發現我們孩子的優缺點。
A: But we would be isolating our children from social interaction in that way.	A：這麼做的話會讓我們的孩子很孤立，不會社交。
B: I still need consider gravely to make this decision.	B：我還需要認真考慮才能做出這個決定。

★**temper** [ˋtɛmpɚ] **n.** 性情，脾氣

★**public** [ˋpʌblɪk] **adj.** 公眾的，公共的

★**interaction** [͵ɪntəˋrækʃən] **n.** 互動

① **share sth with sb**

表示「與某人分享某物」，此處的with sb 作受詞補語。表示「兩者之間分享某物」也可以用 share sth between sb。

② **can't help doing sth**

表示「情不自禁做某事」，而 can't help to do sth 表示「不能幫助做某事」。

③ **be patient with...**

表示「對……有耐心」， be patient of... 表示「對……容忍」。前者強調耐心，後者強調容忍。

④ **too expensive**

表示「太貴了」，too 修飾形容詞，要放在形容詞的前面。語氣上有點否定的意思。

⑤ **a lot of**

表示「許多」，等於 lots of，在句中可以修飾可數名詞，也可以修飾不可數名詞。類似的表達還有：a number of, a great deal of。

學習英文Fun輕鬆！

1. Instruction knows no class distinction.
   有教無類。
2. It's never too old to learn.
   活到老，學到老。
3. Birth is much, but breeding is more.
   出身誠有力，教養功更高。
4. Education has for its object the formation of character.
   教育的目的在於品德的培育。
5. Teaching others teaches yourself.
   教學相長。
6. Education begins a gentleman, conversation completes him.
   君子開始形成於教育，而完成於交際。

文化小站

教育是一門學問，也是一門藝術。廣義來講，教育包括家庭教育、學校教育以及社會大環境的教育。東方家庭教育的差異還是比較大的。在東方，孩子常常和大人是一體的，孩子的成績常常與父母的臉面聯繫在一起。家長對孩子的要求，在某種程度上是家長的需求。而在西方教育觀念中，孩子是獨立的個體，有獨立的需求。在教育孩子方面，最主要的還是在學校接受的正規教育。說到 school education，東西方的差異也是很大的。東方的 education model 多以訓導式為主，以教師為教育主體，上課方式多是灌輸式，這與我們數千年的文化傳承有千絲萬縷的關係；而西方多是嘗試教育，以學生為教育主體，師生關係是平等的，上課方式也比較自由，多是討論式、自主式。如果學生提出一個問題，而老師答不上來，東方老師很可能受「師道尊嚴」的影響，不肯承認自己不會，只好避重就輕蒙混過去；同樣的情況發生在西方，老師就可能會承認自己不會，解釋說「God is not almighty, either.」並引導學生一起討論，這樣就真正做到了「教學相長」。值得慶幸的是，華人的教育工作者也在學習西方，去其糟粕，取其精華，打造真正適合當下華人學生的教育。

婚姻

Unit 44

Divorce 離婚

世界上沒有任何東西可以永恆。正如婚姻，有的可以白頭偕老，有的卻不能一直走到最後，於是選擇了離婚。那麼如何委婉地提出離婚呢？

精選實用會話例句

❶ 這個女士離婚有充分的理由。
The lady had adequate grounds for her divorce. Track 790
重要詞彙 adequate [`ædəkwɪt] adj. 足夠的，適當的

❷ 琳達提出了離婚申請。
Linda filed a petition for divorce. Track 791
片語釋義 file for 申請

❸ 我們離婚吧。**Let's get divorced.** Track 792
重要詞彙 divorce [də`vors] n. & v. 離婚

❹ 這個家庭的所有人最後都離婚了。
All of marriages in this family ended in divorce. Track 793
重要詞彙 family [`fæməlɪ] n. 家庭

❺ 最近有關離婚的電視劇太多了。**There have been so many TV dramas about divorce recently.** Track 794
重要詞彙 recently [`risntlɪ] adv. 最近，近來

❻ 麗娜的第一次婚姻維持了三年。
Lena's first marriage ended after three years. Track 795
同義表達 Lina's first marriage lasted three years.

❼ 金錢上的問題讓他們離婚了。**It was the money trouble that made them break a marriage.** Track 796
重要片語 make sb do sth 讓某人做某事

8 他們的父母結婚二十週年了，現在正在鬧離婚。After twenty years of marriage, their parents are divorcing. Track 797

重要詞彙 parent [`pɛrənt] n. 父親或者母親，先輩

9 法官簽了離婚法令。
The judge signed the divorce decree. Track 798

片語釋義 divorce decree 離婚法令

10 這對新婚夫婦前天離婚了。The new couple divorced the day before yesterday. Track 799

片語釋義 the day before yesterday 前天

11 這首歌是他離婚時寫給妻子的。The song was written to his wife when they divorced. Track 800

重要片語 write to sb 寫給某人……

12 他們應該到婚姻登記處申請離婚。They should file for divorce at the marriage registration office. Track 801

片語釋義 the marriage registration office 婚姻登記處

13 這個男的上個月和他的妻子離婚了。The man got a divorce from his wife last month. Track 802

片語釋義 last month 上個月

14 湯姆的婚姻以離婚收場。
Tom's marriage ended in divorce. Track 803

片語釋義 end in 以……而告終

15 他們婚姻破裂不是他的錯。It is not his fault for the breakdown of their marriage. Track 804

重要詞彙 breakdown [`brek͵daʊn] n. 分解，損壞

16 離了五次婚以後，她開始認為自己不適合結婚。
After five divorces the lady started to think the marriage didn't suit her. Track 805

重要片語 start to do sth 開始做某事

17 他們在離婚後經歷了一段痛苦的時期。They went through a difficult period after the divorce. Track 806

片語釋義 difficult period 痛苦的時期

⑱ 在經歷了十年的婚姻後，這對夫婦突然決定終止婚姻關係。**The couple suddenly decided to call it quits after ten years of marriage.** Track 807

重要片語 decide to do sth 決定做某事

⑲ 大家都知道他們的婚姻破裂了。**Everyone knows that their marriage has broken down.** Track 808

片語釋義 break down 失敗，損壞

⑳ 離婚後，孩子們歸麥克斯照顧。**Max was given custody of the children after his divorce.** Track 809

重要詞彙 custody [ˈkʌstədɪ] n. 監管，撫養權

㉑ 他們中的多數人來自婚姻破裂的家庭。**Most of them are from broken families.** Track 810

同義表達 Most of them come from broken families.

看情境學對話

Track 811

	中譯
A: Hello. I haven't seen you for a long time. I am really happy to meet you here.	A：你好！好久沒見你了。很高興在這兒遇見你。
B: I am happy, too. Have you heard? Jerry is going to divorce his wife. I am sorry to tell ① you about that.	B：我也很高興。你聽說了嗎？傑瑞要和他的妻子離婚了。很抱歉告訴你這些。
A: Really? I can't believe that. I'm so surprised. Why did they decide to end ② their marriage suddenly?	A：真的嗎？我簡直不敢相信。我很驚訝。為什麼他們突然決定要離婚呢？
B: I heard that they didn't get along well with ③ each other and fought a lot ④ .	B：我聽說他們倆合不來，還經常吵架。

A: That's not what I know. I thought that they were happy together.	A：我知道的不是這樣。我還以為他們在一起很幸福呢。
B: That isn't true. To tell you the truth, Jerry told me that they had been separated for half a year.	B：並不是那樣。事實上，傑瑞告訴我他們已經分居半年了。
A: I still can't believe it. But if they both determined to divorce, I hope they will have an amicable split.	A：我還是不相信。但是如果他們雙方都決心要離婚，我希望他們能夠好聚好散。
B: I will tell Jerry what you said.	B：我會把你說的話轉告給傑瑞的。
A: What about the children?	A：小孩怎麼辦？
B: Jerry was given custody of the children after his divorce.	B：離婚後，孩子們歸傑瑞照顧。
A: Their marriage is really a mistake.	A：他們的婚姻真是一個錯誤。
B: What a pity! ⑤	B：真遺憾啊！

【程度提升，加分單字】

★**surprise** [sɚˋpraɪz] **v.** 使驚奇 **n.** 驚奇
★**suddenly** [ˋsʌdənlɪ] **adv.** 意外地
★**separate** [ˋsɛpəˏret] **v.** 分開，分離
★**determine** [dɪˋtɝmɪn] **v.** 下決心，決定

① **I am sorry to tell...**

表示「我很抱歉告訴……」，該結構中的動詞不定式是表示原因的，也可以改寫成 I am sorry telling...

② **decide to do sth**

表示「決定做某事」，是一個固定的用法。類似的表達還有：make a decision to do sth，make up one's mind to do sth。

③ **get along well with**

表示「與……相處融洽」，get along well with 後邊一般加人，表示一種友好的人際關係。

④ **a lot**

表示「非常多」，常常出現在句末，用來修飾動詞，比如：Thanks a lot.

⑤ **What a pity!**

表示「多遺憾啊！」是一個省略的形式，其完整的形式就是：What a pity it is! 用來表達說話者的同情與安慰。

Chapter 4

休閒娛樂

Part 1 慶祝節日

Part 2 放鬆心情

Part 3 美容美髮

慶祝節日

Unit 45

New Year

新年

新年，嶄新的開始。新年，對於每個人來說都代表著新的希望。所以在這裡祝大家在新的一年都能展示新的面貌，新年新氣象。而學生呢，要學習進步，健健康康，上班族更是要事業有成。

精選實用會話例句

❶ 你今晚會放鞭炮嗎？
Will you let off firecrackers this evening? Track 812
片語釋義 let off 引發，引爆，讓……下車

❷ 我希望你度過一個很棒的春節。
I hope you have a great New Year. Track 813
同義表達 Wish you have a wonderful New Year.

❸ 新年快樂！**Happy New Year (to you)!** Track 814
片語釋義 New Year 新年

❹ 希望你在新的一年裡取得更大的成就。**May you achieve greater success in the coming new year.** Track 815
重要詞彙 achieve [ə`tʃiv] v. 實現，取得，獲得

❺ 你新年都做些什麼？
What do you do on new year's day? Track 816
同義表達 How do you spend new year's day?

❻ 你們是如何慶祝新年的？
How do you celebrate the new year's day? Track 817
重要詞彙 celebrate [`sɛlə͵bret] v. 慶祝，祝賀

❼ 你們什麼時候慶祝新年？
What time do you celebrate the new year? Track 818
片語釋義 what time 幾點，幾時

⑧ 新年就要到了。A brand new year is approaching. Track 819

同義表達 The new year's day is drawing near.

⑨ 新的一年意味著新的開始。A new year means a new start. Track 820

重要詞彙 mean [min] v. 意思是，意味

⑩ 新年你有什麼打算？
What's new for the New Year in your plan? Track 821

同義表達 Have you made your new year's plans?

⑪ 你應該和我們全家一起慶祝新年。You should join our family to celebrate the new year. Track 822

重要詞彙 join [dʒɔɪn] v. 加入，參加

⑫ 恭喜發財！May you come into a good fortune! Track 823

片語釋義 good fortune 福氣，幸事

⑬ 我們新年不能在一起度過真是太遺憾了。It's really a shame we can't celebrate the New Year's Day together. Track 824

重要詞彙 shame [ʃem] n. 遺憾，可惜，羞恥

⑭ 提前祝你新年快樂。
Happy New Year to you ahead of time. Track 825

片語釋義 ahead of time 提前

⑮ 請接受我誠摯的問候。
Please accept my sincere greetings. Track 826

重要詞彙 sincere [sɪn`sɪr] adj. 真摯的，誠摯的

⑯ 希望快樂幸福永遠伴隨你左右。May the joy and happiness surround you forever. Track 827

同義表達 May joy and happiness follow you wherever you go!

⑰ 今年春節去旅遊怎麼樣？
How about going on a trip this Spring Festival? Track 828

片語釋義 go on a trip 旅行

⑱ 她回家和父母一起過年了。
She has gone back to her home to celebrate the Spring Festival with her parents. Track 829

片語釋義 go back to 回去，歸

⑲ 春節是中國一個很重要的節日。

Spring Festival is a major holiday in China. Track 830

重要詞彙 major [ˋmedʒɚ] **adj.** 主要的，重要的

⑳ 我們都知道現在過年的一些習俗都已經變了。

We all know that some customs of the Spring Festival are changing now. Track 831

重要詞彙 custom [ˈkʌstəm] **n.** 風俗，慣例，風俗

㉑ 鐘聲迎來了新的一年。**The bells ushered in the New Year.** Track 832

片語釋義 usher in 迎接，開創

看情境學對話

\中譯/ Track 833

	中譯
A: Steven, time flies ① . A new year starts again. What are your resolutions for the New Year?	A：史蒂芬，光陰似箭。新的一年又開始了。你新年的決心是什麼？
B: Well, I have plenty. But my top priority ② is to get the scholarship for this semester.	B：我有很多，但我的首要任務是獲得這個學期的獎學金。
A: You're right. As college students, this not only means that our scores are improved, but also that we can ease the burden. ③	A：沒錯。作為一名大學生，這不僅意味著我們的分數提高，還表示我們能減輕一些負擔。
B: That's right. By the way, how did you spend your New year?	B：是的。對了，你是如何度過新年的？
A: As usual, I went back to my hometown to spend it with my parents. My father bought a lot of fireworks and my mother made many dumplings.	A：和往常一樣，我回到家鄉和我的父母一起過了新年。我爸爸買了很多煙火，我媽媽包了很多水餃。

B: How happy you are! Can I spend the New year with your family next year? I'd like to see how you spend your most important festival.	B：真幸福。明年我能和你的家人一起過新年嗎？我想看看你們如何度過這麼重要的節日。
A: Sure. My parents will be very pleased with your coming.	A：當然可以。你來了，我的父母一定會很高興的。
B: I like Chinese culture and want to know more about the customs of Chinese New year.	B：我喜歡中華文化，也想瞭解關於新年的風俗習慣。
A: Well, I'm sure you'll fall in love with ④ it. And if you're in my family next year, you will get red envelopes from my parents.	A：好啊，我相信你一定會深深愛上的。而且，如果你明年在我家過年的話，我父母還會給你發紅包呢。
B: Great. I know the money given to me is for good wishes.	B：太棒了。我知道那代表著美好的祝福。
A: So clever you are! I hope you will achieve good results in the new year.	A：聰明。在新的一年裡，希望你能獲得好成績。
B: So do you. ⑤ But what I hope most is that I have the opportunity to paste Spring Festival couplets.	B：你也是。不過我最希望的是能有機會體驗一下貼春聯。
A: No problem.	A：沒問題。

【程度提升，加分單字】

★**resolution** [ˌrɛzəˋluʃən] n. 決心

★**priority** [praɪˈɒrətɪ] n. 優先，優先考慮的事

★**semester** [səˋmɛstɚ] n. 學期

★**burden** [ˋbɝdn] n. 負擔

★**hometown** [ˋhomˋtaʊn] n. 家鄉，故鄉

① **time flies**

意為「時光飛逝，時間過得真快」，是一個比較特殊的感歎句，應是How (fast) time flies，但在口語中常用time flies 和 how time flies 來表示。

② **top priority**

意為「最優先考慮的事」，與其相近的片語有 give priority to，意為「優先考慮」。

③ **ease the burden**

意為「減輕負擔」，可直接作為片語使用，也可以在 burden 前加上形容詞來表示「減輕……的負擔」，如：financial burden（經濟負擔）， environmental burden （環境負擔）。

④ **fall in love with**

意為「愛上，傾心於」，強調愛上某人或某物，用fall in love 來強調「愛上」的動作。

⑤ **so do you**

意為「你也是，你也一樣」，so + 助動詞 + 主語，構成倒裝句，若是 so + 主語 + 助動詞，則表示「確實」。富生活知識的基礎。

學習英文Fun輕鬆！

1. As the new year begins, let us also start anew.
   一元復始，萬象更新。
2. May you always get more than you wish for.
   年年有餘。
3. Hope everything goes your way.
   萬事如意。
4. I wish you good fortune and every success.
   大吉大利。
5. May you succeed in whatever you try.
   心想事成／馬到成功。

由於文化和習俗的不同，中西方對新年的定義和理解有所不同。在東方，元旦是新的一年的開始，人們會在元旦這一天辭舊迎新，為親朋好友在新的一年裡送上最好的祝福：身體健康，萬事如意等。但在西方人眼中，耶誕節才是他們最大的節日，不過新年也有著不可替代的作用。他們會選擇在除夕夜用各種活動慶祝新年的到來，最受歡迎的當屬化妝舞會，他們的打扮稀奇古怪，用舞會帶來喜氣洋洋的氛圍，高高興興地度過一年的最後一個夜晚。在英國，午夜 12 點鐘聲響起的時候，人們還會手拉著手唱蘇格蘭民歌《友誼地久天長》。在中國，春節才是真正意義上的新年。人們迎接新年的活動很是豐富，大都是從古代繼承下來的風俗習慣。例如：貼春聯，放鞭炮，敲鑼打鼓等。人們還會在一年的最後一個夜晚也就是除夕夜，看春節聯歡晚會以及陪家人守歲。當然，發紅包也是必不可少的活動，人們通常是在大年初一的早上發紅包，以求健健康康，大吉大利。而且在某些地區，大年初一的早上晚輩要向長輩拜年，鄰里之間也會相互拜年，送出美好的祝願。

慶祝節日

Unit 46

Valentine's Day

情人節

在情人節這一天，成雙成對的情侶們會抱著鮮花現身街頭，單身者們則會感到孤獨。不過這也給足了他們告白的馬力——下個情人節不單身！

精選實用會話例句

1 情人節快樂。**Happy Valentine's Day.** Track 834

片語釋義 Valentine's Day 情人節

2 作我的情人吧。**Be my valentine.** Track 835

重要詞彙 valentine [ˋvæləntaɪn] n. 情人，心愛的人

3 你應該在情人節這天為你女朋友製造一點浪漫的氣氛。**You ought to create a romantic mood for your girlfriend on Valentine's Day.** Track 836

重要詞彙 romantic [rəˋmæntɪk] adj. 浪漫的，浪漫主義的

4 你應該做一些浪漫的事。**You are supposed to do something romantic.** Track 837

重要片語 be supposed to do 應該做某事

5 我每次都是被迫買花和巧克力給我女朋友。**Every time I was forced to buy flowers and chocolate for my girlfriend.** Track 838

重要片語 be forced to 被迫做某事，迫不得已

6 我會一直愛你的。**I love you all the time.** Track 839

同義表達 I love you forever.

7 你昨天收到情人節卡片了嗎？**Did you get the Valentines cards yesterday?** Track 840

片語釋義 valentines cards 情人節卡片

❽ 你情人節怎麼過的？
How did you spend this Valentine's Day? Track 841
同義表達 What did you do on Valentine's Day?

❾ 我沒有勇氣表白。I have no courage to confess. Track 842
重要片語 have no courage to do sth 沒有勇氣做某事

❿ 你應該向她表白。
You should confess your love for her. Track 843
重要詞彙 confess [kən`fɛs] v. 坦白，承認

⓫ 我深深地愛著你。I'm deeply in love with you. Track 844
重要片語 be in love with 迷戀，愛戀

⓬ 他的確約我出去吃飯，但我拒絕了。
He did call me to eat out, but I refused. Track 845
同義表達 He invited me to dine out last night, but I turned it down.

⓭ 能認識你我很幸福。I'm happy to have known you. Track 846
重要片語 be happy to do sth 很高興做某事，樂意做某事

⓮ 你是我的一切。You're everything to me. Track 847
同義表達 You are the whole of me!

⓯ 我可以約你出去吃飯嗎？May I ask you to eat out? Track 848
片語釋義 eat out 在外吃飯，默默忍受痛苦

⓰ 你送了或收到什麼禮物嗎？
Did you give or get any presents? Track 849
重要詞彙 give [gɪv] v. 給予，贈送

⓱ 這盒糖果是給你的。This box of candy is for you. Track 850
片語釋義 a box of 一盒

⓲ 這束花送給你。Here's a bunch of flowers for you. Track 851
片語釋義 a bunch of flowers 一束花，花束

⓳ 今天有很多男孩送我玫瑰花。
Many boys send roses to me today. Track 852
同義表達 There are so many boys sending me roses today.

⑳ 如何在情人節這天打動你愛的人呢？How to impress your loved one on Valentine's Day? Track 853

重要詞彙 impress [ɪm`prɛs] v. 給……深刻印象

㉑ 我已經喜歡你很久了。
It's been a long time since I fell in love with you. Track 854

片語釋義 long time 長時間，好久

㉒ 原來送我那張情人節卡片的人是你！
It was you who sent me that Valentine's card! Track 855

重要片語 send sb sth 送給某人某物

看情境學對話

Track 856

	中譯
A: Hi, Johnson. You got a minute? ①	A：嗨，強森。你現在有空嗎？
B: Yes, what's up?	B：有的。怎麼了？
A: I want to ask you something.	A：我想問你一件事。
B: What? Ask away. ②	B：什麼？問吧。
A: Valentine's Day is coming, but I don't know what I should give my girlfriend for gift. Any suggestions? ③	A：情人節快要到了，但是我不知道應該送我女朋友什麼禮物，你能給我一點建議嗎？
B: Is this a difficult question for you? You can give her something she likes, such as chocolate and roses, or you can invite her to a romantic candlelight dinner.	B：這對你來說是很難的問題嗎？你可以送她喜歡的東西，例如巧克力和玫瑰花，或者你也可以邀請她吃一個浪漫的燭光晚餐。
A: That's right. But I want to give her something special this year because I want to propose to ④ her that day.	A：沒錯。但是我今年想送她一點特別的，因為我想在那天向她求婚。

B: Wow. That's a good idea. Usually, girls will be very moved. Then you can find an empty room and decorate it with a romantic atmosphere. Of course, balloons and roses are essential.	B：哇哦。很不錯的想法。通常情況下，女孩們都會很感動的。那你可以找一個空房間，然後佈置出浪漫溫馨的氣氛。當然，氣球和玫瑰是必不可少的。
A: What should I give her?	A：那我應該送她什麼禮物呢？
B: How about a ring with your and her names on it?	B：送她一個戒指怎麼樣？上面刻上你和她的名字。
A: It's a good idea, but she doesn't like to wear any jewelry. That's why I don't know what to give her.	A：這是個不錯的主意，但是她不喜歡戴首飾，所以我才不知道應該送她什麼了。
B: What about a big teddy bear?	B：那送她一個很大的泰迪熊呢？
A: You think this is romantic? Well, I guess you are also at the end of your wit. ⑤	A：你覺得這很浪漫嗎？算了，我猜你也沒更好的想法了。

【程度提升，加分單字】

★**suggestion** [sə`dʒɛstʃən] **n.** 建議
★**propose** [prə`poz] **v.** 提議，提名，求婚
★**essential** [ɪ`sɛnʃəl] **adj.** 必要的
★**decorate** [`dɛkə͵ret] **v.** 裝飾
★**candlelight** [ˈkændllaɪt] **n.** 燭光

① **You got a minute?**

意為「你現在有空嗎？我現在可以跟你談一談嗎？」其完整的說法是 Have you got a minute? 但在口語中通常用 You got a minute?

② **ask away**

意為「問吧，說吧」，通常用於別人向你問問題時。

③ **Any suggestions?**

意為「有什麼建議嗎？」這個句子的完整說法是 Do you have any suggestions? 在口語中通常用簡化的說法。

④ **propose to**

意為「求婚，對……提出建議」，to 後面可跟動詞原形或者人，跟動詞原形時表示的是「提議／建議做某事」，若其後跟人等，則表示「向某人求婚」。

⑤ **at the end of one's wit**

意為「無計可施」，與其相似的片語是：at one's wit's end意為「毫無辦法，不知所措，束手無策」。

文化小站

雖然東方和西方的情人節都是充滿浪漫和甜蜜氣息的日子，但在很多方面仍存在著差異。華人的情人節也被稱為七夕節，這一天是牛郎和織女在鵲橋相聚，充滿情意的日子，其起源於漢朝時期。而西方的情人節是為了紀念神父瓦倫丁，因為他違背皇帝的旨意堅持和相愛的人結婚卻在 2 月 14 日這天被絞死。東西方的情人節在送禮物方面也有很大的不同。眾所皆知，西方的情人節推崇送巧克力和玫瑰花，中華文化的七夕節則是通過送梳子來表達自己的愛意，還用紅豆來表達自己的相思之情，因此紅豆也可被稱為相思豆。而在西方，情人節主要是男女表達情意的日子，他們互贈禮物，參加各種各樣的活動，已婚的夫婦也會參與到這樣的活動中來慶祝這個浪漫溫馨的節日。隨著東西方文化交流的加深，越來越多的華人也開始過西方的情人節，贈巧克力和玫瑰花。

慶祝節日

Unit 47

Halloween 萬聖節

萬聖節，南瓜、糖果是標準配備。膽小的你敢在萬聖節外出嗎？各路鬼怪紛紛上路，他們對膽小性格的你可是情有獨鍾哦。

精選實用會話例句

1 萬聖節快樂！**Happy Halloween!** Track 857

同義表達 Have a happy Halloween!

2 孩子們今天玩得很開心。**The kids have a lot of fun today.** Track 858

片語釋義 have a lot of fun 玩得很開心

3 所有的小孩一定都很喜歡萬聖節。

All children must love Halloween. Track 859

重要詞彙 Halloween [ˌhælo`in] n. 萬聖節前夕

4 你想裝扮成什麼？**What are you going to dress up as?** Track 860

片語釋義 dress up as 裝扮成，打扮成，扮作

5 孩子們在玩什麼特別的遊戲呢？

What special game are the children playing? Track 861

重要詞彙 special [`spɛʃəl] adj. 特殊的

6 我不知道我要裝扮成什麼。

I haven't figured out what I'm going to be. Track 862

重要片語 figure out 弄明白，想出

7 或許我會扮成巫婆。

Perhaps I will go to the party as a witch. Track 863

重要詞彙 witch [wɪtʃ] n. 女巫，巫婆

❽ 他想打扮得看上去很嚇人。
He wants to look frightening. Track 864
重要詞彙 frighten [ˈfraɪtn] v. 使驚恐，使恐慌

❾ 你想參加萬聖節聚會嗎？
Do you want to come to a Halloween party? Track 865
片語釋義 come to 甦醒，到達，共計

❿ 你今天會化妝嗎？Will you dress yourself today? Track 866
同義表達 Will you dress up today?

⓫ 你嚇了我一跳。You made me jump. Track 867
重要片語 make sb jump 使某人吃驚，嚇某人一跳

⓬ 你想參加萬聖節派對嗎？
Would you like to go to a Halloween party? Track 868
重要詞彙 party [ˋpɑrtɪ] n. 社交聚會，夥伴，黨

⓭ 我買了兩個南瓜和一袋糖果。
I bought two pumpkins and a bag of candy. Track 869
重要詞彙 pumpkin [ˈpʌmpkɪn] n. 南瓜

⓮ 今晚獨自外出時要小心些。
Be careful when you are out alone tonight. Track 870
同義表達 Be careful if you go out alone tonight.

⓯ 萬聖節要到了，是嗎？Halloween is near, right? Track 871
同義表達 Halloween is coming up, right?

⓰ 你能幫我做一個南瓜燈嗎？
Can you help me make a pumpkin lantern? Track 872
片語釋義 pumpkin lantern 南瓜燈，南瓜燈籠

⓱ 我喜歡你的萬聖節裝扮。I love your Halloween costume. Track 873
重要詞彙 costume [ˋkastjum] n. 戲服，服裝

⓲ 人們用很多種方式慶祝萬聖節嗎？
Do people celebrate Halloween in many ways? Track 874
片語釋義 in many ways 在許多方面，用許多方法

⑲ 我會裝扮成一個吸血鬼。**I will dress up as a vampire.** Track 875

重要詞彙 vampire [`væmpaɪr] **n.** 吸血鬼

⑳ 我能看一下你的服裝嗎？

May I have a look at your costume? Track 876

片語釋義 have a look at 看一眼，看一看

㉑ 我認為萬聖節對孩子們來說是個愉快的日子。**I think Halloween is a cheerful occasion for kids.** Track 877

同義表達 I think Halloween is a fun day for children.

㉒ 我今晚玩得很高興。**I enjoy myself tonight.** Track 878

重要片語 enjoy oneself 過得快樂，過得快活

看情境學對話

\中譯/ Track 879

A: Andy, let's talk about Halloween today, shall we? ① What do you think about ② Halloween?	A：安迪，我們今天來談談萬聖節，好嗎？你是怎麼看待萬聖節的？
B: I like it. I think Halloween is a fun day for children, because they can dress up in costumes to go trick-or-treating to get more candy. So, I have a lot of sweet memories of Halloween.	B：我很喜歡。實際上，我覺得萬聖節對孩子們來說是很快樂的日子，因為他們能穿上另類的服裝玩「不給糖就搗蛋」的遊戲來獲得更多的糖果。為此，我有很多美好的萬聖節記憶。
A: Hum, what is trick-or-treating?	A：嗯，什麼是「不給糖就搗蛋」？

B: It means on Halloween, children dress up in costumes, knocking on doors. When someone opens the door, they say “trick or treat ③ ”. If the host gives them candy, they would leave, but if not, they would play a trick on ④ the host. Generally speaking, people are willing to give candy to children now.	B：指的是，在萬聖夜的時候，小孩們會用服裝打扮自己，然後他們會挨家挨戶敲門。當有人開門時，他們就會說「不給糖就搗亂」。如果主人給了他們糖果，他們就會離開，但若是主人沒有給他們糖果，他們就會對房主惡作劇。一般來說，人們是願意給小孩糖果的。
A: How do children play tricks?	A：小孩們是如何惡作劇的？
B: They throw trash and toilet paper into the house, or eggs at the windows.	B：他們會朝房子裡丟垃圾、衛生紙，或者向窗戶上丟雞蛋。
A: Is it just American custom?	A：這只是美國的習俗嗎？
B: No. So far as I am aware, in Canada it is the same as in the U.S. What do you usually dress up for Halloween?	B：不，據我瞭解，加拿大和美國是一樣的習俗。你在萬聖節會扮成什麼？
A: I usually dress up as a vampire or witch. But sometimes I dress up as a bat girl, or a Wonder woman as well ⑤ .	A：我通常會裝扮成吸血鬼或者巫婆。不過有時我也會裝扮成蝙蝠女或者神力女超人。
B: Sounds interesting.	B：聽起來很有趣。

★**memory** [ˋmɛmərɪ] **n.** 記憶
★**trick** [trɪk] **n.** 把戲，戲法
★**trash** [træʃ] **n.** 垃圾

① **shall we?**

這個句子中包含了反義疑問句，用 let's 引導的句子，其疑問部分用 shall we；若是 let us，則疑問部分用 will you，注意區分。

② **think about**

意為「考慮，對……有某種觀點」。當表示對某事物或者某人有什麼看法時，可與 think of 替換。

③ **trick or treat**

意為「不給糖就搗蛋」，萬聖夜時，孩子們會挨家挨戶要糖果，不給糖果的話就會惡作劇。

④ **play a trick on**

意為「捉弄某人，對某人惡作劇」，後面通常跟 sb，與其意思一樣的是 play tricks on。

⑤ **as well**

意為「也」，常用作狀語，相當於 also 或者 too，通常用於句末，不用逗號與句子隔開。在口語中有時也可置於句中，意為「倒不如，也好」。

文化小站

萬聖節是西方的傳統節日。萬聖節前夜是最為熱鬧的時刻，在東方，通常會將萬聖節前夜當作萬聖節。萬聖節主要流行於英語國家，例如北美國家、英國、愛爾蘭、澳大利亞、紐西蘭等。在萬聖夜的時候，孩子們會穿著各種另類的衣服，提著南瓜燈籠挨家挨戶索要糖果，不停地說「不給糖就搗蛋」。別以為小孩子的話就是玩笑，如果你不給他們糖的話，他們就會往你家裡扔垃圾或者往窗戶上扔雞蛋，直到你給他們為止。在萬聖夜，「咬蘋果」是最流行的遊戲，孩子們會在裝滿水的盆裡咬漂浮的蘋果，誰咬到誰就是勝利者。現在的萬聖節基本上都被美式了，是他們大為慶祝的活動，他們會在萬聖節前夕舉辦遊行活動，一群吸血鬼、女巫、僵屍等紛紛出動，還邀請市民和遊客加入這個行列，成為熱鬧的人鬼嘉年華。在萬聖節，南瓜、糖果和蘋果是必備的食物。這個節日最開始出現的意義是為了讚美秋天，但隨著歐洲人對萬聖節理解的轉變，人們就將其變成了鬼怪、巫婆的節日。在中國也會看到萬聖節的影子，每逢節日到來時，人們會在商場或者超市中看到代表萬聖節的各類玩具。

慶祝節日

Unit 48 Thanksgiving 感恩節

闔家歡聚，慶祝感恩節。在感恩節到來時，父母的想法是：快到我懷裡來。所以，不管你是遠在天涯還是近在咫尺，都要早早回家過感恩節哦。

精選實用會話例句

1 你們什麼時候慶祝感恩節？
When do you celebrate Thanksgiving? Track 880
重要詞彙 thanksgiving [ˌθæŋksˋgɪvɪŋ] n. 感謝，感恩節

2 在十一月的第四個星期四。**On the fourth Thursday of November.** Track 881
重要詞彙 November [noˋvɛmbɚ] n. 十一月

3 你們在那天吃什麼？**What do you eat on that day?** Track 882
片語釋義 on that day 在那天

4 通常情況下，人們會在感恩節晚餐時做火雞。**Normally, people cook turkey for Thanksgiving dinner.** Track 883
重要詞彙 turkey [ˋtɝkɪ] n. 火雞

5 感恩節快樂。**Happy Thanksgiving.** Track 884
同義表達 Have a nice Thanksgiving.

6 這是一個團圓的日子。**It's a time of family reunion.** Track 885
重要詞彙 reunion [riˋjunjən] n. 重聚

7 感恩節很快就會到來了。
Thanksgiving will soon come around. Track 886
片語釋義 come around 如期而至，甦醒

8 希望你能度過一個特別的感恩節。**Hope you have a very special Thanksgiving Day.** Track 887
重要片語 hope sb do 希望某人做某事

❽ 先把聖誕樹放在客廳吧。
Put the Christmas tree in the parlor first. Track 911
同義表達 Put the Christmas tree in the living room first.

❾ 你家從來都沒有買聖誕樹嗎？
Your family never bought Christmas trees? Track 912
片語釋義 Christmas tree 聖誕樹

❿ 一定要掛上襪子！
Be sure to hang up the stockings! Track 913
片語釋義 hang up 吊起來

⓫ 耶誕節要來了。Christmas is in the air. Track 914
重要片語 be in the air 即將發生的事情

⓬ 聖誕老人來了。Here the Santa Claus comes. Track 915
同義表達 There is the Santa Claus.

⓭ 這是聖誕老人給你的禮物！
This is your present from Santa! Track 916
重要詞彙 Santa [ˈsæntə] n. 聖誕老人

⓮ 聽，他們正在唱聖誕頌歌。
Listen, they are going caroling. Track 917
片語釋義 go caroling 唱頌歌

⓯ 你小的時候相信聖誕老人嗎？Did you believe in Santa Claus when you were a child? Track 918
重要詞彙 believe [bɪˋliv] v. 相信，信任

⓰ 聖誕老人不存在。Santa Claus isn't a real being. Track 919
片語釋義 Santa Claus 聖誕老人

⓱ 聖誕老人開始分發禮物了嗎？
Did Father Christmas start giving out presents? Track 920
片語釋義 give out 分發

⓲ 哇哦！我的聖誕襪裡裝滿了禮物。
Wow! My stocking is swarming with presents. Track 921
片語釋義 swarm with 擠滿，充滿

⑲ **我們來唱聖誕頌歌吧。Let's sing Christmas carols.** Track 922

重要詞彙 carol [ˈkærəl] **n.** 聖誕之歌，（宗教）頌歌

⑳ **耶誕節就要到了。**

Christmas will come before long. Track 923

片語釋義 before long 不久之後，在短時間內

㉑ **我希望回家過耶誕節。I hope to go home for Christmas.** Track 924

同義表達 I wish I were home for Christmas.

㉒ **何不跟我一起度過耶誕節呢？**

Why not enjoy Christmas with me? Track 925

重要片語 why not 何妨，何不

看情境學對話

\中譯/ Track 926

A: Merry Christmas! Alan.	A：聖誕快樂！艾倫。
B: Merry Christmas! Albert. Today is Christmas. How would you like to celebrate it?	B：聖誕快樂！亞伯特。今天是耶誕節，你想怎麼慶祝這個節日呢？
A: I don't know. Steven and I are discussing how to celebrate it. What are you going to do this Christmas?	A：我不知道，我和史蒂文也正在討論如何慶祝呢。今年的耶誕節你準備做什麼？
B: I will invite all my relatives to get together ① at my house.	B：我會邀請所有的親戚來我家聚會。
A: That's great. Everyone in our family will be back for Christmas except my sister.	A：太棒了。除了我姐姐外，我們家的人也都會回去過耶誕節。
B: Why won't your sister go back?	B：為什麼你姐姐不回去呢？

文化小站

感恩節是西方的傳統節日。嚴格來說，感恩節是美國人獨創的一個節日。是他們闔家團聚吃感恩節大餐的日子。最初感恩節沒有固定的日子，直到 1941 年，美國國會才將每年十一月的第四個星期四定為感恩節。假期則是從星期四延續到星期天。加拿大的感恩節日期也改變了很多次，最終在 1957 年確定每年十月份的第二個星期一為感恩節，也成為了全國性的假日。除了美國和加拿大外，還有埃及、希臘等國家也過感恩節，只是習俗會有些不同，但其實，感恩節並不是一個世界性的節日，像英國和法國這些歐洲國家是沒有感恩節一說的。感恩節是為了感謝上天給予的收穫，加拿大的感恩節日期比美國早的原因是其收穫的季節比美國早。感恩節作為美國的傳統節日，在那天舉國上下熱鬧非凡，會舉辦很多的活動，如體育比賽、化妝舞會以及戲劇表演等。感恩節晚餐更是異常豐富，火雞是家家戶戶必備之物，除此之外，還有南瓜派、馬鈴薯泥、玉米等傳統菜餚。通常情況下，無論家庭成員在哪裡都會趕回家跟家人一起過感恩節，類似於中國的春節，都是團聚的日子。

慶祝節日

Unit 49

Christmas 耶誕節

不知你是否也喜歡過耶誕節？聖誕卡、聖誕樹、聖誕歌以及聖誕老人是否亦能勾起你那美好的回憶？我相信它們與你的故事也一定有著很美好的聯繫。

精選實用會話例句

1 耶誕節快樂！**Merry Christmas!** Track 904

同義表達 Wish you a merry Christmas!

2 我們用松樹做聖誕樹。

Pine trees are used for Christmas trees. Track 905

重要片語 be used for 用來做……

3 聖誕樹上掛了很多禮物。**There are many presents hanging on the Christmas tree.** Track 906

片語釋義 hang on 掛在……之上

4 好漂亮的一棵聖誕樹！

What a beautiful Christmas tree! Track 907

重要詞彙 beautiful [`bjutəfəl] adj. 美麗的，美好的

5 你想怎麼慶祝耶誕節？**What do you want to do to celebrate Christmas?** Track 908

重要詞彙 Christmas [ˈkrɪsməs] n. 耶誕節

6 比爾，耶誕節還遠著呢。

Bill, Christmas is a long way off. Track 909

片語釋義 a long way off 時間距離現在很遠

7 今年的耶誕節是在星期五。

Christmas falls on a Friday this year. Track 910

片語釋義 fall on 落到，輪到

A: If you're interested, you can come with me to Brian's, and his parents and brother will also be there.	A：如果你有興趣的話，也可以跟我一起去布萊恩那裡，他的父母和弟弟也會在那裡。
B: It's very kind of you. Thank you. I'd love to.	B：你真的太好了。謝謝，我願意去。
A: That's wonderful. I'm sure Brian will be happy. We can see how they spend Thanksgiving as well.	A：那太好了。我相信布萊恩會很高興的。我們可以看看他們是如何過感恩節的。
B: Yes. Can you tell me something about Thanksgiving?	B：是的。你能告訴我關於感恩節的一些事嗎？
A: Take it easy ③ . It's just a time of family reunion. We will eat a lot of delicious food, such as turkey and pumpkin pie.	A：放輕鬆。其實，就只是家人團聚的日子。我們會吃到很多美味的食物，例如火雞和南瓜派。
B: It's gonna be great. I can't wait to ④ get to Brian's.	B：那一定很棒。我都迫不及待想到布萊恩家了。
A: Me too. But now you have to tidy up ⑤ some of the things you need.	A：我也是。不過你現在需要快點整理一些你要帶的東西了。
B: Okay.	B：沒問題。

【程度提升，加分單字】

★**roommate** [ˋrum͵met] **n.** 室友　★**arrangement** [əˋrendʒmənt] **n.** 安排

★**wonderful** [ˋwʌndɚfəl] **adj.** 極好的，絕妙的

★**pie** [paɪ] **n.** 餡餅，容易得到的稱心的東西（美俚）

① **not really**

意為「不完全是，不見得」，常用於口語中，具有否定意義，可以用來表達不怎麼忙，不怎麼想去，不怎麼懂等。

② **I see**

意為「我明白了，我懂了」。表示明白某人說的話和做事的目的。

③ **take it easy**

意為「輕鬆點，別緊張，沉住氣，別著急」，多用來安慰他人而說的話。

④ **can't wait to do**

意為「等不及要做某事，迫不及待要做某事」，其後常跟動詞原形。

⑤ **tidy up**

意為「整理，收拾」，是由一個動詞和副詞構成的片語，若受詞是名詞，名詞既可以放在片語中間，也可以放在片語後面，但若受詞是代詞，則代詞只能放在片語中間。

⑨ 記得去感謝那些幫助過你的人。
Remember to thank those who helped you. Track 888
重要詞彙 remember [rɪˋmɛmbɚ] v. 記得，牢記

⑩ 火雞是感恩節的象徵。
The turkey is a symbol of Thanksgiving. Track 889
重要片語 a symbol of ……的象徵

⑪ 沒有火雞和盛裝的加拿大感恩節是怎麼樣的呢？**What is a Canadian Thanksgiving without turkey or dressing?** Track 890
重要詞彙 Canadian [kəˈneɪdiən] adj. 加拿大的，加拿大人的

⑫ 我們經常把火雞和感恩節聯想在一起。
We often associate turkey with Thanksgiving. Track 891
重要片語 associate...with... 把……與……聯繫在一起

⑬ 如果和你一起過感恩節的話我會很感激。**I will be grateful if I have you with me on this Thanksgiving Day.** Track 892
同義表達 I would be grateful if you spend this Thanksgiving Day with me.

⑭ 在感恩節吃火雞是一個傳統。
It's a tradition to have turkeys on Thanksgiving. Track 893
重要詞彙 tradition [trəˈdɪʃn] n. 傳統，慣例

⑮ 我媽媽剛剛烤了火雞當晚餐。**My mother has just roasted a turkey for dinner.** Track 894
同義表達 My mother has just cooked a turkey for dinner.

⑯ 你能找一個裝火雞的烤盤嗎？**Can you look for a baking dish to hold the turkey?** Track 895
片語釋義 baking dish 烤盤，烤碟

⑰ 在感恩節吃烤火雞的習俗是怎麼來的？
How did the custom of eating roast turkey on Thanksgiving Day come about? Track 896
片語釋義 come about 發生，產生

⑱ 這個火雞做的恰到好處。
The turkey was done to perfection. Track 897
同義表達 The turkey was done to a turn.

⑲ 你可以用火雞款待朋友。
You can feast your friends on turkey. Track 898

重要詞彙 feast [fist] v. 款待，宴請 n. 盛會，宴會

⑳ 感恩節晚餐你吃飽了嗎？
Are you full after the Thanksgiving dinner? Track 899

重要片語 be full 飽，吃飽

㉑ 馬上你就能吃到真正的火雞了。You can sink your teeth into genuine turkey meat soon. Track 900

片語釋義 sink one's teeth into 吃

㉒ 感恩節是一年一度的節慶。
Thanksgiving is an annual holiday. Track 901

同義表達 Thanksgiving Day is celebrated annually.

㉓ 感恩節快樂。Best wishes for Thanksgiving. Track 902

片語釋義 best wishes 最美好的祝福

看情境學對話

	中譯 Track 903
A: Happy Thanksgiving Day! Are you busy now?	A：感恩節快樂！你很忙嗎？
B: Not really. ① I'm just planning how to spend this holiday because all my roommates and friends are going home for Thanksgiving.	B：並不會。我只是在安排如何度過這個假期，因為我所有的室友和朋友都要回家過感恩節了。
A: Oh, I see. ② It's like Chinese New year. Almost everyone goes home for Thanksgiving.	A：哦，我知道了，它就像華人地區的春節，幾乎每個人都會回家過感恩節。
B: That's right. Do you have any plans?	B：沒錯。你有什麼打算？
A: In fact, I didn't have any arrangements, but Brian invited me to his home for Thanksgiving dinner.	A：其實，我也沒有什麼安排，不過布萊恩邀請我去他家吃感恩節大餐。
B: Great.	B：很棒。

A: Curry chicken, which is a dish I have learned recently, but my mother spoke highly of it. I can cook it for you if you have time. When you are free, I can do it for you.	A：咖喱雞。這是我最近學會的一道菜，不過我媽媽對它評價很高。你有空的時候，我可以做給你吃。
B: That's great, but I don't think you look like someone who can cook.	B：太棒了，不過我覺得你看上去不像是會做菜的人。
A: I really don't like to cook but if I do it, it will be delicious.	A：我的確不太喜歡做飯，但只要是我做的就會很好吃。
B: Woah!	B：哇！
A: Do you like the birthday present I gave you yesterday?	A：你喜歡昨天我送你的生日禮物嗎？
B: I really love it. How did you know I wanted those shoes?	B：超級喜歡。你怎麼知道我想要那雙鞋子？
A: You've been to that shop three times. I certainly know that. I know you think that pair of shoes is very expensive.	A：你都去了那個店鋪三次了，我會不知道嗎。我知道，你是覺得那雙鞋子很貴。
B: It really got to me. ④ Give me a hug. ⑤	B：我太感動了。讓我抱一下。

★**especially** [ə`spɛʃəlɪ] **adv.** 尤其地，主要地
★**specialty** [`spɛʃəltɪ] **n.** 拿手菜，特長，專業
★**seafood** [`si͵fud] **n.** 海鮮

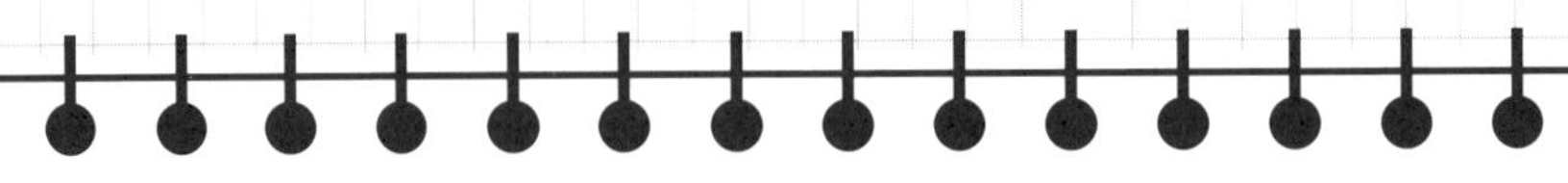

對話解析

① **how do you like sth**

意為「你認為……怎麼樣」，相當於 what do you think of sth。這裡的 like 後面跟名詞或者動名詞。

② **It was the first time that...had...**

意為「這是第一次做某事」，be動詞是 was，從句就要用過去完成時態，be動詞是 is，則從句用現在完成時態。

③ **have a good time**

意為「過得愉快，玩得痛快」，其後可以跟動名詞形式，也可以單獨成句，表示美好的祝願。

④ **it really got to me**

意為「我太感動了」，這是一個固定用法。

⑤ **give sb a hug**

意為「給某人一個擁抱」，hug 前可加形容詞來修飾，例如 bear hug（熊抱）。

❽ **請幫我切一塊蛋糕。Please cut me a slice of cake.** Track 934

片語釋義 a slice of 一片，一份

❾ **結果這個蛋糕很好吃。The cake turned out fine.** Track 935

片語釋義 turn out fine 轉好

❿ **請接受我的生日祝福。**

Please accept my birthday wishes. Track 936

重要詞彙 accept [ək`sɛpt] v. 接受，同意

⓫ **你對這個聚會滿意嗎？**

Are you satisfied with the birthday party? Track 937

重要片語 be satisfied with 對……感到滿意

⓬ **你的生日願望是什麼？What is your birthday wish?** Track 938

片語釋義 birthday wish 生日願望

⓭ **讓我們一起為麥克唱生日歌吧。**

Let's sing birthday songs for Mike. Track 939

重要詞彙 birthday [`bɝθ͵de] n. 生日，誕辰

⓮ **要是每一天都是我的生日該有多好！**

If only everyday were my birthday! Track 940

重要詞彙 If only 但願，要是……多好

⓯ **我很喜歡這個聚會。I really enjoyed this party.** Track 941

重要詞彙 enjoy [ɪn`dʒɔɪ] v. 享受，喜歡

⓰ **別忘了許願。Don't forget to make a wish.** Track 942

同義表達 Do remember to make a wish.

⓱ **你許願了嗎？Did you make a wish?** Track 943

片語釋義 make a wish 許願

⓲ **你應該抽出時間舉辦生日派對。You should take some time off for a birthday party.** Track 944

重要片語 take some time off 抽出一部分時間

⓳ **一口氣吹滅所有蠟燭。**

Blow out the candles with a single puff. Track 945

同義表達 Snuff out the candles in one breath.

⑳ **這是你的生日禮物。Here is a present for you.**

Track 946

重要詞彙 present [`prɛznt] **n.** 禮物，現在

㉑ **你會怎麼過自己的生日？**

How will you spend your birthday?

Track 947

重要詞彙 spend [spɛnd] **v.** 度過

看情境學對話

Track 948

	中譯
A: Julie, how do you like ① your birthday party last night?	A：你覺得昨晚的生日聚會怎麼樣？
B: I really enjoy it. It was the first time ② in five years that I had this birthday party with all my family and friends.	B：我很喜歡。這是五年來我第一次和所有家人朋友一起辦這個生日派對。
A: Although we had known each other for three years, I had never been to your birthday party. I mean, I had never had a birthday party for you.	A：雖然我們已經認識了三年，但是我從來沒有參加過你的生日聚會。我的意思是，我從來沒有為你舉辦過生日派對。
B: Thank you. I had a good time ③ last night. It's my honor to meet you. By the way, the dinner last night was really delicious, especially the French seafood soup. Did your mother make it?	B：謝謝你，我昨晚過得很開心。認識你真是我的榮幸。對了，昨天的晚餐真的很好吃，尤其是那個法式海鮮湯。是你媽媽做的嗎？
A: No, it's me. This is one of my specialties.	A：不是，是我做的。這是我的拿手菜之一。
B: What else do you have?	B：你還有什麼拿手菜？

文化小站

耶誕節，又被稱為耶誕節，是一個宗教節，為了紀念耶穌的誕生，起源於基督教。耶誕節是在每年的12月25日，而前一天晚上也就是12月24日晚上是平安夜。

在耶誕節期間，聖誕老人必定是一個不可或缺的角色，被小孩認為是真實存在的，是一個會在平安夜分發禮物的神奇角色。但等真正長大後他們會發現其實聖誕老人分發禮物只是大人為了哄孩子開心編出來的。聖誕老人的原型人物據說是尼古拉斯，此人常將自己的財產捐給貧苦可憐的人，並且獻身教會，後來還暗中送錢幫助了三個小女孩。後人為了紀念他，就將其尊為聖徒，形象是頭戴紅帽、身穿紅袍的白鬍子老頭。在西方故事中，每年的耶誕節他都會駕著由幾匹鹿拉著的雪橇趕往各家各戶，然後從煙囪進去，把聖誕禮物裝進紅色襪子裡放在孩子們的床頭或者火爐前。隨著世界文化交流的不斷深入，現在的日本、中國以及韓國等亞洲國家都受到了耶誕節的影響，不同程度地過著耶誕節。在華人地區，每逢耶誕節來臨之際，你都會在商店或者超市里看到耶誕節的影子。不過對華人地區影響最大的是平安夜，基本上每個人都會送親朋好友代表著美好祝福的平安果——蘋果。當然，耶誕節購物也是重要的一部分。

慶祝節日

Unit 50 Birthday 生日聚會

相信每個人過生日的時候都能獲得美好的回憶，不管是與朋友還是家人。希望你在過每個生日的時候都能快快樂樂的。

精選實用會話例句

1 你想吃點蛋糕嗎？Will you have a bit of the cake? Track 927
同義表達 Would you like some cake?

2 生日快樂！Happy birthday (to you)! Track 928
片語釋義 happy birthday 生日快樂

3 讓我們開始許願和吹蠟燭吧。
Let's make a wish and blow out the candles. Track 929
片語釋義 blow out 吹滅

4 奶油蛋糕太甜了，所以我不喜歡吃。
Cream cake is so sweet that I don't like to eat. Track 930
重要詞彙 cream [krim] n. 奶油

5 我要舉辦一個生日派對，你會來嗎？I'm going to throw a birthday party. Would you like to come? Track 931
重要詞彙 throw [θro] v. 舉辦

6 我們今晚就痛痛快快地玩吧。
Let's have a spree tonight. Track 932
片語釋義 have a spree 狂歡作樂

7 把蛋糕切成幾塊？
How many pieces will the cake be cut into? Track 933
片語釋義 cut into 切成，削減

A: She's going to her mother-in-law's for Christmas this year.	A：今年她要去她婆婆家過耶誕節。
B: That's too bad! ② What kind of Christmas present do you want this year, a computer or books?	B：那太可惜了。今年你想要什麼聖誕禮物呢？電腦還是書？
A: Actually, I want a new computer table and some computer games this year.	A：實際上，今年我想要一個新的電腦桌和一些電腦遊戲。
B: I also want a new computer desk. I gave my parents a long Christmas list too.I hope you can get what you ask for ③ .	B：我也想要一個新的電腦桌。我給了父母一個很長的聖誕禮物清單。希望你能得到自己想要的。
A: Thank you. You too. ④ By the way, I'm going to a Christmas party later. Will you join us?	A：謝謝，你也是。順便問一下，稍後我會參加一個聖誕晚會，你要來嗎？
B: I'd love to, but now I have to move the Christmas tree into the house, see you later.	B：我願意去，不過我現在要先把聖誕樹搬進家裡，一會見。
A: See you. ⑤	A：一會見。

【程度提升，加分單字】

★**merry** [ˋmɛrɪ] **adj.** 愉快的

★**relative** [ˋrɛlətɪv] **n.** 親戚

★**discuss** [dɪˋskʌs] **v.** 討論

① **get together**

意為「聚會」，其後也可跟 with sb 意為「與某人相聚」。

② **that's too bad**

意為「那太糟糕了」，表示同情惋惜，與 I'm sorry to hear that 有相似之處。

③ **ask for**

意為「請求，要求」，for 是介系詞，後常接名詞，ask for 也可用於 ask sb for sth 中，意為「向某人要求某物」。

④ **you too**

意為「你也是」，使用的範圍很廣泛，例如當對方說 Have a nice day! 的時候你就可以說 You too.

⑤ **see you**

意為「再見，回頭見」，完整說法是 see you later。

❽ 我最大的愛好就是音樂了。
My greatest interest is in music. Track 979
重要詞彙 interest [`ɪntərɪst] n. 興趣，愛好，利息

❾ 任何布蘭妮的演唱會我都不會錯過。
I won't miss any Britney's concert. Track 980
重要詞彙 miss [mɪs] v. 錯過，漏掉

❿ 這首歌很好聽。The music is easy on the ear. Track 981
重要片語 easy on the ear 好聽，動聽

⓫ 我聽說這次演唱會的場地很寬敞。I heard the venue of the concert was very spacious. Track 982
重要詞彙 venue [`vɛnju] n. 會場

⓬ 你願意這週末跟我一起去看演唱會嗎？Would you like to go to the concert with me this weekend? Track 983
重要詞彙 weekend [`wik`ɛnd] n. 週末

⓭ 他把薩克斯風演奏得很完美。
He plays the saxophone to perfection. Track 984
片語釋義 play the saxophone 薩克斯風演奏

⓮ 這次的演唱會讓人印象很深刻。
The concert was very impressive. Track 985
同義表達 The concert left a deep impression on me.

⓯ 你最喜歡哪個樂隊？Which band do you like best? Track 986
片語釋義 like best 最喜歡

⓰ 你聽說過西城男孩嗎？
Have you ever heard of Westlife? Track 987
重要詞彙 hear [hɪr] v. 聽到，聽說

⓱ 我偶像這週六會在體育中心舉辦演唱會。
My idol will hold a concert at the sports center this Saturday. Track 988
片語釋義 hold a concert 舉行演唱會／音樂會

⑱ 這首歌很難聽。**The music is unpleasant to the ear.** Track 989

片語釋義 be unpleasant to the ear 不入耳

⑲ 真遺憾！這次演唱會的票售完了。

What a pity! The tickets for the concert were sold out. Track 990

片語釋義 sell out 賣光

⑳ 你能買到演唱會的門票嗎？

Can you get tickets for the concert? Track 991

重要詞彙 ticket [ˈtɪkɪt] n. 票，入場券

㉑ 那個歌手能輕易帶動現場的氣圍。

The singer can easily stir up the atmosphere. Track 992

片語釋義 stir up 引起，激起

㉒ 在我心裡，他是美國的搖滾界之王。**In my heart, he is the King of Rock Music in America.** Track 993

片語釋義 rock music 搖滾樂

看情境學對話

Track 994

	中譯
A: Alan, are you free this Sunday?	A：艾倫，你這週日有空嗎？
B: It seems there is nothing to do that evening, but I need to pay a visit to ① our professor with my classmates during the day ② . What's up?	B：那天晚上貌似沒有事，不過白天我需要跟同學們一起去拜訪教授。怎麼了？
A: Great! I'd like to invite you to a concert.	A：那太棒了。我想邀請你看一場演唱會。
B: What kind of concert is that? And where?	B：那是一場什麼類型的演唱會？在哪裡？
A: It is a rock concert at the sports center near your home.	A：那是一場搖滾音樂演唱會。就在離你家很近的體育中心。

① **couch potato**

意為「電視迷，花大量時間看電視的人」，美國人通常比喻為「沙發馬鈴薯」，指的是整天像馬鈴薯一樣蜷縮在沙發上看電視的人，也指「懶惰的人」。

② **rely on**

意為「依賴，依靠」，其後可跟名詞或者動名詞。

③ **prey on**

意為「捕食，掠奪，折磨」，若構成 prey on sb 則指「折磨某人」，若構成 prey on sth 則指「捕食某物」，sth 通常指動物、昆蟲。

④ **except for**

意為「除了……以外」，與 except 的區別在於，except for 後接的詞跟主語不是同類的，而 except 後接的詞跟主語一般是同類的。

⑤ **sounds good**

意為「聽起來不錯」，原句是 it sounds good，在口語中省略了主語it，表示對別人的觀點或者建議等表示贊同。

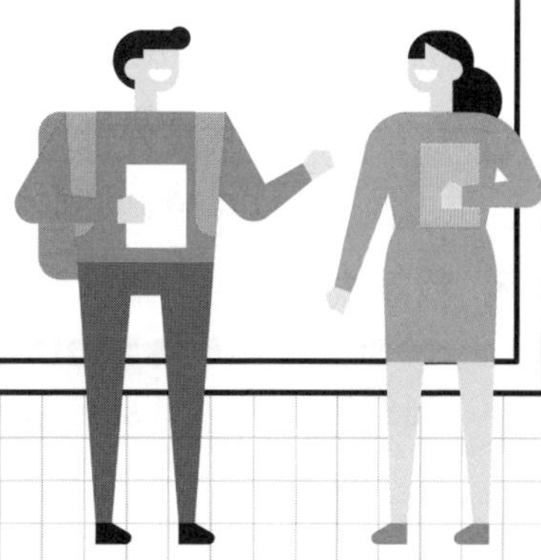

放鬆心情

Unit 52 Concert 演唱會

歌迷們，與我們的偶像一起互動吧，讓他感受到我們的熱情和對他的喜愛。讓我們與現場的燈光一起，為偶像點亮激情。

精選實用會話例句

1 那場演唱會真令人失望。

The concert was a letdown. Track 972

重要詞彙 letdown [ˋlɛtˏdaʊn] n. 失望，令人失望的事物

2 我希望將來有一天可以去現場聽戴安娜的演唱會。

I wish I could go to Diana's live concert someday in the future. Track 973

重要詞彙 concert [ˋkɑnsɚt] n. 演唱會，音樂會

3 我經常去聽演唱會。I go to a concert frequently. Track 974

同義表達 I often go to a concert.

4 我知道你對音樂有鑒賞力。

I know you have an ear for music. Track 975

重要片語 have an ear for 對……有鑒賞力，對……聽覺靈敏

5 你的偶像對音樂很有天賦。

Your idol has a natural bent for music. Track 976

片語釋義 natural bent 天賦，天生的喜好

6 在音樂方面我是外行。I'm no judge of music. Track 977

重要片語 be no judge of 不能判定

7 我無法忍受搖滾樂。

Rock music is more than I can bear. Track 978

同義表達 I can't stand rock music.

⑲ 你老公真是一個電視迷。
Your husband is such a couch potato. Track 967
片語釋義 couch potato 花大量時間看電視的人，電視迷，懶惰鬼

⑳ 你喜歡的電視節目是什麼？
What is your favorite TV program? Track 968
重要片語 TV program 電視節目

㉑ 這部電視劇的最後會在這週日播放。The last episode of this series will be on this Sunday. Track 969
重要詞彙 episode [ˋɛpəˏsod] **n.** 一集，插曲

㉒ 你能不能切換到頻道五。Would you change/switch to the channel five? Track 970
重要詞彙 channel [ˈtʃænl] **n.** 頻道，海峽

看情境學對話

Track 971

	中譯
A: What do you often do when you are free?	A：當你有空的時候，你經常會做什麼？
B: I often watch TV. I am a real couch potato ①.	B：我經常看電視。我是一個十足的電視迷。
A: What program attracts you so much?	A：什麼節目那麼吸引你？
B: I like watching “Animal World” and “World News” best. Of course, I love watching soap operas, too.	B：我最喜歡看《動物世界》和《世界新聞》。當然，我也很喜歡看肥皂劇。
A: I also like watching “Animal World”. I think the world of animals is very interesting.	A：我也喜歡看《動物世界》。我覺得動物的世界很有意思。

B: Sure, especially the ants who live underground. Their underground castles shock me.	B：沒錯，特別是生活在地下的螞蟻，他們的地下城堡著實讓我震驚。
A: Yes, but my favorite animals are hyenas because they rely on ② cooperation to prey on ③ large and medium herbivores.	A：是的，不過我最喜歡的動物是鬣狗，因為他們懂得依靠合作來捕食大中型食草動物。
B: Indeed. How long do you watch TV every day?	B：的確。你每天會看多久的電視？
A: I spend most of my time watching TV except for ④ work hours. I feel relaxed when I sit on the sofa watching TV after work.	A：除了上班時間我基本上都在看電視。我覺得下班後坐在沙發上看電視令我很放鬆。
B: You're right. But I prefer to relax myself through movies.	B：你說的很對。不過我更喜歡透過電影來放鬆自己。
A: Yeah, it's one of the ways to relax. Where do you prefer to see movies, at home or at the cinema?	A：是的。那也是放鬆的方式之一。你比較喜歡在哪裡看電影？家裡還是電影院？
B: Cinema. I think when I watch movies in the cinema there is more atmosphere. I enjoy watching movies with so many people.	B：電影院。我覺得在電影院看電影會更有氛圍。我享受那麼多人陪我一起看電影的感覺。
A: Sounds good ⑤.	A：聽起來不錯。

★**program** [ˋprogræm] **n.** 節目
★**underground** [ˋʌndɚ͵graʊnd] **adv.** 地下的
★**hyena** [haɪˋinə] **n.** 鬣狗
★**herbivore** [ˋhɝbə͵vor] **n.** 食草動物

放鬆心情

Unit 51

Movie and TV 電影電視

你問哪個方式放鬆好，我說就電影電視最好。那些電影迷電視迷統統都出來吧，讓我們一起享受生活！

精選實用會話例句

❶ 電影什麼時候開始？**When does the film begin?** Track 949

重要詞彙 film [fɪlm] n. 電影，影片

❷ 這部電影會持續多長時間？

How long does the movie last? Track 950

重要詞彙 movie [`muvɪ] n. 電影，電影院

❸ 這個電影什麼時候上映？

When will the movie be released? Track 951

重要詞彙 release [rɪ`lis] v. 發佈，上映

❹ 你覺得那部電影怎麼樣？

What do you think of the film? Track 952

同義表達 Have you any comments to make on the film?

❺ 去看電影怎麼樣？

What about going to the cinema? Track 953

片語釋義 go to the cinema 去看電影

❻ 有什麼好看的節目／好片子嗎？

Is there anything good on? Track 954

重要詞彙 anything [`ɛnɪˌθɪŋ] pron. 任何東西

❼ 那是我看過的最好的電影。

It is the best film I have ever watched. Track 955

重要詞彙 watch [wɒtʃ] v. 注視，觀看

8 我最喜歡看動作片。I like action films best.

片語釋義 action film 動作片

Track 956

9 你最喜歡看哪部電影？

Which movie do you like best?

同義表達 What's your favorite movie?

Track 957

10 這部電影值得一看。

This film is really worth watching.

重要片語 be worth doing 值得做

Track 958

11 你知道這部電影是誰演的嗎？

Do you know who is in this movie?

重要詞彙 know [no] v. 知道，瞭解

Track 959

12 我想知道廣告之後放的是什麼。

I wonder what's on after the advertisement.

重要詞彙 advertisement [ˌædvɚˋtaɪzmənt] n. 廣告

Track 960

13 我們轉到頻道10吧。Let's switch to the channel 10.

片語釋義 switch to 切換到，轉換

Track 961

14 如果你每天都看新聞的話就會增長知識。You shall enrich your knowledge if you watch news every day.

重要片語 enrich one's knowledge 豐富某人的知識

Track 962

15 我們能打開電視看一些綜藝節目嗎？Shall we turn on the TV and watch some variety shows?

片語釋義 variety show 綜藝節目

Track 963

16 他正在看足球比賽。

He's watching the soccer game now.

片語釋義 soccer game 足球比賽

Track 964

17 你浪費了太多時間在肥皂劇上了。

You've wasted too much time on soap operas.

重要片語 waste time on... 浪費時間在……

Track 965

18 大衛很喜歡看電視。David is keen on watching TV.

同義表達 David likes watching TV very much.

Track 966

A: Do you still remember the moves now?	A：那你現在還記得那些舞步嗎？
B: Of course, as long as you put on ④ Latin music, I can dance to it.	B：當然了，只要你放拉丁音樂，我就能隨之起舞。
A: Does your talent come from your family?	A：你的舞蹈天分來自於你的家人嗎？
B: I think so ⑤ . My mother is good at dancing. She likes tango, but she prefers ballet.	B：我想是的。我媽媽很會跳舞，她很喜歡探戈，不過她更喜歡的是芭蕾。
A: So you learned tango and ballet from your mom when you were a kid?	A：所以你在小的時候也跟著你媽媽學了探戈和芭蕾舞？
B: Yes, and then I learned some other dances, such as waltz and cha-cha. But I learned these from my teacher.	B：是的，之後我還學了一些其他的舞蹈，例如華爾滋和恰恰。不過這些是跟我的老師學的。
A: I heard you've been a dance teacher for seven years, haven't you?	A：我聽說你已經當了七年的舞蹈老師，是嗎？
B: Yes, I love dancing, so I want to spend the rest of my life dancing. I hope my spirit will inspire more people.	B：沒錯。我喜歡跳舞，所以我想把餘生用在舞蹈上。我希望我的這種精神也能激勵更多的人。

【程度提升，加分單字】

★**emigrate** [`ɛmə͵gret] v. 移居國外
★**melody** [`mɛlədɪ] n. 旋律，曲調
★**benefit** [`bɛnəfɪt] v. 使受益，得益
★**inspire** [ɪn`spaɪr] v. 鼓舞，激勵

對話解析

① become interested in

意為「對……開始產生興趣」，這個片語強調「開始」，表示從某時開始對某物有了興趣，而 be interested in 只是表明「對……有興趣」。

② emigrate to

意為「移居到」，指的是移居出境。

③ benefit sb a lot

意為「使某人受益匪淺」，benefit a lot from 則表示「從……中受益匪淺」。

④ put on

意為「穿上，上演」，與 music 搭配構成 put on some music 時意為「放一些音樂」，也可以用 put some music on 來表示。

⑤ I think so

意為「我也這麼想，我想是如此」。so 指前面某人說的某件事，用 I think so 來表示同意。

❾ 約翰跳霹靂舞很有天分。
John has a flair for break dancing. Track 1003
重要片語 have a flair for 有……的天分

❿ 沒關係，跟著我做，我教你。
Never mind, follow me. Track 1004
重要片語 never mind 沒關係，不要緊

⓫ 跳舞使我感覺很有活力。
Dance makes me feel energetic. Track 1005
重要詞彙 energetic [ˌɛnɚˋdʒɛtɪk] adj. 精力充沛的

⓬ 這些舞者舞姿很優美。
These dancers are graceful. Track 1006
重要詞彙 graceful [ˋgresfəl] adj. 優美的，優雅的

⓭ 我沒有舞伴。**I have no partner.** Track 1007
重要詞彙 partner [ˋpɑrtnɚ] n. 夥伴

⓮ 他的招牌舞步是太空步。
His signature moves is moonwalk. Track 1008
片語釋義 signature moves 招牌舞步

⓯ 我很高興成為你的舞伴。
I'd be delighted to be your dance partner. Track 1009
重要片語 be delighted to 高興，高興做某事

⓰ 你對現代舞感興趣嗎？
Are you interested in modern dance? Track 1010
同義表達 Do you have an interest in dancing?

⓱ 五歲時我就開始學芭蕾舞了。
I studied ballet when I was five years old. Track 1011
重要詞彙 ballet [ˈbæle] n. 芭蕾舞，芭蕾舞劇

⓲ 老實說，這並不屬於現代舞範疇。
Frankly speaking, that does not belong to modern dance. Track 1012
片語釋義 modern dance 現代舞

⑲ 你是和你的舞伴一起來的嗎？

Did you come with your dance partner? Track 1013

片語釋義 dance parter 舞伴

⑳ 學跳舞很難嗎？

Is it difficult to learn dancing? Track 1014

重要詞彙 difficult [ˋdɪfəˏkəlt] adj. 困難的

㉑ 我只是一個業餘舞者。

I am just an amateur dancer. Track 1015

重要詞彙 amateur [ˋæməˏtʃʊr] adj. 業餘的，外行的，非職業的

㉒ 我們俱樂部有很多專業的舞者。**There are many professional dancers in our club.** Track 1016

重要詞彙 club [klʌb] n. 俱樂部，社團

看情境學對話

Track 1017

A: Fedman, how did you learn to dance?

\中譯/

A：費得曼，你是怎麼學會跳舞的？

B: Well, when I was ten years old, I became interested in ① dancing. Then my parents signed up the dance class for me. But then my parents emigrated to ② Spain, a Latin American country where people love dancing. So I started to learn tango with my professional teacher, who taught me how to dance and listen to music and melody. To be honest, I really learned a lot about tango there, and it benefited me a lot ③ .

B：我十歲的時候開始對舞蹈產生興趣，然後父母替我報名了舞蹈班。不過，之後我父母就移民到了西班牙。西班牙是拉美國家，那裡的人們很熱愛跳舞。於是我也開始跟著我的專業老師學探戈，他教會我舞步以及如何聆聽音樂和旋律。老實說，我在那裡真的學會了很多關於探戈的知識，讓我受益匪淺。

學習英文Fun輕鬆！

文化小站

中西方在演唱會方面本也存在著一些差異。華人看演出喜歡坐著，但由於西方人相對比較開放、熱情，在演唱會上，通常歌迷都是站著的，就算他們有凳子也會選擇站起來，與歌手一起唱，一起跳，一起互動。歌手發佈新歌曲，就會開小型或者大型的演唱會，有的歌手甚至開世界巡迴演唱會，這持續的時間很長，通常都得好幾個月。關於演唱會門票，需要先確定演唱會的日期，然後透過網站提前購票。在演唱會現場，基本上都是離舞臺越近票價越高。如果你沒有買到票的話，可以購買二手票，當然價格肯定會高一點。現今，中西方在演唱會方面的差異則是越來越小。

放鬆心情

Unit 53

Dances
舞蹈

讓我們跳起來吧，不用在乎節奏，不用在乎動作，就這樣灑脫一點，將自己的好心情激發出來，釋放自我，得到真我。

精選實用會話例句

❶ 讓我們高高興興地跳舞吧。Let's dance happily. Track 995

重要詞彙 happily [ˈhæpɪlɪ] adv. 快樂地

❷ 我跳舞跳得很好。I do well in dancing. Track 996

片語釋義 do well in 在某方面做得好

❸ 去跳個舞怎麼樣？How about going dancing? Track 997

片語釋義 go dancing 跳舞，去跳舞

❹ 舞蹈可以讓人的身體靈活。

Dancing can keep people physically flexible. Track 998

重要詞彙 flexible [`flɛksəbl] n. 可彎曲的，有彈性的

❺ 老師教會了我們新舞步。

The teacher taught us new dance moves. Track 999

片語釋義 dance move 舞步

❻ 我能有幸邀請你跳一支舞嗎？

May I invite you for a dance? Track 1000

同義表達 Can I have the honor to dance with you?

❼ 能和你跳下一支舞嗎？May I have the next dance? Track 1001

重要詞彙 dance [dæns] n. & v. 跳舞

❽ 我聽說你的拉丁舞跳得很好。

I hear you can dance Latin dance well. Track 1002

片語釋義 Latin dance 拉丁舞

B: You know, I prefer classical music.	B：你知道，我更喜歡古典音樂。
A: Yes, I know that, but I want you to feel the atmosphere of a live rock concert. You can sing and dance with the singer to release your stress.	A：是的，不過我想讓你感受一下現場搖滾演唱會的氣氛。你可以跟歌手一起跳舞、唱歌來釋放壓力。
B: How do you know I've been stressed out ③ lately? I never told you.	B：你怎麼知道我最近壓力很大？我從來沒有告訴過你。
A: I know you're pretending to ④ be strong. But in front of me, you don't have to pretend. Let's go back to ⑤ the subject, will you go to the concert with me?	A：我知道你在假裝堅強。不過在我面前，你不需要偽裝。回到那個話題，你會跟我一起去看演唱會嗎？
B: All right. You convinced me. I'll try.	B：好吧。被你說服了。我會嘗試一下的。
A: Wonderful. The concert will start at eight o'clock at night.	A：太棒了。演唱會在晚上八點開始。
B: OK. Have you bought tickets?	B：你買票了嗎？
A: Yes, I just got the tickets this morning.	A：是的，我也是今天早上才拿到票的。
B: Well, see you that day.	B：好的，那天見。
A: Okay.	A：好的。

【程度提升，加分單字】

★**professor** [prə`fɛsɚ] n. 教授 ★**pretend** [prɪ`tɛnd] v. 假裝，偽裝
★**convince** [kən`vɪns] v. 使相信，說服

① pay a visit to

意為「拜訪，參觀，探望」，後可接人，表示「拜訪某人」，也可接地點，表示「參觀某地」。

② during the day

意為「在這天當中，在白天期間」，特指某一天，而 during a day 則泛指某一天。

③ stress out

意為「承受極大的壓力」，若構成 stress sb out 則指的是「使某人緊張，令某人焦慮不安」。

④ pretend to be

意為「假裝是……」，通常還可構成 pretend to do sth 意為「假裝做某事」，或者 pretend to be doing sth 表示「假裝正在做某事」。

⑤ go back to

意為「回到」，to 後可跟名詞、動名詞和動詞原形。go back to do sth指回去然後做什麼事情，而 go back to doing sth 則指之前被打斷後，回去繼續做剛才的事情。

學習英文Fun輕鬆！

On the way back to school after watching a ballet show, a kindergarten teacher asked her students, " What do you think of this ballet show?" "I hope the ballet dancers grow taller, so that I don't have to stand on tiptoe all the time," replied the youngest girl in the class.

在觀看完芭蕾舞表演回學校的路上，一名幼稚園老師問她的學生們：「你們覺得這次的芭蕾舞表演怎麼樣？」班上年齡最小的女孩回答說：「我希望芭蕾舞演員能再長高些，這樣我就不用一直踮著腳看她們了。」

文化小站

舞蹈，有多元的社會意義和作用，包括運動、社交、祭祀等。舞蹈可分為生活舞蹈和藝術舞蹈。顧名思義，生活舞蹈是為了生活需要而進行的活動，而藝術舞蹈是為了表演給觀眾欣賞。不過在現代人們的觀念中，舞蹈通常都被認為是一種表演藝術，它能表現人們的情感和思想。舞蹈的種類多樣化，各個國家也都有自己獨特的舞蹈風格。例如美國的街舞，是美國黑人貧民的舞蹈，後來被歸為嘻哈文化的一部分，具有較強的表演性和競爭性。街舞流行於全世界，不過由於不同的人們對它的定義不同，它也相對會有些改變。另外，芭蕾舞你肯定也有一定的瞭解，產自於歐洲，女演員穿上芭蕾舞鞋向人們展示優雅，被稱為「腳尖上的藝術」。爵士舞現在也很流行，也是美國現代舞，是一種外放性的舞蹈，比較活潑又富動感。它由被販賣的非洲黑人們帶到美國本土，逐漸發展為大眾化的舞蹈，其中麥可・傑克森為爵士舞舞者的傑出代表。

放鬆心情

Unit 54

Reading

看書

書中自有黃金屋，書中自有顏如玉。可見，書裡包含了多麼多寶貴的知識。所以讓我們多多地沉浸在知識的海洋裡，感受書中的世界吧。

精選實用會話例句

❶ 你有看書的習慣嗎？
Do you have a way of reading books? Track 1018
重要片語 have a way of 有……的習慣

❷ 我酷愛讀書。I have a passion for books. Track 1019
重要片語 have a passion for 對……非常喜好

❸ 我經常用看書來消磨時光。
I often loiter my time away in reading. Track 1020
重要詞彙 loiter [`lɔɪtɚ] v. 消磨（時光），閒逛

❹ 讀書使我快樂。Reading makes me happy. Track 1021
同義表達 I am happy when reading.

❺ 你在讀什麼書？What are you reading? Track 1022
同義表達 What book are you reading?

❻ 我正在讀一本書叫《孤雛淚》。
I am reading a book called Oliver Twist. Track 1023
重要詞彙 read [rid] v. 閱讀，研究

❼ 你看書快嗎？Are you a fast reader? Track 1024
重要詞彙 reader [`ridɚ] n. 讀者

❽ 我只有週末才有時間看書。
I don't have time to read except weekends. Track 1025
重要片語 have time to do 有時間做某事

❾ 看完這本書後你學到了什麼？
What have you learned after reading? Track 1026
重要詞彙 learn [lɝn] v. 學習，學會

❿ 我看書看得好累。I am tired of reading. Track 1027
重要片語 be tired of 厭倦，厭煩

⓫ 他從不看書。He never reads. Track 1028
同義表達 He never reads books.

⓬ 他正在專心看書。He is absorbed in reading. Track 1029
重要片語 be absorbed in 專心於，全神貫注於

⓭ 你更喜歡哪本書？
Which book do you find more attractive? Track 1030
重要詞彙 attractive [əˋtræktɪv] adj. 招人喜歡的，迷人的

⓮ 我女兒最喜歡看漫畫書。
My daughter likes comic books best. Track 1031
片語釋義 comic book 連環漫畫冊

⓯ 這本書值得仔細研讀。
This book deserves careful perusal. Track 1032
重要詞彙 deserve [dɪˋzɝv] v. 值得，應得

⓰ 那本書我已經看了很多遍了。
I've read that book more than once. Track 1033
片語釋義 more than once 不止一次

⓱ 這本書讀起來很費力。
This book is heavy to read. Track 1034
片語釋義 heavy to read 讀起來很費力

⓲ 誰是你最喜歡的作家？Who is your favorite writer? Track 1035
重要詞彙 writer [ˋraɪtɚ] n. 作家，作者

⑲ **他正在專心看書。He is burying himself in a book.** Track 1036

重要片語 bury oneself in 埋頭於，專心於

⑳ **我正在看一本關於人類文明起源的書。**
I am reading a book about the origins of the human civilization. Track 1037

重要詞彙 civilization [ˌsɪvlə`zeʃən] **n.** 文明

㉑ **她很愛看書。She has a strong love of reading.** Track 1038

重要片語 have a strong love of 對……有強烈的喜愛

看情境學對話

Track 1039

	中譯
A: I often see you reading in the garden. Do you like reading very much?	A：我經常看到你在花園裡看書，你很喜歡看書嗎？
B: Yes, I love it. Reading not only makes me calm, but also enriches my knowledge ①. And I can learn about the culture of different countries and experience the author's thoughts.	B：是的，我很喜歡。讀書不僅能讓我平靜，還能豐富我的知識。並且我可以瞭解到不同國家的文化和體會作者的思想。
A: That's right. Did you read a lot of books?	A：沒錯。那你讀了很多書嗎？
B: Yes, I read a lot. In fact, the main reason is that I have no TV. I have the ability to ② buy it, but in my heart I prefer reading.	B：是的，我讀了很多。其實，主要的原因是我沒有電視。雖然我有能力買，但是在我的內心深處更傾向於讀書。
A: Oh, how many books do you get through ③ a week?	A：你一週能讀多少本書？

B: I'm not sure, it's probably one, because I only have time to read after work.	B：我不太確定，大概一本，因為我只有下班後才有時間看書。
A: Pretty good.	A：很不錯啊。
B: Another reason is that reading gives me imagination, but TV can't.	B：我喜歡看書的另一個原因就是讀書能給我想像力，但電視不能。
A: I hear you ④ . What kind of books do you usually read?	A：我明白。你通常都看什麼類型的書呢？
B: Let me see ⑤ , probably a little more detective fiction. Of course, there are world-famous books as well.	B：我想想，大概偵探小說多一點。當然還有世界名著。
A: Great. Where do you like reading best?	A：很棒。你最喜歡在哪裡看書？
B: On the trains, because I travel a lot. It is worth mentioning that some passengers will look over at my book.	B：我喜歡在火車上看書，因為我經常出差。值得一提的是，有些乘客也會看我的書。
A: Cool.	A：很酷啊。

【程度提升，加分單字】

★**enrich** [ɪnˋrɪtʃ] **v.** 使富有，豐富 ★**imagination** [ɪˏmædʒəˋneʃən] **n.** 想像力
★**detective** [dɪˋtɛktɪv] **n.** & **adj.** 偵探的 ★**passenger** [ˋpæsndʒɚ] **n.** 乘客

① **enrich one's knowledge**

意為「豐富某人的知識」，若表示「拓展某人的知識」可用 broaden one's knowledge 和 expand one's knowledge。

② **have the ability to**

意為「有能力做……」，to 在這裡是不定式，後面跟動詞原形，這個片語用 the 表示特指，特指有某能力，have the ability 還可構成 have the ability of，後常跟名詞或者動名詞。

③ **get through**

意為「通過，完成」，可與 go through 通用。

④ **I hear you**

意為「我明白，我懂你的意思了」，其在口語中單獨成句時也需要根據語境分析。

⑤ **let me see**

意為「讓我想想，讓我看看」，常用在口語中。

學習英文Fun輕鬆！

1.Traveling thousands of miles is better than reading thousands of books.
讀萬卷書，行萬里路。

2.Knowledge is power.
知識就是力量。

3.The reading of all good books is like a conversation with the finest men of past centuries. -Rene Descartes
讀好書就像是我們與過去幾個世紀最傑出的人談話。──雷內・笛卡爾

4.Without reading, the mind will stop. -Diderot
不讀書的人思想就會停止。──狄德羅

5.Reading without reflecting is like eating without digesting. -Edmund Burke
讀書而不思考，就像食而不化。 ──艾德蒙・柏克

文化小站

書能增長人們的知識，拓展人們的視野。那些我們無法親身體會的事物我們可以先從書中瞭解到，然後有機會的話就進行實踐。1995年，聯合國科教文組織將每年的4月23日定為「世界讀書日」，也可稱為「世界圖書日」，可見書成了全世界都在提倡的事物，各個國家也透過不同的活動來響應這個號召，例如英國會舉辦故事人物模仿大賽或者各類型的書展等。說起書，西方人讀書是比較積極的，他們在坐火車、飛機、地鐵或者公園休息的時候都喜歡拿出書來閱讀，儘管近年來這種風氣稍有退化，但是與華人地區相比，讀書的風氣還是要濃得多。在華人地區，書一般都放在書房內，而美國人則經常將書放在隨時能拿到的地方，以方便閱讀，他們可以在沙發上，也可以在陽臺上。美國人比較重視寫作能力和獨立思考的能力，因此很多人都是通過閱讀來培養自己的這些能力，他們從小就會被要求讀大量的經典作品。由此也希望中國的「低頭族們」能多將心思放在閱讀上，少玩手機。

放鬆心情

Unit 55

Karaoke

KTV

讓我們高聲歌唱吧，不管你是五音不全還是歌王，都可以在這裡盡情嘶吼，讓自己的心情得到釋放，感受來自歌聲的力量。

精選實用會話例句

1. 讓我們先唱這首歌。Let's sing this song first. Track 1040
   同義表達 Let's begin with this song.

2. 我的愛好就是唱歌。My hobby is singing. Track 1041
   重要詞彙 hobby [ˈhɒbɪ] n. 興趣，業餘愛好

3. 我喜歡唱她的歌。I like to sing her songs. Track 1042
   重要詞彙 song [sɔŋ] n. 歌曲

4. 你總是唱歌跑調。
   You always sing out of key. Track 1043
   重要片語 out of key 與……不和諧，與……不合拍

5. 離我們家最近的 KTV 在哪裡？
   Where is the nearest KTV to our home? Track 1044
   重要詞彙 nearest [nɪrɪst] adj. 最近的，最親近的

6. 我今晚要跟同事去 KTV， 你要來嗎？
   I'm going to KTV with my colleagues tonight. Wanna come? Track 1045
   重要詞彙 colleague [kɑˋlig] n. 同事，同行

7. 你已經幫我們預約過包廂了嗎？
   Have you reserved a room for us? Track 1046
   同義表達 Have you made a reservation for us yet?

❽ 我記不清這首歌的節奏了。I can't remember the rhythm of this song clearly. Track 1047

重要詞彙 rhythm [ˈrɪðəm] n. 節奏，韻律

❾ 你能幫我把音調降一下嗎？
Could you lower the tone for me? Track 1048

片語釋義 lower the tone 降低音調／格調

❿ 把麥克風給我！Give me the microphone! Track 1049

重要詞彙 microphone [ˋmaɪkrə͵fon] n. 麥克風，話筒

⓫ 你先從點歌單裡選歌。
Choose songs from the song list first. Track 1050

片語釋義 song list 歌曲列表，點歌單

⓬ 這裡可選擇的歌曲很多。
It has a large selection of songs. Track 1051

重要詞彙 selection [səˋlɛkʃən] n. 選擇

⓭ 你應該注意這首歌的歌詞。You're supposed to pay attention to the lyrics. Track 1052

片語釋義 pay attention to 注意

⓮ 你想唱英文歌曲嗎？
Do you want to sing English songs? Track 1053

片語釋義 English song 英語歌曲

⓯ 把音量調大一些。Turn up the volume. Track 1054

重要詞彙 volume [ˋvɑljəm] n. 音量，體積

⓰ 請大聲唱出來。Please sing out. Track 1055

片語釋義 sing out 高聲唱，喊出

⓱ 你可以跟著曲子哼唱。You can sing along with the tune. Track 1056

片語釋義 sing along 跟唱

⓲ 《昨日重現》這首歌怎麼樣？
How about "Yesterday Once More"? Track 1057

重要片語 once more 再，又，再次

⑲ 記得這首歌嗎？Remember this song?

Track 1058

同義表達 Do you remember this song?

⑳ 你應該用心唱這首歌。

You should sing the song wholeheartedly.

Track 1059

重要詞彙 wholeheartedly [ˌholˋhɑrtɪdlɪ] **adv.**

全心全意地，一心，真心誠意

㉑ 離麥克風近一些。Be closer to the microphone.

Track 1060

重要片語 be closer to 更接近，更親近

㉒ 我跟不上這首歌。I can't keep up with the song.

Track 1061

片語釋義 keep up with 跟上

看情境學對話

Track 1062

	中譯
A: You sing high notes ① perfectly; you are such a good singer.	A：你高音唱得是如此完美，你真的很會唱歌。
B: Erm, stereo system helped a lot. And I'm familiar with ② the song, so I don't have to be distracted from ③ the lyrics.	B：是立體音響設備起了作用。而且我對這首歌很熟悉，所以我不用分心在歌詞上。
A: Come on. ④ You are too modest. Let me take a look at the song list and order a song for you. What kind of songs do you like to sing?	A：得了吧。你太謙虛了。讓我翻閱一下點歌單為你點一首歌。你喜歡唱什麼類型的歌曲？
B: Maybe you can order me a rock song. I want to try a crazy feeling.	B：或許你可以給我點一首搖滾歌曲。我想嘗試一下瘋狂的感覺。
A: No problem. Wow, there are so many rock songs here that I don't know which one to choose. Can I choose one at random for you?	A：沒問題。哇哦，這裡的搖滾歌曲真多，我都不知道選哪一首了。我能隨便給你選一首嗎？

B: OK. Oh, I love this song. It's by my favorite singer.	B：可以。哦，我很喜歡這首歌，這是我最喜歡的歌手唱的。
A: But it is a duet.	A：但是這首歌是一個二重唱。
B: I know. Come on! Pick up the microphone and sing along.	B：我知道。來吧，拿起麥克風跟我一起唱。
A: No, I need a break ⑤ . I've been singing for a long time, so I'm tired now. Maybe you can invite Alan with you.	A：不了，我需要休息一下。我已經唱很久了，所以現在很累。你可以邀請艾倫一起。
B: Good idea. But he's been calling outside, and I haven't seen him for half an hour.	B：想法不錯，但是他一直在外面打電話，我已經半個小時沒見到他了。
A: Well, I didn't notice it. Does he have an emergency?	A：好吧，我都沒注意到。他有急事嗎？
B: No, he's just coaxing his girlfriend.	B：不是，他只是在哄他的女朋友。

【程度提升，加分單字】

★**modest** [ˈmɒdɪst] **adj.** 謙虛的，謙遜的
★**random** [ˈrændəm] **adj.** 隨意的，隨機的
★**emergency** [ɪˈmɝdʒənsɪ] **n.** 緊急情況

① **high note**

意為「高音」，常構成 sing a high note, sing high notes 或 hit the high notes 表示「唱高音」。

② **be familiar with**

意為「熟悉，認識」，後面跟的受詞必須是無生命的東西。

③ **be distracted from**

意為「被……轉移了注意力，被……分神」，與 be distracted by 有所區別的是，前者指從什麼上轉移了注意力，後面接的是在注意力轉移之前關注的對象，後者指被什麼轉移了注意力，後面接的是轉移你注意力的對象。

④ **come on**

此時意為「得了吧，來吧」，該片語可表達的意思還有很多，具體意思要根據語境分析。

⑤ **need a break**

意為「需要休息」，其等同於 need a rest。

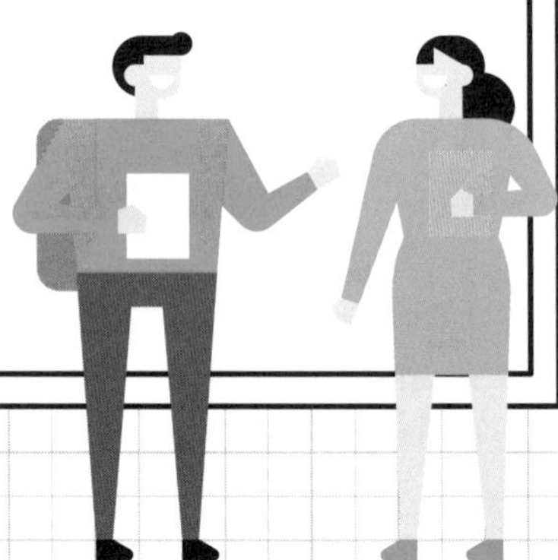

放鬆心情

Unit 56

Amusement Park 遊樂園

來啊，來玩啊，反正有大把時光。一旦踏入遊樂園，整個人都能感受到活力和年輕。此刻，已經關不住那顆內心深處的躁動心靈。

精選實用會話例句

1. 坐纜車怎麼樣？How about taking the cable car? Track 1063
片語釋義 cable car 纜車

2. 你喜歡坐旋轉木馬嗎？
Do you enjoy riding the merry-go-round? Track 1064
片語釋義 merry-go-round 旋轉木馬

3. 我想去開碰碰車。I want to drive bumper cars. Track 1065
片語釋義 bumper cars 碰碰車

4. 記得繫上安全帶。Keep in mind to fasten your seatbelt. Track 1066
片語釋義 fasten the seatbelt 系好安全帶

5. 迪士尼是一個主題樂園。Disneyland is a theme park. Track 1067
重要詞彙 Disneyland [ˈdɪznɪlænd] n. 迪士尼樂園

6. 我兒子很喜歡露天遊樂場。
My son loves fairground very much. Track 1068
重要詞彙 fairground [ˋfɛrˌgraʊnd] n. 露天遊樂場

7. 對我來說，最刺激的就是海盜船。For me, the greatest thrill is playing sea rover. Track 1069
重要詞彙 thrill [θrɪl] n. 緊張，激動

8. 我沒有膽量玩雲霄飛車。
I don't have the guts to ride a roller coaster. Track 1070
片語釋義 roller coaster 雲霄飛車

9 我不怕坐摩天輪。
I have no fear to take the Ferris wheel. Track 1071
片語釋義 Ferris wheel 摩天輪

10 你敢玩高空彈跳嗎？
Do you dare to go bungee jumping? Track 1072
片語釋義 bungee jumping 高空彈跳

11 海盜船和高空彈跳哪個更有趣？**Which is more fun, the sea rover or the bungee jumping?** Track 1073
片語釋義 sea rover 海盜船

12 在摩天輪上俯瞰這個城市很讓人興奮。**It is so exciting to overlook the city on Ferris wheel.** Track 1074
同義表達 Overlooking the city on the Ferris wheel is so exciting.

13 坐這個雲霄飛車把我嚇壞了。
The roller coaster horrified me. Track 1075
重要詞彙 horrify [ˋhɔrə͵faɪ] v. 使感到恐怖

14 我打算在遊樂場待一整天！**I am going to stay at the amusement park the whole day!** Track 1076
片語釋義 the whole day 整天

15 我最喜歡的項目是海盜船。**My favorite item is sea rover.** Track 1077
重要詞彙 item [ˋaɪtəm] n. 項目

16 我們中午就會到遊樂園了。
We'll reach the amusement park at noon. Track 1078
片語釋義 at noon 在中午

17 他特別喜歡高空彈跳。**He has a particular fondness for bungee jumping.** Track 1079
重要片語 have a particular fondness for 特別喜歡

18 你們昨天在遊樂園玩得高興嗎？**Did you have lots of fun at the amusement park yesterday?** Track 1080
同義表達 Did you have a good time at the amusement park yesterday?

⑲ **我從來沒有去過遊樂園。**
I have never been to an amusement park. Track 1081
片語釋義 amusement park 遊樂園

⑳ **乘旋轉木馬會讓我頭暈。Riding the merry-go-round will make me feel dizzy.** Track 1082
重要詞彙 dizzy [ˈdɪzɪ] **adj.** 眩暈的

㉑ **讓我們坐纜車到達山頂吧。Let's take a cable car to the top of the mountain.** Track 1083
重要詞彙 mountain [ˈmaʊntn] **n.** 山

看情境學對話

Track 1084

	中譯
A: Jason, I heard you went to the amusement park yesterday, didn't you? ①	A：傑森，我聽說你昨天去遊樂園，是嗎？
B: Yes.	B：是的。
A: How did you feel?	A：你覺得怎麼樣？
B: I was really tired, but I had a good day.	B：我覺得很累，不過我還是度過了很愉快的一天。
A: Well, how do you like it? ②	A：你覺得那裡怎麼樣？
B: Marvelous! A lot of tourists arrived there in a stream ③ of private cars and buses every day, that is to say, it's really crowded, but I still want to go there again because that's a fascinating place.	B：很棒！儘管那裡每天都有很多遊客隨私家車和巴士蜂擁而至，換句話說，那裡真的很擁擠，但我還想再去一次。因為那裡是個讓人著迷的地方。
A: What attracts you so much in Disneyland?	A：在迪士尼樂園裡是什麼如此吸引你？

B: As far as I am concerned, the Magic Kingdom is the most exciting thing for me. I think it attracts me the most.	B：就我來說，神奇王國是最讓我興奮的了，我覺得它最吸引我。
A: What age occupies the largest proportion?	A：什麼年齡的人占最大比重？
B: I'm not sure, but there are people of all ages ④ , from children to old people.	B：我不確定，不過那裡有各種年齡層的人，從小孩到老人都有。
A: I see. How long does it take to play there? Is one day enough?	A：我明白了。在那裡玩需要多長時間？一天夠嗎？
B: If you want to take a good look at it, it doesn't seem enough.	B：如果你想好好看看的話，貌似不太夠。
A: But I only have one day. How should I visit?	A：但是我只有一天的時間，我應該怎樣遊覽呢？
B: In that case, I suggest you take the tour bus, which will save you a lot of time. I have a guidebook here, which may help you.	B：如果是這種情況的話，我建議你坐遊覽車，這樣你會節省很多時間。我這裡有一本旅遊指南，或許會對你有幫助。
A: Thank you so much.	A：謝謝你。

★**amusement** [ə`mjuzmənt] **n.** 娛樂，遊戲
★**marvelous** [`mɑrvələs] **adj.** 不可思議的，非凡的
★**crowded** [kraʊdɪd] **adj.** 水泄不通的，擁擠的
★**fascinating** [`fæsn͵etɪŋ] **adj.** 迷人的，有極大吸引力的
★**occupy** [`ɑkjə͵paɪ] **v.** 佔領，使用

對話解析

① **I heard you went to the amusement park yesterday, didn't you?**

這句話中包含了特殊形式反義疑問句，疑問部分應是對受詞子句的反問，受詞子句是肯定句和一般過去時態，故疑問部分用否定形式的一般過去時態 didn't。

② **how do you like it**

意為「你覺得怎麼樣」，等同於 what do you think of it，一般用來詢問某人對某事的評價。

③ **in a stream**

意為「川流不息地，連續不斷地」，此處表示「蜂擁而至」。

④ **people of all ages**

意為「各個年齡層的人」，與其有些相似的片語是 all walks of life，意為「各行各業，各界」。

文化小站

美國人對遊樂園的興趣非常濃厚。在美國，遊樂園很普遍，大大小小有400 個，每年大約有 3 億人進遊樂園玩，是美國最受歡迎的娛樂場所了。又因為美國人偏愛極限運動，愛刺激，所以遊樂園裡的各項設施，例如雲霄飛車、高空彈跳以及海盜船等都少不了，他們要的就是這種刺激的感覺。全世界最受歡迎的樂園當屬迪士尼了，它也是主題公園，來這裡的人一般都是帶著自己的孩子或者女朋友，體驗別樣的樂趣。目前，在美國加州和佛羅里達州、日本東京、法國巴黎、中國香港以及上海都建立了迪士尼樂園，其帶來的收益很是可觀。

放鬆心情

Unit 57 Picnic 野餐

一起來野餐吧，水果、小餅乾、壽司、麵包等等應有盡有，讓你在欣賞美景的同時還能大飽口福。還在等什麼？加入我們吧！

精選實用會話例句

1. 這週日去野餐怎麼樣？
   How about going for a picnic this Sunday? Track 1085
   片語釋義 go for a picnic 去野餐

2. 讓我們來定一下野餐時間。
   Let's fix a date for the picnic. Track 1086
   片語釋義 fix a date 定日期

3. 我們去哪裡野餐？**Where shall we go for the picnic?** Track 1087
   重要詞彙 picnic [ˈpɪknɪk] n. & v. 野餐郊遊

4. 這週末我想去野餐。
   I want to have a picnic this weekend. Track 1088
   片語釋義 have a picnic 去野餐

5. 如果天氣允許的話，我們明天就去野餐。**If the weather permits, we will have a picnic tomorrow.** Track 1089
   重要詞彙 permit [pɚˋmɪt] v. 允許，許可

6. 我們可以去附近的公園野餐。
   We can picnic in the park nearby. Track 1090
   同義表達 We can go to the park for a picnic nearby.

7. 我們需要帶一些食物和炊具。**We need to bring some foods and the cooking utensils.** Track 1091
   重要詞彙 utensil [juˋtɛnsəl] n. 器具，用具

8 你能幫我準備一下野餐需要的東西嗎？Could you do me a favor to prepare for the picnic? Track 1092

重要片語 do sb a favor 幫某人一個忙

9 我來負責生火。I will be in charge of the campfire. Track 1093

重要片語 be in charge of 負責

10 我想知道你們是否所有東西都帶齊了。
I wonder if you have got everything. Track 1094

同義表達 I want to know if you have taken all the things with you.

11 你能幫我們找一些木柴嗎？
Could you find some firewood for us? Track 1095

重要詞彙 firewood [`faɪr͵wʊd] **n.** 木柴，柴火

12 我們一起來烤些牛排和火腿片吧。Let's roast some beef steaks and sliced hams together. Track 1096

重要詞彙 steak [stek] **n.** 牛排

13 我們來收拾一下野餐的剩餘物。
Let's tidy up the remains of our picnic. Track 1097

重要詞彙 remains [rɪ`menz] **n.** 剩餘物，遺體，殘骸，遺跡

14 你決定去哪裡野餐了嗎？
Have you decided where to have the picnic? Track 1098

重要詞彙 decide [dɪˋsaɪd] **v.** 決定

15 你應該穿一件厚外套。You should wear a heavy coat. Track 1099

重要片語 heavy coat 厚外套

16 帶上些飲料否則我們會口渴的。Bring some drinks with you or we will be very thirsty. Track 1100

重要詞彙 thirsty [ˋθɝstɪ] **adj.** 口渴的

17 請拿些醬汁過來。 Fetch some sauce, please. Track 1101

重要詞彙 fetch [fɛtʃ] **v.** 取來，拿來

18 你最好現在就開始搭帳篷。
You'd better start to put up tent now. Track 1102

片語釋義 put up tent 搭帳篷

⑲ 你對這次的野餐有什麼建議嗎？Do you have any suggestions for the picnic? Track 1103

同義表達 Do you have any idea about the picnic?

⑳ 在湖邊野餐很吸引我。Picnics by the lake have great attraction for me. Track 1104

重要片語 have great attraction for 吸引

㉑ 這個食物合我的胃口。This food is quite to my taste. Track 1105

重要片語 be to my taste 合我的胃口

看情境學對話

Track 1106

	中譯
A: My friends and I are going to have a picnic ① this weekend. Would you like to go?	A：我和朋友們打算這週末去野餐，你要去嗎？
B: I'd love to. Have you decided where to have a picnic?	B：我想去。你們已經決定去哪裡野餐了嗎？
A: Not yet ② . Which do you think is better, the park or the lakeside?	A：還沒有。你覺得哪個比較好，公園還是湖邊？
B: Personally, I prefer the lake; we can still choose a place where there is grass.	B：我個人更喜歡湖邊，我們依然可以選擇有綠草的地方。
A: That's right. Do you have any good advice?	A：沒錯。你有好的建議嗎？
B: I just thought of ③ a suitable place for a picnic; I used to go there a lot.	B：我剛剛想到了一個很適合野餐的地方，我以前經常去。
A: Do you remember how to get there?	A：那你還記得怎麼去嗎？

B: I don't remember clearly, but I can ask my friend Mary.	B：我記不太清楚，不過我可以問問我的朋友瑪麗。
A: OK. It's up to you to decide. Moreover, remember to put on your heavy coat that day.	A：好的。這事由你來決定。另外，記得在那天穿上厚外套。
B: Yeah. Have you checked the weather forecast?	B：好啊。你看過天氣預報了嗎？
A: Yes, it says it will be a little cold that day.	A：是的，天氣預報說那天會有點冷。
B: I know. Have you got everything ready for the picnic?	B：好的，我知道了。你們準備好所有野餐的東西了嗎？
A: Yes, we are all set ④ .	A：是的，我們都準備好了。
B: By the way, if it's convenient, please bring your camera and enough films.	B：太好了，我都有點迫不及待了。對了，如果方便的話，請帶上你的照相機和足夠的膠捲。
A: I'm sorry. My camera was borrowed by my friend, but I can bring my brother's.	A：不好意思，我的照相機被朋友借走了，不過我可以帶我哥的。
B: It couldn't be better.	B：那就再好不過了。

★**lakeside** [ˋlekˏsaɪd] **n.** 湖邊　★**forecast** [ˋforˏkæst] **n.** 預測，預報

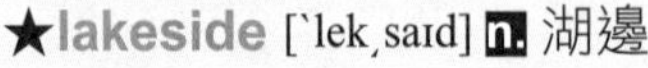
★**film** [fɪlm] **n.** 膠片

① have a picnic

意為「去野餐」，等同於 go on a picnic 和 go for a picnic，這幾個片語基本上沒有什麼差別，可以通用。

② not yet

意為「尚未，還沒有」，在口語中可單獨成句，用於回答完成時態的詢問。

③ think of

意為「想到，想起」，後常接名詞、代詞和動名詞。

④ we are all set

意為「我們都準備好了」。all set 在美俚語中表示「準備就緒」，在口語中可單獨使用。

文化小站

野餐，是人們熱衷的戶外休閒活動，其最早始於 18 世紀的歐洲，那時是一種較正式的皇家社交活動。然而，現在的野餐則是作為一種大眾休閒娛樂的戶外活動，其在發達國家相對流行。野餐時的環境很重要，春暖花開時節，郊外公園或湖邊等環境優美的地方是人們的首選。野餐後，人們還可以在這樣的環境中小睡一下，這也符合西方人愛享受的性格。對於野餐的食物，有的人會選擇從家裡自帶食物，有的人則選擇在野外親手烹飪，總之都要事先安排好帶哪些東西。野餐在西方電影中是男女社交活動的重要選擇，很多電影中都會出現野餐的場景。近年來，越來越多的亞洲人開始喜歡野餐，享受郊外的休閒快樂。

放鬆心情 Unit 58

Bar and Pub 酒吧

來到酒吧的人通常都有不同的目的，有的是為了美酒，有的是為了美人，而有的人是為了社交，那你，是為了什麼呢？

精選實用會話例句

1. 我們今晚去酒吧怎麼樣？
Shall we go to the bar tonight? Track 1107
片語釋義 go to the bar 去酒吧，當律師

2. 今晚我能請你喝杯酒嗎？
May I buy you a drink tonight? Track 1108
重要片語 buy sb sth 買給某人某物

3. 給我來一杯威士忌。A glass of whisky, please. Track 1109
片語釋義 a glass of 一杯

4. 給我倒杯啤酒。Pour me a glass of beer. Track 1110
重要詞彙 beer [bɪr] n. 啤酒

5. 我想要一杯加冰的威士忌。
I'd like a glass of Whisky on the rocks. Track 1111
片語釋義 on the rocks （酒等飲料）加冰

6. 讓我們來個一醉方休！Let's tie one on! Track 1112
片語釋義 tie one on 喝得大醉，暢飲

7. 再來一杯怎麼樣？How about another cup? Track 1113
同義表達 Would you like a refill?

8. 我再給你來一杯？Can I get you another drink? Track 1114
重要詞彙 drink [drɪŋk] n. & v. 酒，飲料，喝酒

9 我的酒量很小。I get drunk easily.
Track 1115

片語釋義 get drunk 喝醉

10 我還清醒著呢。I am still sober.
Track 1116

重要詞彙 sober [ˋsobɚ] adj. 頭腦清醒的，冷靜的

11 我有點暈。I am a little dizzy.
Track 1117

同義表達 I feel a little woozy.

12 他爛醉如泥。He is as drunk as a lord.
Track 1118

片語釋義 as drunk as a lord 爛醉如泥

13 為我們的友誼乾杯。Let's toast to the friendship.
Track 1119

同義表達 Here's to our friendship.

14 威士忌賣完了。Whisky is out of stock.
Track 1120

片語釋義 out of stock 無貨存的，賣完了

15 我們何不開一瓶香檳慶祝一下？Why not open a bottle of champagne to celebrate?
Track 1121

片語釋義 a bottle of 一瓶

16 我想要一瓶低卡啤酒。I'd like a bottle of light beer.
Track 1122

片語釋義 light beer 淡啤酒，低卡啤酒

17 你要不要試一下這杯雞尾酒？
Would you like to have a try at this cocktail?
Track 1123

片語釋義 have a try 嘗試一下，試試看

18 我喜歡和你一起喝酒。I like drinking with you.
Track 1124

重要片語 drink with sb 和某人一起喝酒

19 他一定喝了讓人易醉的酒。
He must drink the heady wine.
Track 1125

重要詞彙 heady [ˋhɛdɪ] adj.（酒等）易使人醉的

20 我更喜歡生啤。I prefer draft beer.
Track 1126

片語釋義 draft beer 生啤酒

㉑ 你喜歡國產的還是進口的啤酒？**Which do you prefer, domestic or imported beer?** Track 1127

重要詞彙 import [ˋɪmport] v. 進口

㉒ 請再給我來一杯。**Please give me one more cup.** Track 1128

片語釋義 one more cup 再來一杯

看情境學對話

Track 1129

	中譯
A: Luke. It's been a while. ①	A：嗨，盧克，好久不見了。
B: Yes, it's been five years. You've changed a lot. What a coincidence ② to meet you at this bar.	B：是的，五年了，你變了很多。能在酒吧遇見你真的好巧啊。
A: Yes, you're still as handsome as ever.	A：是的，你還是跟以前一樣帥氣。
B: Thank you. Lisa, are you free tonight? Can I buy you a drink? ③	B：謝謝。麗莎，你今晚有空嗎？我能請你喝一杯嗎？
A: Of course. Let's tie one on.	A：當然可以了，讓我們來個一醉方休。
B: Are you sure? You will drink the heady wine in this bar.	B：你確定？你在這個酒吧會喝到很容易讓人醉的酒。
A: Yes, I'm sure. We haven't seen each other for five years, so I want to get drunk with you tonight.	A：是的，我很確定。我們已經五年沒見了，所以今晚我想跟你一醉方休。

B: We hit upon the same idea ④ . What would you like, whiskey or cocktail?	B：我們有一樣的想法。你想喝什麼，威士忌還是雞尾酒？
A: I'll leave it up to you.	A：這個由你決定。
B: What do you usually drink?	B：那你通常喝什麼酒？
A: Champagne.	A：香檳。
B: Okay. Waiter, two bottles of champagne. By the way, are you here alone?	B：好的。服務員，來兩瓶香檳。對了，你是一個人來的嗎？
A: No, sitting on the sofa at the door are my friends, but they have all brought their own boyfriends, except me.	A：不是，坐在門口沙發上的是我的朋友們，不過她們都帶著自己的男朋友，除了我。
B: Is that okay? Won't your friends be mad at you?	B：這樣沒關係嗎？你的朋友不會生你的氣嗎？
A: It's all right. I just don't want to be the third wheel ⑤ .	A：沒關係。我只是不想當電燈泡。
B: All right, would you like a refill?	B：好吧，再來一杯嗎？
A: Sure.	A：當然了。

★**coincidence** [ko`ɪnsɪdəns] **n.** 巧合　★**cocktail** [`kɑk͵tel] **n.** 雞尾酒

★**wheel** [hwil] **n.** 輪子　★**refill** [ri`fɪl] **n.** 續杯

① **it's been a while**

意為「好久不見」，是美國的地道俚語，a while 指的是「一段時間」，並沒有表明多長時間，但若放在此句中就表示很長時間。

② **what a coincidence**

意為「好巧啊」，可以用作感歎句，也可以後跟 that 從句或者 to do sth。

③ **Can I buy you a drink?**

意為「我能請你喝一杯嗎？」這裡的 drink 作為名詞，通常是「酒」的意思。

④ **hit upon the same idea**

意為「有一樣的想法」，hit upon 指的是「突然想到，偶然想出」。

⑤ **third wheel**

在美國俚語中指的是「電燈泡，累贅」，也就是兩個人約會時在旁邊的多餘的第三人。

美容美髮

Unit 59

Consultation and Requirement

諮詢與要求

你想要美麗帥氣的髮型嗎？你想要精緻的五官，滋潤出水的膚質嗎？那就快到我們店裡諮詢吧，我們還能根據您的要求量身定製哦。

精選實用會話例句

❶ 短髮又開始流行了嗎？
Is short hair fashionable again? Track 1130
重要詞彙 fashionable [ˋfæʃənəbəl] adj. 流行的，時髦的

❷ 我只想把頭髮剪短。**I just want to get a haircut.** Track 1131
片語釋義 get a haircut 剪頭髮

❸ 我想把我的頭髮染黑。**I want to dye my hair black.** Track 1132
重要詞彙 dye [daɪ] v. 染色

❹ 你覺得哪個髮型最適合我？
Which hairstyle do you think suits me best? Track 1133
重要詞彙 hairstyle [ˋhɛrˏstaɪl] n. 髮型

❺ 我想要冷燙。**I want a cold wave.** Track 1134
片語釋義 cold wave 冷燙

❻ 需要多久時間？**How long will this take?** Track 1135
同義表達 How long do I have to wait?

❼ 我能看其他髮型的圖片嗎？
Can I see pictures of other hairdos? Track 1136
重要詞彙 picture [ˋpɪktʃɚ] n. 圖片

❽ 我需要眼部護理。I need eye health care.
片語釋義 eye health care 眼部護理
Track 1137

❾ 這樣的力道可以嗎？How about the strength?
同義表達 Is the strength alright?
Track 1138

❿ 我想知道如何能提升我的膚質。I wonder how I can improve my skin.
重要詞彙 improve [ɪm`pruv] v. 提高，改善
Track 1139

⓫ 最簡單的美容方法是什麼？
What is the simplest beauty method?
重要詞彙 method [`mɛθəd] n. 方法
Track 1140

⓬ 你知道最經濟實惠的美容方法嗎？Have you got any idea about the most economical method of beauty?
重要詞彙 economical [ˌikə`nɑmɪkəl] adj. 節約的，經濟的
Track 1141

⓭ 你能告訴我一些肌膚補水的方法嗎？Could you tell me some ways to moisturize my skin?
重要詞彙 moisturize [ˈmɔɪstʃəraɪz] v. 給……增加水分，使濕潤
Track 1142

⓮ 我需要多久做一次臉部按摩？
How often do I need to do a facial massage?
片語釋義 facial massage 面部按摩
Track 1143

⓯ 一次皮膚護理需要多少錢？
What will I pay for a Skin Care?
重要片語 Skin Care 皮膚養護
Track 1144

⓰ 你能推薦給我一款眼霜嗎？
Can you recommend an eye cream to me?
片語釋義 eye cream 眼霜
Track 1145

⓱ 你會在我的頭髮上塗哪種髮膜？What kind of hair mask will you put on my hair?
片語釋義 hair mask 髮膜
Track 1146

⓲ 我的眉毛是不是很難定型？
Is it difficult to shape my eyebrows?
重要詞彙 eyebrow [ˈaɪbraʊ] n. 眉毛
Track 1147

⑲ 臉部按摩會幫我放鬆神經嗎？**Will the facial massage soothe my nerves?** Track 1148

重要詞彙 soothe [suð] v. 緩和

⑳ 我想換一個髮型。**I want to change my hair style.** Track 1149

片語釋義 hair style 髮型

㉑ 做這種電燙需要多長時間？**How long will this permanent wave take?** Track 1150

片語釋義 permanent wave 燙髮

㉒ 你對魚尾紋有什麼辦法嗎？**Can you do something about the crow's feet?** Track 1151

片語釋義 crow's feet 魚尾紋

看情境學對話

Track 1152

	中譯
A: Good afternoon. What can I do for you? ①	A：午安。有什麼需要幫助的嗎？
B: Good afternoon. I'd like to try a new haircut. Do you have any suggestions?	B：午安。我想嘗試一下新的髮型，你能給我點建議嗎？
A: Judging from ② your costume, I think you must often attend business banquets, so I suggest you have a more refined hairstyle.	A：從您的穿著上看，您一定經常出席商務宴會，所以我建議您做一個精緻點的髮型。
B: We hit upon the same idea. Can you show me the album of waves? I wonder if there is anything I like.	B：我們真有默契。你能把髮型圖集給我看看嗎？我想知道上面有沒有我喜歡的。
A: Sure. Here you are. ③	A：當然可以了。給您。
B: Can I have this wave?	B：我能要這種波浪狀的嗎？

A: This hairstyle is perfect for ④ you, but if you want it, you need to dye your hair. Because if you don't do it, you'll look old.	A：這個很適合您，不過如果您想要這種髮型的話，就需要染髮。因為如果您不染髮的話就會顯得老氣。
B: Well. Do you think this color will suit me?	B：好吧。那你覺得這個顏色會適合我嗎？
A: No, I suggest you choose this. Not only does it make your hair look more beautiful, but it also shows your good skin.	A：不，我建議您用這種。它既能給這個髮型增彩，也能襯托出您很好的皮膚。
B: How long does it take to do this hairstyle?	B：做這個髮型需要多長時間？
A: About three hours.	A：大約三個小時。
B: What about dyeing my hair?	B：那染髮呢？
A: It will be shorter. About an hour and a half.	A：這個時間會短一些。大約一個半小時。
B: Okay, I get it. But I don't have much time today. I'll come some other day ⑤ .	B：好的，我知道了，但是我今天沒有這麼多時間，我改天再來。
A: Yeah. Here's my card. You can call me at any time.	A：好的，沒問題。這是我的名片，您可以隨時給我打電話。
B: OK, thank you.	B：好的，謝謝。

★**banquet** [ˋbæŋkwɪt] **n.** 宴會
★**costume** [ˋkastjum] **n.** 服裝，衣服
★**refined** [rɪˋfaɪnd] **adj.** 精緻的
★**dye** [daɪ] **v.** 染（髮） **n.** 染料

① **what can I do for you?**

意為「能為您效勞嗎？有什麼需要我幫忙的嗎？」這句話在口語中出現的頻率很高，通常都是服務用語。

② **judging from**

意為「從……判斷，根據……判斷」，一般用在句首，from也可替換by。

③ **here you are**

意為「給你，你要的東西在這裡」，在口語中是很常用的句子。

④ **be perfect for**

意為「對……是完美的，對……是適合的，對……是理想的」， perfect 在這裡作形容詞。

⑤ **some other day**

意為「改天，改日」。

美容美髮
Unit 60

Effects
效果

來我們店裡吧，在我們店裡你可以享受美容美髮的服務，保證你在親朋好友面前都能自信洋溢，精神做人。

精選實用會話例句

1 按摩使我精神好多了。
The massage made me refreshed. Track 1153
重要詞彙 refresh [rɪ`frɛʃ] v. 使恢復精神

2 按摩可以緩解我們臉部的肌肉緊張。A massage may relieve muscular tone on our face. Track 1154
片語釋義 muscular tone 肌肉緊張

3 臉部按摩可提前預防我們衰老。Massaging our face will prevent ageing in advance. Track 1155
重要詞彙 massage [mə`sɑʒ] v. & n. 按摩

4 如果你持續做臉部按摩的話就能消除臉上的皺紋。
If you persist in doing facial massage, it can smooth away your wrinkles. Track 1156
重要片語 persist in doing 持續做某事

5 臉部按摩有助於促進血液循環。Facial massage is good for promoting blood circulation. Track 1157
片語釋義 blood circulation 血液循環

6 我覺得你的捲髮很漂亮。
I think your hair waves are beautiful. Track 1158
同義表達 I think the barber perms your hair beautifully.

7 **捲髮使你更有魅力了。**
Curly hair makes you more attractive. Track 1159
片語釋義 curly hair 捲髮

8 **你的頭髮看起來更有光澤了。** **You hair looks shiner.** Track 1160
同義表達 Your hair looks more shiny.

9 **燙髮後你顯得更年輕了。** **You look much younger than before with a curly hair.** Track 1161
重要詞彙 younger [`jʌŋgɚ] **adj.** 更年輕的

10 **這種髮色使你更年輕了。**
This hair color takes years off you. Track 1162
重要片語 take years off sb 使某人顯得年輕

11 **這種爽膚水使我的皮膚感覺細膩光滑。** **The skin freshener makes my skin feel soft and smooth.** Track 1163
片語釋義 skin freshener 爽膚水

12 **眼影會讓你的眼睛顯得更大一些。**
Eye shadow will make your eyes look bigger. Track 1164
片語釋義 eye shadow 眼影

13 **這個抗皺霜會使你的皮膚有彈性。** **This anti-wrinkle cream will make your skin flexible.** Track 1165
片語釋義 anti-wrinkle cream 抗皺霜

14 **這是個很有個性的髮型，不是嗎？**
It is a very special haircut, isn't it? Track 1166
重要詞彙 haircut [`hɛr͵kʌt] **n.** 理髮，髮型

15 **你的新髮型很引人注目。**
Your hair style is an eye catcher. Track 1167
片語釋義 eye catcher 引人注目的事物

16 **你贊成我的新髮型嗎？**
Do you approve of my new hairstyle? Track 1168
片語釋義 approve of 贊成，贊同

⑰ **我對你給我做的新髮型很滿意。I am very satisfied with the hairstyle you have done for me.** Track 1169

重要片語 be satisfied with 對……很滿意

⑱ **刮完鬍子後你會感覺很有精神。You'll feel very energetic after having a shave.** Track 1170

片語釋義 have a shave 刮鬍子

⑲ **我的臉現在光滑了。My face is smooth now.** Track 1171

重要詞彙 smooth [smuð] adj. 光滑的，流暢的

⑳ **我的頭髮是不是剪得太短了？**
Is my hair cut too short? Track 1172

重要詞彙 short [ʃɔrt] adj. 短的，短暫的

㉑ **我的頭髮燙完後太乾燥了。**
My hair is too dry after a perm. Track 1173

重要詞彙 dry [draɪ] adj. 乾的，乾燥的

㉒ **我的新髮型跟我想像的不一樣。My new hairstyle is different from what I expected.** Track 1174

重要詞彙 expect [ɪk`spɛkt] v. 期待，預料

看情境學對話

Track 1175

	中譯
A: Lisa, you have your hair cut?	A：麗莎，你剪頭髮了？
B: Yes, my beautician said this hairstyle will make me look more elegant.	B：是的，我的美容師說這個髮型能讓我看起來更優雅。
A: It does. You look very beautiful.	A：確實是的，你看起來很漂亮。

B: Really? Actually, I'm in a bad mood ① today.	B：真的嗎？其實，我今天的心情很糟糕。
A: Why?	A：怎麼了？
B: To be honest, I had meant to ② have my hair curled, but the barber made my hair too dry and I was very dissatisfied, so I asked him to cut that part off.	B：老實說，我本打算把我的頭髮燙成捲髮，但是由於理髮師不專業把我的頭髮弄得太乾燥了，我很是不滿意，所以我就要求他把捲髮部分剪掉了。
A: Well. Why didn't you say that earlier? I know a very professional salon.	A：你怎麼不早說？我知道一家很專業的美容美髮店。
B: All right. It was recommended to me by my colleague. I thought I would have a beautiful curly hair.	B：好的。這個店是我同事推薦的，我本以為我會有一頭美麗的捲髮呢。
A: Fortunately, however, your new hairstyle really suits you.	A：不過，幸運的是，你現在的新髮型真的很適合你。
B: That's good. You know what? ③ I was afraid to go out after I had my hair cut.	B：那就好。你知道嗎？我剛剪完頭髮後都不敢出門。
A: But you look really nice. This is a blessing in disguise ④ .	A：不過你現在看起來真的很好看。這叫：塞翁失馬，焉知非福。

B: You're right. You really gave me a lot of confidence. Thank you.	B：你說的沒錯。你真的給了我很大的信心。謝謝你。
A: You're welcome. But if you want to find a good salon in the future, you can call me. I know some very good barbers, and as my friends, they can give you a discount ⑤.	A：不客氣。不過如果以後你想找一個好的美容美髮店的話，你可以打電話給我。我認識幾個很不錯的理髮師，而且因為他們是我的朋友，他們還能給你優惠呢。
B: That's great. Thank you very much.	B：那真的太好了。多謝了。

★**elegant** [ˋɛləgənt] **adj.** 優雅的，美麗的
★**barber** [ˋbɑrbɚ] **n.** 理髮師
★**disguise** [dɪsˋgaɪz] **n.** 偽裝

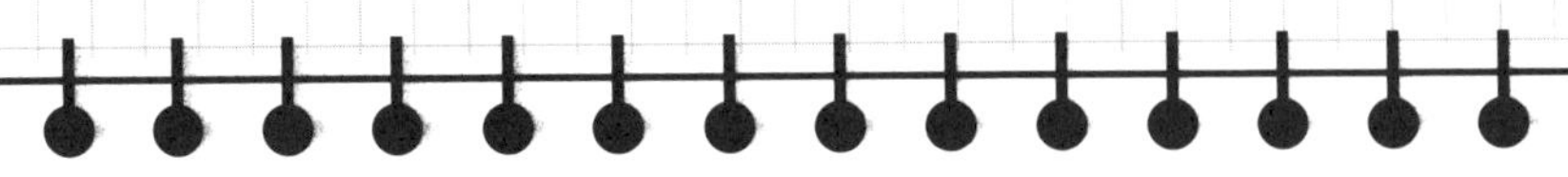

對話解析

① be in a bad mood

意為「心情不好，不高興，情緒很差」，be in a good mood 意為「心情好」。

② have meant to

意為「本打算」，後跟動詞原形，表示「本打算做某事」，指本打算做某事，但沒有做成。

③ You know what?

意為「你知道嗎？」是很口語化的說法，用於接下來要說的話之前。

④ a blessing in disguise

意為「塞翁失馬焉知非福，因禍得福」，是習慣用語，其本意是「原本以為是件倒楣事，後來發現是好事」， disguise 意為「掩飾，隱瞞」。

⑤ give sb a discount

意為「給某人優惠，給某人折扣」，若想表示具體的折扣，可將數字置於 discount 前，例如：give you a 20% discount（給你打八折）。

美容美髮

Unit 61

Perms

燙髮

燙髮，能使你體驗一種不一樣的感覺，或許你會很性感，很嫵媚，很優雅，但你也有可能頂著爆炸頭走在街上，承受別人異樣的目光。

精選實用會話例句

❶ 你想做什麼髮型呢？
How would you like me to style your hair? Track 1176
重要片語 style sb's hair 給某人設計髮型

❷ 我想燙髮。I'd like a perm. Track 1177
重要詞彙 perm [pɝm] n. 燙髮

❸ 我覺得捲髮最適合你。
I think curly hair will look best on you. Track 1178
重要片語 look best on sb 最適合某人

❹ 你捲髮看起來更好看。
You look more beautiful with curly hair. Track 1179
同義表達 You look better with curly hair.

❺ 燙髮使你顯得更年輕。
You appear quite young with a perm. Track 1180
重要詞彙 appear [əˋpɪr] v. 出現

❻ 你想要什麼樣的燙髮？
What kind of perm would you like to have? Track 1181
同義表達 What kind of perm do you want?

❼ 你想要哪個，冷燙、直燙還是捲髮燙？Which do you prefer, cold perm, straight perm or pin curl? Track 1182
重要詞彙 straight [stret] adj. 直的，連續的

❽ 你能把我的頭髮弄成大波浪式的嗎？
Can you have my hair in big waves? Track 1183
重要片語 have sb do 讓某人做某事

❾ 我想要輕燙。I'd like a light perm. Track 1184
重要詞彙 light [laɪt] adj. 輕的

❿ 我想燙成中捲的。I want to have it medium. Track 1185
重要詞彙 medium [`midɪəm] adj. 中等的

⓫ 你想剪髮還是燙髮？Do you want a haircut or a perm? Track 1186
重要詞彙 want [wɒnt] v. 想要，希望

⓬ 你想要跟上次一樣的燙髮嗎？
You want the same perm as last time? Track 1187
片語釋義 last time 上次

⓭ 過多的燙髮會對發質造成傷害。Too much perm will do damage to the hair texture. Track 1188
片語釋義 do damage to 損害，破壞

⓮ 你不能再燙髮了，否則你的頭髮會很乾燥。You can't perm any more, or your hair will be very dry. Track 1189
片語釋義 any more 再，又

⓯ 如果我現在燙髮，到時候會不會看起來自然點？If I have a perm now, will it look natural by then? Track 1190
片語釋義 by then 到時候

⓰ 如果你想燙髮的話，我建議你也染色。
If you want a perm, I suggest you dye it too. Track 1191
重要詞彙 suggest [sə`dʒɛst] v. 建議，提示

⓱ 燙髮後你需要定期做護理。
You need regular hair care after the perm. Track 1192
重要片語 hair care 護髮

⓲ 你最好定期整理頭髮。
You'd better take care of hair regularly. Track 1193
片語釋義 take care of hair 整理頭髮

⑲ 燙髮使你顯得一點都不老。
Perm doesn't make you look old at all. Track 1194
片語釋義 not at all 一點也不

⑳ 我的朋友說你的捲髮像羊毛。
My friend says your curly hair is like wool. Track 1195
重要詞彙 wool [wʊl] n. 羊毛，羊毛製品

㉑ 雖然燙髮很漂亮，但是每天整理也是一件麻煩事。
Perm is beautiful, but shaping it every day is a real nuisance. Track 1196
重要詞彙 nuisance [`njusns] n. 麻煩事，討厭的東西／人／行為

看情境學對話

Track 1197

	中譯
A: Sorry to keep you waiting so long ① . Today is the second anniversary of our barbershop, so there are a lot of regular customers.	A：不好意思讓你久等了，今天是我們店的兩週年紀念日，所以來了很多老顧客。
B: That's OK. ② Do you have any discounts in your shop today?	B：沒關係。今天你們店裡有優惠活動嗎？
A: Yes, you can get a 50% discount on both haircuts and perms. And, if you apply for a membership card today, you will enjoy free haircuts ten times.	A：是的，剪髮和燙髮都能享受五折優惠。而且，如果您今天辦會員卡的話，會享受十次免費剪髮的服務。
B: That's a good deal ③ .	B：真划算啊。
A: Sure. What do you want, young lady?	A：是的，您想做什麼頭髮，小姐？
B: I'd like a haircut and a perm.	B：我想先剪一點再燙一下。

A: You are just in time ④ . If you come a little later, I won't have time to do it for you.	A：您來的正是時候。如果您再來晚一點點，我就沒有時間給您做了。
B: Why?	B：怎麼了？
A: Just now, a dozen regular customers called for a perm.	A：剛剛有十幾個老顧客都打電話說要燙頭髮。
B: All right. I'm really lucky.	B：好吧。我真的太幸運了。
A: Yeah. Erm, how long do you want to cut your hair, young lady?	A：是的。小姐，您想剪多少頭髮？
B: Just cut a little off, mainly because ⑤ the end of my hair is too dry.	B：剪一點就好了，主要我的髮尾太乾燥了。
A: Indeed. Do you want a curly hair or having it in big waves?	A：的確。那您想要小捲還是大捲？
B: Frankly, I prefer the latter.	B：老實說，我想要後者。
A: Sure. That's a nice haircut, but what I need to tell you in advance is that if you want it, you need to shape your hair every day.	A：可以啊。那個髮型很好看，但是我要提醒您，如果您想要大波浪型的話，您需要天天整理它。
B: It sounds like a lot of trouble.	B：聽起來很麻煩。

★**anniversary** [ˌænəˋvɝsərɪ] **adj.** 週年紀念日 ★**barbershop** [ˋbɑrbɚˌʃɑp] **n.** 理髮店

★**customer** [ˋkʌstəmɚ] **n.** 顧客 ★**trouble** [ˈtrʌbl] **n.** 麻煩

① **sorry to keep you waiting so long**

意為「抱歉讓你久等了」，sorry 前還可加 so表示抱歉的程度。

② **that's OK**

意為「沒關係，那沒什麼」，常用來回應別人的道歉，it's OK 意為「好的，沒問題」，通常表示對別人的贊同。

③ **that's a good deal**

意為「太划算了」，deal 作名詞有「交易」的意思，good deal就作為「划算，好交易」來理解。

④ **you are just in time**

意為「你來得正是時候」，指的是在時間上很剛好。

⑤ **mainly because...**

意為「主要是因為……」，because 後面跟原因。mainly 是副詞修飾 because，也常用於 It is mainly because... 句型中。

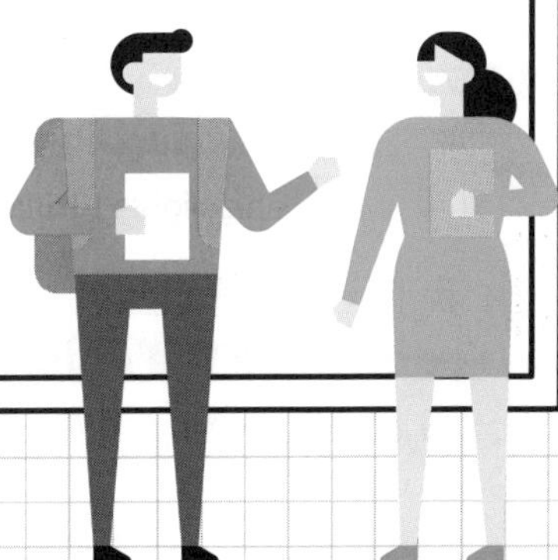

美容美髮

Unit 62

Hair Dye

染髮

你想染什麼顏色呢？黃色？紅色？彩色？還是黑色？不管你選什麼都是可以的，所以還等什麼？這會讓你看到多彩的自己。

精選實用會話例句

❶ 你想染成什麼顏色的呢？
What color do you like to dye it? Track 1198
同義表達 What color do you want?

❷ 我想把我的頭髮染成金色。
I like to dye my hair blonde. Track 1199
重要詞彙 blonde [blɒnd] **adj.** 金色的

❸ 這個顏色看起來相當不錯。**This color looks quite nice.** Track 1200
重要詞彙 color [`kʌlɚ] **n.** 顏色

❹ 我能把我的頭髮染一下嗎？
Can I have my hair dyed? Track 1201
同義表達 Can I dye my hair?

❺ 這種顏色會使你的頭髮看起來不自然。
This color will make your hair look unnatural. Track 1202
重要詞彙 unnatural [ʌn`nætʃərəl] **adj.** 不自然的

❻ 大約兩個星期後染過的顏色會淡下去。**The highlights would grow out in about two weeks.** Track 1203
重要詞彙 highlights [`haɪlaɪts] **n.** 頭髮挑染部分

❼ 我不太喜歡這個顏色。
I don't like the color very much. Track 1204
片語釋義 very much 很，非常

8 你要染頭髮嗎？
Would you like to get your hair colored? Track 1205
重要詞彙 colored [`kʌlɚd] adj. 有色的，彩色的

9 會褪色嗎？ Will it fade? Track 1206
重要詞彙 fade [fed] v. 褪去， 失去光澤

10 染個髮怎麼樣？ What about doing hair coloring? Track 1207
片語釋義 hair color 染髮

11 棕色一直是我喜歡的顏色。Brown is always my favorite. Track 1208
重要詞彙 brown [braʊn] adj. 棕色，褐色

12 你還是選擇便宜的染髮劑嗎？
Are you still choosing cheap hair dye? Track 1209
片語釋義 hair dye 染髮劑

13 你有好牌子的染髮劑嗎？
Do you have a good brand of hair dye? Track 1210
重要詞彙 brand [brænd] n. 商標，牌子

14 紅色太怪異了。Red is too erratic. Track 1211
重要詞彙 erratic [ɪˈrætɪk] adj. 不穩定的，古怪的

15 顏色取決於你選擇什麼髮型。Color depends on what hairstyle you choose. Track 1212
重要詞彙 choose [tʃuz] v. 選擇

16 我如果選擇這個顏色，你覺得怎麼樣？
What would you say if I choose this color? Track 1213
重要片語 what would you say 你會怎麼說

17 我想洗個頭，然後把我的頭髮染成金色。I would like a shampoo and have my hair dyed blonde. Track 1214
重要詞彙 shampoo [ʃæm`pu] n. & v.洗頭，洗髮劑

18 請把我的頭髮染成淺色的。
Please dye my hair in light color. Track 1215
重要片語 light color 淺色

⑲ **我覺得棕色會讓你顯白。**

I think the brown will make you look brighter. Track 1216

重要詞彙 brighter [braɪt] adj. 明亮的

⑳ **你可以從這裡面選擇你喜歡的顏色。**

You can choose the color you like from here. Track 1217

重要詞彙 like [laɪk] v. 喜歡

㉑ **你覺得什麼顏色適合我？**

What color do you think look good on me? Track 1218

片語釋義 look good on 看上去適合，好看

看情境學對話

Track 1219

	中譯
A: Good morning. What can I do for you?	A：早安。有什麼需要幫忙的嗎？
B: Good morning. I want to dye my hair.	B：早安。我想染頭髮。
A: Well. What color do you want to dye it?	A：你想染什麼顏色？
B: The most I've seen are red and brown, but I don't know if they are right for ① me.	B：我見過最多的就是紅色和棕色，但是我不知道是否適合我。
A: Here's an album including all kinds of colors; would you like to have a look? ②	A：這裡有一本包含各種顏色的冊子，你要看看嗎？
B: Yes, but there are too many colors on it. Can you give me some advice?	B：好啊。但是上面的顏色太多了，你能給我點建議嗎？
A: Okay. Nowadays, there are a lot of girls choose to dye their hair blonde.	A：可以。現在有很多的女孩都選擇染金色。

B: I don't think blonde suits me very well. It doesn't make me look white and it makes me look like I have very little hair, personally.	B：我覺得金色不太適合我，不僅讓我顯得很黑，還會顯得我頭髮很少。
A: No. If you choose this color, I suggest you perm it, which will make you look more attractive.	A：不會的。如果你選擇這個顏色的話，我建議你燙一下。這樣就會顯得你很有魅力。
B: Forget it. Anything else?	B：算了。還有其他的嗎？
A: Then how about pink?	A：粉紅色怎麼樣？
B: Are you kidding me? ③ I'm still a college student, and if I dyed this color, my roommates would probably laugh at me. What would you say ④ if I choose this color?	B：你在開玩笑嗎？我還是一名大學生，如果染了這個顏色，恐怕我的室友都會笑我。如果我選擇這個顏色，你覺得怎麼樣？
A: Light orange? It seems to suit you very well.	A：淺橘色？貌似很適合你。
B: Great, I choose this one. Do you have any good brands of hair dye?	B：好的，那我選這個。你有好牌子的染髮劑嗎？
A: Yes, I have several brands, but not many. Which one do you want?	A：有幾個，但不多。你想要哪一個？
B: I want the best one.	B：我選最好的。

【程度提升，加分單字】

★**album** [ˋælbəm] **n.** 冊

★**personally** [ˋpɝsnəlɪ] **adv.** 就個人而言

★**orange** [ˋɔrɪndʒ] **n.** & **adj.** 柳丁，橘子，橙色

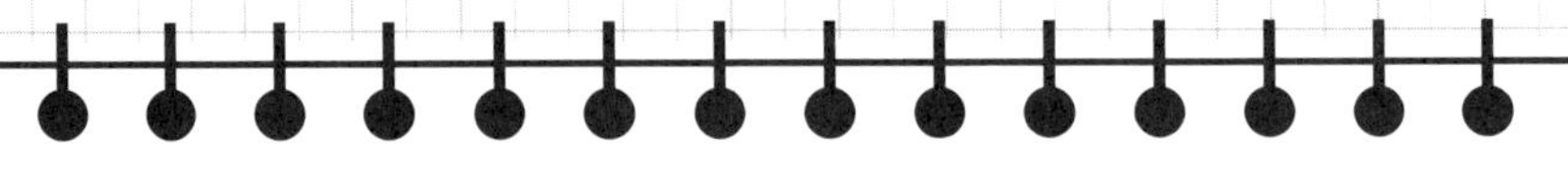

對話解析

① **be right for**

意為「適合」， be right for sb 意為「適合某人」，如構成 it's right for sb to do sth 則意為「某人做某事是正確的」。

② **Would you like to have a look?**

意為「你要看一眼嗎？」用來詢問某人是否對某物感興趣。look 後面可以加 at sth，指出具體的東西。

③ **Are you kidding me?**

意為「你在跟我開玩笑嗎？」常出現在美劇裡，能表示類似意思的是：You must be kidding me. / You must be joking. 你一定在開玩笑。

④ **What would you say...**

意為「你認為⋯⋯怎麼樣呢？」後面通常跟 if 引導的從句。在口語中常出現 What do you say... 意為「你認為怎麼樣？你有什麼看法？」

美容美髮

Unit 63 Cosmetics 化妝品

亞洲有四大邪術，分別是：泰國的變性術、韓國的整容術、日本的化妝術以及中國的 PS 術。化妝術也是其中之一，化妝品在其中扮演了重要的角色。

精選實用會話例句

❶ 我想買一瓶保濕霜。I'd like to buy a moisturizer. Track 1220

重要詞彙 moisturizer [ˋmɔɪstʃəraɪzɚ] n. 保濕霜

❷ 你能給我推薦一款睫毛膏嗎？

Could you recommend mascara to me? Track 1221

重要詞彙 mascara [mæsˋkærə] n. 睫毛膏

❸ 我能看下這個口紅嗎？

Can I have a look at this lip rouge? Track 1222

片語釋義 lip rouge 口紅

❹ 我急需一支眉筆。

I'm in great need of an eyebrow pencil. Track 1223

重要片語 be in great need 急需

❺ 這款護手霜的功能是什麼？

What effect does this hand cream have? Track 1224

片語釋義 hand cream 護手霜

❻ 這個化妝品的作用是什麼？

What's the function of this cosmetic? Track 1225

重要詞彙 function [ˋfʌŋkʃən] n. 功能，作用

❼ 你知道你的皮膚類型嗎？

Do you know your skin type? Track 1226

片語釋義 skin type 皮膚類型

❽ 你應該根據自己的皮膚類型選擇化妝品。You should choose products according to your skin. Track 1227

同義表達 Choose cosmetics based on your own skin type.

❾ 哪款化妝品適合我的皮膚？
Which kind of makeup fits for my skin? Track 1228

重要詞彙 makeup [ˋmekˏʌp] n. 化妝品，組成，補考

❿ 這款產品適合乾性皮膚。
This product is suitable for dry skin. Track 1229

片語釋義 dry skin 乾性皮膚

⓫ 你們有什麼類型的粉底？
What kind of foundation do you have? Track 1230

重要詞彙 foundation [faʊnˋdeʃən] n. 粉底

⓬ 這種粉底霜能遮蓋你臉上的雀斑。This foundation cream can hide the freckles in your face. Track 1231

重要詞彙 freckle [ˋfrɛkəl] n. 雀斑

⓭ 這種柔膚水能改善你皮膚的乾燥狀況。This smoothing toner can improve the dryness of your skin. Track 1232

片語釋義 smoothing toner 柔膚水

⓮ 這種爽膚水會使你更加清爽和美麗。The skin freshener will make you more fresh and beautiful. Track 1233

片語釋義 skin freshener 爽膚水

⓯ 它有護膚的功能。It has a function of skin care. Track 1234

片語釋義 skin care 護膚

⓰ 這種產品有抗衰老的效果。
This kind of products have anti-aging effect. Track 1235

同義表達 This product has effect on anti-senility.

⓱ 這些化妝品都是純天然的。
These cosmetics are all natural. Track 1236

重要詞彙 cosmetic [kɑzˋmɛtɪk] n. 化妝品

⓲ 化妝品有副作用嗎？Do cosmetics have side effects? Track 1237

片語釋義 side effect 副作用

⑲ **這能消除我的皺紋嗎？Will it remove my wrinkles?** Track 1238

重要詞彙 wrinkle [ˋrɪŋkl] n. 皺紋

⑳ **眼影能使你的眼睛看起來更大。**
Eye shadow can make your eyes look bigger. Track 1239

片語釋義 eye shadow 眼影

㉑ **這種產品有助於改善你的膚色。This product makes for improving your complexion.** Track 1240

重要詞彙 complexion [kəmˋplɛkʃən] n. 膚色

看情境學對話

Track 1241

	中譯
A: Welcome to the cosmetics shop. Can I help you?	A：歡迎來到化妝品店。請問您要買點什麼嗎？
B: I'm just looking around. ①	B：我只是隨便看看。
A: Well, we have a range of ② products from cosmetics to skin care products.	A：嗯，我們有一系列的產品，從彩妝到護膚品都很全面。
B: Actually, I don't know what cosmetics I should buy. But my skin is not very good, and my cheeks are a little dry, I want to improve it.	B：事實上，我不知道應該買什麼化妝品。我的皮膚不是很好，而且我的臉頰有些乾燥，我想改善。
A: You must rarely care for your skin, do you?! Your skin lacks moisture and you need some moisturizing products to moisturize your skin.	A：您肯定很少護理皮膚吧？！您的皮膚缺少水分，您需要一些保濕產品來滋潤皮膚。
B: That's it. ③ Can you recommend some for me?	B：就是這樣。那你能推薦給我嗎？

A: Of course. The emollient cream is perfect for your dry skin. I'll put some on your hand. You can try it.	A：當然可以了。我們這款滋潤霜就很適合您的乾燥型皮膚。我塗一點在您手上，您可以試一下。
B: Yes, it's nice. Anything else? I'll take it. ④	B：是的，挺不錯的。還有其他的嗎？我買這個了。
A: But if you buy a package, I think it would be more cost-effective. It includes an emollient cream, a bottle of lotion and a skin freshener, which is $120.	A：不過如果您買套餐的話，我想會更划算一點。這個套餐包含一個滋潤霜、一瓶乳液和一個爽膚水，這樣是120美元。
B: How much is this emollient cream?	B：那這個滋潤霜多少錢？
A: 60 dollars.	A：60美元。
B: All right, I'll take this package. By the way, I'd like to buy an eye shadow.	B：好的，那我買這個套餐吧。對了，我想買眼影。
A: How about this one? It will make you look natural.	A：這個怎麼樣？它能讓您看起來自然些。
B: Forget it. I don't like it very much.	B：算了。我不太喜歡。

★**cheek** [tʃik] **n.** 臉頰
★**cost-effective** [kɔst ɪˋfɛktɪv] **adj.** 划算的，合算的
★**shadow** [ˋʃædo] **n.** 陰影，影子

① **I'm just looking around**

意為「我只是隨便看看」，是購物時的日常用語，當店員問你需要什麼或者想給你推薦某物的時候，你就可以用這句話表示自己的態度。

② **have a range of**

意為「有一系列的……」，後面可跟名詞，have a wide range of意為「……範圍很廣」。

③ **that's it**

表示對某人的肯定，意為「就是這樣，那正是問題所在」，還能表示反感，意為「夠了，好了」。

④ **I'll take it.**

意為「就要它了。／我買了。」店員向你介紹或者推薦某產品時你很滿意而想買下的時候就可以用這句話來表達你的意思，也常用 I'll take this...。

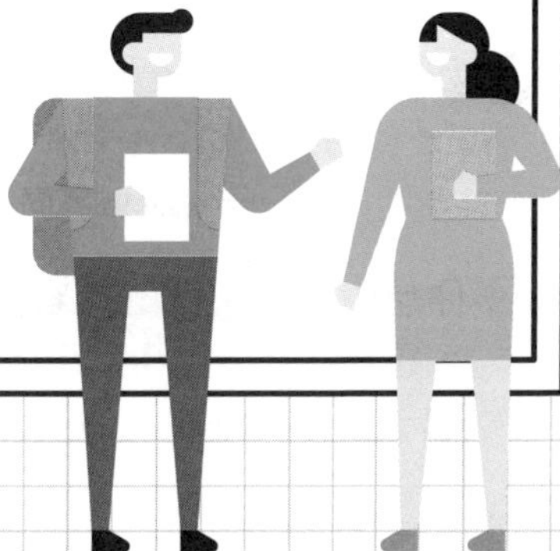

美容美髮

Unit 64

Beauty Care 美容

在美容方面，我們依然任重而道遠。可以說，這是我們一輩子都在堅持或者應該堅持的事情。為了美麗，為了獲得別人的羨慕或者一見傾心的目光，就讓我們在美容道路上越走越遠吧。

精選實用會話例句

1 你需要面部按摩嗎？Do you want a facial massage? Track 1242

片語釋義 facial massage 面部按摩

2 美容能緩解壓力。

Beauty treatment can alleviate pressure. Track 1243

片語釋義 beauty treatment 美容

3 據說蘆薈能用來美容。It's said that aloe can be used for facial care. Track 1244

片語釋義 facial care 面部護理

4 首先，我們會給您做面部清潔。

Firstly, we will give you a facial cleaning. Track 1245

同義表達 We will cleanse your face firstly.

5 閒暇時我會幫自己做臉部按摩。I do face massage by myself in my spare time. Track 1246

重要片語 in one's spare time 在某人閒暇時間

6 我想知道如何能改善我的膚質。

I'd like to know the way to improve my skin. Track 1247

重要片語 the way to 通向……的路

7 你想使用什麼樣的美容產品？What kind of skin-care products would you like to use? Track 1248

片語釋義 skin-care product 護膚品

❽ 我多久需要做一次面部按摩？
How often do I need to do a facial massage? Track 1249
同義表達 How often should I make a facial massage?

❾ 你想修眉嗎？**Do you want to trim your eyebrows?** Track 1250
重要詞彙 trim [trɪm] v. 修剪，整理

❿ 我需要拔眉毛嗎？**Do I need to pluck my eyebrows?** Track 1251
重要片語 pluck one's eyebrows 拔眉毛

⓫ 我想把眉毛染深一些。
I'd like to have the eyebrows darkened. Track 1252
重要詞彙 darken [`dɑrkn] v. 使變暗

⓬ 你多久去一次美容院？
How often do you go to the beauty parlor? Track 1253
片語釋義 beauty parlor 美容院

⓭ 大部分女性都熱衷美容。
Most women are into cosmetology. Track 1254
重要片語 be into 喜歡，對……感興趣

⓮ 這個護膚品中含有大量的化學成分嗎？**Does this skin-care product contain a lot of chemical ingredients?** Track 1255
重要詞彙 chemical [`kɛmɪkəl] adj. 化學的

⓯ 這款面膜可以修復因太陽灼傷的皮膚。**This mask can help repair the skin from sunburn.** Track 1256
重要詞彙 sunburn [`sʌn͵bɝn] n. 曬傷

⓰ 這家美容院擅長除皺。**This beauty parlor is good at removing wrinkles.** Track 1257
重要詞彙 remove [rɪ`muv] v. 去除， 拿下

⓱ 我應該如何改善我的皮膚狀況？**How should I improve my skin condition?** Track 1258
片語釋義 skin condition 皮膚狀況，皮膚問題

⓲ 我已經來過這個美容院很多次了。
I've been to this beauty parlor many times. Track 1259
片語釋義 many times 多次，常常

⑲ 我想修臉。I'd like to have a shave. Track 1260

片語釋義 have a shave 刮鬍子，修臉

⑳ 你要不要我幫你刮臉？

Would you mind me shaving your face? Track 1261

重要詞彙 shave [ʃev] v. 剃，削去

看情境學對話

Track 1262

	中譯
A: Amy, could you hand me ① a facial mask? I'm extremely tired. ②	A：艾米，你能幫我拿一個面膜嗎？我太累了。
B: Your skin has been in poor condition ③ lately. Why don't you do a facial massage?	B：你的皮膚狀況最近很差，為什麼你不去做個面部按摩呢？
A: Yeah, I've been working overtime lately. It's no wonder that my skin looks like this. Actually, I want to do it, but I don't know which beauty parlor I should go to.	A：是啊，我最近一直加班熬夜，難怪我的皮膚會變成這樣。其實，我想去做，但是我不知道應該去哪家美容院。
B: I know a nice beauty salon near our house. Do you want to go?	B：我知道一家很好的美容院，就在我們家附近。你要去嗎？
A: Sure. Will you go with me?	A：好啊，你要跟我一起去嗎？
B: No, I have to go back to school to write my paper.	B：不了，我還要回學校寫論文呢。
A: Well, let me know the address.	A：好吧，那你把地址告訴我。

B: OK, I've written it down. You can go there by this.	B：好的，我已經寫下來了。你可以依照這個去那裡。
(20 minutes later)	（二十分鐘後）
C: Hello, can I help you?	C：你好，有什麼需要幫助的嗎？
A: Hi, I want to have a facial massage.	A：你好，我想做一個面部按摩。
C: Okay. This way, please. ④ What package would you like to choose?	C：好的，這邊請。您想選擇什麼套餐呢？
A: Which is the most economical?	A：哪一種最經濟實惠？
C: I suggest you experience this. It is best for your skin condition and is also the cheapest.	C：我建議您體驗一下這個。它最適用於您的皮膚狀況，而且也是最便宜的。
A: How long does it take?	A：它需要多長時間？
C: About an hour. We will clean your skin with the cleansing cream first. Then rub it on your face with a massage cream and do the massage for you.	C：大約 1 個小時。我們會先用清潔面霜清潔您的皮膚，之後用按摩霜塗在您的臉上給您按摩。
A: OK, I get it. Just do it. ⑤	A：好的，我知道了。就這麼做吧。

【程度提升，加分單字】

★**condition** [kən`dɪʃən] n. 狀況，條件 ★**address** [ə`drɛs] n. 地址
★**package** [`pækɪdʒ] n. 套餐 ★**massage** [mə`sɑʒ] n. & v. 按摩

① **Could you hand me...?**

意為「你能把……遞給我嗎？」me 後跟要某人遞送的事物，其與 Could you pass me...? 用法一致。hand 作名詞時可構成 Could you give me a hand? 意為「你能幫我一個忙嗎？」

② **extremely tired**

意為「使極度勞累，精疲力盡」，其也可構成 tire sb out 意為「使某人精疲力盡或厭煩」。

③ **be in poor condition**

意為「狀況不佳」，be in good condition 意為「狀況好」。

④ **This way, please.**

意為「這邊請。」，通常是服務人員為客人指路時的用語。

⑤ **Just do it**

意為「說做就做！就這麼做／辦／做吧！」是很能讓人鼓起勇氣的一句話，也是 Nike 的一句廣告語。

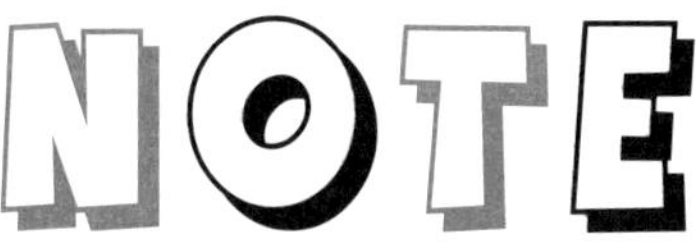

NOTE

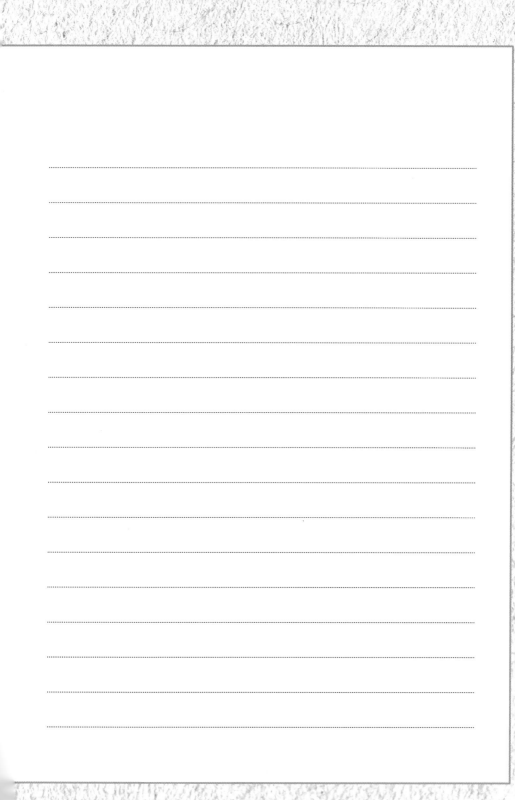

易人外語 系列 E0017

零基礎學生活英語會話，一本就掌握：
讓你從「不敢說話」到「自信開口」的64個日常英語情境大破解

從現在起，一本書提升你的生活英語會話實力！

作　　者　吳悠（Giselle）
總 編 輯　黃璽宇
主　　編　吳靜宜、姜怡安
執行編輯　李念茨、陳儀蓁
美術編輯　王桂芳、張嘉容

初　　版　2019年09月
出　　版　含章有限公司
電　　話　（02）2752-5618
傳　　真　（02）2752-5619
地　　址　106台北市大安區忠孝東路四段250號11樓-1

定　　價　新台幣400元／港幣133元
產品內容　1書

總 經 銷　昶景國際文化有限公司
地　　址　236新北市土城區民族街11號3樓
電　　話　（02）2269-6367
傳　　真　（02）2269-0299
E-mail:　service@168books.com.tw
歡迎優秀出版社加入總經銷行列

港澳地區總經銷　和平圖書有限公司
地　　址　香港柴灣嘉業街12號百樂門大廈17樓
電　　話　（852）2804-6687
傳　　真　（852）2804-6409

▶本書部分圖片由Shutterstock圖庫、freepix圖庫提供。

國家圖書館出版品預行編目資料

零基礎學生活英語會話，一本就掌握 / 吳悠著．
-- 初版．-- 臺北市：含章，2019.09
　面；　公分（易人外語：E0017）

ISBN 978-986-98036-3-2(平裝)

1. 英語　2. 口語　3. 會話

805.188　　　　108011515